Pale F &

The Raven

By

Stacey Dighton

DEDICATION

For my beautiful wife Jo and my two wonderful children, Jayden and Harley. I was inspired to make this leap into the unknown by the courage and confidence you have shown in the career choices you have made.

CONTENTS

PROLOGUE

The deity was angry. It was enraged. It snarled and spat like an asp, backed into a corner and ready to fight to the death, its face was a contorted grimace of ferocity and defiance.

The daevas were being slaughtered in their hundreds by the treacherous creator and his army of winged avengers, their glimmering arrows pouring from the heavens like molten gold. *His* own benevolent forces were on the verge of a calamitous and devastating defeat.

He had devised a glorious plan to unleash the sixteen deadly scourges, forcing those above ground into an eon of pestilence and suffering. The serpent lord had crossed *Him* but had been defeated with deception and fire.

The daevas had served *Him* well in halting the season of rains and turning the above ground into a barren and ashen wasteland, but someone had usurped *Him*. Somebody had spoken of *His* plans to the creator in hushed tones in private, bejewelled corridors. Someone who *He* had trusted. Someone who *He* had loved.

Now *He* stood, on the edge of the precipice, the fiery underworld behind *Him* and the army of godly spirits ahead, their swords drawn and their bloodthirsty desires dripping from their lips, their lurid gazes steadfast. They would have *Him* cast asunder into the eternal blackness, tumbling through the nothingness for eternity, and for what? For daring to be ambitious. For even considering the possibility that the two legged were lesser beings, filthy animals that should be treated as lowly slaves and should tend to their every whims and desires.

The creator stood before *Him*, his bow drawn, his neck muscles bulging and his jaw set firm. His eyes were a bright, luminous green and his face glowed with both a deep love and a pure and terrifying rage. *He* would have his revenge. *He* swore that even if it took *Him* until the dawn of a new time, *He* would be avenged.

As the arrow left the bow, *He* cried out with an anger so visceral and infinite that the earth cracked, the sky split, and the seas boiled. There was a boom of tumultuous thunder, a flash of burning light, an eruption of fire that turned the land into molten rock.

And then nothing.

Just a breath.

ACT 1: THE AWAKENING

Chapter 1: The Body

She was dead alright. No confusion there. No need to confer with the medics or obtain a cautionary second opinion. He may not have worked many cases involving the deceased before but one look at the girl lying against the damp, moss-riddled tree told him that she had been dead for a while. Her throat cut from ear to ear, her naked and pale torso, black and purple marks around her neck and shoulders, dark blood around her upper chest. Not a nice way to start the week, he thought. Not for her and not for him.

He'd been called at around four thirty that morning. Officially he was on call. Personally, he couldn't give a fuck. He'd been screwed so hard by the powers that be in the previous two years that the idea of diligently keeping an eye on his woefully outdated mobile phone for the hint of an emergency made him chuckle to himself.

He'd been half in a dream, in a nightclub with some girl, the music pounding so hard that it was difficult to make out what she was saying. Whatever it was she had been desperate to make him listen. Kept pulling at his sleeve and pointing. Couldn't make out what she was pointing at. Some shadow in the corner. The lights were bright and they were surrounded by people. Crammed in, sweaty bodies all around him, all he could think was that she was hot. Hotter than his usual 'companions'. Hotter than Lisa. Much hotter. He loved the song too. 'The Omen' by the Prodigy. One of his all-time favourites and, coincidentally, the ring tone on his phone. He still mourned the loss of Keith.

And that was when he realised that the whole bloody thing was only a dream and his cell was ringing. He swore under his breath.

'Bastards.'

Half falling out of bed he'd grabbed the phone out of the pocket of his jeans which were screwed up on the bedroom floor from the night before. That *morning*, more specifically. He vaguely remembered putting the key in the lock of his flat, falling through the door, one leg out, the other leg still caught up in the tight fitting, scuffed denim, and eventually stumbling into his double divan. Now his head hurt and the pounding noise from the phone, the Prodigy at full blast, was causing him mild nausea.

It was the station and they wanted him pronto. A body discovered in Westhampton Common. Some kids out way too late had stumbled across it. Apparently one of the girls had puked all over the crime scene, but other than dropping some litter, energy drink cans (lord knows what the kids saw in those things) and a fag packet, they had made the call and left. He knew he was going to have to talk to them. Once he'd had a coffee and gotten rid of his damned headache. Christ, half of him was still standing in that nightclub, arm around the mysterious woman, body moving to the tunes. He often wondered how things could turn to shit so quickly.

He looked at the body. The poor girl, probably no more than mid-twenties. Slim, blonde and almost certainly extremely attractive when she was alive. Unfortunately, that ship had sailed.

The crime scene was being taped off, forensics were suiting up and getting ready to start work. It was cold. October mornings usually were, but other than the morning dew it was dry. That would make things easier, he thought. There was nothing worse than working a scene when it was pissing it down. But the combination of the outside air temperature and the image in front of him made him shiver. One of those shivers that really got down to your bones. One of those shivers that was difficult to shift.

He looked over and saw Damian. He had just pulled up in his

VW. Young guy, new to the squad but keen and enthusiastic. On his way up for sure, he thought, for now in any case. But in spite of that, not because of it, Luke liked him. Liked his enthusiasm and dynamism. Not that it motivated him in any way of course, but in many ways it gave him energy that he couldn't seem to find from any other source. The elixir of youth perhaps.

'Hey Damo,' he said as the young detective zipped up his coat, blew out a plume of early morning breath and trotted over.

'What we got, boss?'

'Take a look for yourself but I suggest you take a moment first. It's not nice. Some scumbag did a real number on her and he didn't leave anything to chance.'

Damian brushed past him and looked down at the young female, completely exposed to the bitter elements of the cold October morning. Legs crossed awkwardly, arms spread across her lap, placed uncomfortably at the base of the gnarly trunk of an old sycamore.

'Jesus, Luke. Jesus fucking Christ,' he turned sharply.

'I know. Not nice. I got the call earlier this morning. I reckon she's been there for a few hours at least. You okay, kiddo?'

'Yeah, yeah, yeah,' he clearly wasn't. A little green around the gills and ashen in the cheeks, 'just a bit of a shock to the system this early in the day.'

'She was found by some local herberts. Two boys and a girl. Think they are all teens. I'm going to need you to find out who they are and round them up. We need to determine whether they saw anything. It's unlikely but let's cover all of the bases, do the legwork, all that good stuff. And we need to get some of the team together to search the area. Find out if she, or the piece of shit that did this, left anything for us.'

Luke Raven, Detective Inspector for the Hampshire Constabulary, looked across from the body. Deep gouges in the earth immediately informed him that she hadn't been killed there. Whoever had done it to her had dragged her across the woodland and laid her at that place deliberately. The placement of the body seemed odd. Why sit her up like that? Why not just dump her, or cover her up in the bushes, maybe a shallow grave under the mulch and damp earth. Why present her to them like that? It was almost like the killer wanted them to find her, wanted them to know that she was there.

'I'll get on it, boss,' Damian looked over to him and smiled, 'you look awful. You want a coffee?'

'Damo,' the D.I. sighed grimly, 'I could kill for one.'

Chapter 2: The Writer

Tony was bored. *Christ*, he was bored. He'd gotten up early that morning to get cracking. He needed this, needed it so bad. But motivating himself had always been tough.

He was never a good student at school. He'd done okay. Worked his way through GCSEs, A Levels and his Bachelor's degree, but he would be kidding if he said it had been easy. It had been tough. And, if he was honest with himself, he'd scraped through with minimal effort.

Jane had woken him. That bloody alarm. Every weekday morning at six a.m. Blam, blam, blam, blam, blam! Some mornings he wanted to lean over, rip it out of the wall socket and throw the bloody thing through the window. Which of course he couldn't as the window was double glazed, and the alarm-radio would just bounce right back at him. Probably bounce right off his head on the way back, *blamming* all the way.

She was great though. Always brought him up a coffee, a plate with a couple of rounds of toast on it and his laptop. His bloody laptop. The bane of his life but also his supposed ticket to a new one.

He hated the white screen. He hated the fact that it stared back at him, taunting him, bellowing at him 'Go on then. Do something! Amaze me! Show me how talented you are! Do something FUCKING INTERESTING!'

Every morning since the first of January, when he had made his repeat new year's resolution that he was going to really try this year, the laptop had spoken to him. He had sworn to himself that he was going to really put the effort in and, if he failed, he could look at himself in the mirror and say; 'At least I gave it my best shot'. And yet his mind and his soft, pudgy fingers had not responded. Had not responded at all.

Jane encouraged him. She had never given him any reproachful looks. Never pressurised him. Never bitched or moaned that she was out working, earning them a living while he was at home, eating Cheerios by the bucket, watching Loose Women, Peppa Pig and Jeremy Kyle and drinking endless cups of tea. That made it worse.

She really believed in him. She was forever telling him that he just needed to mine the wonderful talent that she had seen at University. She knew it was there. She had seen it with her own eyes and all he needed was time and the right inspiration.

He wished he could believe in himself as much as she believed in him.

They'd moved into the house six months ago. They had been an item for four years now, since the second year of University, and it seemed like the right time. Rented, of course, because neither of them had anywhere near the right level of savings to put a deposit down on a house to buy.

Jane had gotten her job at the school a year earlier but that just about paid for them to live. Their social lives were expensive and his takings working behind the bar at Stooges were never going to make much of a difference. But they had scraped enough money together to put the first month's rent down on the house, a small semi in Highfield.

And they had a plan. She would take on a teaching job at a local primary while he worked on his novel. And once he was a successful novelist, with two or three best sellers in the bag, they would buy their dream home in the countryside, probably down at Brockenhurst or Lymington, get married, have kids and live the dream '2.4 children' family existence. That was their goal, their ambition if you like. It was what they were planning ahead for. Jane had it all mapped out. He just needed to get his arse in gear.

Well that morning he'd had a breakthrough. He'd finally gotten pen to paper so to speak. Or, at least, fingers to keyboard. And whilst it wasn't James Patterson or Kathy Reichs, it was something. His first creative chapter since walking out of Westhampton University two years prior. And that needed to be celebrated and so, as a little reward, he'd put the kettle on and took the lid off of the biscuit barrel. And that, as the old saying goes, was all he wrote. He'd been vegetating on the settee ever since.

Geniuses, it seemed, couldn't be rushed.

Chapter 3: The Neighbour

Tony awoke at around five p.m. He'd dozed off without realising it. The telly was on mute, his empty cup still sitting in his lap, the late afternoon summer sun starting to sink low in the sky.

Jane was still out. Spin class after work. He leaned over and looked out of the dining room window. Looked like Billy was home from work, he thought. Somebody was certainly out in next door's back garden trimming hedges. Could only be Bill. Sally worked late on a Monday.

He jumped up, knocking his cup onto the floor, cursing as he scrambled to pick it up before the dregs of tea spilt onto the rug. He stood up and looked down at himself. Still in his bloody PJs. He couldn't go outside like that.

He launched himself upstairs to his bedroom, threw on a pair of shorts and a crumpled T-shirt and came back down, crashed through the back door and tumbled down the rickety path. He wanted to share his news.

Billy West was a big unit. Built like a prop, he was around sixteen stone, five-foot-ten in height, almost four-foot-wide and with a head that seemed to rise from the shoulders without a hint of a discernible neck. Red, curly hair sat atop his almost permanently flushed face with a ginger moustache to match. He was wearing a white polo with khaki-coloured combat shorts and a pair of sandals.

Stylish he wasn't, but Bill was the type of neighbour that really didn't give two hoots.

'Hey Bill, how you doing?'

'Oh, hi Tone. I'm doing pretty good. Just got home from work,' his cheeks flushed scarlet, 'I tell you, things ain't what they used to be. Seems like everyone's an electrician nowadays, 'cept no-one does a decent job. Exposed wires, no earth cable, electricians tape holding things together by a thread. And I get the bitch of a task of going round fixing all the mess that do-it-yourselfers and cock-it-up cowboys have made. One day it's going to be the death of me. How's your book going?'

'Novel Billy, novel. And it's going okay thanks. Wrote my first chapter today,' Tony smiled casually as he aired the good news.

'Shit a brick. Jane will be pleased. Jesus, seems like you've been cogitating on that novel for forever. Hope it's a good one. Don't forget me when you collect your Booker prize.' Billy stepped down from his ladder and walked over to the waist-high fence separating the gardens. He pointed one short, stubby cigar of a finger at Tony, 'You could be the next Stephen King.'

'It's a crime thriller, Billy. Not a horror. And, anyway, I've got a long way to go yet. One chapter does not a novel make.' The idea was pretty irresistible though. He had to admit, getting his first words down had really gotten his juices flowing. Keeping them flowing, he knew, was the tricky part. 'Effort, effort, effort, Anthony,' he could hear his mother saying, 'nobody gets anywhere without hard work and sweat.'

'Yeah, well,' Billy waved his hands dismissively, 'let me have a read when you've got something worth sharing. In the meantime, Sal's going to kill me if she gets home and I haven't sorted out the garden. She keeps on at me. Says she can't get down the path without feeling like she's walking through the Congo,' he hacked off a large branch from a bright green conifer as he spoke. 'You, er, coming over tonight?'

'I'm not sure, Bill. That last stuff you got was pretty lethal.'

Bill West was, despite his homely appearance, a casual user of what some might call the sweet leaf. Nothing too heavy, but whoever he was getting the stuff from seemed to be gradually upping the potency. Tony had his suspicions about who the dealer was, but Billy was extremely protective over his source. Almost violently so.

'Plus,' Tony continued, 'now I've started I don't want to stop. Reckon I might get another two or three chapters down this evening.' He didn't know whether he really believed that, but he needed to at least make an attempt to keep the wheels rolling.

'OK. But this new batch is pretty decent, and I've got the new Fast and Furious on DVD. I'll be out in the den at around eight thirty. If you change your mind just pop over. Otherwise, good luck with your book. If I look over and see the dining room light on, I'll know that you're hard at it.' He laughed heartily, 'Anyway, best get on.'

With that, Billy's mobile phone went off. The loud, irritating, Nokia ring tone that made Dom Joly so famous, 'Yeah, I'm out in the garden now… no, I'm not just sitting around drinking tea… yeah, I got the milk… no I didn't see your sister… why would I have said that? … no… look, I should be done in a little while…' he winked at Tony, waved his hand and gesticulated at the phone, shuffling up the path as his face grew more and more crimson.

Chapter 4: The Girlfriend

I wasn't late that night. Home by around seven. Tuesday night was spin class night and I never missed it. Got me out of the house and out of the classroom. Sometimes you need that, don't you? You just need a change of scenery, a change of people and a change of...well a change of air, really. Breathing the same air day in and day out can be pretty stifling.

I'd been spinning for around three months. Some of my workmates had encouraged me to join them. Isobelle, Jemima and Nick. They had all been going for quite a while and raved about it in the staff room. Jemima, in particular, swore by it. Said she felt like a new woman after a few weeks. I'd resisted the urge to join in, but after many, many instances of cajoling over the coffee machine, Nick had finally convinced me to give it a whirl. So to speak.

Tony didn't mind. Didn't mind at all. Which was nice. It was nice to be supported in a hobby, you know? He could have easily pushed against it. After all, he was at home all day, hunched over that bloody book. I was the main presence in his life, in a human sense, and with me being out of the house for most of the day he must have looked forward to me coming home. Someone to talk to and to be with. We weren't the most outstandingly romantic couple in the world, not even in the whole of Westhampton, but we were a unit and the family unit stood for a little at least.

I remember something being different when I walked in. Not 'out of this world' different but just a sense that things had changed. I wasn't sure whether it was for the better or not but there was certainly a shift. A movement in the atmosphere if you like.

He was sitting at the dining room table when I came through the door from the lounge. He was smiling, his arms folded and a cup of tea, my cup of tea, resting on a table mat. He'd even laid out a couple of my favourite cookies.

'What are we celebrating?' I was a little apprehensive. He'd been pretty down recently. Every night the same look of disappointment and unease on his face.

'I'm up and running. I've got a story and I've started to get it down. Not much but enough to get me going.' He held out his arms like he'd just won the heavyweight championship of the world. Not that he was a heavyweight but, hey, you get my drift.

'That's great news, sweetheart. Really great,' I was pleased but we had had false starts before. Stories that he had laid out to me, ideas that he promised he would be fleshing out, tales that he had elaborated on but which never made it to the page. He must have caught on to my cynicism because he whirled the laptop around.

'See for yourself. It's no epic but now that I've got chapter one put to bed I already feel that I know where it's going. What this guy's going to do next.'

He was really animated and, whilst I didn't actually sit to read it, I could definitely see that he had started something. And something, anything, was good.

'That is really terrific, Tone. Really, really terrific. So, so good,' I put my hands to his stubbly face and kissed him hard. Not passionately, but greedily. I was happy. Not ecstatic because, let's face it, he had a long way to go and many writers, the majority possibly, had faltered after the first few pages. This had to pick up some real steam if it was going to go anywhere. But, still, this was further than he had gone before. Further than since before the writer's block had hit him straight out of University. It was like the pressure of life, real life, had sewn his imagination shut with unbreakable thread. And now finally that stitch had given a little. And I, for one, was hoping it would tear all the way open. God knows we needed the money.

'I really feel it, Jane. I just woke this morning with the story in my head. I just knew that, after you went off to work, I would be able to do something. I haven't felt like that in so long,' he was up and moving around the kitchen, 'I know that it's not much, but I figure it's like one of those guys in Alien, you know? Like Sigourney Weaver, John Hurt and all those guys. They're in the Nostromo and they've just come out of suspended animation after all these years of travelling through space and then, suddenly, something calls to them and the ship wakes them up. And it takes them a while to figure out where they are. It takes them a while to wake up and get moving, you know? I reckon that's what I am. Someone coming out of suspended animation. I need to ease into it. But I feel it. I feel it. Almost like it's going to write itself. Like it won't take me much effort. Like the wheels are starting to grind into life. At least,' he paused, reflecting, 'I hope I'm right.'

I hadn't seen him like that in such a long time that it all felt a bit surreal. He had gotten himself into such a black hole of inertia that I had, I admit, started to think he might never get going again. But this was good. It was really good.

'I tell you what, why don't you get back to it and I'll get us a takeaway in to celebrate. Maybe a curry from the Rogan. I'll get your favourite, Chicken Jalfrezi, extra hot,' I was so over the moon that a curry after spin class, whilst a tad counter-productive, felt intuitively right.

'Yeah, yeah. That sounds good,' he grabbed hold of the laptop hungrily, 'I'll see if I can get a few pages down while you ring it in. This could be it, babe,' he jumped up and grabbed me by my shoulders, my grey sweatshirt ruffling under his firm grip, 'this could be us back in the game.'

I laughed childishly. I wasn't sure that we had ever been in the game, but I was happy nevertheless. Happy for him. Happy for us both.

A little fearful too.

Chapter 5: The Dream

He was back in the nightclub. He was back with the same girl. She had her hands on his arse. Firmly, caressing. He was pushing his hands through her hair, moving his pelvis against hers in time with the music. It was loud, the atmosphere was hot and sticky, her scent was tantalisingly sweet.

She looked up at him longingly. She looked like she wanted him, and God knows he wanted her. Her long blond hair was slick; her red lipstick was thick and glossy. She wore a tight black dress and had a tattoo on her left shoulder. He couldn't quite see what it was. Some kind of emblem. But who cared? It just added to her all-round appeal, an appeal that was arousing him in all the right places.

He bent down to kiss her. He felt the heat from her breath and the smell of her sweat and perfume. He wanted this, she wanted it. Sure, he would feel guilt but who didn't? This was the twenty-first century after all, a time where swiping left was a natural and easy motion.

She was teasing him. Moving towards him and then moving away. Her eyes were locked with his, never breaking contact, her mouth drawing him in, pulling him into its sweet abyss. He was transfixed and completely at one with her. She was all he wanted, all he desired and needed.

She groaned and he groaned with her. It was getting pretty intense and a little too hot for the dance floor. He was starting to feel that it was time to take it somewhere else. The next level beckoned.

Their lips almost touched when she pulled away. Her eyes were wide. Her body tense, resisting the magnetic force that was drawing them together. She was looking over his shoulder, her mouth agape. She was pointing. *Look, look, look! Look at him, he is here!*

He turned but couldn't see. Just a mist, flashing lights, bodies writhing to the music, hair and sweat and limbs.

But he saw a shadow. A long thin shadow. And the white half-moon of a face. Was it a face? Was it a smile? Was there someone there, way back in the club? Someone or something, long and sleek, partly hidden, smiling, grinning. The air was shimmering and flexing like ripples on a lake, waves of anxiety distorting the thick and smoky atmosphere.

He squinted, looked back at the girl who, by now, had let go of his backside and was sliding in reverse towards the exit. She had lost all of her colour. Her eyes were unnaturally wide, and her mouth was turned down in a gruesome, grotesque grimace. He could see all of her teeth, her tongue, her throat, the fear etched across her face in deep ravines. She staggered back haphazardly and tripped. Fell sprawling into the sea of dancing bodies where he lost sight of her.

He looked back and the shadow was moving, floating towards him. He still couldn't make out any details, but he sensed it. He sensed that whatever it was it was malicious, evil even, and it was hell-bent on causing him and all those around him immeasurable harm.

It floated upwards and loomed over him, and he could see a ghostly white face, long black arms, ghoulish grin, black eyes as black as the depths of hell, and it was reaching out to him. Reaching out with limbs that extended and extended, long, black fingers with long, yellowing hooked nails. And it was calling him, 'Luke, Luke, LUKE, LUUUUUUKKKKKKEEEEE!'

That was when he screamed.

Chapter 6: The Find

'Luke, LUKE!' Damian Barber had his hands on Luke Raven's shoulders, shaking him awake from what was a pretty lucid and unwelcome dream. He had been thrashing his head violently and moaning. Damian had had to stifle a fit of hysterics through the back of his hand.

Luke jumped and glared at the young detective. His eyes, dilated and bloodshot, took a few moments to focus on his junior partner's semi-amused face.

'Sorry mate, sorry. Nodded off.'

He sat up in his car. He had taken a time out over lunch while the crime scene crew did their thing. He'd finished his Mcmuffin, licking the greasy paper to relieve it of the left-over melted cheese and egg yolk and had laid back in his seat to rest his eyes. Sleep time hadn't been too good for him recently and he had taken to having the odd power nap or two during the day. Not exactly departmental procedure but needs must and all that.

Round two of that bloody dream didn't help. What was all that about anyway? He shook it off, rubbed his dry, sore eyes, tried to adjust his focus to the here and now and push the now fading nightmare out of his thoughts. Although, oddly, he could still smell the perfume and the sweat and he pondered how the mind could be such a bizarre and twisted thing.

All of a sudden, he felt all of his thirty-eight years. He glanced at himself in the rear-view and saw the deep crevices around his green/grey eyes, salt and pepper short but shaggy hair and three-day old stubble. He sighed wearily.

Yesterday had been a tough day. Getting yanked out of his slumber so early and finding the body of that poor girl was pretty rough, even for him. He didn't have any kids, but he still felt he could empathise. Learning that your daughter had been disposed of in such a horrendous manner, in such a disrespectful and brutal way, would tear any parent apart.

They hadn't had any joy with the kids who discovered her. Damian had located them and had encouraged them, somewhat forcefully, to join him at the station. Luke had met up with him there to question them.

They were all in their mid to late teens and pretty vacant about the whole thing. The boys were nonchalant, almost disinterested, and the girl was both shocked and intrigued at the same time. Their attitude was beyond him, but he had given up trying to rationalise the actions of youths. They were either too naïve for words or frustratingly and worryingly cynical. Of course he was generalising, but he had yet to find an exception to his rule.

According to the two lads, they had literally stumbled across the body while trying to scare the living daylights out of the young girl, Tina. The oldest boy, Max, had attempted to revive the victim using mouth to mouth. He said he had seen it on TV. Holby or some other hospital show. If he had taken the time to look, he would have noticed the large slash mark across her neck, the congealed blood pooling in her breasts and lap. No amount of oxygen was going to heal that. He had also inadvertently and carelessly screwed up their crime scene.

Tina said she had screamed and screamed until her throat gave out, but by the look and the sound of her Luke doubted it. Her voice seemed fine to him. High pitched and annoying. She also had the grim look of a rubbernecker. He blamed the internet. People nowadays were rarely shocked by anything; too many images of car crashes, shootings, executions in some far away land, explosions in arenas and racially motivated attacks in mosques and such like. Luke got the impression that Tina found this all too morbidly interesting.

Either way, none of them saw a thing, and he suspected that once the coroner's report came in later that day the time of death would be some hours earlier. Meaning that their murderer was unlikely to have been anywhere near the scene when the hapless trio arrived.

A strike out but not one that he hadn't anticipated.

The cordoned off area around the park was awash with fully equipped crime scene investigators. White-suited trained operatives moving in an organised fashion within a white, forensic tent collecting whatever microscopic evidence they could lay their hands and test tubes on. There were unlikely to be finger prints, the damp mossy earth was hardly a hot bed for greasy human residue, but there were almost certainly footprints and possibly human hair and fluids. It was these titbits of evidence that he was counting on. Whoever had dragged her there had to have left some memory or mark.

He had officers out questioning locals on what they might have seen, but this area was so far off of the normal beaten track that, depending on time of death, there were unlikely to be any passers-by. And there was just something about how the body was arranged that told him that this was more than a random act. It was planned. And the killer wanted to make a statement.

A one off? Maybe. Serial? Possibly. Meticulous? Almost certainly.

He was also waiting on an ID. His team were checking all of the missing person reports in and around the area and he was hoping that her fingerprints might also give him a lead. She had no personal effects on her at all and that made it all the more difficult. It had been less than thirty-six hours however and often people didn't ring in until two or three days after the initial disappearance. People were mobile nowadays.

'Boss, the guys may have found something. But, it's a bit…odd.'

Luke zipped up his jacket and followed Damian around his car to the cordoned off area.

'What do you have?' he was intrigued. He hadn't expected anything so soon.

'I don't know. One of the officers was investigating the ground immediately underneath where the girl was lying and found this wedged in a piece of loose bark from the tree.'

Damian held up a plastic bag with what looked like a capsule inside. It was the size of a cigarette lighter but smooth and oval shaped. It was black and hinged down one side, the hinged half laying open to reveal a stained slip of paper inside, beige in colour, almost like it had been soaked in tea. There was a single word written on the paper that Luke struggled to make out. It was written in large italic handwriting.

'What does it say?' Luke had left his glasses in the glove compartment.

Damian leaned in closer. Through the crumpled clear plastic, he could vaguely make out the words;

Aka Manah

Damian read it out to him, pronouncing the second word 'manner'. He looked a bit bewildered. Luke was sympathetic. After all, he thought, this upped the 'weirdness' level quite considerably and Damo was new to this shit. Most new guys in the job expected to be dealing with the usual GBH, knife crime and drunken pub fights, not premeditated, pre-calculated and now 'sub-titled in a foreign language' murder.

Luke sighed. It was just what he needed. Some voodoo bullshit on top of all the other crap he had going on.

'Take your phone to somewhere that actually has a signal and see if you can Google what the hell that means. Seems to me like our perpetrator had some sort of interest in some weird occult shit that probably bears absolutely no relation to the atrocities he's inflicted on that poor young girl.'

Luke just hated this kind of thing. It seemed like all the nut-jobs nowadays wanted some kind of interesting tagline. If it wasn't the occult it was religion, if it wasn't religion it was some allegiance to another nut-job. Just fucking lunatics as far as he was concerned. And now his head hurt.

'I'm going back to the station to brief the Chief. Keep an eye on this lot and give me a call as soon as the coroner's report comes in. I want to know cause and time of death. Find out if she was sexually violated in any way, both ends. And get me an update as soon as you hear anything on the ID. The quicker we know who she is the better.'

Damian nodded and waved his hand. Good kid, Luke thought, does what he's told. Needed more like him. *He* needed more like him.

He smiled and turned back to his car. His headache was getting worse. He could feel the burning behind his eyes and dull ache across the back of his skull.

Sure, he was heading back to the station, but he was going to make a pit-stop first.

Chapter 7: Boys Night In

Tony felt good. Really good. He was really steaming now, like a Maserati on steroids. Jane was so pleased. He could see it in the way she looked at him, smiling at him over her chicken passanda. He might have been imagining it, but he thought he might be in for a treat tonight, and that would be the first time for such a long time.

Intimacy for them had pretty much slowed to a crawl around four months ago and he suspected much of the reason for that was that she was subconsciously losing patience with him. Sure, on the surface it was all sweetness and light, but underneath she couldn't help but be disappointed with her choices. God knows her parents were.

But now he was actually producing something. He felt that if he could keep it up then that would help him to keep it up, so to speak. And the fact that she had held his hand over the table, engaging in upbeat conversation and laughing and smiling while they chatted, gazing at him while he spoke, stroking the top of his hand, made the situation all the more sweet.

Jane had cleaned up after dinner, scraping the plates and loading the dishwasher while Tony headed back to the dining room to fire up the computer. Microsoft Word was his new friend. How quickly an old enemy could change allegiances in the heat of the battle. Just with a few strokes of the keyboard and a spattering of grammar and punctuation.

He had cranked out a couple of chapters in little under an hour, the prose coming to him as if it was already written within his head. How the hell it had been contained in there, unwilling to come out or even to pull the curtains a crack, really puzzled him. An agoraphobic imagination. It had gone so well today that at times he struggled to prevent his fingers from fizzing over the keyboard. He half expected to see smoke emanating from his finger-tips. He had also suddenly become an expert typist, hardly hitting a wrong letter or accidently pressing 'delete' or 'enter'.

But he didn't want to overcook it. It was good to write but it was also good to stop. Stories needed structure; a beginning, a middle and an end. A through line, character studies, emotion, twists and taglines and, above all, a compelling plot. All the things he had studied during his Creative Writing and English Literature degree. And he wasn't going to spoil what he was doing through tenacity, over-eagerness and spunk.

Plus, he had that invitation from Bill to consider. And, man, did he deserve a celebration.

'Jane, I'm popping over to Billy's,' he mumbled sheepishly. She usually didn't mind but his night time trysts to his neighbour's den had started to become more of a habit than spontaneous and occasional events.

Jane popped her head through the door, 'Oh, okay. Are you done?'

'I've been doing pretty good. Another couple of chapters in the bag and some real story developments. I'm, er, feeling pretty okay about it,' he grinned at her, all of his slightly uneven teeth showing.

'OK, but don't be late. You don't want to sleep in too long in the morning. You've got work to do now. Plus, I've had a long day and don't want you waking me up drunk again.'

'I won't, I won't. I'm just popping over to watch a film and have a chat. I think he's having a tough time at work.'

Jane smiled, 'Billy would moan even if he wasn't having a tough time. That's his natural demeanour. Seriously, I don't know how Sal' puts up with him.'

'I think she just switches off,' he laughed, 'not everyone's as lucky as me, having a beautiful and understanding gal like you.' With that he stood up, grabbed her hand and pulled her to him. They kissed passionately. He held her shoulders and looked down at her earnestly. From his six-foot-four elevation her five-foot-five frame looked delicate and frail.

'I know I've been hard to be with at times but it's all going to change, Jane. I'm going to make you proud; you wait and see. I'm going to pay you back in spades. I love you darling.'

She hugged him then. Hugged him tightly around his waist, her face buried in his chest.

'I know you will, sweetheart, I know.' She stifled unexpected tears and turned back to the kitchen, 'I'll see you later on tonight. Behave yourself over there,' and she was gone.

*

Tony knocked on the door.

Bill's den was separated from the house by the full length of his garden. Around fifty feet of lawn, shrubs and bedding plants. The den was a brick-built outhouse; flat roof, breeze block construction, heavy wooden door and one UPVC window. Around ten feet by ten feet internally, it was perfectly big enough for a flat screen, a beer fridge, a three-seater sofa and several pictures of scantily clad women. Tony would be lying if he claimed he wasn't jealous. It was what many people now referred to as the perfect 'man cave'.

Billy opened up a crack and looked out, 'That's not the secret knock.'

'Oh…sorry,' Tony knocked again while Billy looked on. Rat, rat, raaaat, rat, rat, tat taaaaaaat. Smoke on the Water. Who didn't love that riff?

Billy opened up wide, standing there bareback, dark glasses on, khaki shorts and flip flops, arms open in a welcoming gesture. He looked like a slightly more eccentric version of Richard Attenborough in Jurassic Park. He always cranked the heat up high in the den and insisted on being topless. A large spliff burned brightly in the ash tray next to the couch.

'Come in…come iiiinnnnn my maaaaan.'

Tony entered and closed the door behind him, hoping that Jane wasn't looking out of the rear window. He'd promised to be sensible.

The TV was blaring, Vin Diesel pulling a few gees in a large American Hotrod, some half-dressed actress (somebody Rodriguez) draped over him while he shifted gears. It was good to see that the art of using automotive phallic symbols was alive and well in Hollywood.

Billy turned the volume down, the sound bar shifting from a loud booming thud to a small tinny mumble.

'Not as good as the last one,' he declared as he crashed back on to the sofa, 'didn't think you would make it out tonight. Thought Jane would have you chained to the keyboard.'

'Oh now, come on. Bill. She's not like that. And anyway, I've put down some more pages and we both thought I deserved some time out.'

'Glad to hear it, glad to hear it,' he handed Tony the joint, 'Sally's away tonight, round her mums for the evening. Something about arranging some family event. Anniversary or some shit. I dunno, I struggle to keep up with that lot.' He crossed his hands behind his head, 'So, I've got the whole night to myself. Might not even go back in tonight. Might stay out here,' he smiled, looking at Tony over the top of his glasses.

'You really have it made, Billy. An understanding wife, a bat cave of your own and your own business. You've got it all sorted. Wish I had,' Tony took a hit and almost instantly felt a wave of nausea mixed with exultation and delirium.

'Holy shit,' he exhaled, 'what the fuck is that?'

'Some Mexican skunk I got from my guy,' he laughed like a kid, 'he reckons it's the strongest weed he's ever sold, and I tend to agree with him.'

'Jesus Billy, I'm not sure I could do any more of that,' he laughed and fell backwards into the sofa, 'man, that's got to have some pretty high-octane THC.'

'Sure has. I've been using it for a little over a week and it blows your mind. Can't over-do it though. Makes you see weird shit.' He pulled down his sunglasses and rolled his eyes comically.

Tony laughed uneasily, 'It's even better with tunes on, listen, I've got the latest Chemical Brothers download. Check this out.'

With a flick of a button Billy's Bang and Olufson kicked into life. Immediately thumping bass and pounding electro-synth rattled from the eight speaker plus sub-woofer sound system. He thought it was a good job that Bill had spent the money sound-proofing the den. The neighbours, of which Jane was one, would go ballistic.

Tony could hardly hear himself think let alone speak, but Billy was right. This helped a lot. Helped ease the mind.

Billy threw him a bottled Stella Artois. Tony ripped the lid off, took a swig and another hard toke on the spliff. Boy this was good, he thought. Really chilled him out. It was good to feel this way. He was on his way to fulfilling a professional dream and he had the right to celebrate, goddam it. He was doing nothing wrong. He was his own man and he could do his own thing. Fuck everyone else. He deserved to feel good and right now he felt, in the words of Tony the Tiger, 'Grrrreeeaaat!'

Billy was up, another spliff lit, his bare belly sagging over his combat shorts, arms aloft, raving to the beat, joint clamped between his teeth. The room was getting smokier and smokier, smelling more and more like wet, week-old socks, but the atmosphere was great. Tony leapt up and joined him, waving his arms in the air like an ape, laughing infectiously.

'Life doesn't get much better than this, Tony my man! We are at one with the world! Happy days are here to stay! Let's celebrate! Cheers!' They clinked bottles as the music pounded.

'Here's to your book, Tony!'

'Here's to your 'guy' Bill! And here's to the Mexicans! Viva Mexico! And by the way, it's a novel. NOT A FUCKING BOOK!'.

Chapter 8: Aka Manah

He didn't feel guilt. Didn't really feel anything. Just calm. A calm that seemed to fully encompass his mind, body and soul. Odd. He expected to feel guilt. Remorse. Shame.

It had all happened quite quickly, which surprised him. It surprised him at how cruelly adept he was at it. How quickly he turned from mister to monster. He didn't even feel the change; it was like it was in him all along.

He hadn't meant to kill her. Well, not at first anyway. But she wouldn't stop screaming. Just went on and on and no matter what he did or how he tried to stop her she just kept doing it. Silly.

It was a shame. He had wanted the sex. It wasn't all that he wanted but he had wanted it nonetheless. And she wanted it too of course. That's how they had happened to be there in the first place. He had asked and she had accepted. Offered her the proverbial coffee, which of course she didn't want. But they both knew that he hadn't really offered her coffee in any case. He just wanted to be inside. Inside his bedroom and inside her.

And accepting his offer was her big mistake. Her last big mistake because *he* had arrived. Just as he had made it up the stairs, almost as soon as he had opened the door of his room. *He* had seen it and *he* had made an entrance. It had confused and confounded him. He had been told that it would happen but seeing, or feeling, was believing.

He had penetrated him. Entered his body and used him as his vehicle. Like a drone pilot, *he* directed him from some far-away place. It was a weird feeling. Odd but strangely comforting, like a mother's hug or a father's stern hand. *He* took him to a place, a place where there were no consequences. Where you could do whatever you wanted, and no-one cared. He was the autonomous vehicle carrying out the deeds. The deadly deeds. She was just in the wrong place at the wrong time.

But unlike a drone pilot, *he* could be seen. *He* wanted to be seen. Wanted her to feel fear, dreadful unabated fear that would tear through her like a virus. Incapacitating her so that she couldn't move, couldn't flee, couldn't think.

And he had enjoyed it too. On some level. He didn't resist, he simply did *his* bidding. And with a tightening of his hands and a little thrashing and contorting she was gone. Simple. Her God delivered her into this world, and *he* took her away. So easy.

And *he* wanted them to see. All of them. Show her to them. Let them see what he could do. Let them know *his* power. They had no ability to stop *him*. They could try with all their resources, their technology and their theories but *he* would do what *he* wished. And he would do what *he* wished.

Of course, there were complications. People who had seen him and who had witnessed him with the girl. Unavoidable really. They had met in public, had spent time together out in the open, in front of and amongst others. Couldn't be helped. It was not how he had planned the evening, but it was how it had unfolded, nevertheless. But people could be swayed. Minds could be manipulated. Phone records could be erased. *He* would see to that. *He* had told him not to be concerned. *He* would use his unique gifts to cast a web of invisibility and manipulate the recollections of the weak.

And of course this was only the beginning. He knew it. Now that *he* had started, *he* would not abate. *He* wanted it so badly and he was the only way that *he* could get it. They were bound by a common and unbounding desire. He knew that *he* wouldn't allow him to move too fast but that *he* would allow him to have what he wanted when all was said and done. The thrill was in the chase after all. Don't be too premature. Take your time. Hakuna Matata. There were plenty of fish in the sea, plenty of lives to be ruined, rivers of human blood to be spilt in *his* name.

They had crossed *him* and they would be made to pay.

Chapter 9: The Hangover

I have no idea what time he came in. I didn't hear him. I'd gone to bed at around ten thirty while he was still outside with that overgrown child, Billy West. I have to admit, I was a little annoyed but I let it go. Things were better and I didn't want to spoil it by going to bed on an argument.

I woke that morning at my usual time, six a.m. Tony was lying diagonally across the bed, completely butt naked apart from a pair of old black, holely socks. Not very attractive. And he stunk of alcohol and weed. He thought I didn't know but I knew. My mother didn't raise an idiot.

I went downstairs, like I did every day, to make both of us a tea. The early morning sun streamed through the blinds in the kitchen window. It really was beautiful that time of year. Much nicer than during the winter months when the sun seemed to always struggle to pick itself up off of the floor. A little like Tony that morning.

I also made him some toast because he looked like his stomach would need some serious lining. I really cared for him, you know. Okay, things hadn't been that great in the recent months, but I was committed to making them better. Nick would understand. I really had hoped that Nick would understand.

Tony's laptop was open on the dining room table, and I felt sure it had been closed and put away when I went to bed. The battery was flat so I couldn't read anything he'd written, but I'm not sure that I would have anyway. I wanted Tony to have the freedom to write his novel without any pressure or fear of reprisal. It had been the pressure that had dried him up, and because his creative valves were open and free flowing, I didn't want to twist them closed again. I was afraid that the rust might set in, sealing them shut forever.

I looked out of the kitchen window and saw a large chunk of our wonderfully blooming red hydrangea lying across the garden path. It seemed that Tony was a little worse for wear when he climbed over the low garden fence to get back to our side. Bloody thing had taken me ages to get right, pruning and tying so that it flowered in just the right places. I wasn't much of a gardener but what I did I did meticulously and to an order. I planned to admonish him later.

The kettle boiled and the toaster pinged, and I took him up his breakfast. I gently rubbed his back to wake him.

He jumped with a start, 'No, no, no, it's not like that. I was just talking, we…we were just talking…'

'Tony, Tony, it's me. I've made you some tea.'

His glazed eyes stared at me through his tousled and shaggy blonde hair. It took him a few seconds to come back to this earth from whatever planet he had been occupying.

'Oh, hi babe. Hi,' his voice was gruff and deep, 'sorry, I was, er… dreaming.'

'That's OK, honey. Here's your breakfast.'

He sat up in bed, pushed the pillows against the headboard so that he could sit upright and took the toast. He looked like he'd been literally dragged through the hydrangea backwards. He pulled the duvet up across his lap in order to cover his manhood and then munched hungrily into the roughly cut bread, making a low humming sound as he did so.

'What time did you make it home last night?'

'Oh,' he spoke through hunks of crust and buttery wholemeal, 'around two, I think. Sorry darling, I got chatting and time got away from me. Bill's done a nice job in there you know. Very homely.'

He looked sincere. I buried my pissiness as far down as I could, hoping that it didn't show on my face. I thought that if that overweight juvenile next door had ruined that day's planned literary productivity then I was going to be less than pleased. Pretty flipping angry in fact.

'I'm going to take a shower,' I turned to him, sitting there with crumbs all the way down his chest, slurping and gurgling on a large mug of hot Typhoo. Milk, one sugar. He looked so innocent, 'It looked like you did some more on your novel when you came in this morning. I hope you were in a fit state to write.'

He looked up sharpish, 'Oh... er... did... erm... yeah. I, er, told you, it was a quiet one. Just some nachos and a couple of beers. We're getting quite civilised in our old age.' He looked both worried and troubled and that told me all I needed to know.

As I turned on the shower in the en-suite, adjusting the mixer to get the water temperature just right, I cursed under my breath. I remember thinking that if he'd logged in and deleted the whole bloody thing while stoned and off his face I would be knocking on our neighbour's door. Billy West would feel the unholy wrath of a very tired and unhappy woman. And that would be something he would not forget in a hurry.

Chapter 10: The Surprise

Tony was sitting at his laptop. His head throbbed and his throat burned. He was pretty sure he smelt rotten too, and he hoped that Jane hadn't picked up on that. Just put it down to a bad case of the early morning death breath.

She had left for work about twenty minutes earlier and she had seemed in an okay mood. A little short with him but that wasn't unusual. She wasn't an early bird after all. Didn't really get going until after her second or third cup of coffee. He couldn't complain. She had the nine til' five job and paid most of the bills after all. Sure, he had his measly wage but that didn't even cover the cost of the shopping. Food bills certainly weren't what they used to be. The pressure had been on her for some time now and she did a pretty good job of coping with it, silently beavering away and keeping her own counsel for the most part.

What had really gotten to him was his novel. She was right. He had been writing after he had got back this morning. Some pretty weird shit too.

He was amazed that he had been in a fit state to write anything at all. Christ, he couldn't even remember coming home. Sure, he had told Jane that he had gotten back at around two, and that may have been right, but he had no way of knowing. He was actually pretty astounded that he had found his way back home.

That was the trouble with spending an evening with his excitable and slightly needy neighbour. He was such a welcoming host that it was extremely difficult to get away and after a while you just went along with whatever it was he was doing and time just washed away from underneath you. And, he thought, with the help of a little South American mumbo jumbo it certainly hadn't taken long for that to happen last night.

The last thing he remembered was downing a few shots of tequila while Sabbath Bloody Sabbath boomed out from the sound system. Nineteen seventies stoner rock, the type of music that only ever suited that type of occasion. Billy always had the right tunes for the right moment. Tony wondered whether he was still out there, crashed out in the den with empty bottles of beer and tequila lying around his rotund and half-naked torso, unused rizlas stuck to his face like band aids. He must have taken the day off or had a late start which was one of the clear benefits of working for yourself. No boss to answer to, although he was sure he would complain about it later on. Jane was right. When he was sober Billy complained about pretty much everything.

Tony had rushed downstairs after he had nonchalantly kissed Jane goodbye in the bedroom and then waited for the front door to swing shut. He glanced out of the landing window to be sure she had gone, getting into her beaten up Corsa and driving slowly down their congested street. He had been in such a hurry that he had almost tripped over a pair of slippers on the landing and crashed down the steep staircase. That would have been just spiffing, he cursed under his breath. Budding novelist found dead from a fall in his home, neck broken, naked except for a pair of yellow stained boxer shorts and hole-ridden socks. Not really the way he wanted to check out.

Once he'd composed himself, he had booted up the laptop. It took a minute or two as it was completely out of charge. For a few, hair-raising moments he silently panicked that he hadn't saved his work and he would be reliant on Windows auto-save to rescue the few pages that he had managed to complete during his recent rush of creativity.

He breathed a sigh of relief when, after he had gone through the log in ritual of mis-typing, swearing out loud, mis-typing again and then re-typing his password, the Word document opened and everything was still intact.

Except there was an addition. A new chapter and one that he didn't recognise. He sat down at the table, half cold mug of tea in hand, and read what the stoned/drunk him had written, presumably a few hours earlier.

And whilst it wasn't what he had planned (he had been planning to flesh out one of the main characters next, give the story some depth), he considered it to actually not be half bad. Not much of it there, he thought, just a couple of pages, but what was there was both interesting and surreal, a turn of narrative and a nice change in pace. It appeared that even when intoxicated the new creative him was able to knock out something passable. This really was new, he thought to himself. Very new and very useful indeed. Good to know, he might say.

He sat back smugly in the dining room chair, jumping slightly as the cold pine struts of the chair's upright met his naked back. That didn't matter. This was good. He was very pleased. It felt like things were looking up after all. He smiled to himself, a small chuckle emanating from his hoarse vocal cords. Inwardly he now felt a little better about last night. A little more productive. He had felt pretty guilty when Jane had been looking down on him this morning, with eyes that said 'I know what you did last night you lazy, good for nothing waste of space. Thought you were finally worth something, did you? Well guess what asshole, you were wrong!'

But now that feeling had passed. Now he felt like he was unstoppable. Impervious to the dangers of drinking on a school night. Justified in his perilous actions. Unbreakable and victorious, ready for whatever that day, the week and even the rest of the month could throw at him. What was it that Vince Vaughan said in that film – 'dodge, dip, dive, duck and dodge'? He was doing all of those things and, like Elton John, he was still standing. This opened up a whole new world of possibilities for him.

He smiled as he contemplated a bacon sandwich and a fresh cup of tea, the whole day stretching out ahead of him like a long, silent road, the end of which dipped beyond the horizon.

Chapter 11: It's Five O' Clock Somewhere

Luke ordered another. It was going to take more than one rusty nail to shift his headache. Last night was another in a long string of late nights and, what was it that Lisa said to him? Something like, 'If you keep burning the candle at both ends eventually you're going to scorch your fingers.' Wait, he thought, was that it? Who knew and who cared? All he really knew was that he needed a drink, and he needed one pretty badly.

Daisy was behind the bar. She looked up at him through her scruffy blonde boy's cut and scowled. They had had a thing once. Purely off the record of course, and it hadn't turned out too well. Raven had gotten a little handy with one of the punters who insisted on constantly stroking and massaging her arm, rubbing her back and tugging on her hair. He'd thrown him across the dance floor and smashed his head repeatedly against the stage. The landlord had intervened and threw the punter out, blood pouring from a gash above his eye, but he had made it very clear that he held Luke responsible and that Daisy was equally to blame. He had even docked her that evening's wages. Luke had apologised and she had eventually feigned forgiveness, but things had never been the same. He didn't think it had been going anywhere in any case and she was certainly better off without him.

'Drinking a little early in the day, aren't we?' she sniped as she worked a damp rag round the bar. 'Aren't you s'posed to be working?

Aren't there criminals to catch out there? We can't keep relying on Batman you know.'

He threw his second scotch back and smiled, the remaining ice clinking in his glass as he set it down, 'Actually I do, but it's a big one and I need a little sharpening up.'

'You're not as young as you were, Raven. Your body can't take it the way it used to. And in any case, haven't you been in enough trouble recently?'

He had to admit, she was right on that score, but the train-wreck of his professional and personal life was contributing heavily to his overcast state of mind. This latest encounter at the Common was just another nail in the coffin, ready and waiting for the hammer to fall.

'There's nothing wrong with my body, Daisy, and you of all people know that. I can deal with my problems, thanks. Everybody's got 'em. I just happen to be an avid collector of the best ones.'

'Well,' she smiled ruefully, 'as much as I like the company, this ain't no way for you to sort yourself out. I've told you before, they ain't gonna put up with you for much longer. Just don't wanna see you down and out. Not that it's any business of mine, but you're a good punter and it would be a shame to lose you.'

There was a hidden meaning there, he was sure of it. Did she still like him? It had been a long time, but who knew?

'Hey, don't get any ideas,' she glared at him accusingly, 'I'm just looking out for you, that's all.'

Luke stared at the bottom of his glass and sighed, 'You concentrate on your issues, lady, and let me deal with mine,' he paused and looked up, 'how is your mum by the way?'

The shot hit home. Never could miss with that one.

Daisy's mum was a crack addict and lived at home on her own in one of the less salubrious parts of town. Daisy was her only daughter and because of that she took the sole burden of her care. It was a full-time job for her on top of the full-time job she had at The Golden Swan and it controlled her life. If she wasn't here she was there, and if she wasn't there she was catching up on what little sleep she could get. It had been tough on her, but Luke knew that, and it was, ashamedly, his favourite come back line. Levelled the playing field in a battle.

'Fuck you, Raven! That's a low blow and you know it,' her eyes were red with rage mixed with more than a little shame, 'don't expect to come back here when your life is down the shitter and nobody wants you.'

He managed a false laugh as she turned to walk away.

'Oh, come on. You know I didn't mean it. I'm sure she's fine. Just ribbing you, that's all,' he raised a hand in fake surrender, 'I'll take one more for the road and then I'll get out of your way.'

'Never knew a copper who didn't like the odd drink before he got behind the wheel. It's one rule for you lot and another for the rest of us.' She grabbed his glass and threw in a shot of scotch, followed by Drambuie. She put it down hard on the beer mat, 'That'll be four pounds twenty-five please sir,' she spat as she held out her hand.

'I tell you, no wonder you lot are all going out of business. Used to be that you could have a drink or two and still leave the pub with the shirt on your back.'

She ignored him. There were three other punters in the pub. He recognised them all. All sitting on their own, two men at the bar and a woman at a table, all in there every morning at opening time, all of them retiring home for bed every day at around four or five to sleep off their beer buzz. AA was for amateurs. This was the real alcoholics meeting. It wasn't anonymous and no-one spoke, but they all knew each other, and they all knew how the others felt. In the grip of a vice that got tighter and tighter every day.

One of them, an old guy with a hat, clinked his glass. Daisy dutifully poured him a Dark and Mild. He pushed his change, lots of silver and copper, across the counter. She gathered it up and counted it into the till. He smiled to himself. There was no need for a 'tap and go' machine in this place.

'By the way, your girlfriend was in here earlier. Think she's looking for you.' She smiled and grabbed another punter's glass, pouring him a pint of Guiness. She knew the locals like the back of her hand, and they all appreciated her for it. She was what every good boozer needed. A hard as nails bar lady with a heart of gold and a soft touch.

So, he mused, Lisa had been in. He hadn't seen her for a few days, but it didn't bode well. She didn't often venture into the town centre looking for him, so either he was in trouble or she needed something. In neither instance did he see a good outcome for him. He decided that it was time to dance and avoid the confrontation, not feeling in any fit state to face up to her any time soon.

And anyway, he inwardly justified, he had a case to crack and a boss to brief. He reached into his jacket pocket and pulled out a packet of extra strong mints, shovelling two into his mouth and chewing them hard. He would need a few of those on the way back to the station to hide the stench of alcohol and regret.

'Thanks for the heads-up, Dais'. I still owe you dinner, don't forget.'

'You owe me an awful lot more than that, Raven, and you know it.'

Chapter 12: The Doctor

Damian was standing in the coroner's office, a large square room with an oversized bay window facing a well-groomed garden area. The office contained a sizeable mahogany desk, a large bookcase and two huge leather swivel chairs. He was watching the chief pathologist manoeuvre herself around the office, a pretty twenty something from London with a clipped, preppy accent and a nice arse. He was pretty sure he could see her knickers through her tight, grey, thigh-length skirt and felt his hands go clammy. While he hated the way that Raven left all of the work to him, he never passed up the chance to visit Doctor Jasmine Chandur's office. She always smelt great and looked fantastic.

'You will be interested to know, Detective, that the subject was asphyxiated before the blade cut through her carotid artery,' the doctor shot him a look of grim resignation, 'she was dead long before the final assault occurred.'

Damian couldn't take his eyes off her legs, long and dark with tiny ankles atop black Jimmy Choos. He concluded that she obviously earned herself a good salary working with the dead, far more than he earned working with the barely living. He felt her eyes on him. Busted.

'Er... that's very interesting, Doctor. How long had the victim been deceased before her, ahem, throat was cut?'

The doctor sat back in her chair, the soft leather back and arms dwarfing her tiny frame. She swiped across the face of her tablet and looked down at her report, her brow furrowed as she searched for what she was looking for. God he would like to see that face first thing in the morning. He shoved his hands in his pockets to hide the growing swelling.

'I would say about thirty minutes to an hour. Heavy bruising around the neck, she was most probably strangled by hand given the damage to the muscle tissue and the crushing to the oesophagus and vocal cords. No other damage to the torso or limbs. No other cuts or contusions. We have checked for any signs of a struggle but there are no traces of skin or hair under her nails. That is quite unusual. The body appeared to have been very well cleaned prior to being, erm, deposited.'

Damian started taking notes in his pocket book, not because he had to, all of this would be in her report of course, but because he needed to occupy himself. He was having trouble focussing his mind. What was that scent she was wearing? It was a musky smell of berries in the spring. Not something that he had ever smelt on anyone he had dated or met, but then he didn't mix in the same circles as the doctor. She was most certainly a level or five above his usual dates. He wondered what that dark skin would look like with no clothes on and with the lights dimmed, sweat gleaming from her body while she leant over him, eyes gazing down and hair swinging side to side while her slight bosom gently heaved. He coughed and sought to compose himself.

'That's a real shame, Doctor. We were hoping that she could give us some kind of clue on who her assailant was. Any other points to note?'

'Yes,' she had a fascinated and slightly bemused look on her face, 'one disturbingly interesting point. The victim had lost a lot of blood. An awful lot.'

'That's not really surprising, is it, Doc? She'd had her throat cut after all. That's a sure-fire way of losing blood pretty quickly, right? A fast checkout and all that.'

'No detective. You're missing my point. The human body, a living human, contains around eight pints or four and a half litres of blood, varying dependent upon height and weight, age, diet etcetera. The victim is... was... around five feet five inches and somewhere between eight and nine stone. Therefore, four and a half litres would be a reasonable assessment of normal blood levels.'

'Er, okay. Thanks for the update on all things blood related. I'll clock those details for any future police-force wine and wisdom events.'

The doctor frowned and tapped the tip of her pen on the heavily lacquered desk, 'This is certainly not a laughing matter detective.'

'Sorry Doc.'

She sighed, 'Anyway, with the type of injury the victim had sustained one would expect her blood level to drop by around fifty to seventy percent depending upon orientation, how fast the heart was beating, coagulation etcetera. This would typically take just a few minutes,' she smoothed a strand of dark hair behind her ear, 'however, in this case, as I have already advised, the victim's heart had already stopped beating. The blood loss would therefore be far less prevalent and would take much longer. What surprised me when the victim was brought to me was that there was very little blood around the wound and almost none on her body, a slight pooling of old blood but no dried fresh blood around her upper torso. Even with an inactive heart the initial cut would cause quite a spray, causing a covering from the chest down to the waist.'

This biology lesson was helping. Damian hadn't looked at Doctor Chandur's cleavage for at least three minutes.

'But you've already said that the body was cleaned before being moved to the Common. Seems to me like the killer had watched CSI and knew that we would be looking for clues, DNA and such like.'

The doctor swung her chair from side to side as she chewed the end of her pen. Her glasses rested on the tip of her delicate nose. Damian blinked. Was she trying to tease him or what?

'That is correct, detective. But what is really interesting is that when we investigated further, we found that the body contained less than five percent of what we would consider to be a typical blood level.'

'Five per cent. How much is that?'

'Detective, the young girl had around two hundred millilitres of blood left. That's just over a third of a pint,' the Doctor was rocking side to side on her chair whilst considering her sentence, 'that is to say that she was almost completely empty. That could not have been caused solely by a natural bleed out.' Damian put his notebook back in his pocket.

'What are you saying, Doc?'

The doctor leaned forward, her elbows resting casually on her desk, her small hands folded neatly under her chin.

'This girl was drained, detective,' her words hung in the air like a heavy fog, 'for whatever reason, your murderer strangled her to death, cut her throat and drained almost all of the blood from her body, post mortem. This isn't your usual crime of passion, I'm afraid. Whoever did this was a very, very sick individual indeed.'

Damian gulped and grimaced. This was not good, he thought, not good at all. He flipped open his notebook and scrolled back a few pages. The capsule in the evidence bag flashed forward in his mind's eye. The words which eluded him but which he had made a note of that morning were written in his scrawled handwriting.

Aka Manah. Evil Spirit.

Chapter 13: The Chief

He loved to sit in his office, back to the door, binoculars raised, peering across the wide expanse of lawn and assorted trees and shrubbery that surrounded Westhampton Central. It took his mind off the detritus of slime and filth that passed across his desk day after day after day. The never-ending sea of decay that gave off a foul stench and sat in the pit of his stomach like a three-day old, sixteen-ounce steak that he just couldn't digest. No, the birds gave him his centre, gave him his peace and freedom of thought. He only had to spot a Pied Wagtail or a Spotted Flycatcher circling overhead and his mind was at ease. Temporarily, but at ease all the same.

He was looking down at a group of birds about two hundred yards out, sitting on a makeshift bird table that one of the PCs had brought in, apparently homemade in his garage. The haphazard wooden structure leaned acutely to the right, but it was sturdy enough for some of the office staff to hang fat-balls and seed trays from.

It was difficult to tell with the sun behind them, but he was convinced he could make out a yellow breast, black and white hood, tipped wings, possibly a Great Tit. He wasn't sure, could be a Coal Tit he considered as he zoomed in. He reached behind himself for his Twitcher's Bible and almost knocked his half-drunk coffee on the floor. Cursing, he flipped open the book and lifted his 32X Olympus binoculars back to his eyes to double check.

At that precise moment he caught a glimpse of the navy-blue

Mondeo as it pulled into the car park, skidding to a halt across two parking spaces. The driver's door swung open with a load crack and the single occupant heaved his large frame out into the open air, eyes blinking rapidly like a prisoner of war emerging from an underground bunker. The chief sighed at the driver's appearance; tousled dark, greying hair, unshaven face, crumpled charcoal suit with a light blue shirt, collar unbuttoned.

Raven, he cursed, the rather large and unsightly thorn in the chief's rather large and unsightly arse.

He considered Raven to be a good cop. No, a very good cop. But a very good cop with very big issues. And those issues appeared to him to be getting bigger and more complicated and as a result Luke Raven was slipping further and further into a rather large, wet and cavernous hole; one which Chief Inspector Dave Simmons was feeling less and less confident that he could ever climb out of.

The chief leaned back in his chair and rested his binoculars on the table. It had never been great with Raven, but things had taken a significant turn for the worse when his father, a very well-respected local businessman, had died suddenly. The guy was worth a load of money, earned it all through a furniture business that he had built up from its humble beginnings. A simple market stall that had become a string of shops that littered the surrounding Hampshire area. He had left it all to Raven and his mother, but Raven had rejected it. Had absolutely renounced it in fact. It had always seemed to the chief that Raven and his father had never got on. Un-reconcilable differences. Nobody knew what they were, but it all appeared to stem from Luke's parents separating when he was in his early teens.

Raven had always been a drinker, was always the last to leave a knees up after a big bust, but the last two years had seen him turn up to work drunk on several occasions, make irrational and inconceivable decisions on big cases, fight with colleagues both in the office and in public and generally be an arse to be around.

It had gotten close to being the end of the line a few times but Simmons had held back. Sure, he had given him a few warnings, had docked his overtime and given him lesser cases, but the chief had always resisted making it final. He couldn't say why, particularly. Maybe, he often thought to himself, just maybe he saw something in Raven that he subconsciously admired, maybe he felt that despite his problems he considered him an asset to the department. Or maybe he was just an over sentimental idiot who should have done the right thing a long time ago and shown him the door. Only time would tell, he pondered, but what he did know was that his afternoon was going to get a hell of a lot worse as soon as his office door opened.

And when it did it was with a load bang and a chaotic fluttering of papers.

'Jesus Luke, can't you ever come in quietly? Didn't they teach you that at spy school?'

'Never went to spy school, chief. Didn't have the nose for it,' he chuckled and slumped into a chair opposite the chief's desk.

Chief Simmons poured a coffee into a Styrofoam cup from the percolator on the pedestal next to his desk and handed it to Raven.

'Looks like you could use one.'

'Thanks chief. Yeah, I could. Hell of a mess out there. Just got off the phone to Barber. It sounds like we have a sick son of a bitch on the loose.'

He filled the chief in on the gory details. The body, the way it was carefully laid out for them, the capsule with the scrawled handwriting, the strangulation, the slicing of the girl's throat post mortem and the draining of her blood.

Chief Simmons took a large swig from his coffee, black two sugars, and exhaled loudly. He rubbed one hand across his eyes as he considered the very complicated and emotional press briefing that was ahead of him. He just knew that the local rag were going to be all over him like an irritating and uncomfortable rash.

'Tell me you have an ID.'

'We do. Got that about an hour ago. The girl is a student from the local Uni. Twenty-one years old. She was studying literature. Her name is,' he paused and let out a long breath of regret, 'was, Tracey Webb. She's not from the area. She had moved here to study. Her parents live in the Lake District, Ullswater I think. I've got an officer from the region visiting them now.'

To tell the truth Raven was relieved that the parents weren't local. It was not a home-call that he had been looking forward to.

47

'Oh Christ. I'm going to have the Mayor on my back about this. The last thing this town needs is bad press for the University. If I've been told once about the economic benefits of the student fraternity, I've been told a thousand times.'

Chief Simmons stood and paced his office, rubbing his hands together in agitation.

'It gets worse I'm afraid, boss,' Raven swung his chair around to face the chief who was now standing behind him, 'whoever did this knew what they were doing. No fingerprints, no debris on the torso, crime scene was clean aside from some boot prints, generic size elevens, no eyewitnesses, no clues at the victim's room back at campus. Our only lead is that her friends confirmed that they were all out at a local club, Gold-Diggers, when she disappeared.'

Luke was not enjoying this. He hated being in a position where he had nothing positive to say. He liked to be the problem solver, the guy that the team could rely on to find the unfindable, to uncover the one piece of the puzzle that nobody else could locate. He could see Simmons was getting tetchy, his face was turning crimson and his body language was jerky and unsettled. He knew that this was possibly his last chance at rewarding the chief's faith in him, and yet he was drawing a blank.

'We've checked the club's CCTV but it's got a huge time-lag between frames. Some cheap shit system that the owner had installed a few years ago. One minute she's there, the next minute she's gone. We're continuing to work it but at the moment we're not seeing anything unusual. We're going to have to put out a wider announcement, ask the local community if they saw anything at all, no matter how trivial. This is going to take manpower, and a lot of it. And based on what we have so far, I would say that there is a better than average chance that this maniac will do this again,' the chief huffed at this, 'and soon.'

Simmons could feel his blood pressure escalating, his ears starting to ring and the backs of his eyeballs beginning to ache. Think birds, think birds he thought to himself, you're out in a field and they're circling around you. You've got a flask of coffee, lunch in your rucksack. The spring air is fresh and clean. Stuart's with you. And the dogs. You're enjoying the sunshine, the calming relaxation. The view is magnificent. You can see the sea from here, the yachts, the sun reflecting on the water. You have no worries, no pressure.

Fuck it, he swore under his breath, it wasn't working.

'OK. I need a full report and a press briefing for the morning. Any chance of getting the parents down here to make an emotional plea?'

'I'll get Barber onto it.'

'And get something out to the campus. Let's assume this nut-job has a thing for young women. Don't panic them but ensure that the University instructs the students to be on their guard. Get a few patrol cars to scan the area at night. Keep working that CCTV footage. There must be something there that we're not seeing. Check people entering and leaving the building at all times during the day. Run background checks on all the staff. We've got to shut this thing down quickly and cheaply. The budget's already creaking, and a long running and costly murder case is not going to do us any favours.'

Raven was working all of those angles of course. He wouldn't be very good at his job if he wasn't, but he was relieved to hear Simmons get engaged and not enraged. He was always impressed with how quickly Dave Simmons formulated a damage limitation plan. He sure knew how the politics worked and he could see that he was considering all the permeations. He guessed that was how he had risen to the position he now occupied. Attention to detail, play the game, grease the wheels and oil the pistons.

'I'll get onto it, boss.'

'And Raven?'

'Yeah?'

'Lay off the fucking sauce. You smell like a distillery. I'm going to need you all over this and you can't do that with one foot in the sewer.'

Luke crumpled the packet of mints in his pocket and decided that he needed to think of a better way of covering his tracks.

'Will do, Chief. One hundred percent.'

Chapter 14: The Visitor

There was a knock on the door. Tony thought it was unusual to be disturbed in the middle of the day. In fact, it was almost unheard of.

He got up from the dining room table, pulled down the screen of his laptop and walked through the hallway to the front porch.

He opened the door.

Standing there was a short man, unshaven, scruffy brown shoulder length hair, wearing a black hoody and tracksuit bottoms with beaten and dirty white trainers.

His brother.

'Hiya Mitch. You OK?' Tony hadn't seen his brother in a couple of weeks, and he was shocked at the sudden and unexpected interruption, 'What's up?'

Mitchell Richards wiped a hand across his stubbly chin.

'Can I come in? It's about Mum.'

*

They were drinking tea. Mitch hated coffee and Tony couldn't be arsed to faff around. And, anyway, his mind was running on overdrive.

'It's cancer, Tone. Lung cancer. They've given her three months and that's optimistic. She's a mess. She struggles to get herself up out of her chair every day, I've been missing shifts just to keep an eye on her. It's only going to get worse… I… I don't know what to do.'

Mitch's eyes were red raw, and his appearance was even more unkempt than usual. Tony could see that the news had taken its toll on him both physically and emotionally. He had been relaying the facts to him for the last thirty minutes and he just kept repeating the prognosis, like the act of saying it would eventually make it less real.

Tony considered Mitch to be a tough kid but he knew that a hard shell didn't protect you from a harsh reality, particularly when that reality lived in the same house as you and made you your dinner every day, washed your clothes, cleaned your room and wiped your bloody arse.

Tony was shocked, sure he was shocked. And upset too. But he hadn't seen his Mum in over three years, and they hadn't parted on the best of terms. She had made it pretty clear during their last conversation that he was a disappointment, an anomaly even and that she would not be held responsible or accountable for how his life turned out. She had been the monkey on his back for so long that at the time it was a huge relief to let her go, to feel the weight of expectation lifting from his shoulders. She wasn't even his real mum, her and her husband had taken him in at the age of three, and since his dad had left when he was ten she had come down on him like a crushing and imposing weight, like somehow the crap in her life was in some way his fault. He had never fathomed what he had ever done to make her so reproachful to him. He was just a kid for God's sake.

So they didn't speak. Didn't see each other at Christmas. Didn't celebrate the other's birthday. Didn't Skype or email. Were definitely not Facebook friends. And now she was going to die, and he didn't know how he felt about that.

'You've got to come and see her, Tony. You've got to make your peace with her before she goes. She's changed. She often talks about you, even asks me how you and Jane are doing. I think she realises what she's lost,' he stifled a sob, 'especially now that the end is staring her in the face. She…she won't want to leave it this way.'

'Has she…has she had a second opinion? I mean, are you convinced, is *she* convinced that it's really terminal? They can do an awful lot nowadays, Mitch, with the right doctor and the right medication.'

'Second opinion, third opinion. They're all saying the same thing.

Tumours on both lungs, advanced stages. They offered chemo but told her it might give her another couple of months, but they won't be good months. Understandably she's turned it down and wants to go with her dignity intact.'

Tony winced. He wasn't sure what else he could offer his brother. If that was it then that was it. What else could he do? Make another cup of tea?

'You need to go see her, Tone.'

Tony put his cup down, 'I...I need to think about it, Mitch. I can't just turn my feelings off. She has been a bitch to me for so long that at the moment that's how I still see her, the woman that never had a good word to say to me or about me. The woman who pushed so much negativity onto me that I felt like a piece of shit all day, every day for so long,' he reached a hand out to his brother, 'I need time.'

'But she hasn't got time, Tone. She hasn't got any time. She could be gone tomorrow for all I know, for all anyone knows. If you're going to do this, you've got to do it now!'

Mitch stood up and leaned against the kitchen worktop, arms folded. He looked like the little kid that Tony remembered from when they were little. Bottom lip stuck out, defensive posture, eyes turned down to the ground, hair all over his face. He'd gained some weight and some facial hair, but other than that he was the same little boy, hurt at not being able to get his own way and right now he was vulnerable. After all, he was a real Richards, wasn't he? She was his real mum. They shared the same blood, the same DNA. Tony resented him for that but loved him too.

'Look Mitch. I'll think about it. I really will. But I've got to figure out what to say to her. Let me let the news sink in,' Tony was trying to look Mitch in the eye, to show him he was being sincere, but his brother kept his focus firmly on the kitchen linoleum as if there was something of interest there, 'I'm a little bit shocked here you know. You've known this for a couple of days. I've only just found out.'

Mitch slammed his hand on the worktop, 'And that's always been the problem, Tony! I'm left to pick up the pieces. You two argue, I sweep up behind you. You upset her, I'm the one calming her down. You walk out, I'm the one left in that house, just me and her. You were never there! I've *always* been!'

Tony leaned back in his chair and sighed. Shit, he'd just started to get his life back on track and this huge, greasy spanner had been thrown in the works. He really didn't know what to do. He considered whether he should go and make peace with her and bury the hatchet after years and years of turmoil. But, he thought, should he stay away and avoid upsetting his mother at a moment when she needed to make the most of all the time she had left? Or should he just say fuck it, it's not my problem, and walk away? He wiped his hand across his forehead which was damp with perspiration. It felt hot in his house, stifling even and all he really wanted was Jane to come home.

He looked out the window onto the back garden. He was happy there. Happy with the way things were right now. He didn't want to go back, back to her. He knew how it would unfold. He would walk in, the room would turn icy. Her with her cold silver hair and hard face, pursed lips, angular frame, pointy hands. The way she looked at him, with hard, granite eyes. He would regress, turn back into the boy that always looked up at her hopefully for some praise or some words of comfort, a hug. She would be strong, despite her terminal illness. He would be weak. He didn't want that, to be that. He wanted to be in his safe place, in his new life, with his new home and his loving girlfriend.

'I… I can't commit to anything, Mitch. I'm really sorry about all this. I really am. But I can't commit to it. Not right now. I just can't.'

His brother lifted his head and glared at him, his anger barely hidden behind a cowl of brown curls, fists clenched. He whispered through gritted teeth, 'Fuck you, brother,' and wheeled around, storming out the door and slamming it hard behind him.

Tony buried his head in his hands and cursed under his breath, 'Fuck, fuck, fuck, fuck, fuck.'

Chapter 15: Nick

I finished up around four-thirty at the school that night. Classes had finished at three-twenty, but I had prep to do for the next day and some homework to mark. Those times were always the quiet times and I could sit at my desk, drink coffee and catch up with everything. Not a lot of teachers did it, I knew plenty of the younger school teachers in particular who left at finishing time and turned up at the last minute the following day. Isobelle called them the clock in and clock out brigade and I'd always dreaded becoming like one of them.

Tony was due at work that evening. He usually worked Tuesdays, Thursdays, Fridays and Saturdays. Not the best job in the world, Stooges was a shit-hole after all, but the money helped, and it kept him occupied. And I was so hopeful that his book would get off the ground and we could really kick our life together into gear. Christ, I couldn't stay at that school forever. The headmistress was a bitch.

I cleaned my desk and collected up all of my papers. I planned to finish the last of the marking at home while Eastenders was on as I knew I'd have the house to myself until around midnight with the TV remote firmly by my side. I planned to throw a lasagne-for-one in the microwave and open a bottle of merlot, Sainsbury's own because beggars couldn't be choosers, and slowly inebriate myself.

That was when Nick waltzed in.

'Hi sweet-cheeks. Still here? I thought you might be.'

Nick Waters was a year six teacher. My class was year three, younger and less volatile. Year six always seemed a little too close to teenage angst for my liking and I never felt I could deal with the drama of it all.

'Yeah, just sorting out some stuff for tomorrow. We're doing some work on religions around the world and I needed to print off some hand-outs.'

'Such a workaholic. Anybody would think you enjoyed it.'

I smiled. I suppose I did, really. I didn't like the hierarchy and unnecessary bureaucracy but that didn't mean I didn't like my job, the bit that I was in control of. And the kids were great, not a naughty one among the lot of them, not really and that made my job a hell of a lot easier.

'Well, you know. You can't do enough for a good boss.'

He laughed and sat on the corner of my desk. I could smell his aftershave, David Beckham I think, and could see his biceps through his tight shirt. He worked out a lot and made no bones of telling people about it. He was older than me, twenty-nine, but he had a real zest for life, a real can-do attitude. I never saw him down in the dumps or without zest or energy and I liked that about him.

'That class was pretty cool last night. I saw you were really going for it. It's amazing how far you've come in such a short space of time,' he smiled at me, all white teeth, bright eyes and dimples.

'Yeah. Yeah, it was good. I think I'm starting to feel the benefit now; I feel a little fitter and less tired,' I leant over and shut the desktop PC down.

'Well, you look pretty fit to me,' I knew what was coming, 'you know, that offer is still there. A drink or two after work,' he touched my hand gently and I pulled it away, feeling the colour rise sharply in my cheeks and neck.

'I know, Nick. Thanks for the offer but you know I can't.'

He stood up and pushed the door to the classroom closed. He turned to face me.

'No pressure, Jane. I just don't want you to think that just because you've turned me down that the offer's withdrawn. Any time you change your mind don't hesitate to let me know. I'm really not going anywhere.'

I had thought about it, I couldn't lie. He was a really attractive guy, short, dark hair, nice physique, about five eleven and tanned. He even had a nice car, an Audi A6, and a nice place up in the hills. Superficial I know, but we also got on like a house on fire; he made me laugh and he was always so positive and upbeat. His attitude was contagious.

But when all was said and done, I wasn't a cheater. I loved Tony, despite all of his faults, and I didn't want to give up on what we had even if what we had wasn't much at all and wasn't showing much sign of improving in the near future. Not until the last couple of days at least, but who knew if that was going to continue. It had already hit a blip.

'I appreciate that. And I do like you, you know that. I think you're a really nice guy. But I'm with Tony and that's just the way it is.'

I turned away from him, but I could feel his eyes on me, his forced smile, could still smell his aftershave and see his rugged, handsome face.

'I'm not saying you should be with me, Jane. Jesus, I wish you were, but you deserve better, you know? You deserve to have someone looking after you, not the other way around.'

I snapped a little at that, instantly wheeling on him.

'He's not a bad person, Nick, and yet you seem to have a real low opinion of him. You've only met him a couple of times, but you don't know him like I do. He is really kind and caring. And, anyway, he is writing his novel and he's already had some interest in it. A couple of big publishing companies,' I lied but I lied for all the right reasons. I didn't want to have to justify my life choices but for some reason I felt I had to.

'Okay, okay. I crossed a line. I'm sorry,' he held his hands up, palms out as if surrendering, 'I'm just… disappointed, that's all. I just… just wish it was me with you and not him.'

I crumbled at this. He looked so vulnerable. I stood closer to him and held his hand tenderly.

'You'll find someone, Nick, I can't believe you haven't already.

You are such a sweet guy. And when you do, we can all be good friends and hang out together. You... you and Tony would get on so well, you're very similar really.'

'I'd like that,' he said softly and leaned in, 'I really would.' He bent down and kissed me on the cheek and I could feel the slight rasp of his day old stubble, could smell his scent and felt the softness of his smooth lips against my skin. My legs trembled.

The door opened suddenly, and I took a sharp intake of breath. I let go of his hand and immediately all of the sexual tension in the room evaporated.

'Hi girlie! Oh, *oh* hi Nick.'

It was Jemima, my Teaching Assistant friend. She was looking at me quizzically and I frowned at her, knowing that I was in for an interrogation and more than a little embarrassment.

'Just popped in to see if you could give me a lift home. My car's at the garage having the exhaust done,' she was still looking at me intensely, the corner of her mouth turned up like she had uncovered a deep secret and was desperate to know the details.

'Yeah... yeah, no problem. Of course,' I could feel my cheeks turning red again, the blood rushing to my face.

Nick looked at Jemima, then back at me. He was still smiling but I could see his suppressed anxiety, assessing the moment for his next move. He made a decision.

'I'll see you later, Jane,' Nick stepped towards the door, 'thanks for the advice on that... that thing,' he turned to me, 'and about what you said. I... I really would like that. I really would,' the pause was excruciating, the silence deafening. He grabbed his stuff, 'See you, Jem.'

'See you, Nick. Looking good as ever,' she turned to me as he left, big grin on her face, eyes wide with excitement. 'What... the fuck... was that?'

I grabbed my bag and my keys.

'That was nothing,' I laughed.

'Yeah right, and my arse is a size eight. Have a little bit of heat there did we?' She was skipping around like an excited child. Jesus, she was such a snoop, but I loved her in spite of it.

'No, nothing like that. He just wanted to know something, and I gave him the answer.'

'I bet you did, you horny bitch.'

I slapped her arm and laughed, 'You can assume all you like but I'm spoken for and you know it.'

'But a little sexual tryst wouldn't hurt now, would it?' she giggled.

'Jemima Carter, you're such a tart! You know that's just not going to happen. We're friends and that's all there is to it,' I smirked but I could still feel his lips on my cheek, the warmth of his hand in mine.

'Yeah, yeah. I know. Can't blame a girl for wanting a bit of soap opera drama in her life though.'

'You want drama, make your own. There's none here.'

I was smiling inwardly as we left the classroom. It was good to feel wanted. It was good to know that I still had it, whatever it was.

Chapter 16: Stooges

Tony was surprised how busy the place was for a Tuesday night. Usually the jam night attracted ten or fifteen musos, all wanting to outshine the next one with their licks or their riffs, all firmly of the belief that they could have turned professional had they had the right breaks at the right time. Long hair, faded T-shirts, ragged blue or black jeans, smoking spitty roll ups and drinking real cask ale or red wine. None of that factory-made lager shit. And some of the songs were really out there, not one of the musicians were interested in playing something 'popular' or, worse still, 'commercial'. The more obscure the better. If you knew it and could sing along to it, they had failed. 'Look at this guitar', 'check out the intonation on that', 'Jimi played this one', 'this amplifier runs on real glass valves', 'this plectrum was once touched by Brian May', 'this guitar has the best sustain', etcetera, etcetera.

Tony looked around. There must have been forty or fifty people in the house, most of them simply there to watch and that was good. That meant that someone with a modicum of popularity was going to play, which usually meant they played well and sang a good song or two. Something he could get into while he poured beer, spirits and, later on, shots for the locals.

Tony had clocked in at six, he and Jane passing each other like ships in the night as he left for work. She looked good, a big grin on her face as she kissed him on the cheek. The last couple of days had really put the colour back in her eyes and he was happy about that. Even he had to admit that he had been pretty bone idle recently. Too much TV, too much cereal while in his dressing gown and not enough effort. He was really stoked about the whole writing thing and even if it came to nothing, he was going to enjoy the moment.

But he had to admit the business with his mum had knocked him for six. He didn't know what to make of it and it seemed to have just thrown him into a whirlwind of unexpected and unusual emotions. He hadn't mentioned it to Jane. He would tell her later. She looked so happy that he didn't want to rain on her parade. It could wait, it could wait just as long as he felt it had to. He needed time to digest the news and he was in no way sure whether he was ready to talk about it.

Mitch was really pissed with him. He thought he was a spunky little shit at the best of times, but he rarely lost it the way he had lost it earlier. Tony needed to consider his next move as a wrong move could have relationship changing ramifications.

His mother was a real piece of work and had done more than a number on him over the last twenty years. Jesus, he thought, that was the understatement of the century. And he couldn't let that go, even if Mitch wanted him to. Even if he wanted himself to. You just couldn't turn that shit on and off like a light switch. No way.

He poured a glass of Doombar for a punter, took the change and looked up at the stage. It was a small venue, no bigger than fifty feet by forty feet, and the stage area was not much more than a small raised step. You could get two or three guys up there with guitars, but once you put a drum kit on it the majority of the band had to stand on the floor. Tonight, there was a drummer tuning his Pearl kit, alternatively hitting the snare, tom and bass drum, a bass player warming up with some Thin Lizzy riff and a guitarist adjusting the volume on his amp. The rest of the musicians waiting patiently for their chance in the spotlight would eventually take turns, swapping their guitars, changing symbols on the kit, adjusting the stool height on the drums. A couple usually brought along trumpets and saxophones. God, he'd even seen a guy playing the spoons before.

The place was dark and dusky. It was in the cellar space of a shopping centre and consequently had a low ceiling, no windows and a metal staircase at one end which served as the only way in and out.

There was a fire escape at the back, but lord knows when that was last used. Big Al would stand at the bottom of the stairs all night, taking three quid off of every punter as an entrance fee. It was the only way the place could stay open; charging locals who craved live entertainment for the privilege of watching average musicians, who all played for free, playing less than average tunes. God, he hated his job.

'How you doing, small dick?'

Billy West stood before him, decked out in a nineties Faith No More T-shirt, khaki shorts and Converse trainers. He had dark glasses on and looked like a pimp. He was with Sally.

'Alright Bilbo. You know it's dark in here, right?'

'Yeah but these make me look cool, give me an air of mystery,' he had that permanent adolescent grin on his face.

'You alright Sal'?'

Sally was dressed in a smart black, short sleeved top and tight-fitting black leggings. She had a short dark bob of a haircut which always made her look very professional. She was four years older than Billy at thirty-five, but you wouldn't know it. She looked good. Far too good for his gimp of a neighbour.

'Yes, thanks Tony. I'm doing okay. Except that this big oaf has dragged me out to watch some mate play tonight. I don't even know him, let alone want to listen to him. God, how do you work down here? It's like the bat cave,' she looked mildly concerned.

'Oh well, you know. You get used to it. Just don't let me out into the sunlight or I'll catch fire.'

'Is that a ginger joke?' Billy laughed, his red moustache bobbing up and down on his top lip like a caterpillar with epilepsy. Tony knew the guy was a prat at the best of times, but he always made him smile.

'Who's your mate?'

'Oh, fat Steve from the wholesalers. Reckons he does a mean Paul Weller. Keeps going on at me to come and watch him. You've probably seen him before; I think he's done a few jam nights down here.' He had; Tony recalled. He was shit.

'No, can't remember it. We get a lot of musicians down here.

After a while I just tune them out.'

'Well,' Sally said, 'he'd better be worth watching. I'm missing the Apprentice for this.'

'Oh, stop moaning. You always say I never take you out. Well, I'm taking you out. What more do you want?' Billy looked at Tony as if to say 'women'.

'I'm sure he'll be fine, Sally. It's normally a good night down here.'

Tony poured Billy a bitter and Sally a red wine and Billy threw him a pound coin tip as he winked at him and dragged his beleaguered wife over to a small table in the corner. Tony sighed. It was going to be a long night.

*

The singers had come and gone. Plenty of Ed Sheeran and Sam Smith wannabes Tony regretted. The odd Pink Floyd guitar whiz, two guys doing a fairly good Proclaimers impression, Dire Straits, The Who, the Stones, Mumford and Sons and all things in between. All of the standards, the songs he'd heard a million times with varying degrees of success, plus a few folkies. Sally had left partway through fat Paul Wellers set. Two songs. Changing Man and Wildwood. Guitar... out of tune. Vocals... out of tune. Look... all wrong.

She was not pleased, not pleased at all, shooting Billy an accusatory look as she stood up, necked her wine and stormed up the stairs. That woman is independent as hell, Tony thought to himself. He often wondered why she stayed with Billy. Was it the money? Well he wasn't the richest guy in town. Was it the sex? He looked over at Bill's rotund belly. Unlikely. Perhaps, he considered, it was his quirky sense of fun and enthusiasm.

The musicians were packing up, and a few of the punters were leaving. Tony knew that would leave the die-hards, staying back to talk everything muso, the size of your instrument, the tone on your guitar, the boom of your bass drum, the wing on your wang. Tony hated it. He had to fake interest, make out like he knew his stuff and hope that his 'play nice' act got him some tips or even a drink or two.

'Shit he was *baaad*,' Billy had made it back to the bar, 'why didn't you warn me? Sally was pissed.'

'I didn't want to spoil your evening out.'

'Well he sure did. I'm going to have to tell him. Bloke's making a prat out of himself.'

'I'm sure he enjoys it. You don't want to burst his bubble, I mean, he looked like he was having fun at least.'

'I think he burst my fucking ear drums.'

Tony laughed. He was right, the mixture of Paul's jangly guitar and wailing voice really set his teeth on edge, like sharp nails down an old blackboard.

Billy pointed at the shelf behind the bar, stocked full of spirits, liqueurs and beverages of dubiously bright and assorted colours.

'You wanna drink?'

'Yeah why not. Thought you'd never ask.'

Billy propped himself up at the bar and the two of them chatted for the next hour, sinking drinks as they alternated between telling jokes, laughing about their respective partners and generally taking the piss out of the locals. Strictly speaking Tony wasn't supposed to drink when manning the bar, but Al really wasn't that much of a disciplinarian. As long as Tony didn't take advantage he was pretty easy going and if the job got done the job got done.

The place was thinning out. Tony was slightly the worse for wear, still sober enough to serve the punters and take their money but loose enough to tell Billy about what had happened that day. He needed an ear and Billy was more than happy to be one, especially when the spirits were flowing, and Tony knew Billy wouldn't judge. His own morality was questionable at times and it made him a good candidate for sounding out his options. It wasn't as if Tony expected advice as such. Just a means to get it all off of his chest. It had been weighing down on him all day like a lead weight across his lungs.

'I say to hell with her, Tone. If she really wanted to see you, she would have been over by now. You haven't spoken to her in years. Do you really want to be dragged into all of that again?'

'Yeah I know. But she's dying, Bill. She won't be around much longer. And at the end of the day she put a roof over my head when I needed one. No-one else did. I don't know, am I going to regret it if I let it go?'

Billy swigged his vodka, 'Are you going to regret it if you don't? From what you've said it's not likely to be a happy meeting.'

He was right. Tony knew it. He knocked back a Teachers, the liquid burning his throat and warming his body as it slid down his oesophagus.

'Shit, I don't know. I know I don't want to lose my brother.'

'He'll come around. He's just emotional at the moment. Once he's settled down, he'll start to see your point of view. You said it yourself, he's not an idiot.'

'You don't know him like I do. He's a stubborn git. Could take a while.'

'Give it a few weeks and bring him over to the den. We'll cheer him up,' he grinned impishly.

'I don't think that's appropriate, do you?'

'Nah, only kidding. Unless he's got weed. In which case get him over straight away,' he chuckled, and Tony sniggered with him.

Big Al wandered over, 'You'd better clean up, Tony, we're closing. I've got gym first thing and anyway,' he gestured to the almost empty room, 'Everyone's leaving'. He was a big guy, taller than Tony with a rugby player's chest and biceps. Tony always thought that Al could crush a Ford Fiesta with his bare hands and so always ensured he stayed on his good side.

'Okay Al. No problem,' Tony wasn't up for arguing. He took a moment just to get his legs together and called over Seamus, the sixty-year-old Irish soundman/cleaner/all-round helper with a limp, to help pack away.

Tony loaded the dishwasher and wiped down the bar while Seamus packed away the PA system and swept the floor. Billy helped stack the chairs. It took less than ten minutes to clean down.

'Quick one for the road,' Billy was looking at the Sambuca.

Tony turned to see where Al had gone. He was in the loo, probably snorting a line or two. Al thought Tony didn't know, but he did. Everyone did. Al was a user alright. Coke, steroids, you name it. It explained why the guy looked like something out of the Avengers.

Avengers on speed.

'Yeah, why not.'

He quickly poured two shots of Sambuca each and they necked them in double quick time, both grimacing as the aniseed flavour hit their tonsils and intoxicated their brains.

Seamus silently sipped at a bourbon.

'That oughta give you some perspective, Tony, my man. In the morning everything will be much clearer.'

'I doubt that very much. But cheers, Bill.'

Tony grabbed his jacket from behind the bar and raised a salute to the freshly chemically enhanced Al as he and Billy climbed the rusty staircase, winding up through the ceiling like a slightly worse for wear stairway to something like heaven. Except that it wasn't heaven. It was the Starlight Shopping Arcade, with its boarded up empty units, grimy pound shops and 'fleece me quick' bookies. Salubrious it wasn't, but Tony always thought that it felt like the perfect setting for the interminable Stooges, with its dank interior, shady corners, sticky tables and wayward punters.

Billy slung his arm over Tony's shoulder as they exited the shallow entranceway into the dark and vacant street. Streetlights speckled the narrow road ahead, drizzly, cold rain poured down on them and litter hung around their feet like a particularly bad bug infestation.

'You gotta love this place, Tony. Why emigrate to Spain when you can have all of this?' he swung his free arm out extravagantly, 'This… is… paradise!'

'I think your version of paradise and mine are slightly different, but I get your point,' the fresh night air had hit Tony like a sledgehammer and he could feel the alcohol he'd consumed in the last hour beginning to gnaw at his brain, 'where else could you spend the evening listening to a racket like that, which by the way you paid for, and then exit into such a beautiful evening, dog shit and all?'

'You said it. What would we do without the dog shit?' Billy hopped over a mound of canine faeces on the pavement in front of him, 'Which reminds me… Kebab?'

Tony laughed, 'Sounds like a great idea.' He clapped Billy on the back, hard enough to knock the wind out of him. 'Chilli Sauce?' they both yelled in unison as they sauntered off down the narrow street, following an invisible and random yellow brick road.

Behind them, at the corner of where Pilgrims Way met the High Street, a tall, slim and silent watcher observed, collar pulled up to his ears, rain coat zipped all the way to his chin. He pulled out a book of matches and lit a slim cigar, inhaling deeply and blowing out a thick plume of smoke which merged with the night mist forming a foggy halo. He waited a few moments before following them, keeping to the shadows. Watching, listening, planning.

Chapter 17: Second Helpings

This one was easier, much easier. Not that the first was hard, it was just that the leap into the unknown was more difficult. He didn't have that threshold to cross, the conscience threshold. His conscience was now redundant, something that she could take the full and terrible blame for.

She was a pretty red head, a little older, a bit more meat on her. He hated those skinny girls, with their bony elbows, long fragile limbs, rib-cages jutting from their torso. Although *he* didn't care either way. They were all just a means to an end. Nothing more, nothing less. Just a media, a canvas, for *his* work.

She had come willingly also. It seemed, somewhat bizarrely, that he had the knack with women. Who knew? Knowing that, he thought, would have come in handy some years ago, particularly at school where he could have used a friend. Anyone really. But, anyway, that line of thought was for another time and perhaps another mind.

She hadn't suspected a thing, possibly because *he* always waited until he was alone with their guest before arriving or, more specifically, springing out from his hiding place to show himself, like a dramatic artiste, fanning himself out like a horrific, shadowy and yet splendid debutante.

Once that happened there was no turning back. She had become paralysed with fear, terror emanating from her body, her skin trembling in tiny ripples, her voice shrill and breathy.

She knew. She knew immediately that her moments on this earth were numbered. The profound inevitability of it all was right there in her eyes and she was instantly resigned to her fate, no fight left in her small, fragile frame.

He waited until *he* gave him the signal, staring down at her from *his* lofty perch like the undead almighty, taking *his* time to pass *his* judgement, thumbs up or thumbs down. Except it was never thumbs up. He would make *his* move, and *his* move was decisive, swift and powerful.

And then the real work began. The delicate work, the thorough, cleansing work, the precise work. The reason, the real reason, why they did this. The reason why *he* made him do this. And then came the art, the display, the imagery. So that they all knew. So that there would be no doubt.

Chapter 18: The Discovery

Shit.

Shit a brick.

Luke Raven was standing next to Damian Barber in a disused warehouse off of Commercial Street. The place had an air of despair, angst and solitude, an early nineteen hundreds building with bare brickwork, rotting window panes, broken glass and damp and uneven flooring. Rafters hung around fifty feet above them from a roof that was as holey as a colander with extra holes in it. The main warehouse doors, rusted metalwork with sharp edges, peeled paint and graffiti, stood wide open. The homeless lady that had discovered... *this*... stood in the corner, arms folded round her chest, ratty old green duffel coat hanging from her aged and bedraggled body, eyes staring ahead dumbly as if in morbid disbelief.

She had called it in, had enough sense about her to get to a pay phone, a rare thing around those parts, and call 999. Luke had gotten a call at around seven that morning.

He wasn't surprised. Horrified, repulsed, but not surprised. He had known that it was coming.

Luke looked around, taking care not to touch or disturb anything.

'What do you see, Damo?'

His young partner looked visibly shaken. It was an awful lot to take in, especially during his first, full year on the job. Most D.I.s didn't get to see this in a career, in *ten* careers. Barber was getting his feet held firmly to the flames and he was finding out it burned.

'I see a girl, late twenties early thirties,' he paused and swallowed, 'she is… hanging from a hook… by her hair I think. Red headed.'

Raven circled the body hanging above him, all the time taking care of where he stepped. Aside from a few drops of blood the floor around him was quite clean.

'What else?'

'It looks as though her throat and wrists have been cut, large gashes through her arteries. She is naked, and there looks to be bruising around her throat and shoulders.'

'Just like the last one?'

Damian paused, 'Yeah… just like the last one.'

'Except the last one wasn't hanging around and didn't have any injuries to her wrists. The MO has been…upgraded.' Damian nodded, mouth agape.

'She is very pale.'

'Yep, extremely pale, almost waxy. Looks like she's been here for a few hours, maybe since yesterday evening. No clothing on the ground around her and no sign of a disturbance. The crime scene team will cordon off the area and carry out a thorough search so be careful where you step and what you touch. Did you call them?'

'Yeah. They're on their way.'

Raven shuddered. It was a typical English autumnal day on the south coast. Damp, cold and breezy. He needed a coffee. Scratch that. He needed a drink.

'Isn't the Chief holding the press conference today?' Damian asked.

'That's right. And we've got victim number one's parents giving an emotional plea to the public. Our investigation is counting an awful lot on somebody coming forward as a result of today's big event. This is not going to make Simmons happy. It ramps the whole thing up from a nut-job with a grudge to a nut-job looking for a career.'

'Could be a copycat.'

Raven blew out air, 'I doubt that very much. The media frenzy won't start until after today. This is too early for a copy-cat. Far too early.' Luke looked over at the vagrant, 'You want a coat, sweetheart?'

'Tall, very tall,' her hair stood out at all angles, seemingly it hadn't been washed in months and had taken on a life of its own. Luke half expected it to jump off her head, run down her back and scurry away into the shadows. She pointed at the body.

Damian looked up. The young girl didn't look that tall, he thought. Average height, maybe a little over.

'Yeah, yeah. We are going to need you to make a statement,' Luke talked slowly and succinctly, as if he suspected the woman's first language wasn't English, 'we need to know what you saw.'

'Very tall, went up and up and up,' she stared at Luke, wide dark eyes, lips curling out in a snarl, arms pointing at the body, 'White face, veiny face. Scared me.'

Luke turned towards Damian and frowned, a smile forming at the corners of his mouth, 'Er... okay. I didn't think she looked that bad, but I guess I get your point.'

'A man. A tall, ghostly man.'

Damian walked over to Raven. 'I think she's talking about the murderer, boss. I think she saw something. Did... you... see... something?'

'Okay Barber, she's not an imbecile. No need to talk to her like that,' he turned to face the woman, 'What... did... you... see?'

'He was here, here with her,' she pointed, 'I saw him leaving, except he didn't leave. He just...,' she waved her arms, 'went.' She looked around her, as if whatever it was would reappear at any moment. 'He didn't see me, but I saw him. I saw him. Tall, veiny, black. White, white face. Evil eyes, black eyes.'

This was beginning to creep Luke out. Barber didn't look too comfortable either. He hadn't seen this woman at the Swan before, but he bet his last month's pay that she had been on the sauce, probably drank from a green bottle in a brown paper bag.

'Okay, okay sweetheart.'

A police car pulled up outside, along with two crime scene vans.

'I'm going to ask the nice PC to get you back to the station and get you a nice coffee. You drink coffee?'

'White, two sugars.'

'White, two sugars. Great. Yeah, as I was saying, we'll get you in the warm and ask you a few questions. Is that okay with you? It would be really good if you could help us out.'

She nodded as a young male PC came over, put his arm around her and walked her back to the car. She looked back over her shoulder at the two detectives.

'He didn't see me. But I saw him. White face, black eyes, evil eyes.'

Damian looked at Raven. His jaw hanging, his eyebrows floating about three inches above his head. They watched her leave.

'What the hell was that about?'

Luke laughed, 'I think she might be a little inebriated. Get them to give her a breathalyser test, would you? I don't want us to waste our time looking for some phantom,' he laughed, 'I mean, this isn't fucking Scooby Doo for god's sake.'

Damian remained silent, 'I don't know, boss. She seemed pretty spooked.'

'Oh, come on, Damo. I know you're new on the job, but I don't believe that ghost hunting is something they specialise in at inspector school nowadays, is it? Did you pass that module? Get an A star?'

Damian looked hurt, 'Okay, but she convinced me. She probably got the details slightly confused, but I think she's telling the truth. It seems to me that some of what she is telling us is based on fact and we shouldn't ignore it.'

Raven zipped up his coat, and walked out into the open air, 'We'll see. In the mean time you know the drill. Let's brief this lot and then get the whole scene locked down. We need to broaden our enquiries to a circular mile from here. Let's see if anyone else saw or heard anything, anything at all. Including ghosts and goblins.'

Raven looked at his watch. Eight thirty. He needed to make a call.

Chapter 19: Lisa

I was in bed when the phone rang. It was my day off, I worked at the supermarket, Aldis, and it was the only day of the week where I could lie in bed beyond five thirty in the morning. I fucking hated being woken on my day off, especially that early. It was only eight forty-five. I wondered who could be calling at that ungodly hour.

I slept alone most nights. My shit of an on-off boyfriend only turned up when he wanted something, and even then he would usually be half drunk. He either wanted feeding, watering or shagging.

I ignored the first two rings. The first time it just got lost in my dream. I was dreaming that I had won the lottery and somebody from the Lotto was calling me to tell me I was now worth over five million pounds. I was fantasising about what I could spend it on. A holiday, a house, one of those top down cars. But no such luck. The second time I heard it more consciously than before but decided that if I ignored it that it would go away. The third time I answered.

'Yes?'

'Lisa, it's me.'

'Me who?'

'Let's not play that game. Me, Luke. Luke, remember me?'

I huffed loudly, 'Kind of. Heard of the bloke. Haven't seen him in a while.'

'Yeah, yeah. Sorry 'bout that. Been caught up in something. In a case.'

'In a beer glass more like.'

'No, no. It's not like that. I promise. I've got a big case, an important case.'

I laughed at him mockingly, 'They wouldn't put you on a big case. Not after last time. Big case? I think you mean basket case. They couldn't trust you to solve a crossword.'

'Very funny. No, honestly. I'm here now. That's why I'm calling. I wanted to make sure you were okay.'

I rubbed my eyes with the back of my hand and yawned loudly.

'Why? You don't normally bother. In fact, I haven't heard from you in a week. Thought you'd dropped off the face of the earth.'

'I know, I know. And I'm sorry. I've just been so caught up in… this. But I was going to pop round later. If I can get away, I'll come round for dinner. Tonight.'

'Yeah, well. I can't guarantee anything. You're not the only one who's busy you know. I've got other friends. People I see when you're not around.'

'Yeah, of course, I know. But just promise me something?'

I couldn't believe the cheek of him. Calling me before nine on my day off, waking me up and making demands. 'What? What could you possibly ask of me?'

'Just be careful. Don't go out on your own. Especially not at night.'

I spat down the phone, 'Don't fucking phone here out of the blue on my day off and tell me what I can and what I can't do, Raven! You've made it quite clear that I am no more to you than a fuck buddy, for when the drink wears off and you need a pick me up. Well news flash, asshole, I will go out when I want and with who I want!'

'Okay, okay, okay. Peace, okay. Peace. But please promise me you'll stay safe.'

'Is that some kind of safe sex thing? Because the last I remember you didn't religiously follow that rule yourself.'

'No, no, I didn't mean that. I mean stay safe, keep yourself safe. There are some dangerous people out there and you need to be careful. Just...just make sure you are with someone, and if you can't be with someone make sure you are in crowded areas and it's during the day time. Will you do that for me?'

I paused, 'What's this about, Raven?'

'Just a case I'm working on. It's got me a little spooked.'

I looked out of my bedroom window. The postman was making his rounds. If it wasn't some idiot phoning me it was this guy, crashing letters through the letterbox as if I was at a demolition derby.

'I'll bear it in mind.'

'Okay. Good.'

'I mean it, I don't know what I'm doing tonight. I might be busy. I've got a few things I've been invited to.'

'That's okay. I'll come round anyway. On the off chance.'

There was another pause. I could hear voices in the background, animated voices, people rushing around, scraping of metal on concrete, engines revving, frantic footsteps.

'Okay. Well, if I'm here I'm here.'

'Yeah. If you're there you're there. Maybe I'll see you later.'

'Yeah, maybe.' I hung up.

I laid back on the bed, pulled the duvet up to my neck, ruffled the pillows and stared at the ceiling, yellow and cracked. I rubbed my tattooed hand gently across my abdomen and shut my eyes, forcing myself to get back to my dreams. I wasn't going to let this asshole ruin my day or my life. Not for some random misplaced concern that made no sense. I made a mental note to spit in his coffee when he turned up later that night.

I smiled.

Chapter 20: The Press Conference

Chief Simmons sat uncomfortably at the table, wringing his hands together in agitation. He didn't like this at all. It was bad fucking timing.

He'd just taken the call from Raven. Another dead girl, only this time the scene was more fucked up, like an image from one of those Hollywood horror stories. And he didn't need it today. Definitely not today. He had carefully managed the attendees, the layout, the timing and the statements that Mr and Mrs Webb were due to give in around fifteen minutes. And now this? No, he didn't need it at all. What he needed was something on par with a dull BBC2 documentary about carp fishing. Simple, quiet and oh so calm.

The room was filling up. Local press and national press. If word got out about that morning's discovery then he would have the international press to deal with too. The Mayor was there, standing in the corner at the back of the room in his oversized tweed jacket, some effeminate young man running around him with what looked like a feather duster, making sure that the mayor looked the part. There were a few Joe Public milling around at the back; probably relatives or friends he assumed.

This needed to go well, it had to go well.

He could feel damp patches forming under his arms and chanced a quick but discreet sniff down there. It was okay, he thought. Musty but no discernible body odour. Dry stick does the trick after all, he thought to himself.

What to do, what to do.

He took a sip from his water. It felt good, the icy liquid trickling down his throat and cooling his fiery insides. He closed his eyes and took a deep breath. Calm, soothing thoughts. Walks out in the country, just the two of them. The two of them and the dogs. And the birds.

Fucking Raven! He was like a train wreck waiting to happen. If it could go wrong, it would go wrong. Sure, he couldn't blame him for some sicko taking his perverse fantasies out on young, vulnerable women, but bad luck followed him like a bad smell. And the smell was pretty pungent today.

He could see the parents of that poor girl in the cloak room off to one side of the main hall. The mother was crying and one of his female PCs was comforting her. He had asked her to try to keep the woman as calm as possible. Tears were good in these circumstances. They tore at the heart strings, brought members of the public out of their shells. Enticed the reluctant witnesses, those that were distrustful of the authorities. But too much and the message wouldn't come across. He felt for them. This was tough.

He would get through this part, his introduction, the parents' plea, question time, and then he would announce today's latest discovery. A quick statement and then a 'no further comment.' He would deal with the fallout later.

He glanced at his watch. Ten fifty-five. It was almost time to roll. He looked over at Molly, the young PC who was going to shepherd the parents into position. He gave her a nod. She smiled sheepishly and uncomfortably. Nobody was used to this kind of situation around these parts. It wasn't a normal event. Completely not normal in fact. But they were the local law enforcement, and this is what they were trained for. Sure, they had to deal with the mundane, the annoyances, the traffic incidents, the scuffles, and the arguments between neighbours. But this was the real deal, the big one and he could do without it. Particularly at this stage of his career when retirement was beckoning.

He tapped his microphone. It gave a loud knock-knock and a whistle. It was on. He took a swallow.

'Okay, okay, settle down now everyone. Settle down. If you could all take your seats, we will get going.'

He tightened his tie and looked around. There was the usual shuffling, lots of people lugging around cups of coffee and heavy camera equipment, members of the press jostling for position and circling like carrion round a corpse. He could never fathom the human subconscious and what it was about death and despair that mesmerised people. It didn't matter how grim or gruesome, the crowds flocked to a murder like flies around a turd. It both amazed and saddened him.

And the biggest fly of all, his D.I. Luke Raven, was there at the back, purveying the scene before him like a conductor inspecting his orchestra. Raven put a hand up in acknowledgement. Simmons chose to ignore it. He leant forward, his chair creaking and groaning beneath him.

'As you are all aware, at approximately three thirty A.M. on Monday the **21st of October** we received a call informing us of…'

And off he went. Cool, calm and fighting to keep it together. His statement took around ten minutes, give or take. There was a hushed silence in the room as he spoke, only interrupted by the noise of camera shutters clicking away furiously. He stuck to the facts, like any good chief inspector should. No emotion, no conjecture, no supposition. He glanced over at the mayor, standing stock rigid, his hands folded at his groin, a look of faux sadness sitting heavily on his brow. Yeah right, the chief thought to himself. He's thinking about how he can get a public relations angle on this.

'And now I would like to ask the parents of Tracey Webb, David and Suzanne… are you ready, guys? Yes? Okay, take your time. Take your time,' he looked across at Molly who was nodding, 'I will ask David and Suzanne Webb to make a public statement regarding the terrible events of the last few days.'

The cameras swung to his left, at the pathetic image of two emotionally destroyed parents, clinging tightly to each other as if they knew that they were doomed to a future of tears and remorse. These were the worst of times. Dealing with family tragedy was the most gut-wrenching and stress-inducing part of his job.

They managed to hold it together for the most part, the father doing most of the talking, pausing occasionally to gather himself.

Molly had done a good job and he glanced over at her. Whatever she had said it had worked. She stood behind them, ready to step in if either of them crumbled. She was going to get on, that girl. He made a mental note.

The mother finished up, 'Please, if you saw or heard anything, no matter how unimportant it might seem, please, please call the police. Don't let this monster do this to anyone else. Don't let our baby's… our baby's death be in vain…'

Suzanne Webb broke down and sobbed loudly into her husband's shoulder. He gripped her tightly and they both shook with grief. Cameras clicked, flashes lit up the room like fireworks, murmurs and mutterings started to escalate into a vocal crescendo. This was going to make front page news alright.

'Okay, okay guys,' the chief stepped in to spare the parents any further torment, 'I'll answer any questions that you may have.'

'Any clues on who might have done this, chief?'

'Can you provide any more details regarding the cause of death?'

'Who found the body? Are they suspects?'

'Do you think the murderer is still in the local area?'

'Will the University be closing down while investigations continue?'

The chief answered each question as dutifully as he could, providing the facts as he knew them. Any off the wall question without a clear answer he responded to with a 'no comment at this time.' Any inappropriate question was ignored. He glanced around and noticed that Raven had made his way to the front of the room and he silently wondered with a heavy heart whether it was for moral support or whether he had yet more bad news. He braced himself for the reaction of the crowd.

'Okay, thanks for your time this morning ladies and gentlemen. And… erm… well…' he looked up at his expectant and blissfully ignorant audience and cleared his throat, 'Before we wrap up here I would like to bring you up to speed with a further incident that occurred this morning at around seven A.M.'

The room was filled with movement and excited voices. He could see the confused faces, turning to each other, quizzing the person next to them. Simmons looked across at Raven. They both shared an uneasy glance.

'I am afraid to say that another body has been discovered in a warehouse in the Commercial Road industrial district. We are yet to identify the body, but we can say that the victim is also a young woman. Cause of death is, as yet, unconfirmed.'

The room erupted with noise. Reporters hurled questions at him like heavy projectiles. The camera shutters doubled in intensity. Flashes went off like strobe lights at a rock concert. People were out of their seats, standing up, craning their necks above the amassed throng, desperate to get a soundbite from someone in authority. The mayor was apoplectic, glaring across at Simmons as though he had just called his mother a dirty whore. Raven urged him on.

'We... we... WE DO NOT yet know whether the incident is linked with that of Tracey Webb, but clearly we are keeping all possibilities open.' More noise, more questions, more yelling and hollering.

'Clearly our investigations are ongoing and until we know more it would be foolish to make any further comment. We will be in touch with further news as it becomes available. Thank you.'

He stood up, signalling with his arms for the baying crowd to calm down. They were like scavengers around rotting flesh. Raven walked over to him and they headed for the rear door. He nodded to Molly to escort the astonished and distraught parents away.

'Good job, boss.'

'Jesus, I'm too old for this.'

He could hear his officers behind him attempting to usher the still raucous and agitated crowd out of the building.

'Thanks for the fucking heads up, Simmons.'

It was the Mayor, all coiffured hair and trimmed goatee. A waft of aftershave made its way up the chief's nostrils, acrid and pungent. His manservant tottered along behind him.

'I agree that the timing wasn't great, Mayor Wood, but there was not an awful lot I could do about that.'

'That mob is baying for blood, Simmons. Just a quiet word

beforehand, that's all I'm asking for.'

Raven chipped in.

'We did the best we could with the situation, Mayor. This was going to make its way into the public domain, with or without our help. The best thing we can do is to take control of the information flow and get ahead of it.'

Mayor Wood looked Raven up and down.

'Don't tell me that you're the D.I. in charge of this case, Raven? Simmons, you've got to be kidding me!'

Raven whirled around.

'Do you have something to say to me?'

The Mayor stuck his chest out, 'Yes, yes in fact I do. This is now the biggest situation in this town's recent history. We haven't had a murder here in years and now we have two in the space of a week. And we're going to trust the town's safety, the safety of all of our citizens, to a raging alcoholic? Christ, if I had my way you would have been kicked out after the last fiasco!'

Raven got himself in the Mayor's face, up close and personal, close enough for his breath to ruffle the gentle lie of the Mayor's facial hair, and grunted. His eyes were wide and wild.

'Is that so?' Raven had his hands by his side, fists opening and closing, 'You want someone else on the job? Then be my guest.'

'Now, now Raven. I'll make that call,' the chief glared at the Mayor, 'I and nobody else. And, mister Mayor, if you have any concerns then of course you are always more than welcome to come and see me in my office.'

The Mayor dabbed a handkerchief across his face, 'My concern is only with ensuring we provide the best service to the people we serve. If you think that this,' he waved a hand at the D.I. 'is the best person for the case then so be it. But if he fucks up,' he smiled through gritted teeth, 'then you and I will be having a much more difficult conversation.'

'Understood. And he, *we*, won't.'

Raven was biting at his lip hard enough to leave a red and sore welt.

'And next time, Dave, just a fucking call. I've now got to go into PR overdrive to keep these clowns quiet. You know how it is. They don't see the work we're putting in. They just see the chaos.'

Simmons cursed under his breath. The work *we* are putting in? The only work this joker put in was in getting his PA to organise dinners with local businessmen, attending charity functions and generally gorging himself on five-star dinners and expensive riocha.

'Point taken. And we sincerely hope that there won't be a next time. We'll be working night and day to ensure that we get the perpetrator into police custody before he or she can strike again.'

'Let's hope you do,' the mayor waved to his manservant, 'come on Leo, we need to get back to the Office. I've got several thousand calls to make.'

Raven turned to the chief as Mayor Wood wafted out of the room, waving a hand at the remaining photographers and shooting the ladies in the room his expensive, winning smile.

'That guy needs to be taken down a peg or two.'

'Yeah, he does. But not by you. You want to get taken off the force for good? Then smack that guy upside the head. Is he annoying? Sure is. Does he work hard enough to earn his sizable salary? No way. Is he stupid? Unfortunately not. He can play the politics better than most bureaucrats I've had the misfortune to encounter and he has some very powerful allies, including your late father, so don't under-estimate him.'

Raven grunted, 'Just doesn't seem right. We do all the legwork, and people like that get all the glory.'

'Welcome to public service, Luke.'

Chapter 21: Lunch

I told him that he had to see her. There was no question in my mind. For god's sake, she was his mother. He couldn't just ignore it. I knew it and I think that he knew it too. If it had been my mum, I wouldn't have hesitated. But I knew this was different. That their relationship was very different. I never could quite get my head around it and for the majority of our time together she had been a distant, unwelcome presence.

We were sitting at a table in the local Wetherspoons having lunch and a coffee. He'd called while I was at work and said he wanted to meet with me, that he had something to talk over. I hadn't known what to expect, but him telling me that his mum had terminal cancer wasn't top of my list of possibilities.

'You've got to go over there, Tony. You will regret it if you don't and… well, you know.'

'I knew you'd say that. I guess I'll have to go round there later this week. I think Mitch wants me to do it sooner.'

'Well just do it when it feels right for you. You don't want to go in there half cocked.'

'He doesn't seem right at all. He really went overboard the other day. I know he can fly off the handle but even for him this was extreme. It's really hit him hard.'

'Well, he always has been a mummy's boy. You can't let his hard man act fool you. She's always looked out for him and that means he relies on her, a little too much possibly, but I think she likes it.'

I paused and looked at him. He tried to make eye contact but failed miserably. He glanced around the pub as if looking for something.

'And how about you, Tone? Are you okay?'

He pushed greasy bacon and a half-eaten egg white round his plate. He looked a little pale. He had arrived back from work late the night before and, I suspected, had had a few after-hours drinks. It had been some music night at Stooges. I hadn't heard him come home. But despite what I suspected to be at least a moderate hangover I knew a headache wasn't the cause of his dour demeanour.

'I'll probably head over on Sunday or something. Give myself a couple of days to get my thoughts together.'

'Probably for the best.'

He smiled half-heartedly.

'How did it go this morning?' I'd left him at home in his pyjama bottoms when I'd gone to work, his eyes bloodshot, tea and toast on his lap, not going anywhere.

'Yeah, yeah. Pretty good, I think. I'm still hard at it. Still tapping away.'

I looked at him curiously. There seemed to be a nervous uncertainty in his eyes, not the confident bravado that I'd seen earlier that week. I thought it odd. I feared that perhaps the 'cynical me' had been right and that his recent efforts were just a flare of enthusiasm which would dull down into low, smouldering embers. Inwardly I cursed. If it wasn't going to happen now, then it probably never would and where did that leave us? With me putting in all the hours that god sent, him sitting at home wearing out the TV remote and partying the nights away with his reckless friend.

I brought myself back to earth. He was giving me bad news, earth-shattering news, and I was thinking about my life, how it all affected me. I scorned myself for my pathetic self-pity and considered that perhaps I was wrong, perhaps it was all just a setback. And who could blame him? I mean his mum was dying for god's sake.

'Oh, Hi Jane. Hi Tony.'

I looked up over Tony's head and saw a pair of sunlight-framed silhouettes in the pub's large glass door. It was Nick from school. And some… woman.

'Thought we'd grab a quick sandwich before we head out. I've got this afternoon off, gonna do a bit of shopping,' he smiled, and I couldn't help thinking that he looked like the smug cat that had gotten the cream, 'Have you met Wendy?'

Tony held out his hand, 'Hiya Nick. Nice to meet you, Wendy.'

I held my hand out, not moving from my seat. 'Hello,' she shook my hand warmly, 'nice to meet you,' and then awkwardly, 'and you are?'

'I'm a friend. We met online a month or so ago. This is only the second time that Nicholas and I have actually met in person,' she giggled like a school girl, 'he is very handsome, no?' she took my hand and smiled, 'Very nice to meet you.' I wondered whether it was some eastern European accent. With a name like Wendy?

She was tall and dark. Very attractive and very slim.

Tony smiled. 'Online eh? All the rage nowadays. Cuts out all that small talk crap. Well it's good to see you both,' he looked her up and down, 'did you two want to… er… join us?' Well, I thought, his mood had certainly improved.

Nick looked at me, quizzically.

'Er, well, don't forget, Tone,' I jumped in hastily, 'I've got to get back to work. We haven't all got half days off you know,' I half smiled at Nick and then hastily back at Tony, 'And you've got to get back too,' I scraped the food off of his plate onto mine and stacked the dishes, clattering the cutlery and knocking leftovers onto the floor.

Tony looked at me, frowning, his face confused and wary.

Nick smiled and interjected, 'Never mind. Perhaps another time.' He knew he had made an impact and was pleased with himself.

Wendy spoke, 'Yes, perhaps another time,' there was a sultry and seductive air to her voice which put me on edge. 'Perhaps we can meet up one evening. Nick's always talking about his friends at the school. It would be good to see if everything he says is true,' she giggled again and shuffled her feet, her heels tapping on the hard floor.

'I'm sure it is, we are really all as nice as he says we are,' I stood and gestured to Tony, 'enjoy your lunch,' I grabbed my jacket and bag, 'and your afternoon,' I wiped the hair from my face and smoothed down my blouse, 'and, Nick, I'll see you at work tomorrow.'

'Yeah, see ya Nick,' Tony held out his hand and gripped Nick's firmly, 'and we'll see you some other time, Wendy,' she waved at him with her long, eastern European fingers and Tony smiled bashfully. He looked like a bloody idiot. He leaned in and kissed her on the cheek. I couldn't believe it. What the hell was he playing at?

We all waved, and Tony and I left through the big double doors. I'd parked my car down the road, so we beat a hasty retreat through the High Street, Tony half a step behind.

'Well, that was… rushed,' he was struggling to keep up, 'did you know her or something?'

'No!' I snapped, 'I've just got to get back. I've got a heavy schedule this afternoon, my class is preparing for a school assembly next week. I took the time out to come and see you because I knew something was wrong. I haven't got time for a long lunch and a chit chat.'

I beeped the car as we got closer.

'I'm sure ten minutes wouldn't have hurt.'

'And how would you know, Tony?' I whirled round and confronted him. Shocked, he took a step back and almost fell into the road while a white van came hurtling past, 'You've never had to hold down a steady nine to five job, have you? Noooooo…I get that privilege, up at the crack of dawn, make you your breakfast, get washed and dressed, do a hard day's work with a bunch of kids, some of whom will probably grow up to be crack dealers someday given the state of their parents, mark homework all night, deal with bullshit and drama and more bullshit and what do you do? Get up, watch TV, maybe open your laptop, drink tea, have a chat with the bloody next-door neighbour,' I could feel my face flush, the heat rising to my cheeks and forehead. People were staring. Tony was standing there, mouth wide, hands by his side.

I stopped. What was I doing? What was getting me so riled? Shit, I even had tears welling up in my eyes. I turned around and got in the car, slamming the door behind me. I gripped the wheel. I couldn't believe how I could be such a selfish bitch.

Tony got in next to me and gripped my hand. His eyes were on me, I could sense his compassion. A flood of guilt suddenly washed over me.

'It's okay, babe, it's okay. I've made my mind up, you're right,' he spoke in a low, calming voice, 'I'll go around tomorrow. I'll deal with this, and I'll deal with Mitch. I'm the eldest after all. I'll do the right thing, I promise.'

I kept my eyes on the wheel and nodded, wiping one hand across my damp cheeks. I couldn't face him. I didn't know why, to this day I don't know, but I couldn't even bring myself to look at him. I turned the key and pulled away.

Chapter 22: Mother

Tony got off the train at Briars Oak. The old place had had some work done, a new platform, a nice new overpass, a coffee shop and a plush new internal seating area. What did they say, he pondered, money goes to money?

It was an overcast June day, not cold but not warm. He was wearing jeans and a T shirt, a hoody just to keep out the chill. He had his earphones in, listening to the new Foo Fighters album. Anything to keep his mind off of what was about to go down.

He hadn't called ahead. Didn't think he needed to. She wasn't going anywhere soon, not on this earth anyway. She'd refused any form of treatment, wanting to go with her dignity intact, and so aside from visits from the nurses he knew that she would be holed up indoors.

It was a short walk from the station to his home, his mum's house. He hummed as he walked. He didn't really have a plan, more an ethos. He would go in, he would be polite, he would make sure that she was comfortable, ask her if she needed anything and then he would leave. His duty would be fulfilled, and he could get on with his life. His brother would be happy, and he would leave guilt free. That wasn't so difficult now, was it? And Jane would get out of the funk she had been in for the past couple of days.

He thought about his work. It was going pretty well, the words still seemed to be coming to him, his characters were still developing, and his plot was thickening. Sure, he had had a bit of setback when he'd got the news. That was hardly surprising, but he had gotten back to it. And, for some reason, whenever he'd had a good chat with Billy, normally greased with some form of intoxicant, his creativity really shone. Odd but true. Jane didn't seem to like it but, shit, what did she want? She wanted him to write and he was writing.

It started to spit with rain. Wonderful. He knew he should have brought a jacket. Not that it mattered, his mum's detached Victorian chateau was just around the corner.

It stood on its own, unusual in this day and age but not unusual for this town.

Briars Oak was an affluent part of Hampshire. Lots of upwardly mobile couples had moved out there to be close enough to the city but far enough away to live the kind of suburban blissful existence that only city slickers could. There were no slums, no council house estates, no 'two meals for the price of one' pubs, no budget shops. The place was chock full of boutiques, high end supermarket chains, antique traders, wine bars and brasseries. Not a fag butt on the pavement, not a crisp packet in the dahlias. The kids went to private schools, they drove their own BMWs and Porsches, they drank Prosecco and cocktails and they even swore politely. There was a farmer's market on a Wednesday, a craft fair on a Friday. There were banners proclaiming that Briars Oak had been voted the tidiest village in the south of England, there were large scale pedestrian zones in the middle of town to keep the riff raff out, there was a bowls club, the lawn variety, a cricket club and a rugby team. And the houses were all detached and had character. Nice driveways, front lawns, sculpted hedges and iron railings. None of those cheap new builds. And his mum's place fit right in.

She came with her own money, her father had been wealthy, a stockbroker who had moved his family down south in the forties. She had moved out at a young age, they had fallen out over her choice of male friends, but he had still seen fit to leave her everything when he died. And everything was a lot. She had never wanted for anything all of her adult life, other than a husband who loved her.

He opened the low gate and walked up the long pathway to the large front door. No doorbell. He took a deep breath, reached up to the black door knocker, a gargoyle with its mouth wide open like it was attempting to swallow him whole, and knocked once, twice, three times.

He stood there with his hands in his pockets like he had done as a kid. He felt like he'd just gotten home after playing with his friends, up to some mischief, playing knock door ginger, pulling the wings off of butterflies or snogging the girls at the park. And he was late. Again.

Suddenly all the years washed away and he was eleven years old, his blond hair bowl cut around his ears, his white dirty face, his lanky frame. He was afraid. She was going to scold him, smack his bottom and send him to bed at six thirty without any tea. Mitchell would be laughing at him as he came through the door, tears in his eyes. There would be shouting. 'Why do you do this to me?' 'Am I really that horrible to you?' 'Don't you love me?' 'Why, I took you in when you had nowhere to go, you wretched boy!' 'What have I got to do to get through to you?' 'You know I don't want to smack you; it hurts me to do it, but you just won't do as you are told!'

The door opened. It was Mitchell. He looked Tony up and down, his face passive, unmoving.

'You came.'

'I did.'

'Didn't think you were going to.'

'Neither did I.'

They stood staring at each other for what seemed like an eternity.

'Are you going to let me in or what?'

Mitchell opened the door and stood to one side to let Tony through.

The house smelt musty. The wallpaper hadn't changed, beige with dark brown swirly patterns. The steep stairs led upwards into the gloom, worn brown carpet lined the floor. The living room door was to his left, the dining room door dead ahead, the kitchen beyond. The ceilings were as high as he remembered them, reaching up and up as if to the heavens. White cornices with sculpted angels gazed down at him.

'Where is she?'

'She's through there,' Mitchell pointed down the hallway to the dining room, 'be nice.'

Tony looked back at him, 'I'm not here for an argument, Mitchell. I'm doing what you asked.'

'You should be doing it because you want to.'

Tony ignored him. He opened the door.

The large dining area lay before him, a dark oak table with solid leather backed chairs, an open fireplace with a family portrait, his mother and her family, hanging above it. The floor was wooden, years of abuse scored into its every groove, the walls papered with light grey wallpaper, black, swirly images embedded in the thick vinyl. The kitchen door was off to the right, the rear of the dining room opened to a large conservatory, the dim daylight pouring through into the space beyond. Tony shuddered. He remembered every moment of his childhood spent in that dark and gloomy room. He felt the marks on his back, the sharp stinging sensation on the upper part of his thighs, the shouting, the turmoil.

He walked across the cavernous space and saw his mother out in the conservatory, thin and frail but somehow strong. Sitting upright in a floral-patterned armchair with stiff arms and a straight back. She was reading, her glasses perched on the end of her nose. She wore a blouse and charcoal-coloured trousers, a heavily embroidered shawl over her shoulders, white open-backed slippers on her tiny feet. Never casual. 'Dress to impress, my dear.'

He stood in the entrance, not knowing what to say, not wanting to disturb her until she was finished. Suddenly his sketchy plan escaped him and words evaded him. He just stood there in silence.

'Hello Anthony.'

He jumped with a start.

'Hello Mother.'

She looked up from her book, her piercing blue eyes boring into his soul.

'So, you've heard.'

'Mitchell told me.'

She closed her book and set it down on the coffee table beside her, her long bony fingers caressing the cover as she laid it to rest.

'You've put on weight.'

'I guess I have,' he looked down at his bloated stomach.

'It suits you. Would you like a tea?'

'No thank you, I'm fine.'

'Nonsense, of course you do. Mitchell!'

Mitchell appeared at Tony's side, his arms folded.

'Make a pot, dear, will you? Your brother wants a tea and so do I.'

'Okay Mum,' he glanced ruefully at Tony as he headed back to the kitchen.

'Well,' she held her arms out and coughed, a loud raspy, wheezy cough, 'how do I look? Like death warmed up I suppose.'

Tony felt all of the fight leave his body. He didn't know what to say or how to say it. She just looked like his mother. A little older, a little skinnier, but the same woman who he both hated and loved in equal measure.

'I don't know what to say, mum. You look good, but I… I know you're not.'

'It comes to us all, dear boy. There's not much I can do about it,' she reached out and grabbed her cigarettes. She lit one and inhaled deeply.

'Should you really be doing that?'

She blew out the smoke and laughed. It was a crackling, breathy laugh.

'Well, it's not going to make much of a difference now, is it? Forty years of,' she nodded to the smouldering cigarette in her right hand, 'these are what has caused this, or so the doctor says. A few more won't do me any harm now.'

He shrugged. He guessed she was right, but it just seemed wrong, like she was giving up.

'Sit down, Anthony. You're making the house untidy.'

He took the other armchair across from his mother. He folded his hands in his lap. Jesus, why did he feel so inadequate?

'Do you need anything?'

'A few more years would be nice. Other than that, no. I don't think so. Mitchell is looking after me and the nurses come in from time to time,' she flicked ash in the crystal ash tray on the arm of the chair, 'I am going to relax and enjoy the time I have left.'

'What about the pain? Are you... comfortable?'

She laughed again and coughed, 'I won't lie to you, my boy. The drugs help.'

He looked around the conservatory, brown wooden beams with large glass panes, tiled floor. The garden beyond was vast and overgrown, Mitchell hadn't been keeping up with the lawn. A large, lonely willow tree stood in the middle of the lawn, its long droopy fingers caressing the ground. The times he had hidden out there, shrouded by its furry beard, imagining, day-dreaming. It was where he escaped. He wished he was out there now.

'How's your... girlfriend?'

'Jane? Yeah, Jane's good. She's a teacher now you know?'

'What does she teach?'

'Primary school. Saint George's. She enjoys it I think.' His mother huffed.

'Young minds need a firm hand. Discipline. Let's hope she knows that. Too many children nowadays are left to their own devices, wayward, roaming the streets like orphans.'

She took another large drag from her cigarette and exhaled. There was a silence between them. He felt the urge to fill it but couldn't. It just lay there, like a thick fog, filled with the odour from her cigarette and years of resentment.

Tony heard the kitchen door open and footsteps echoing across the wooden floor as Mitchell brought a tray out to them. A teapot, milk jug, sugar cubes and two cups, plus a plate of biscuits. He set it down on the coffee table and poured.

'Sugar?'

'Yes please, two.'

His mother frowned at him.

'Biscuit?'

'No thanks.'

He reached out for the cup and saucer and took a sip of the hot liquid. It burned his throat, but he relished the warmth. It was cold in here, wasn't it?

The wind picked up outside, the willow was waving its long arms at him, or was it calling to him? *'Come out, come out and play. I will keep you safe and warm. Come to me and I will hold you tight, I won't let her get to you. Not again. You can stay with me for as long as you want, forever and ever if you need to. I would never hurt you.'*

He blinked. Mitchell had left. His mother had stubbed out her cigarette and was munching on a digestive biscuit, crumbs rolling down her chin and onto her lap. She brushed them away.

'Have you been… working?'

'I'm writing. Writing a novel actually.'

'Is it any good?'

'I think so.'

'Does anybody else think so?'

'Nobody else has seen it yet.'

'So how do you know if it's any good?'

Silence again. He sipped his tea. The wind whistled. The willow gestured to him.

'Is that it?'

'Is that what?'

'Is that all that you've been doing?'

'I work at a bar.'

'Doing what?'

'Serving drinks mainly.'

'Is that your career choice?'

'Well no, not really. It's just to tide me over while I…'

'While you what?'

'While I write my novel.'

She took a long gulp from her tea and put it down, 'You always were a dreamer.'

He bit his tongue, almost hard enough to pierce the skin.

'What does Jane think of this?'

'She supports me.'

'Financially?'

'Well... yes. But emotionally really. She wants me to succeed.'

She huffed again and reached out for her cigarettes, 'A woman keeping her man. Wouldn't have happened in my time.'

'She's not keeping me. I pay my way.'

'With your bar work, I suppose.'

'Yes, with my bar work.'

She lit her cigarette, inhaled and coughed loudly again, this time a hacking cough which went on and on. It finally subsided and she looked up at him through the fog, her eyes shining brightly through the haze, eyes watering from her desperate gasp for clean oxygen.

'You could have done so much more if...'

'If what?'

'If you had listened to me. I raised you single-handedly you know, tried my best. But you just... resisted.'

'I wasn't a bad boy.'

'You were a naughty boy.'

'You were too strict.'

'I had to be. You were stubborn,' she wiped spittle from the corner of her mouth, 'still are.'

Silence again. This was not going well, and he knew it. He shouldn't have come.

'What do you want from me? I'm here, aren't I? I'm making myself available to you.'

'Too little, too late I'm afraid, Anthony. We will always have our... differences.'

He felt dark emotion rise up in him like bitter bile. Sorrow overwhelmed him, tinged with rage and hatred.

'You never let me be... me.'

'And who are you, my boy? Who is it that you think you are?'

'Your son! Your adopted son, but your son nonetheless!'

She laughed, cackled, cigarette flailing side to side, head back against the stiff upright of the armchair, a loud crackling laugh that echoed off the glass walls and reverberated around the house. The willow whipped itself into a frenzy behind her, calling to him, '*Get out, get out, get out!*'

'My adopted son! That's right, like Moses from his basket, I fished you out of the river and gave you a home, food, warmth. And what did you do for me? What did you ever do for me?'

She glared at him across the empty space between them. There had always been a space between them. He glared back.

'I loved you.'

She cackled, coughing out smoke like a fearsome dragon emerging from its fiery and forbidden lair.

'Loved me? Loved me? And why would you do that, Anthony? Why would you love me, the mother that you terrorised for so long? The woman who I know you feared more than anything else on this earth.'

'Because you are my mother!'

'Is that right? But I adopted you, Anthony, didn't I? You believe that I chose you, picked you out from all the other children that I could have taken under my wing? Ha! Chose you? Do you think I would choose you? I tolerated you, put up with you. But I didn't *choose* you. You were thrust on me. Thrust on me like an unwanted gift. Violently forced on me,' she was spitting as she spoke, 'Driven into me like a disease, like a virus, a horrible twisting, curling thing that burrowed into me!'

The willow tree was thrashing furiously now, the clouds overhead darkening, the wind swirling around the garden like a mini tornado, the hedges swaying side to side like a singing quartet, the long grass thrashing side to side like a storm at sea, the garden furniture rocking frantically on the patio. The conservatory creaked like a galleon in heavy weather.

Tony was confused by her crazy ramblings. What was she trying to say? Were these the mad rants of a dying woman? She was saying something but saying nothing. He shouldn't be here, should never have come. Jane was wrong. Mitchell was wrong. This was bad. Bad for both of them.

'This is why I stayed away. We are not good for each other, mother. We bring out the worst in each other.'

'The worst in each other! Ha ha, that's right. You are the worst of me, and I am the worst of you,' she shrieked into the dark space before them, 'all of the bad bits, all of the best bits. You took all of the best bits when you came into this world and I lost them all. I lost everyone, and I was left…with you.'

'What do you mean? What are you talking about?'

'All on my own, no husband, no companion, no family, no friends! You saw to that. I tried, I had a man, we had a son together, but even he left me. He couldn't bear to be around me, all because of what you did!' she pointed her long bony finger at him, her arm shaking with exertion and her eyes red with rage. He thought she was going to leap up and put her frail hands around his quivering throat.

'I didn't do anything. I was just a child!'

'A devil child!'

'A normal child!'

'A bastard child! A bastard child that nobody wanted. And I was cursed with raising you!'

'You didn't have to take me in, you know. I could have stayed an orphan! I might have been happier that way!'

She smiled through yellow, rotting teeth and thin decaying lips.

'I didn't adopt you, Anthony. That's the great big lie, the blockbuster of a scam. That's why you are here, so I can let you in on my little secret. The awful truth that I've been keeping from you for all these long, hurtful years,' she gripped the arms of the chair, her knuckles white and her thin, fragile biceps trembling. 'You are mine, *all mine!*' her piercing, dying eyes burrowed into his head like tapeworms as she hissed at him like an angry serpent.

'But… I… didn't… want… you!'

His jaw dropped; his eyes bulged. He was shaking now, with rage and with shock. What?

'He forced you into me against my will and then he abandoned me, cold, alone, full of his semen and hate! *And then there... you... were.*'

The wind wailed, the willow cried, and Tony fled.

Chapter 23: The Watcher

He could see her through the window at the back of the house. She was in the kitchen making tea and she looked lovely. Beautiful some might say. He would say. He could smell her, her scent, sweet and enticing.

She looked out at the garden longingly. She couldn't see him of course; it was dark, and he was purposefully wearing dark clothing. He was sitting on a plastic patio chair, just far enough away that the gloom enshrouded him, hands folded at his lap. She was looking for something, for someone. For him, maybe?

He watched as she tucked her hair behind her ears and rested her chin on her hands. Her soft features, large blue eyes, slightly plump, pale pink lips. He loved her.

The sky was clear, full of stars, no moon. The perfect night for him to silently sit and watch over her, like a guardian. *He* wasn't there tonight, preoccupied elsewhere, so he could sit quietly, gazing and dreaming. No-one out there but him. And the stars.

The door behind her opened and she turned. A stranger's set of arms enveloped themselves around her shoulders. She looked up and smiled cautiously. He kissed her on the forehead, then on the lips. Him. *The fucker.* He could see that she was giving herself to him reluctantly. She wanted a way out, someone to lead her to an open doorway without fear of reprisal. He could give her that. If only she knew.

STACEY DIGHTON

What did he have that she could possibly want? What did he have that drew her to him? What could he give her that he couldn't?

Mind games. He had brainwashed her, seduced her, into giving into him. Schmaltzy charm and flash like a firework with no bang. The guy was a fucking fraud and he wasn't smart enough to see that she was better than that, that she would never fall, not for long anyway, for such superficial, paper-thin bullshit.

But there she was and there he was. In her fucking kitchen. Making out.

He clenched his hands tight enough for his nails to leave deep, red marks. He gritted his teeth, pursed his lips and kept his counsel. And yet he could feel his heart beating hard in his chest, like it was going to combust and rip his rib cage wide open.

He had to be careful. Keep his cool. Maintain his composure and not give up his emotions. If he was unable to do that then sure as eggs were eggs *he* would pick up on the rage and anger and *he* would come. And once that Pandora's box was opened it could never be closed. *He* would never be stopped.

He took a mental picture and stored this one for later.

No, he would sit out there until she retired to bed. Make sure she was safe. He couldn't bring himself to think of what they might get up to up there, in the bedroom, his hands all over her, slipping the straps of her nightdress from her slight shoulders, kissing her neck, running his disrespectful hands down her spine and over her delicate hips, laying her onto the bed as he gently caressed the inside of her silken thighs. He felt himself harden and pushed those thoughts to the back of his mind. Not now.

She looked out into the dark night once again, unblinking, gazing at the vast emptiness. He could almost touch her then, reach out and touch her face, rub his caressing fingers down her cheek, feel her soft, porcelain smooth skin, her warm, scented breath on his face.

Then, in an instant, she reached out a hand and twisted the blinds shut. She was gone.

He sighed to himself.

It was chilly but he wasn't cold. He didn't care. He would sit there until all the lights went out. He wasn't afraid of the dark anymore.

100

ACT 2: THE RISING

Chapter 24: Nightmares

He was out in the open. The air was damp and there was a low, swirling mist sitting just above eye level. It was dark.

There was a clearing, somewhere in a forest or a park. There were cars parked at one end, somebody had built a campfire and a few kids, teenagers or young adults, were dancing around it like fools. Some of them, male and female, had their tops off. Music was playing, some random drum and bass tune and the erratic way the amassed throng were moving suggested that many or most had had way too much to drink, smoke or both.

He was at the other end of the clearing, away from the lights and the chaos of the party. She was looking at him intensely like she wanted to tell him something, something personal, something meaningful. He desperately wanted to know what she had to say but she was hesitant. Part of him wanted to hold her, to tell her it was going to be okay, it would all be alright but deep down in the pit of his stomach he knew that wasn't true.

He recognised her, he'd seen her face somewhere, maybe at a bar or out on a call. He was rummaging through his memory banks but it all seemed foggy, dulled somehow.

She took a swig from a bottle of cheap red wine. Her lipstick left a mark around the rim. She was smiling but it was a melancholy smile.

He wanted her, wanted her so badly, but his legs felt like lead weights and he couldn't move them. It felt as if someone had glued him to the ground. He started to panic.

She saw it first. Her smile switched in an instant and, all of a sudden, her face contorted. She looked around for help, started to turn to flee. He floated behind her, his legs were still useless to him, but he stayed with her. She ran through the thick brambles, thorns tearing at her clothes, weeds pulling at her legs as she forced her way through the dense thicket.

There was a darkness around him, darker and more foreboding than before. It seemed to be reaching to the girl from behind him, long thin tendrils of blackness, stretching fingers that grasped the air behind the young girl's fleeing form. She turned back as she ran, naked fear etched into her very being, eyes wide and bloodshot, her mouth silently screaming. She looked at him imploringly, 'Help me, please', but he couldn't, no matter how desperately he wanted to and how hard he tried.

She didn't watch where she was going, her trainers caught on a tree root and she toppled, arms flailing as she crashed into the sodden earth beneath her. Nettles and brambles grabbed and clawed at her, branches whipped at her face and arms, the soil and mulch encased and sucked her in like quick sand, pulling her down, down.

She rolled onto her back in time to see the blackness envelope her. She let out a hissing scream, her throat ragged and dry. He frantically tried to free himself from his paralysis to get to her, but it was in vain. He was helpless, useless.

Her hands clutched at thin air, trying to push the thing off of her, desperately trying to fight her way through its shadowy form and to some safe place, but it was fruitless. It had engulfed her in its dark misery, thrusting at her with fierce intensity again and again.

He cried out.

Chapter 25: Morning

'NOOOO!'

He sat bolt upright, wincing into the blackness, cold sweat encasing him, his body and face damp, his heart pounding. Where had she gone? Where were his clothes? He felt around him, the earth was soft, cushioned somehow. Had he fallen onto some patch of mossy earth? His head was a blur, confused. He moved his arms. He wasn't paralysed any more. Whatever it was that had held him rigid had faded.

'You okay?'

It was a whispered female voice, husky, and there was a hand on him. He jumped.

'It's okay, it's okay, it's me. You were dreaming.'

There was movement and then a bright orange light to his right-hand side. He was in a room. Wardrobe, bed, door. Bedroom. Reality came back to him with a whoosh and a pop. He was in Lisa's bedroom. He looked down at her, her hair was a mess, her face pudgy, worry lines etched into her cheeks and brow. He remembered; he had stayed over the previous night. She had cooked spaghetti and meatballs. He could still taste the garlic and rosemary. He remembered some kind of herb bread.

'Yeah, yeah. Nightmare I think,' he grunted nonchalantly.

'You okay now? You want a glass of water?'

'Please. My mouth's as dry as sandpaper.'

She sat up. She was naked. They had made love last night; he could still taste her on his lips and feel her soft caress on the nape of his neck. She pulled the covers back and stood up. He could see her in all her glory, petite but not too skinny, short punky red hair, tattoos on one arm and on the side of one hand, pale skin, large brown eyes, silver piercings in her ears and through her lip. He watched her bum cheeks jiggle as she walked into the other room to get him his water.

He rubbed his eyes and cursed at himself. What was with the god-forsaken nightmares? Could it be the case he was working? Maybe, he pondered, he needed to recognise the distinct possibility that it was getting to him more than he had previously considered. He needed a lead and he needed one fast. He knew that he couldn't let the maniac strike again, if only to prevent the chief having a major coronary.

He checked his phone. No messages, no emails. It was only four thirty A.M. but he was wide awake. He'd only been asleep for a few hours, but he felt like he'd slept for a week. He felt the urge to get moving, to get active and do something useful.

He heard the tap running and glasses clinking.

He had gotten there at about ten thirty. He'd spent the day interviewing residents, quizzing the innocently ignorant and generally looking for leads that weren't there. They'd had some calls but most of them were crack pots living out some TV fantasy. Time wasters. Damo had manned the latest crime scene, making sure no stone was left unturned. They'd found another of those damned capsules, what appeared to be the killer's call sign. This one, it seemed, contained different words but the same handwriting and the same old crap. At least, he told Damo, they could be almost completely certain that it was the same perp.

Lisa had been pretty pissed that he was so late, but he'd sweet talked her into forgiving him. Kind of. But then wasn't make up sex the best kind?

The dinner was nice. Lisa wasn't a great cook, he knew the sauce was out of a jar, but it was warm and tasty. He'd washed it down with a few bears and a few large glasses of scotch and the fuzz in his head nullified his anxiety. Lisa hadn't drunk, said he could drink enough for the two of them and he tended to agree. She hadn't gone out for a smoke either which was odd although it was something he'd complained at her about on occasion. He thought she was probably on some kind of health kick or something and, he had to admit, she was looking good for it.

'I had some ice in the freezer. Here,' she handed him his water. He had a dull ache in the front of his skull but that seemed to be a permanent fixture these days, as attached to him as his smile, his body odour and his fractious personality.

'Thanks Lis'. Sorry for waking you.'

She was still drowsy; her eyes were puffy. She laid back on the bed and pulled the duvet around her.

'S'okay. Didn't want to sleep anyway. Just wasting the day away.' She smiled languidly at him, 'What was the dream?'

'Oh, just a nightmare. This murder case must be getting into my psyche or something. Third one in a week.'

'You were calling out some girl's name you know,' she eyed him up and down with curiosity.

He frowned, searching his frazzled brain for the fading contents of his dream, 'Was I?'

'Yeah, Truly or Trudy? You know someone with that name?'

He relaxed. He didn't, he honestly didn't, 'No, never met anyone with either of those names. Truly? Isn't that the one from Chitty Chitty Bang Bang? She was sweet.'

She slapped his arm softly, 'Don't be a prick. Well, whoever it was you wanted her to stop what she was doing. Kept shouting 'no' and 'don't'. Was it a dirty dream? Was she abusing you sexually? Is that what you like?' She kicked him hard enough to spill his drink, narrowly missing his groin,

'Yeah, you know I do,' he smiled at her wryly.

'Knob.'

'I've got one.'

'Not one to speak of.'

He got out of bed and stretched.

'What you doing?'

'I'm gonna take off.'

'Something I said?'

'No, but now I'm awake I feel the urge to get moving.'

She was agitated by that, 'Typical Luke Raven, can't spend more than ten minutes in any one place. Will I see you again anytime soon?'

He pulled on his jeans. 'Yeah, I'll give you a call or a text.'

'Don't do me any favours.'

He picked up his crumpled shirt from the floor and flapped it to shake out the creases. 'Now come on. Last night was great. The food. The sex.'

'Don't flatter yourself. I've had better.'

'Maybe you have, but I keep coming back.'

'Maybe one day I won't be here.'

He smiled with a hint of cynicism, 'That's your choice.'

He buttoned his navy cotton short-sleeve and tucked himself in while pulling his belt around his slowing growing waste line.

'Where are we going with this, Luke?'

'What do you mean?'

She sat up, arms folded to cover her breasts, 'This. Where's it going? You come round every now and again, we eat, we drink, we shag. Is this it or is there more?'

He stopped and looked at her.

'I can't really think about that now, Lisa. There's a loony out there and I need to get him caught and banged up in a cell somewhere, preferably far away from here.'

She laughed sarcastically, 'You can't keep using your fucking job as an excuse to avoid any kind of commitment.'

'Commitment to what?'

'Commitment to this… this relationship.'

He smiled and grabbed her foot from underneath the covers, 'Is this what this is? Are we in a relationship? Are we grown-ups?'

'One of us is at least,' she smiled back, but she wasn't joking.

He grabbed his shoes, 'Look, I like you, Lis'. I really do. We have fun. *I* have fun. I love… being around you. You're good for me. We have a heat to us, a fiery heat. But I've got a lot on my plate at the moment,' he looked in the mirror and brushed his hair to one side, 'one more false move and I'm out of a job. The Mayor's gunning for me, Dave's got my back but for how much longer I don't know, and I've got a crazy on the loose. I will make time for… us, but not right now.'

She exhaled loudly and glared at him, 'Just don't be surprised when you come over and I'm gone. I can't keep putting my life on standby waiting for some drunk cop to turn up at my door. You're either with me or against me, and if you're against me I'm out of here. I don't need any more shit in my life.' She pulled the covers over her head and slunk down into the bed.

He grabbed his bag.

'I'll see you, Lisa. I'll give you a call.'

She grumbled something from under the duvet.

He looked back at her, sighed, and decided to file this one under 'problems to resolve at a later date.'

Chapter 26: Angra Mainyu

He was with her, was holding her gently in his arms.

She had fought the most, had thrashed about wildly and torn a chunk from his cheek. He hadn't liked that. That had really pissed him off. He probably shouldn't have done what he did. *He* had chastised him for it, but the bitch had clawed him like a fucking wildcat. That had enraged him. He had lost control. *He* would always tell him never to lose control because *he* said if you lost control you showed weakness in temperament and the weak did not rise to power.

He was sorry, so sorry that he had struck her so many times, but the red mist had descended. Now she was damaged like a broken doll. *He* would not accept damaged goods, and neither would he. Never could, not even when he was little. If a toy was broken it went in the bin. If someone crossed him, they would be cast aside or faded out of his circle of friends. He couldn't bear to have things that were...compromised.

He was like a farmer who discarded bruised or rotten fruit. She was bruised. Bruised and rotten.

He knew that he wouldn't need to do the other thing now. She would just be tossed aside. Cleaned and discarded. He thought it was a shame. She was pretty.

He had said that they would soon move on from their appetisers. This was a little wrinkle in their dress rehearsal. He wouldn't let it happen again. He was unprofessional tonight and had been slow and clunky. Next time he would be slick and sharp. Sharp as the knife he carried, strapped to the inside of his wrist with a leather holster and hidden from the eyes of those who could not see.

He laid her down. He had made a hell of a mess and knew that it now needed to be cleaned. If he didn't clean, good and thorough, then he was well aware that the copper from the TV would find something, something incriminating and perhaps damaging. Their plan would be ruined and all the hard work, risk taking, and self-sacrifice would have been for nothing. *He* would get mad and he certainly didn't want to be the cause of that. It could only end badly for him.

He looked at her. She was pretty before but she wasn't as pretty now, hair matted with blood, face crushed and bleeding. He felt a pang of sorrow and guilt. He touched his cheek and looked at his hand. There was blood on his fingers. His blood. She had really left her mark.

He looked around at his tiny home. This had become his kill-zone and he hated the place. It reminded him of death. Of both death and of fear. The fear he had felt as a child. The rage, burning in him like a simmering flame, occasionally erupting like an awakening volcano. The fear his victims felt when they finally realised what was about to be unleashed, when they saw *him* appear from the murk and the shadows. The fear that he always felt when he saw what he had done.

They would have to get on to the real work and soon. Time was running out and if they didn't work quickly then she would get away and he knew that if that happened he would never get her back.

He looked at the floor around his feet, ceramic tiles running with dark liquid, hair and urine. He hated it.

It was time to clean.

Chapter 27: The Chase

Luke wiped the sleep from his eyes. The sun was just peering out from behind the horizon as he left Lisa's building, like the face of naughty child spying on its parents. Low orange flame reflected from the windows of the Victorian terraced buildings, their brickwork red and scarred, their old wooden frames splintered and faded. The air smelt fresh and clean like only a good English autumnal morning could. It had a hint of the sea, freshly cut grass, morning-dew mixed with the tepid odour of a town that was long past the heady days of its boom years.

He smiled to himself. Last night had been good. It hadn't been that good with Lisa for quite a while and that was mainly his fault. He hadn't been paying attention. He had not been a good... what... boyfriend? Is that what he was? Christ, if he didn't know that then what chance did they have? He considered the questioning, her probing of him like she was looking for something. She had never used the 'R' word before, she had never seemed to have been the type, but when he thought about it he really hadn't considered it would have lasted as long as it had. He had to admit to himself that he kind of liked the idea.

He zipped up his jacket and blew out condensed, and probably less than perfumed, morning breath. The air still had that early morning damp chill. He would walk back to his place, wash and freshen up and throw on a change of clothes before heading in to the office. He wanted to read Damo's latest report on their second victim. She had been identified as a Billy Roper, thirty-year-old shop worker from town. She lived on her own, her mother lived locally, father was dead. She had been out the night before with friends at a pub in the town centre and had left them at about midnight to walk home. She never showed up for work the next day, no-one at home. Damo had the team doing the usual CCTV checks, interviewing anyone that had been in or around the pub at the time, traced her route home, interviewed her neighbours. With a little luck he thought that something would come up.

Shit, he cursed, he hated this. But he felt a deep-seated responsibility to bring the bastard in. They hadn't had anything like this in Westhampton for fifty years or so, not since the Seafront Strangler who had killed five, and he was damned if he was going to let that record be broken. Not while he was still on the case, not on his watch, although he knew that if the Mayor had his way that wouldn't be for much longer.

There were hardly any cars on the road and not a soul on the streets. He liked it that way, he could think as he walked without any interruptions. Even his mobile phone was keeping its own counsel and he knew in a little while all of that would change.

He could still smell Lisa on him. He breathed it in as he walked, and it was good. Something about last night was different. Sure, he thought, she had given him the cold shoulder that morning but what did he expect? She could be a temperamental so and so at the best of times but, regardless of all of that, he could sense something had changed. It was just that he couldn't put his finger on it, whatever *it* was. He decided to let the day's events unfold before he would come back to ruminating on what could be and what might have been.

He reached into his jacket for his hip flask. He was yearning for just a little nip to get his electrons charged and his protons rattling. He intended to get some results today and he was going to need all of his available inner resources to do it. He pulled the flask out, unscrewed the lid and inhaled deeply, tasting the whiskey on the back of his throat even before the flask had touched his lips. He promised himself that it was just a sip and then that would be it until later that night.

A clang and clatter down one of the alleyways startled him and almost made him let go of his flask.

He could hear a muffled dragging sound but couldn't quite make out the direction from where it was coming from. There were two alleyways leading between derelict buildings to a wide expanse of waste land, overgrown with tall reeds and randomly scattered brambles. He didn't know if it was the left alley or the right one. Didn't matter, he said to himself, it was probably foxes rummaging through boxes or bin bags. The bloody things had been infesting the neighbourhood since fox hunting had been outlawed. Not that he had anything against nature and all of god's creatures, great and small but when the poxy things were spreading litter all over his doorstep and crapping on his lawn he had to fight to keep his inner hunter in check.

He put his flask back in his jacket pocket, shrugged and turned to leave.

That's when he saw the dark shape rise up from about halfway down the alleyway to his left. He stopped, turned and peered into the gloom. It was hunched over, tall, sinewy and almost semi-translucent. It reminded him of something, something he had seen before. The dawn sun wasn't making it all the way down there yet and he struggled to picture any distinguishing or obvious features. It appeared to be positioning or stacking something, stooping down to make some final adjustments to something, a piece of street art perhaps. He stepped between the two buildings either side of him and immediately the light dimmed, and the temperature dropped. He couldn't make out whether it was a man or a woman. It looked like it had a long black parka coat on, black hat, black gloves. Like an undertaker.

He took a step toward it and unwittingly kicked a semi-crushed beer can. CLANG! He swore under his breath and froze.

The shape turned and looked at him. White face, insecure eyes, sharp angled features. It looked bemused. It seemed to blink, its mouth tightly pursed, brow furrowed as if it were thinking. It stepped towards him, arms held outwards as if to reach for him and he involuntarily took a step back. It seemed to rise, float, gain height and form. It raised its head, tilted to one side, questioning, wondering. The shadows seemed to shift, flicker and jolt as if alive.

'Hey!' his voice was coming from a thousand miles away.

It dropped back to earth. The shadows evaporated and it turned and fled. It was quick.

'Hey! You there! Police! Stop!'

It was running, faster than any man or woman he had had the pleasure of pursuing before. Mind you, he thought, he was usually on the tail of half drunks, tramps or wasters. Before he even moved his feet, it was out of the alleyway and making its way across the two hundred metres or so of misshapen wasteland. He gave chase, leaping over boxes, rubbish bags and battered refuse bins. He almost fell over the body.

He stopped and swore. Fuck, another young girl. Different. Beaten. He paused to check her pulse and quickly confirmed that she was dead.

He raced to catch up. It was vaulting the fence at the far end of the open space, almost clearing it with a single leap. He wondered how anybody would have the agility to do that, but he pushed the thought to the back of his mind. Luke wasn't slow but he certainly wasn't the fittest in his unit and he could feel his heart pounding in his chest as he reached the fence, hauling himself over it, taking a chunk of skin out of his shin in the process. He landed hard on the other side, going down on his knee with a loud crack and a curse. He scraped the palm of his hand on the gravel, drawing blood. He looked up and could see the flap of a coat jacket as his fugitive rounded a corner at the far end of the road.

'Shit,' he leapt up and ran, feeling the pain in his knee shoot up his thigh and onto his hip. He decided that he needed to get to the gym more often, he was way too young to feel this unfit. He launched himself around the corner to see it... him... getting further and further away from him, rounding the back end of a parked lorry and accelerating up the steep hill.

He stopped and put his hands on his knees, taking in deep, long heaves of vital oxygen while his heart threatened to rip out of his chest. In through the mouth and out through the nose he repeated to himself. He reached into his jacket and pulled out his phone, hitting speed dial for the station as he raised it to his ear.

'This is D.I. Luke Raven,' he paused to take in more air, 'I am in pursuit of a suspect on James Street. I have located a body, another young girl,' he sighed, 'in an alleyway off of All Saints Road. He or she is making their way up Trafalgar Hill,' another breath, he was starting to see stars, 'send an ambulance to All Saints Road and scramble all mobile units, I will continue to pursue on foot.'

Who was he kidding? He took in a lungful and started to jog up the hill. He no longer had a visual on the suspect and he cursed.

'Shit!'

Something cracked under foot and he looked down at the weed-ridden pavement. A small wooden object had splintered under the weight of his boot, a piece of crumpled paper stuck to his shoe. Curious, he reached down and plucked it off, unfolding it and holding it in the palm of his bloodied hand. He squinted his eyes in the dim light to read what it said. He frowned, bemused, exhausted and frustrated;

The door of Āz is open.

Chapter 28: Late Morning

He couldn't see! He couldn't see! He was awake, he could feel blood rushing back to the tips of his toes and his fingers, his body starting to recover from the semi-paralysis that sleep had brought to him, but he simply could not see! Whatever he had consumed the night before it had left him blind, had taken his eyesight from him. What the hell had he been drinking? He remembered getting the train home but hardly remembered the journey. He was emotional, sure, perhaps even disorientated. Had he fallen? Was he laying outside in the street or, worse, alone on the train-track? Had he been that distraught that he had tried to take his own life but had even failed at that, blinding himself in some botched attempt at suicide?

He shook his head from side to side in despair, no, no, no, NO! He reached up to wipe his eyes and felt loose skin over them, something dry and soft, some kind of black veil, a pelt of some kind that he could pinch between his fingers but without any feeling.

Wait, he thought, and then…what? He exhaled loudly in relief as he pulled his underpants from his face. Jesus, he thought, where was he? He winced as the light from a single window penetrated his pupils. It burned. The whole space around him appeared to be on fire from some supernatural light.

He lay there a second while his eyes adjusted. Where the fuck was he?

He turned his head to one side. A couch that had seen better days.

He rolled his head to the other side. A TV stand, DVDs, action films, documentaries, an assortment of porn.

Lots of porn.

He shook his head. He knew it could only be one place. Bill's place.

He was naked. Someone had stripped him completely bare and stolen his clothes. Of course, he considered, there was the distinct possibility that he had done that to himself.

'What the fuck did you get up to last night?'

Billy was standing behind the sofa, mug of coffee in one hand, resplendent in shorts and T-Shirt, a Star Wars Episode IV original, with both an intrigued and amused look on his face. Tony jumped up, trying to cover his flaccid manhood, and swiftly pulled on his boxers.

'Where did you spring from, you bastard?'

'Whoa there, cowboy. Put that lasso away. The question should be, where did you spring from? This is my den, not yours,' he took a large swig from his coffee, cappuccino foam thickly coating the underside of his moustache.

'I… I don't know. I don't actually remember getting here,' Tony grabbed his jeans and shirt which he had located tucked behind the cushion on the sofa.

Billy flopped back onto the couch, 'Well you were making a hell of a noise,' he scratched under his chin and frowned, 'I'm going to have to find a new hidey hole for my spare key.'

Tony leant against the wall while his vision came back into focus, 'Oh, really? Sorry Bill. I… I must have been pretty out of it.'

'Pretty wasted I'd say. You could barely stand, kept falling into my azaleas. Sal's gonna do one,' he smiled, 'You must have been hitting it pretty hard, you smelt, no you *smell*, like a cheap offy. Some kind of works do?' he shot Tony a reproachful glance, 'And why wasn't I invited?'

Tony waved his hand, the sudden motion causing his head to pound, 'No, no, nothing like that. I… er… went round to see Mum.'

Billy sat upright, 'Oh, shit. How… er… is she?'

Tony took a seat at the desk in the corner. He stretched back into the second-hand, navy-blue office chair and rubbed his temples. 'You got any pills?'

'What kind of pills?'

'Headache fucking pills!'

'Oh, sure. Yeah, hang on,' Billy stood up, walked over to the desk and rifled through a drawer. A drawer full of dead batteries, take-away menus and what looked like two bags of skunk. He handed Tony a packet of 'own-brand' paracetamol.

Tony raised his eyebrows, 'You spend a fortune on Mexican marijuana from your top secret, can't tell a soul, drug peddler but won't fork out for some decent headache pills?'

'You want them or not?'

'Give me that coffee.'

Billy gingerly handed him his Simpsons mug; Homer dressed as a pitchfork wielding devil with fire blazing in his eyes. Tony popped two capsules in his mouth and took a big gulp.

'I guess I'll make myself another,' Billy stood up and popped a pod in his coffee maker, 'you want one?'

'Nah, I'll just finish this one.'

'So… you didn't answer my question!' Billy raised his voice over the whir of the coffee machine.

'What question?'

'About your mum. How is she?'

'She's dying, Billy. How do you think?'

'Well if you're gonna be like that I won't pretend I care.'

Billy took his cup, popped out the empty pod, stirred and slurped. Tony looked at the big Budweiser clock on the wall. It was ten thirty on a Saturday morning. Jane was going to wonder where the hell he was. He sighed to himself ruefully, knowing the day was going to be a long one.

'She told me some home truths. Some truths that I'm going to need to check out,' he sighed, 'turns out the bitch is my real mum after all'

Billy choked on his cappuccino, more milky foam coating his moustache like an iced, cinnamon donut. He wiped his mouth with the back of his hand, brushing spilt coffee from the faded black helmet of the Sith Lord which adorned the breast of his vintage T-shirt.

'You what?'

'You heard me.'

'I thought she adopted you when you were a little 'un.'

'So did I.'

'Why would she lie about that?'

'I don't think she consented.'

'Consented to what? The birth?'

Tony rested his elbows on his knees, put his hands to his head and shook it. After a few moments it dawned on Billy and he uttered a shocked 'Oooooh.'

The room fell silent. Tony could feel Bill staring at the top of his head. The mood in the den shifted, darkened. Some moments didn't need words.

'Shit,' Billy said it anyway.

'Guess I took it badly.'

'Guess you did,' then reassuringly, 'who wouldn't?'

Tony gazed out of the window. He could see Sally in the back garden hanging the washing on the line. He couldn't see any movement from his house, the windows dark, shades pulled. After the last couple of days, he couldn't see Jane being too forgiving about his overnight absence, shocking revelation or no shocking revelation. She just hadn't been right. He'd convinced himself that it was the news about his mum, but that was a stretch. She was… distracted.

'Look, Tone, I really would like to sit and chat about this some more, but I promised Sal' I'd take her shopping. She needs to get some posh frock or something for an estate agents' awards dinner. Excuse for a piss up if you ask me,' he mocked a smile, 'I don't know. She thinks she might be up for a prize, most annoying sales executive probably. But anyway, I said I would take her. Shouldn't be too long.'

'S'okay Bill. I need to get back anyway,' Tony put his cup on the desk and stood up, stars flashing before his eyes and head swimming, the little angry man in his head beating a mallet on the inside of his cranium.

'You can stay in here for as long as you want. I mean,' he smirked, 'you've got the key.'

'No, no. It's okay. I need to get back to Jane. She's gonna be wondering where I am.'

Billy stood up and put an arm around his neighbour, 'She's probably pulling your leg you know. Your mum I mean. The old lady's just giving you grief on her way out. You go round there again and she'll probably laugh the whole thing off.'

Tony smiled, 'Yeah, maybe, mate. Maybe. Go on, you get on out. I'll catch you later.'

They both stepped outside, the mid-morning June sun already pushing the temperature well on its way to the mid-twenties. Tony raised his hand to Sally as he hopped over the fence.

'Be gentle with her, Tony. It'll be fine,' Billy waved as he walked off.

'Yeah, yeah. Off you go Bill, go buy yourself a pretty dress.'

They both laughed. Tony turned back to his house and took a long, deep breath.

Chapter 29: The Row

'WHERE THE HELL HAVE YOU BEEN?'

Tony closed the door and reluctantly turned to face his enraged partner. Her cheeks were a flushed red, her eyes a blazing inferno, her lips pulled back around her teeth, spit spraying.

'Round Bill's?' he offered, lilting his pronunciation as if he were asking a question.

Jane slammed the palm of her hand on the dining room table, almost knocking his opened laptop onto the floor.

'Ooooh! Round Bills! Of course you were! Why didn't I think of that? Well you weren't there last night when I went to bed! And you certainly weren't there at two o' clock this morning when I came down to see if you were home because I was worried sick about you!'

'I... I...'

'You what! You thought I wouldn't notice! Don't you think I worry about you, Tony?'

He paused and shrugged.

'And what is that scratch on your face?'

Tony held his hand to his cheek but couldn't feel a thing.

'The other side!'

He felt the other cheek and ran his fingers down some kind of mild laceration. Odd, he thought.

'I guess I must have caught it on something.'

'Woooooh! What a theory!'

Tony held his hands out, palms facing her, 'Look Jane, I know you're mad but…'

She flew at him, 'But what, Tony? But what? You do this all the time. You just disappear and I don't see you for the rest of the night! If you're not staying late at work you're out in town or round your bloody boyfriend's house! I come back from work, you're gone! You pop out for ten minutes, you don't come back. Don't you want to spend any time with me? Am I that horrible to be with?'

'No Jane. It's not like that. It's not like that at all. If you'd just let me…'

'Just let me, just let me! That's all I do. I just let you do whatever it is you bloody want while I have to do everything else, cleaning up behind you like a bloody housemaid! I'm just fed up with it!'

'Come on, Jane. That's not fair! We both agreed that…'

'That what? That you would stay home while I went to work? That was two years ago, Tony, and all you've written in that time is the fucking shopping list!'

Silence. She was right, but it hurt to hear it from her. She had been so understanding about the whole thing, but he had known that this had been coming, hadn't he? All that buried resentment rising to the surface. He just hadn't realised it was there simmering for all this time. He'd been a fool, a blind fool.

'Do you know what? I don't care. Do what you want!' she grabbed her keys from the table, 'I'm going out. I don't know when I'll be back.' There were tears rolling down her cheeks and a sorrowful look of regret etched on her face. She didn't want to go, it was obvious to both of them, but she had to do something. She stopped and looked at him, imploring him to say something, to stop her from leaving.

He stood there, looking at her, willing her to stay but not knowing what to do.

She turned to the door.

'It's Mum, Jane.'

She stopped with her back to him.

'I did what you asked. I went to see her. She told me things. Horrible, awful things and I... I don't know what to do.' His shoulders slumped, he buried his face in his hands and sobbed.

She turned, dropped her keys to the floor and went to him.

Chapter 30: The Breakthrough

Damian Barber and Luke Raven stood over the body. The poor girl had been beaten up pretty badly. Whoever had done it had apparently been in a fit of intense anger and rage. Her face was a pulp, teeth ground into her cheeks, eye sockets shattered, skull cracked.

'Do you think it's the same guy?' Barber was asking the question.

'Hard to say. Different M.O. but that doesn't necessarily mean it's a different killer. We would have to have some pretty shit luck to have two homicidal maniacs on the loose in Westhampton at the same time.'

'Doesn't mean that we should rule it out.'

Raven sighed, 'No, no you're right. We shouldn't rule it out.'

They were both standing in hospital whites, face masks on, heads covered.

Doctor Chandur was in the theatre, the hospital garb suiting her tiny frame much better than the two lumbering oafs standing before her. She was annoyed that they had insisted on being there while she conducted her work, as if she didn't have enough on her plate. Plus, she thought to herself, the young detective, Barber, kept looking at her oddly. It was unsettling.

'Anything, Doc?'

She looked up, scalpel in hand, blood on her smock.

'It's a little early to say, Detective Inspector. And I wouldn't want to speculate.'

'But if I asked you to?'

'Then I would say that it would be inappropriate.'

The way that she clipped her consonants and rounded her vowels made Barber's heart skip a beat. Several even. He found her tone both soothing and arousing in equal measure. He looked over at Raven.

'I think this was a botched job, boss.'

'Very possibly, Barber.'

'I mean, look at her. Whoever did this had lost all control. I reckon she must have really pissed him off,' he sighed, 'No, I don't think this is what he intended at all. I think this was a reaction to something, maybe the fear of getting caught, maybe a revenge for something she said or something that had happened to him.'

'Him? You're assuming that the attacker is a male.'

Barber looked down at the torso of the young girl, 'Well, look at her. I might appear sexist in saying this,' he glanced up at the doctor, 'but I don't believe a female could, *would*, have done,' he pointed at the young girls face, his own pulled into a sickened gurn, 'that.'

The room fell silent. Raven spoke first.

'What about the head trauma, Doc? Any clue on type of weapon used.'

The Doctor made no secret of her displeasure at the D.I's incessant questioning, 'As I said before, Detective Inspector, I would not want to speculate until I had completed a thorough examination.'

'But you have a view.'

'I am a forensic pathologist detective. Of course I have a view. But that doesn't mean that I'm going to share it.'

'Not even if I ask nicely?'

'Not even if you ask really nicely.'

'What if I asked Barber to ask nicely,' Raven dug an elbow into Barber's ribs. He could feel his partner fidget uncomfortably next to him.

The Doctor let out a sigh of exasperation, 'Especially not if Detective Barber asked nicely.'

Barber shifted his weight from one foot to the other, embarrassed.

Raven looked around at his surroundings.

The room was cold and stark, bare walls and floor, overhead strip light, the single bed and a trolley carrying the Doctor's tools and surgical implements. They stood quietly, hands folded in front of them, listening to the gruesome sounds of blade on flesh and bone.

'You out tonight at the get together?'

Raven frowned at Barber, 'What get together?'

'The department's monthly night out.'

'Is it that time of the month already?'

'Yeah, yeah you know it is. It's always the fourth Friday.'

'Yeah, I guess it is.'

Silence as they watched the Doctor dropping items into a small bowl by the side of the bed. The coldness of the room enveloped them, the bleakness of the scene.

'Where is it?'

'Where's what?'

'The night out.'

'Oh, we're starting at the Swan, I think. Around eight-ish?'

'Who's going?'

'Most of the department. The chief said he might even pop in for one.'

'Oh, he did, did he?'

'Sure did.'

'Mmmm.'

The Doctor muttered under her breath as she investigated the cranium. She wasn't used to such disturbances while she carried out an autopsy. She found it… irritating.

'Well?'

'Well what?'

'Are you coming or not?'

'I don't know. I'm going to see how we get on today. Did you run the new note by forensics?'

'Yeah, they've got it along with the other two. I think they're going to draw a blank again though.'

'Why do you say that?'

'Well, they've looked long and hard at the first two and came up with nothing. Standard printer paper, no fingerprints, no skin deposits. The wooden capsules appear hand-made, carved from some soft wood. Again, no prints. Can't even trace them back to a store or retailer. This guy's got all the angles covered.'

'Well let's see. What about the messages? Any news on what they're all about?'

'Well, it's interesting. Apparently they are Persian or Iranian in origin. The first one, Aka Manah, means evil spirit or evil intention. I'd told you that one already. Creepy,' he paused, recalling what the guy at the library had told him, 'the second, Angra Mainyu, is from the ancient Persian faith of Zoroastrianism.' He spoke the last word slowly and deliberately so as to nail the pronunciation.

Raven looked at him like he was talking gibberish.

'I know, right? Anyway, Angra Mainyu represents the destructive spirit. An evil God. Whoever is writing these notes appears to be either of Iranian origin, or a scholar of these ancient scripts.'

'And what about this last one. The door of Āz? What is that?'

Barber looked at him over the top of his mask, 'Well, Āz is another of the Zoroastrian demons. Except this one is much more identifiable to Westerners like us. In our world we would see Āz as the reaper. He is the demon of death, his door being the door to the other side. Whether its heaven or hell is not clear, but this guy is telling us that there will be more victims, that he's just getting started, that the door is open.'

Raven felt a chill run down his spine. He recalled the tall black figure, the ghostly white face, inquisitive eyes, the way it had risen from the ground like some deathly spirit beckoning him to come closer. Those kinds of things were not supposed to happen in Westhampton and certainly were not supposed to happen around him. If he hadn't seen it with his own eyes, he wouldn't have believed it.

A cracking noise followed by a small tearing sound resonated around the chamber. Raven jumped. Barber felt his stomach flip. He realised that the bacon and egg bap earlier that day had been a bad idea. He turned to Raven, 'I can't believe he got away. Our first big break and we let him slip from between our fingers.'

Raven winced, remembering how he had failed to keep pace with the suspect, 'Yeah, yeah. But he was quick, must have been a sprinter or something. And he had a good head start. By the time the squad cars had arrived he was long gone.' He felt the pain in his knee and the shame of not having kept up with his fitness work at the gym, 'Doesn't mean they won't find him. We've got the whole department working the area. If he makes a move, we'll know it.'

Barber was right though. He had been so close, just a few feet away from nailing the guy, from shutting the whole thing down. He cursed to himself. Now they were back to square one and again hoping for blind luck to throw them a bone.

'That's interesting,' the Doctor was investigating the finger nails of the girl. They were quite long and varnished in pastel pink, adorned with some kind of intricate flower pattern. She had obviously looked after them.

'What's that, Doc?'

'A small amount of tissue and hair under the nail of the right index finger,' she squinted as she used a tiny set of pincers to pull the epidermis fragments out from under the nail and place them into a petri dish. 'Looks like this girl fought back which would certainly not be out of character.'

Raven smiled. Good girl. This was their bone.

Chapter 31: Big Night Out

Simmons was at the bar. It was early, he was there first, but he only intended on staying for one or two, just to show his face. He needed to demonstrate his support; it was his team after all. The mood at the station had been pretty low recently. Cuts being announced, people fearing for their jobs, the threat of the station being closed and relocated to a more central head office. All of that followed by the events of the last week. He wasn't surprised at all that morale had taken a hit.

He sipped on his cider. The cool, refreshing liquid tasted good, and the alcohol buzz was even better. It had been a long few days and, he thought, today had been the toughest. Another body, as yet unidentified, the killer agonisingly close to being in their grasp and then slipping away, more crazy messages, more blood spilt, another family ruined.

He sighed to himself. Perhaps he should have taken that retirement when they had offered it to him. What was it that had led him to turn it down? Pride? The feeling of not yet accomplishing everything he had set out to do? The fear of being left on the scrapheap? The dread of being seen as a failure? What had all of that gotten him? Still in the same job, dealing with the same dregs of humanity, coping with the same bullshit bureaucracy day after day. Stuart had said he was a fool at the time, and he was beginning to think that he had been right.

'Hey Chief,' it was Barber, always one of the first to arrive, his youthful buoyancy always rejuvenating the darkest of moods. He bounded into the pub, his foppish blond hair swaying in front of his piercing blue eyes, the kind of eyes that could get a boy into trouble. He was wearing a light purple polo top and dark blue jeans with blue and white Nike trainers, 'I'll have a Carlsberg, Daisy, when you're free. Thanks.'

Daisy looked up from the other end of the bar, winked and nodded.

'Hi Damian. You're not with Raven?' Simmons eyed him curiously.

'No, he said he had to go freshen up first. He put in a long shift today, you know, after the chase and everything.'

Daisy set his Carlsberg down on a tattered beermat at the bar. She smiled politely as he handed her his money.

Simmons turned to him, 'Any news from forensics?'

'No, not yet. The Doc has sent the skin and hair off for analysis. She expects something back in the morning.'

'Okay, good. We could sure use some good news.'

'You're not wrong there.'

Daisy looked up from pulling a pint of Boddingtons, 'This about the murders?'

Barber looked cautiously at Simmons, 'Yes it is. But, you know. We can't really talk about it.'

'I knew one of those girls. Went to school with her. Shouldn't speak ill of the dead but,' she raised her eyebrows, 'what a bitch.' With that she headed off in the other direction.

Simmons smiled, 'Nice girl that one.'

'Not as nice as you might think,' Raven set himself down at a stool, 'kicks like an angry thoroughbred and punches like a cruiserweight.'

He ordered a scotch, no ice. He gave Daisy a cursory, unreciprocated smile. It had been a rough fifteen hours or so. He looked haggard, tired, despite the shower that he had just had. He had turned the water up hot, almost painfully so, but it soothed him. He'd been with the team all afternoon, scouring the streets, interviewing residents, searching for clues. Aside from the find by the Doctor earlier that day they had again drawn a blank. It was like the guy had simply disappeared.

Over the course of the next hour, several others from the team arrived. Bob 'Spidey' Webber, the Sergeant who had been co-ordinating the search that afternoon, Roger 'Wodger' Dawes, the Junior Inspector who mispronounced his 'r's as 'w's, Alli' 'Crusher' Bailey, the PC of Caribbean descent with an ever-expanding waistline and a vitriolic foul mouth, Ruby 'Tuesday' Cropper, the pretty, young constable who manned the desk and took the calls and Ray 'Lola' Davis, the Inspector who had his ear closest to the ground, the guy they called on when they needed insider information on the local hoods and hoodlums. In one shape or form they all had their part to play in the hunt for 'Angry Manner' or whatever his fucking name was. All of them were involved, all of them shared a desire to bring him to justice. Just a glimpse at the photographs of the face of that young girl brought a real sense of unity amongst them. They all wanted to take him down.

They huddled round a large circular table, a few others joining them from the station, Barber taking charge of the kitty.

'So, you hear about old Teddy Spencer? Took a bullet in the leg in some drugs bust in London. Reckon he's lucky to be alive,' Lola was supping a vodka and coke.

'Bloody idiot taking that job if you ask me,' Spidey downed the dregs of his Spitfire, 'playing with fire messing with the gangs up-town. He's only got three years 'til retirement. Gonna get himself killed.'

'Well, it all sounds pretty exciting to me. Like something off the telly,' Tuesday was eating a packet of dry-roasted and nursing a Corona and lime.

'Except they shoot real bullets and make real holes,' Spidey scowled at her youthful naivety.

'For fuck's sake, Spidey. We don't all want the quiet life you know,' Crusher hollered in her thick Jamaican accent, 'I for one could do with a bit of fucking action, if you know what I mean?' She jiggled her large breasts with her pudgy hands, shiny gold rings on every finger and winked.

Simmons spoke up, 'I think we're getting enough action around here to last us a few years, don't you?'

'How you getting on with hunting down your ghost Wegan? Heard he managed to vanish into thin air this morning. My guys have been putting out feelers all day,' Dawes put his glass down, 'Scurrying around in the alleys like a wodent. You want me to see if I can get hold of Wentokil?' Raven gave him an icy glare.

'If you mean Ghostbusters Wodge, then no thanks. This guy's as human as the next. He just,' Raven knocked back his scotch, 'was a bit quicker than I had anticipated. Caught me on my haunches,' he sneered, 'he won't get so lucky next time.'

'Never was the quickest, were you, Raven?' Spidey smiled at the D.I. through his half-full beer glass. His smile had more than a hint of sarcasm.

'Never pretended to be, Spidey, but that had nothing to do with it. He'll get what's coming to him. We just have to be as determined as he is.'

The table fell quiet, the noise from the rest of the busy pub filling the silence.

Daisy wandered over and started collecting the empty glasses, 'You guys and gals want another?'

They all nodded, a few adding their enthusiastic affirmation. Another was exactly what they needed.

'I'll bring them right over.'

Raven watched her carry the glasses back to the bar. He flinched as he caught Barber eyeing him with interest.

'So where next, Raven? What's our next move?' Simmons was leaning back in his chair, munching on a packet of salt and vinegar crisps.

'Keep up the search, keep taking the calls, carry out more interviews, keep checking the CCTV footage and wait for forensics to come back. We haven't got an ID yet on today's victim. Once that comes in, we'll go round to her place, check out the area, look for signs of disturbance, talk to any friends, relatives, boyfriends,' he looked round the table, 'this thing's got plenty of legs yet. We're just going to need to double the footwork, put in the time. He's already made one mistake. He'll make another.'

Barber nodded silently next to him. Simmons knew he was right, but they'd been checking all the angles for days and, as yet, had only the tiniest of clues to go on. It wasn't hopeless but it was far from an open and shut case.

Raven stood up from the table and walked over to the bar. Daisy was pouring out the drinks.

'You want a hand?'

'From you?'

'Who else?'

'Nah, think I can manage.'

'Look, I didn't mean to have a go the other day. I've got a lot going on, that's all.'

'You and me both, Raven. I can manage, thanks.'

Raven touched her hand, 'I'm sorry Daisy. I didn't mean it. Honest,' he gave her his best, winning smile.

She smirked back, paused and took a breath, 'Whatever. No harm done. Here, you can carry these back to the table.'

He took a tray of drinks, handed them out and then came back for the rest.

'Maybe you can stay back for a drink later. When you finish up,' he perched on a stool, 'I think I owe you one.'

'Oh, you owe me much more than that. And,' she smiled cagily, 'maybe I will.'

He smiled back and returned to the group.

Barber collared him on the way, 'Hey, Raven. I've been meaning to ask you something.'

'What's that Damo? You want a raise? Cause, I don't think the Chief's gonna go for that.'

Barber looked at him confused, 'No, no, nothing like that. Although,' he smiled, 'I wouldn't say no if you offered. No, it's about the Doc.'

'The Doc?'

'Yeah, you know Doctor Chandur? Jasmine, from forensics.'

Raven frowned, 'Yeah, what about her?'

'You, er,' Barber blushed, 'you, er, think I've got a crack?'

'A crack? In the head maybe. What are you going on about?'

Barber sniffed, 'No, a crack. A chance. With her?'

Raven laughed, 'What, you? And the Doctor? What, like on a date?'

'Yeah, that's it. A date. What do you think?'

Raven took a moment to consider it, 'Well, I think you've got about as much chance of scaling Mount Kilimanjaro with one leg,' he chuckled, 'and that's being kind. Don't you think that she's a bit...'

'A bit what?'

'A bit out of your league?'

The crimson in Barber's cheeks intensified.

'Well, I just thought...'

'Thought what?'

'Well, felt really. I felt a... connection.'

'I think the only connection she wants you to feel is the palm of her hand slapping your face. She caught you staring at her earlier you know?' Barber looked shocked, admonished.

Raven put a hand on his shoulder. 'Look, you'll never know unless you try, I suppose. I just...I just don't see it, that's all.'

Barber smiled, taking heart from the tiniest of encouragements, 'But you think I should try?'

Raven sighed, 'Yeah. Why not. What have you got to lose?' he pointed a finger of warning at him, 'Just don't act stupid.'

'Do I ever?'

Raven grinned, 'Come on. Let's have a drink.'

Barber smiled back, 'Sounds like a great idea. I just need to go and drain the main vein first.'

Raven grimaced at the thought as Barber jogged off to the men's room, adjusting his pants as he crossed the bar. He chuckled as he took his place back at the table, the group now animated and chatting loudly.

Crusher looked round at her fellow police officers as he sat down, a pint of Guinness at her ruby red lips, 'Now,' she grinned, her big white teeth brightening the room, 'who wants to hear a filthy joke?'

*

It was dark outside. The street was busy with revellers. He stood on the opposite side of the road, people bashing into him as they hurried from pub to club. He stood still, staring, watching.

He could see them, all of them. Especially that copper who had almost cornered him this morning. The slow copper, the one who couldn't run for toffee.

What to do about him? That was the big question of the day. He was starting to become a pain.

Kill or be killed, that's what *he* would say. But that wasn't always the answer now, was it? There were other ways. If you cut out the cancer it could always grow back. He just needed some discouragement, just needed to be made to back off. There were always ways to achieve the desired end result. You just had to plan it out, like a good game of chess. Strategy, that's what he needed, a good strategy.

He watched them laughing, the big black woman was holding court. The copper, Raven, was laughing at her, drinking his whiskey, patting his comrades on the back. Distasteful, all of them. A bunch of pitiful wasters playing at cops and robbers, not an ounce of integrity between them. It made him sick to his stomach. They wouldn't have got away with acting like this. Not in the old world.

He pulled his hood up and turned away. He had seen all he needed to see. He knew what he had to do.

Chapter 32: Wendy

Nick Waters sat across the table from Walenty Jasinski. They were having a quiet Sunday lunch, Walenty, or Wendy as she liked to be called, wanted to sample the simple English cuisine that she had heard such terrible things about. Nick had rolled his eyes at her acceptance of such a vulgar stereotype. What was the point in trying to explain to the Polish imbecile the finer details of the culinary revolution that had been occurring on Great British shores for the past twenty years or more? All she was interested in was having a pot roast or a steak and kidney pudding followed by jam sponge and custard or a spotted dick. She didn't care that 'pub grub' was only one of a vast arrays of spectacular cuisines which existed in the wonderfully multi-cultural British society, a society which housed one hundred and sixty-two establishments with at least one Michelin star. Four of those with three stars. Gone were the days of the French, Spanish and Italian chefs looking down their noses at their British counterparts. Love them or hate them, Gordon Ramsey, Jamie Oliver, Hester Blumenthal and the like had put British cooking back on the map.

'Oh Nick, this is delicious,' she was wiping her mouth after eating a large forkful of cottage pie. The way she elongated every vowel was really beginning to irritate him.

'That's great, Wendy, really great. I'm glad you like it,' he looked around the little country pub. Aside from the two of them there were only half a dozen others in there, most of whom were obviously local and just there for a pint. 'You do realise I could have taken you somewhere else you know? Somewhere with a bit more…finesse.'

She waggled her fork at him, 'No, no. This is perfect. Exactly what I had wanted and expected. A little English village pub with character. I don't want for you to keep taking me to those posh places, they don't have any atmosphere. This is what I like, somewhere quiet, somewhere quaint.'

He smiled politely, 'Whatever you want. Anything to make you happy, my dear.' He prodded away at his fish and chips. It wasn't even good fish and chips, so obviously warmed up in the oven after sitting out for most of the day. He cracked the batter of his cod with his fork and took a dry and tasteless mouthful. He needed three of four swigs of his diet coke in order to wash it down.

Wendy was munching greedily on her cottage pie. Dry mashed potato, frozen mixed vegetables and reconstituted minced beef with gravy. Did they really eat so badly in Poland that she should take so much enjoyment in such a pitiful, poorly executed meal? He groaned inwardly.

She tossed her jet-black hair over her shoulder so as not to dip it into her lunch, 'Are you not enjoying your fish and chips, Nick? You know, you should have had the steak or the chicken?' She smiled through a mouthful of food. He winced.

Pretty as she was, her table manners were atrocious.

'No, it's fine,' he took another mouthful, 'probably not as hungry as I thought I was when we pulled in.'

Wendy took a sip from a large glass of Pinot Grigio and pointed at him, 'Well, you won't get a big boy if you don't eat your dinner now will you?' And then in a mock English accent, 'If you want to get big and strong you need to eat your din dins,' she laughed loud enough to jolt a few of the locals from their Sunday afternoon slumber.

'Ha ha,' he laughed uncomfortably, 'I have to work hard enough to keep the weight off. I don't tend to have much trouble putting it on.'

He scowled at her silently while rubbing a hand across his stomach. Years of a strict fitness regime kept him in shape. He didn't need a cow like her to poke fun at him. He'd had enough of that at school. Wobbly Waters was his nick-name and it had stuck with him all the way through to year eleven.

He looked up at her over the rim of his glass. Luscious long dark hair, pouting red lips, big eyelashes, boobs that were too big for her clothes, slender hips. She wore a dark vest top, short mini skirt, light grey tights and knee-high boots. He couldn't get over how she willingly went out dressed like a tart and yet seemed to get away with it.

'You want another glass, love?' a rotund barman with a knitted tank-top and handlebar moustache was bearing down on them.

'Oh, no. If I have another I would become a little… what is it you English say, Nicholas… tipsy?'

Nick smiled, 'Yes, that's it, tipsy,' he waved a hand, 'well if you want one, have one. It doesn't count on a Sunday after all.'

'Now, now. Are you trying to get me drunk?' She reached over the table and slapped him hard on his shoulder.

Nick held his hands out as if to say, 'Would I?' He looked up at the barman who was grinning inanely.

'Well if madam would like another glass I'll be just over there, behind the bar. Reading the paper. Just give me a holler and I'll be right over.'

She prodded him in the belly, 'Don't you worry. I sure will. I will just give you a,' she switched again to a mock English accent, 'a HOLLER!' She laughed loudly once more, a long snorting laugh, this time causing the old guy in the booth by the slot machine to jump, almost slip from his stool and knock the reading glasses off the top of his head. He looked up, bemused.

Nick groaned quietly and held his hand up apologetically. He'd almost bitten off more than he could chew with this one. It wouldn't be the first time, but luckily his Irish family heritage brought just enough luck to keep him out of trouble, at least for the time being.

He'd met Wendy online some months earlier, some internet dating website that he'd been using for years. She was of Polska Roma heritage, a Polish Romany gypsy group who had suffered horribly at the hands of the Nazis during World War II. Since the war her family had made a name for themselves buying and selling used cars, but it was obvious that Wendy wanted more than just sitting behind a desk and manning the phones for her father.

They'd struck up a conversation about football or something and one thing had led to another. He wasn't kidding himself. While he thought of himself as a decent looking bloke; young, all his own hair and teeth, reasonable skin and a pretty toned body; he knew that she was only looking for somewhere in the UK where she could stay, rent free, while she found a job and got herself settled. That was fine by him. He knew that he could use that to his advantage.

He thought back to his encounter in the classroom earlier that week. He really thought that he had made a breakthrough with Jane. Why in God's name she was with that loser, Tony, was beyond him, but she was loyal, and he respected that. To a point. Whether she was prick teasing him or whether she really loved her boyfriend remained to be seen, but he figured it wouldn't hurt to give her a little something to think about. And that something, he had decided a few weeks ago, would be Walenty Jasinski. And boy had it worked a treat. He had lit the touch paper and all he had to do now was wait for the firework to go off.

The problem, he rued, was that now that she was here, he had to keep her occupied. And, aside from the obvious, that was proving a challenge. There were only so many medieval castles, shopping centres, countrified villages and coastal towns you could go to before you started to run out of ideas. And he had to be careful. Not that he planned to be doing it for much longer. He was confident. He smiled to himself, placing a hand over his mouth to hide his smug glee from the Polish bimbo. He was sure of it. In less than a month's time he would get his prize, and Walenty Jasinski would be history.

Chapter 33: The Mayor

Chester Wood, *Mayor* Chester Wood, sat on his long, beige leather sofa, leaning over his Oak Hemingway coffee table, belly sagging onto his knees with a rolled up fifty-pound note in his hand. His week was going from bad to worse and that homo of a Chief Inspector wasn't helping in the slightest. Three murders, no clues and an alcoholic in charge of the investigation. He often wondered whether they realised that he had a position to uphold. A position that relied on day to day events in Westhampton remaining calm, its cogs turning smoothly and all of its citizens not getting *FUCKING KILLED.*

He bent down and snorted a long line of white magic dust, cupping his hand under his chin and brushing the white residue from his goatee. He immediately felt the crystals hitting his sinuses and burning his eyes, the instant energy rush smashing into his brain like a wrecking ball into a concrete building. He threw his head back and yelled.

'Aagh! That feels fucking good!'

He looked around at the three scantily clad women reclining in his spacious and fabulously adorned living room. One of each; blonde, redhead and a gorgeous, ebony Amazonian warrior woman. Well, he considered smugly, one holding such a high social status couldn't be seen to be prejudiced, now, could one? They were smiling and pouting at him which was good. Because for the money he was paying the least he could expect was a fucking smile.

'You see, the problem ladies with this situation is that I am letting the monkeys run the zoo,' they continued to look at him, still smiling, still being seductive and gorgeous, 'the hairy arsed, swinging from the trees eating their own shit fucking monkeys. And do you know what happens when you let the monkeys run the fucking zoo?'

The girls looked at each other puzzled, smiled back at him and shook their heads.

'Well, I'll tell you,' he fanned his arms out, resting them on the back of his sofa, his naked legs crossed and covering his manhood, 'you get fucking monkey chaos. And what happens when you've got fucking monkey chaos in your well organised, perfectly maintained and fucking extremely beautiful zoo?'

The girls looked puzzled again, the redhead was clearly bored and starting to play with her hair.

'Well, the other animals get restless. Restless and anxious. They start looking around at each other and wondering who they should be pointing their tiny little animal fingers at. And restless, anxious, pointy fingered animals do not make for happy animal voters,' there were agreeable shakes of the head all round, 'and unhappy animal voters do not continue to vote for the rich, handsome zookeeper.'

This one had really stumped them. Chester Wood frowned, frustrated with the level of ignorance and downright, utter stupidity in the room.

'You don't know who the rich, handsome zookeeper is in this metaphor do you?'

Three shaking heads.

'ME! The one with the money and the drugs?'

They all clapped their hands, giggling excitedly.

'And if the zookeeper doesn't remain in his job then girls like you,' he pointed at each one of them individually, eyeing them up and down and shaking his head, 'cannot expect to keep getting the same kind of... benefits that you've been getting on and off now for the past year. That just couldn't continue to happen,' he shook his head while sticking out his bottom lip, 'you see why that might be a problem to you girls and the very generous zookeeper?'

They all nodded in unison, clearly concerned and more than a little confused by what he was saying.

'That just wouldn't do at all. And why would anyone,' he shrugged his shoulders, his naked man boobs jiggling up and down, 'anyone at all, want to take all of this away? Those people are not friends of ours. They are certainly not friends of mine. And if these non-friends don't start clearing up after themselves then somebody,' he pointed both index fingers at his own chest, 'is going to have to roll up his sleeves and do it for them,' he grunted and ran a hand through his goatee, 'and that could get real messy.'

He pushed in one nostril, bent over the table and sniffed loudly with the other, pinching his nose and closing his eyes. He stopped and looked around, as if something had caught his attention.

'If I have to get my hands dirty then they will get real dirty. It wouldn't be the first time and I'm sure it won't be the last. Those bloody cops think that only they can play God when it comes to matters of a criminal nature,' he paused as he thought about this, 'burglaries, muggings, assaults, break-ins. I've seen all of that and more in my time. And I've always come out on top. This is no exception. When I was a kid if someone tried to get one over on you, you just got in there first. If someone hit you, you hit them harder. If they taunted you, you silenced them. You couldn't let the little shits get away with it. Call me poor, a loser and I'll go out and work my arse off, bend the rules a little, do whatever it takes to get nice and rich, rich and important. Then turn myself into a handsome, desirable playboy and you can come home and find me fucking your mother. That's how it works. That's the order of things. And if this guy wants to fuck with me by killing all the sweet women of my town, he'd better be fucking good and fucking discreet. Because if, *when*, I find him,' he took a long, slow breath, pushing out his chest and fanning out his arms, 'well, I'll get hold of the little cocksucker, rip out his teeth one by one, get my hands round his tongue and pull it so hard that he'll choke to death on his own bollocks!'

He gathered himself, his face red with pent up anger and bent over, took out his black American Express card and chopped out another four long lines of coke.

'Leo!'

There was a pitter patter of feet as a young man servant arrived at the doorway dressed in a black apron and precious little else. His dark hair was slicked back with excess hair gel, his designer stubble expertly trimmed.

'Yes Sir?'

Chester Wood waved a hand at him, 'Bring us a couple of bottles of Dom Perignon, chilled. And four glasses.'

'Of course sir. And will there be,' he glanced around at the three lovely ladies, still reclining leisurely and beaming their model smiles at him, 'anything else?'

Chester Wood rubbed his chin and pondered this, 'Yes, yes there will. Bring in a big bowl of jelly, sour apple flavoured, the one I like,' he smiled impishly at the girls, 'and put on some fucking music. It's like a morgue in here! What do you say, girls?'

The girls yelped with joy and descended on the coffee table like vampires around a fresh, young virgin. Chester Wood smiled with delight and feverishly joined them.

Chapter 34: Writer's Block

Tony had been writing like a madman since the meeting with his mother and the subsequent confrontation with his girlfriend. It was like the emotional train wreck of it all was way too much for his mind to comprehend so it reacted by throwing out paragraph after paragraph of creative text. Not that he minded of course. If he could get something constructive from the whole thing whilst keeping his destructive thoughts from rising to the surface then, hey, everyone was a winner.

He hadn't come up for air in two days. Hadn't even got dressed. He had been munching on cereal, drinking tea, having the occasional, more substantial snack, cheese on toast or a sandwich, and punching away at his keyboard. He hadn't checked what he had written of course, that would come later when he was mentally in a healthier place, but for now just getting it down was a minor miracle.

Day had turned into night, night had turned into day and back again. The cycle hadn't really resonated with him. He was aware that it had happened, but in his zombie-like state it hadn't registered. He had noticed Jane but hadn't paid her any mind. It was as if she was moving around at high speed while he continued to work at normal pace. The hands of the clock were whirring, but he had no idea what the time was or in what order things were occurring.

She had been surprised at his revelations at first, shocked really. How could he have gotten the situation with his mother so wrong?

Had the lie been so good that he hadn't suspected anything during all those years? Surely he must have known, deep down, in some way. And then she had started to get angry. How could she do such a thing? Why would a mother deny her own flesh and blood his birth right? How could someone be so messed up that they deliberately destroyed the childhood years of their own offspring? Rape or no rape, he had deserved to know who his parents were and that he had been living with his real mother since birth.

He had deserved to be loved.

They had hugged, kissed. She had comforted him, sitting with her arms around him for what seemed like an eternity. And then it had turned into passion. She had undressed him; she must have undressed herself because he didn't remember doing it. She had sat astride him, had caressed him, stroked his hair, run her fingernails down his chest and back. But no matter how she tried, and no matter how much he thought he wanted it, his little man wouldn't play ball. Just didn't want to come out to play. And, for some reason that had frustrated her, as if it was his fault. She had gotten up, silently, and walked up the stairs to their bedroom, leaving him on the settee, trousers around his ankles and silently watching her leave.

And that's where he had awoken that morning. He must have been so tired that he had simply crashed out where he sat, the energy he had expended furiously typing at his laptop for forty-eight hours eventually leaving him spent and exhausted.

Jane was gone. It was nine-thirty and he knew that by now she would be well into her morning class. He considered it odd that he hadn't heard her leave, but hardly surprising.

He sat up, rubbed his eyes and looked around him. The place was a mess, a metaphor for his life. He asked himself where was he going with it all? So what if everything he had known had been turned upside down and shaken about. What difference did it make? He had been alone before; he was alone still. The fact that he now knew that he was the result of some violent altercation between the woman that he had thought was his adopted parent and a rapist father that he had never met meant what? She was still a bitch to him. Made no difference. He still hated her. But then…

He got up and got himself showered, washing off two-day old

sweat. It felt good, refreshing. He pondered his next move, if indeed there was a move to make.

He dried himself, shaved and got dressed. He needed something but he couldn't put his finger on what it was. He wandered around his bedroom, picking up clothes that were lying scattered on the floor. He threw them in the washing basket and then went back downstairs. He stood in the dining room, staring at the laptop screen. It was lying open like the yawning mouth of a giant hippopotamus. It looked like it wanted to swallow him whole, to drag him into his created universe. He stood there for a few minutes, just hypnotised by the words on the screen and the bright, backlit colours. He could see language, grammar, punctuation, paragraphs. He could see words, lots of them, long, short, adjectives, nouns, adverbs. What did all of this mean? What was he fucking doing? How could he know where he was headed when he didn't even have a clue where he was from? Twenty-four years old and he realised that there was still so much that he didn't know about his own existence.

He ran a hand across his smooth chin. Thinking. Thinking. He closed the laptop, picked up his phone and dialled.

'It's me. I'm coming over.'

Chapter 35: Billy and the Pusher

Billy West had his head under the staircase. It was dark. He had a flashlight held in one hand, his body bent at a crooked angle, his eyes searching frantically in the gloom. Peering around the pitch-black space, wiping old cobwebs from his eyes, he could make out box-like shapes, all covered in dust and mess. He held the back of his hand to his mouth to prevent himself from choking. God, he hoped there were no rats in there. Where the hell was this fucking fuse box?

He hated working on old properties like this one. You never knew what you were going to find. Probably some old boy's bones buried under the ground, all rotted and decayed.

'You want a cup of tea, love?'

He looked over his shoulder towards the cupboard door, 'Yes please, Mrs Patterson, milk and two sugars.' Small mercies, he thought to himself. A cuppa was the least he deserved for doing this. Probably just an old fuse needing replacing in any case.

He reached his hand out and knocked over a box. The container tumbled onto the concrete floor, spilling out old ornaments wrapped in ancient red and black tabloids. Ceramic shapes of women dressed in Victorian clothes, animals in funny hats, jewellery stands, ornamental clocks. Shit, he swore under his breath. He felt behind where the box had originated from. There was what appeared to be an old record player, vinyl singles stacked ten or twenty high. Probably some value in those, he mused. Maybe, he thought, he could get the old dear to let him have some. An old lamp, gothic and scary, tangled cobwebs draped over it like a veil over a corpse. He shuddered. Another box full of paperwork, spiders and God only knows what hiding under the envelopes and stapled bills.

And there behind all of that was a metal box, bolted to the wall, frayed and tattered cables arcing upwards and into the crumbling wall render. He cursed to himself. The bloody thing looked ancient.

'You… er… had this thing serviced recently, Mrs P?'

'What's that, dear?'

'Your fuse box. It looks like it needs a service.'

'Oh no, dear. My Alf used to do all of that, but he's been dead for twelve years. He was good with all of the house maintenance. He could turn his hand to anything you know. Plumbing, electrics, brickwork. That's how they used to make them back then. That's what we need nowadays. Too many kids now want someone else to do it for them. No, I don't get involved in that kind of thing. Two sugars you said?'

'Yes please. Two it is,' he grumbled. It was probably a death trap. He didn't really want to touch it. It was barely worth his sixty pound, pensioners special call out rate.

He felt a buzz in his pocket. He sat back against the cold wall, took a deep breath and reached into his jeans.

'What's up?'

'You called me, remember?' the voice at the other end of the line was hard, emotionless.

'Oh yeah, yeah. I… er…,' he lowered his voice so as not to be heard. Not that old Mrs P could hear him. The old girl could barely make him out when he was standing next to her, let alone when he was hidden away in her filthy rat-hole of an under stairs cupboard. 'I wanted to get me some more of that gear. You know? The bag you sold me last week. You got any more?'

'That Mexican shit? You like that did you?'

'Yeah, yeah. It was good stuff. The best you've had yet I reckon. Wanted another baggies worth.'

'I'll have to see what I've got. I think I'm all out of that. But I might have some powerful Colombian hash?'

Colombian eh, Billy thought to himself. What, did this guy have some kind of 'in' with the South American drug cartels? Jesus, it was like some really bad-ass Breaking Bad shit.

'Well, I guess that would work. Same price?' The line went quiet.

'Well, I suppose as you're such a good customer I could keep it at the same fee. Normally this top of the range shit would set you back maybe fifteen, twenty percent more. But you can have this and see how you get on. If you like it, you can come back to me for more. You'll think the higher price is worth every penny, believe me.'

He thought that sounded right up his street. He needed something stronger in any case. His tolerance to the run of the mill street weed had built up so much that the usual stuff just didn't cut it any more.

'Sounds great, man. Yeah, I'll take one. Meet in the same place?'

'Same place. Eight o' clock. Don't be late.'

'I won't. See you then.'

He hung up and smiled. Tony was gonna shit a brick when he tried this stuff. It was gonna be party time, big time.

'You still in there, love?'

The voice startled him and he dropped his phone. It clattered on the dusty ground and he swore.

'Yep, still here,' he wondered where the silly cow thought he would be.

'Here's your tea. And I've given you a couple of custard creams as well, my dear. Help you keep your energy up.'

'Thanks Mrs. P. That's great.'

He laughed to himself. Sort the job out, have a quick cuppa, maybe a swift half down the pub and then off to collect his payload. Life didn't get much better than that.

He lifted his flash light and reached out towards the battered old fuse box. He pulled the cover off and peered inside. Shit, he cursed. Old, bare copper poked into some ceramic block, scorch marks covering the face plate, melted insulation tape barely holding the cable in place. Yeah, he muttered to himself, old Alf sure knew what he was doing.

Chapter 36: Spin Class

I arrived at around five thirty with Jemima. Isobelle was already there. It had been another long day in the classroom and I needed the release, especially with everything going on at home. My head just needed clearing.

The class was held at the sports hall in the town centre which I hated because parking was always a nightmare. Normally around twenty of us attended. I'd only been going for a short amount of time compared to my work colleagues, but I was doing okay, managing to keep up most of the time. The lady that took the class was a real ass kicker and so I felt obliged to put my all into it, despite being told that it would be a 'laugh' and that there would be no pressure. Yeah, right.

Jemima burst into the hall with her usual verve and enthusiasm, throwing her sports bag into the corner of the room and waving to the five or six cyclists who were already there, suited and booted. I sauntered in behind her. Isobelle gave us a 'hi'. She was the reserved one of our little trio, a short, plain brunette with a freckly nose and an often cutting wit. A heart of gold to go with it though.

To tell you the truth I was a little apprehensive. Although I had seen Nick from afar at the school this was the first time that I'd had any kind of meaningful contact since my hasty retreat at the pub. I was still reeling from whatever that was and my altercation with Tony shortly after hadn't helped. I was on edge.

'Come on girls, gee yourselves up. You both look like you're about to fall flat on your faces. We haven't even started yet. And the Sergeant Major says we are going for a forty-five-minute burn tonight.' Jemima was pumped but then she always was. I was pretty sure she must have had ADHD as a kid, constantly on the go, always in a rush. She unzipped a hoody and bent down to change into her trainers.

'Forty-five minutes?' Isobelle looked uncertain, 'Jesus Jem. I don't know about that. We did thirty-five last week and that nearly killed me. I've only got little legs.' She was right, her legs were stocky and powerful but not very long. I smiled at her insecurity. I loved her. She just didn't know how great she was.

'You'll be fine, Issy. Just keep those thighs gunning for it. The Sarg will keep you motivated,' she looked at me. 'What about you, Jane? You feeling in the mood for a tough spin?'

To tell you the truth I wasn't, not really. My mind was elsewhere, occupied with other things. 'Yeah, yeah. Can't wait. Need to burn off some fat and energise myself. Forty-five minutes? No problem. It's a shame that it's not the full hour,' I knew that I sounded unconvincing.

'I just hope I don't pass out. I will you know. If she pushes me too hard,' Isobelle looked worried, but it was all in her head. Once she got going, head down, legs working hard, sweat running down her freckly face, she was totally in the zone. She didn't like to admit it, but she was pretty competitive.

'Stop worrying, Issy. You'll be fine. No pain no gain,' Jemima was laughing as she looked over at me, shrugging her shoulders, 'you'd think she'd never been before.'

I stripped down to my track suit bottoms, vest top and trainers. I wasn't big, never have been, but I was far from toned. I'd never been a gym freak either and wasn't at home amongst the avid cyclists, runners and circuit trainers. I was far happier at home with a cup of tea and a chocolate bar, but at that moment my home was a strange place to me.

'Okay, okay, listen up people!' Sergeant Major Jarvis was on patrol, 'As I told you all last week it's a forty-five-minute race day session today. That means it's a com-pe-tition,' she drew out the last word patronisingly, 'the class member who rides the furthest in the allotted time will win the grand prize,' again, patronising and slightly insulting. She looked at Isobelle and I. 'So, for the newcomers in the class you all have the opportunity to put some of the old hands,' she glanced at a couple of blokes at the front of the hall, 'to the sword. They will think that this is a walk in the park for them. You,' she waved her hand at a few of us, 'won't want them to embarrass you, will you? *Will you?*' She paused for an answer. A few of us mumbled a 'no'. 'Well then, I expect to see extra effort, real sweat, muscles straining, red faces. If you don't feel like passing out at the end of this session you haven't tried hard enough.'

Isobelle looked absolutely terrified. I thought she was going to faint there and then before she even got near the cycle. She gave Jemima a reproachful look and mouthed, 'what the fuck?' Jem shrugged her shoulders and smiled. The Sarg clocked the exchange.

'Everything okay, Mannering? You look somewhat...concerned.' She crossed the hall in a few big strides and stood in front of Issy, hands behind her back, chest thrust forward, feet planted shoulder width apart.

Isobelle looked at Jemima and I for moral support, eyes wide, 'I'm...I'm okay. Just didn't realise we were racing today, that's all.'

'Well then I suggest you listen in class. This is not school time now, Mannering. This is the real world. And if you want to survive in the real world you have to be competitive, you have to want to win,' she spun round and faced the rest of the class, 'competition makes us all better! It drives you on! And if you all want to get fit,' she glanced around at each one of us, 'I mean, that is why you are all here isn't it?' A few more nervously positive murmurs, 'Good, good. That's good to hear. Well then you have to have something to spur you on. And nothing spurs you on more than wanting to win!'

'Here, here!'

I whirled round towards the back of the class. It was Nick. And her.

'Sorry we're late. Stuck in traffic,' he winked at me, 'hope it's okay. I brought a...a friend along. This is Wendy everyone.'

The Sarg waved her hand dismissively, 'Okay Waters. Not a problem. Get yourself ready. We're just about to get going. Wendy, is it? Okay Wendy, take the cycle next to Butler, she can show you the ropes.'

I couldn't believe it. There she was, tight black leggings, skimpy vest, long black hair pulled back from her forehead in a large pony tail, pouting red lips and fake eyelashes as long as your little finger. Not an ounce of fat on her. And now she was going to be riding next to me with my frumpy grey trackies, bingo wings and naked, black-head ridden face.

I smiled at her politely, 'Hi'.

'Hi Jane. Lovely to be seeing you again,' she grinned, large, brilliant white teeth, almost bright enough to blind me. 'So, we are to be riding a bicycle?'

Jemima was looking at me, mouth open. She mockingly cupped her boobs and pouted her lips, strutting round her cycle like Beyonce on heat. I gave her the daggers and tried to stop myself from giggling. Bitch.

'Yes, well, sort of. It doesn't move. It's just an exercise thing. Just a bit of fun really,' I laughed nervously and got on my cycle, clipping my feet into the pedals.

'But the lady says we will be racing,' she got onto her bike and flicked her pony tail over her shoulder, 'I love to race. I race all of the time at home with my brothers. I have four of them. They hate it when I beat them,' she laughed loudly, her shrill guffaw reverberating around the hall.

Great, I thought to myself, a pro. Well if she thought she was going to get one up on me she had another thing coming.

Nick walked over and kissed Wendy on the lips. 'Good luck, sweetheart. See you on the other side,' he glanced at me, a big impish grin on his face, 'and good luck Jane. Don't push yourself too hard just because Wendy's here. She's done this kind of thing before you know, and I don't want you to... pull a muscle.' Bastard.

'I'll be fine, Nick. I'm not here to compete. I'm just here to get myself fit.'

'Oh no Jane,' Wendy was frowning at me, 'you must always want to win. I will be wiping the floor with this one.' She ran a long red finger nail down Nick's cheek. He blushed.

'Okay class. Get yourselves on your cycles and let's get going. We haven't got all night. Some of us have other things to be doing!' The

Sarg had her stopwatch at the ready. Nick walked over to his cycle, hopped on and blew us a kiss. I smiled. Annoying as he was, he was also one charming son of a bitch.

Wendy touched my shoulder, 'Good luck, Jane. Try your best,' she looked at me sympathetically like a little girl looking down at a stray puppy. I steadied myself and glanced over at my friends. Jemima was chatting to a young man on the cycle next to her, not a care in the world. Issy was staring dead ahead, a nervous but icy-cold expression etched into her face. What had I gotten myself into?

'Ready... steady... let's ride!'

And we were off. A room full of Bradley Wiggins wannabes pedalling in a cold hall on a hot July evening. Bizarre when you thought about it like that. But I wasn't going to be beaten.

I had to admit it; Wendy was good. All muscly sinew and brute determination. She had the legs of a racehorse and she wasn't afraid to use them, her face was jutting forward, her eyes narrowed and her sleek pony tail flapping around on her shoulders. I felt positively inadequate in comparison.

I looked over at the milometer on her cycle. She'd already cycled well over a mile. I was still at point eight and had some catching up to do.

I glanced up at Nick. He had his head down, his arms taught, his legs powering away. He had a great body. The guy had obviously worked hard at keeping himself in shape. He must have realised I was looking because he looked over at me and smiled. I blushed and turned away.

I could hear Jemima jabbering away at the guy next to her. She was constantly on the go that girl. How she could muster up a conversation while I could hardly breathe was beyond me. Issy on the other hand was pushing herself hard. Her face looked like it was set in stone, her lips pursed, her neck muscles bulging.

I knew that if I wasn't careful I was going to come in last. I took a deep breath and pushed myself on, using every ounce of determination in my body to power my thighs and calves, my feet driving into the pedals, my hands gripping the handle grips so tight that my knuckles were white. I could hear myself grunting but was powerless to do anything about it. A sheen of sweat formed on my arms, neck and face. The miles gradually start to rack up; two, three, four. I started to feel good about myself.

I could feel someone looking at me. It was Wendy. It was a cold look. And then she smiled at me, as if to say 'Come on then. If you would like to race against me, this grand specimen of a woman, then let's race, bitch.'

She gripped the handles tighter, gave a loud 'eurgh' and doubled her efforts.

I wasn't having that, so I did the same, grunting even louder, the pressure on my calves and thighs intensifying to a warm burn, the sweat on my face and neck trickling down my chest and back like a salty, sticky river. I could feel my face hot and flushed, my forehead felt like it was on fire.

The miles continued to flash by as the Sarg paced backwards and forwards at the front of the class, yelling at us to 'keep going, push yourself, be the best, try harder!' Time trickled on to the steady rhythm of rotating pedals and the grunts and groans of the riders.

Jemima was still chatting, flirting, laughing. Issy was silently powering along. Nick was arched over the handle bars, occasionally glancing over and grinning. I could barely see. The sweat was pouring into my eyes, my hair was slick with it, long strands sticking to my cheeks and neck. I knew that I looked a right state.

All I could think was how long this was going to go on for? It felt like every muscle in my body was on fire. Wendy didn't look out of breath at all. She looked like a robot, like she was the Terminator sent there to humiliate and embarrass me. It looked to me like her legs were a blur, wheeling round and round like a catharine wheel on speed.

'Five minutes to go people! If you have any energy left, then now is the chance to burn it all up!'

I looked at Wendy who was already looking at me. Our eyes said, 'Come on then. Let's do this!'

We both gave a loud 'argh!' as we pushed on. I could feel my calf muscles pulled ever tighter as if they were about to snap. Wendy had a grimace spread across her painted face, the red gloss on her lips had smeared, her eyelashes were askew. I started to think that maybe she was human after all. That gave me hope and I pounded my legs harder and harder, my sweaty palms slipping on the grips, the cycle making a clunking sound as I rammed my feet into the pedals. Round and round they went, onwards and onwards I went, harder, harder, harder.

'Five, four, three, two, one, stop pedalling!'

I slumped over the handle bars, my hot cheeks burning my arms. I was absolutely spent. I looked over at Wendy and smiled. I'd got her, I was sure of it. She smiled back, equally as cock sure of herself. I could see stars flashing before my eyes. I hoped they were the stars of victory.

I sat up and swung my legs over the bike, desperate to get my bum off of the uncomfortably hot seat. My feet touched down on the ground as I looked around the room. Nick had his hands on his thighs, head down. Jemima had her arm on the shoulder of the guy next to her, giggling inanely. Isobelle was wiping her face with a towel, her gray top dark with sweat. I looked at the Sarg. She was grinning at us all, hands on her hips, boobs thrust forward. She looked like a circus performer, crazy grin, wild eyes, muscles rippling under her thin T shirt. It felt like the whole room was sliding away, ripples running down the walls and across the faces of the other riders. Bright flashes went off as if there were a hundred paparazzi in the room. I heard Jemima laughing, Wendy breathing heavily, Nick bending down to tie a lace, Issy unclipping her feet from the pedals. The sounds became muted, muffled. I put my hand out to steady myself on the cycle but missed.

And that was when I fainted.

*

'You okay, Jane? You don't look too good.'

I squinted up at the bright fluorescent lights. I could see a face, but it was out of focus. I opened and shut my eyes two, three times until the face came into view. It was Isobelle. My head was in her lap and she was stroking my hair.

'Where... where am I?'

'We're at the class, silly. You...you fainted I think.'

I looked around. Everyone was standing around me in a circle. The Sergeant Major, a faux look of concern on her face. Jem, Nick,

Wendy, *everybody*!

Nick was sombre. He bent down and grabbed my hand. 'We were all really worried then, Jane. Do you want us to take you to the hospital?' I shook my head. I felt completely humiliated.

'Someone get her a drink of water!'

Jemima walked over to the water butt, filled a beaker and brought it over to me. I sat up and sipped eagerly from the cup but in truth I wanted to drown myself in it. Could this be more horrific?

'I think that you were a little bit too eager to win, Jane,' Wendy was peering down at me, that 'little girl finding a stray puppy' look back on her sweaty and smudged face. I wanted to rip her eyelashes off and ram them up her...

'Well, everyone, now that the drama's over I can confirm the winner,' I looked up at the Sarg who had a sheet of paper out in front of her. 'It was a close run, lots of you putting extraordinary effort in. Some of you,' she glanced accusingly down at me, 'a little too much effort. Several of you over the ten-mile mark which is excellent for the time. But with a grand total of twelve point four miles is...' I held my breath and looked up at Wendy who was still looking down at me, her eyes narrowed, her smudgy red lips pursed shut. If she had beaten me it would put the terrible icing on top of the disastrous cake, '...Isobelle Mannering! Well done, Mannering!'

The class clapped. I let out a big sigh of relief. I looked at Issy who was still stroking my hair. She had a shocked, delighted and almost ecstatic look on her face, like a child who had just been given a holiday to Disneyland for Christmas. She obviously could not believe it. I couldn't have been happier.

'Well done, Issy,' I leant over and gave her a hug. 'We knew you could do it.' She hugged me back as Jemima bent down and joined in the hugging. The Sarg reached over and handed Issy a gold coloured trophy with 'Race Day Winner' engraved on the base. Isobelle looked at it like it was the oddest thing she had ever seen and laughed. We all laughed with her.

I heard a swish from behind me as Wendy grabbed her bag, got hold of Nick by the arm and headed for the door. She was grumbling something Polish under her breath.

'Er… see you later all. Good class. See you at school, ladies!' Nick was dragged out of the door, arms flailing and his jacket trailing behind him.

Chapter 37: Mitch

'How is she?'

'How do you think?'

Tony and Mitchell were sitting in the park one street over from their mother's house. It was late afternoon, but the large grassy area was littered with dog walkers, lovebirds holding hands, kids hanging out after school and teenagers kicking half-flat footballs around.

'Well, I know she's dying, Mitch. But how is she holding up?'

'About the same really. The coughing's getting a little worse, but the drugs are keeping the pain at bay, I think.'

Tony took a swig from his can of Red Bull. He needed the energy after his recent exertions and lack of any real restful sleep.

'Why did you storm out like that?'

'We had a row. She… told me some stuff about my…my father.' Tony gave him the low down, about how she had confessed to being his real mother, about how he wasn't adopted after all and that he was the product of a sexual assault on her. Mitchell sat there, taking it all in, his face impassive. There was a silence between them.

'She told you, huh?'

Tony looked up from the floor, startled.

'You knew? *You knew?*' He turned his body to face Mitchell.

'Of course I knew. She tells me everything you know. She didn't want me to let on.'

Tony's eyes widened, 'How... how long have you known?'

Mitchell looked at him, his face still impassive, calm, 'Oh, around five or six years I would say. When I was old enough to understand how important it was to keep certain...things...a secret.'

Tony sat staring at his brother, his mouth agape and his hands clasped tightly together.

'I...I can't believe this. Does... does anyone else know?'

'No, no. Just the two of us. And, I guess... your dad.'

Tony paused. His dad? He hadn't really thought of that. He had a dad somewhere, and his mother knew who he was. A sick son of a bitch, sure, but a dad, nonetheless. He put his head in his hands.

'This is too much, Mitch. Too much for me to take in. Has, has she heard from... him? Does she know where he is?'

There was a longer pause. Tony's fingers were laced through his hair, scratching and pulling.

'She... she knows.'

Tony sat up. She knows, she knows?

'Well, who the hell is he? Who is this guy that has been kept a secret from me for all these years?'

'He's an arsehole, Tony! He raped her when she was at her most vulnerable and left her to look after you on your own! You really want to meet this son of a bitch?'

Tony shook his head in disbelief. He didn't know what he wanted, but he knew that he needed answers. From someone. Everything he knew, everything he thought that he knew, had been a lie, a sham. What he wanted more than anything else was for someone to put some meaning to it all, to give him some clue as to the how, what and why.

'I... I don't know. I think I do.'

Mitchell moved his face close to Tony's. 'You really want to meet the man who forced his penis into our mother so hard that it hurt? So hard that she was hospitalised for a week, battered and bruised, scared for her own safety. A man that denied what had happened so vehemently, got his lawyers involved, threatened her with a very public court case. She was made to back down through her fear of the embarrassment and shame of it all! You really want to meet someone like that?' his face was red with rage, 'You will never know how hard it has been for me to not go to him and wipe him off the face of the earth! But,' he paused, 'she wouldn't let me of course. She didn't want me to have any contact with... him... *at all*. Let sleeping dogs lie and all that. But I still think about it every day. How I would do it,' he was rubbing his hands together vigorously, 'knife, gun, fists. As much pain as I could possibly inflict.' He stopped and looked across at the families and friends enjoying themselves in the summer sun, 'And his seed, his fucking DNA, is sitting right... there... inside... of you!' he turned and pushed his finger hard into Tony's chest, spitting his words into his face.

There was a long silence between them. Tony pushed Mitchell's hand away from him.

'Whoever... whatever he is, he's not me,' Tony spoke in a low, hushed tone, 'and I'm not him.'

'You'd better hope not.'

'Is that some kind of threat?'

'You just leave our mother alone with this. She doesn't need any more upset.'

'Well either you tell me where this guy is, or she will have to.' Another silence. The morning breeze pushed leaves, cigarette butts and empty crisp packets along the broken pavement. A couple of sparrows hopped in front of them, collecting seeds and crumbs. Their world seemed so painless.

'You realise, I've always resented you, you know?' Mitchell was speaking in low, hushed tones.

Tony was taken aback, 'Resented me? Me? Why?'

'You always had something about you that I couldn't place. You were good at school, you got through university, got your degree, you were good with girls. I always thought you got all of that from...from him.' Mitchell was looking longingly across the open lawn. 'I mean, I know who I am. I know who my Mum is, I still fucking live at home with her for Christ's sake. And I know who my dad is, a pathetic loser who Mum took pity on. My genes are set, they are well understood, this is who I am! There's nothing that I don't know about me!'

'I don't really understand where you're going with this, Mitch. You're the one that mother's always treated as her special one. I was always the outcast, the adopted stray who never lived up to her lofty expectations.'

'But that was just it, wasn't it? I didn't know why... how... you acted the way that you did. There's a mystery to you, Tony. I don't know who you are.'

'And neither... do... I!' They stared at each other across the bench, the distance between them never seeming so far, 'And I wish that I did.' Mitchell looked at his watch and stood up.

'I've got to go. I've got an appointment. You want to find out more about your heritage, your history, I suggest you look the prick up on the internet. You'll find him, he doesn't hide from public attention. Robert Charon, with a 'ch' and one 'r'. Knock yourself out. I hope you find whatever it is that you think you're looking for.'

He left and Tony sat alone on the park bench, tired, bleary eyed, wondering.

Chapter 38: The Stakeout

Barber had come through with the lead. It was a long shot, but it was something and the Chief wanted it chased down. And, D.I. Luke Raven pondered, it seemed that whatever the Chief wanted he got, particularly when he was feeling the clammy hands of that scumbag of a Mayor around his throat.

He had been working his way through a quarter-pounder with cheese back at the station when Barber had made his announcement and since then his arse hadn't stopped moving. Some caretaker from the university, Andrew Swaggart, a fifty-five-year-old guy who was a little short in the braincell department, no family, not much of a social life, the archetypal misfit. It seemed a little too stereotypical for Raven. Swaggart was the type of guy in the films who always did it, but in real life rarely did. It was usually the boyfriend, the cousin, the ex-husband, the estranged parent. Not the loser with a Sesame Street lunchbox. No. That was too neat. Too tidy. Except this guy had a link to at least two of the girls; a) he worked at the university and was caretaker for the block that Tracey Webb bunked down in and b) he had been seen on CCTV outside of the nearby fish and chip shop, Paddy's, having a conversation with Billy Roper the night before she had been killed. All they needed was a link to Trudy Yates, the third and most viciously beaten victim, and they had homicide bingo.

He should have been at Lisa's place; she had been expecting him for dinner. He had *promised* he would be there for dinner. But he wasn't. He was there, sat in an unmarked car at quarter past ten, outside the front of a loner caretaker's house waiting for their man to do something, anything. And what made it worse was that he had Barber sitting next to him, munching on a pork pie and talking absolute rubbish.

'… so, what I can't make out is if my arm goes dead when I fall asleep while its lying above my heart, you know, like I've swung it up there in the middle of the night while I'm dreaming or something, then why doesn't my head always feel like that? I mean, I never get pins and needles in my brain.'

'What?'

'Well you know, when you wake up and your arm's all cold, and you don't know what it is because it feels like its detached from your body, and when you touch it it's completely numb, like it doesn't belong to you. Why is that, and why does it only ever happen to your arms? Why not your legs, or your neck, or your shoulders or something? I just don't get it.'

Christ, Raven thought to himself, this guy might be a half decent copper, but he'd obviously had a knock to the head when he was younger. He took a bite from his sandwich, ham and pickle, and wiped his face with a napkin. He yearned for a drink, a very large, stiff one.

'Well that really is a conundrum, Damo,' he said, between mouthfuls of tangy bread and meat, 'I think you've really hit on one of life's great mysteries there. There are probably teams of scientists in Geneva trying to crack that one as we speak, thinking that the answer could help provide us all with the elusive secrets of the universe.'

'Yeah, yeah, okay. Take the Mickey if you like. But you've got to admit, it is a mystery.'

Raven looked out of the window. The upstairs lights in Swaggart's small two-bed semi were out, just the front room light on. He could vaguely see a shadow moving behind the shades from time to time, but nothing to be suspicious about, just a guy going about his regular business in his home after work. Not exactly a case for a warrant he thought as he rubbed his hand across his eyes. God he was tired.

'So, how you getting on with the Doc?' May as well make

conversation, he thought, it might help to keep him awake.

'Oh, nothing doing yet. I'm biding my time, you know? Waiting for the right moment. I don't want to rush into things, take it slow, keep it natural.'

'In other words, you're shitting yourself.'

'Yeah. Don't really know how to approach it.'

Raven smiled to himself and recalled some of his many exploits, 'I always find the direct approach is the most… rewarding.'

'Really?'

Although, he regretted, he had almost been an arse the other night, staying back for a drink with Daisy after the team night out. She had definitely thawed to him, her demeanour much more approachable and friendly. They had shared a few drinks; he had even walked her home. He considered how very gentlemanly that was of him. Quite unlike him really, but it wasn't a good idea. He cared for her, *really* cared for her, but he was desperately trying not to fuck things up with Lisa. Not this time. The other night with Lisa had been revelatory to him and it had lodged something inside of him, a part of him that wanted something…something more. He felt that he and Lisa could have that.

But there had been a moment, as Daisy had put her key in her lock, that he was convinced that she was going to invite him up. It wouldn't have been the first time and what would he have done then? They certainly had a spark, they had proven that on several occasions, and it was addictive, but he had done the right thing and bid her adieu. In some weird way she had looked disappointed. It was strange how things, people, could alter their opinions and perceptions so quickly.

'Yeah, yeah. There's no point beating about the bush, kiddo. You think you can have something with the Doc then why wait to ask. Life's too short to be messing about with social politics and etiquette. Just go for it. The worst she can do is say no.'

'And laugh in my face,' Barber pondered this, 'but I guess you're right. What am I waiting for, I mean, really?'

'Exactly.'

'I could send her flowers, or a gift card, chocolates! Yeah, chocolates. I could parachute them in, like the Milk Tray man or something. All romantic and stuff. She's classy. She'd like that.'

Raven chuckled under his breath. How did this kid know about the Milk Tray man?

'Maybe take her out, somewhere sophisticated. Three courses and coffee for afters. Cappuccino and a biscotti. Really push the boat out. I mean, if you're gonna do it you've got to go all in, right?'

Raven watched Swaggart open his front door and beep the lock on his car; a small, black Punto. He was carrying a holdall.

'I just need to sort out how I'm going to ask her. I mean, do I just walk up to her and say 'Hey Jas, do you fancy a spot of dinner?', or do I break into it casually, like 'Hey, Doctor Chandur, I'm out in town later and wondered if you were free for dinner?' That kind of thing. More formal. Less familiar. Or maybe I could send her an email or text or something.'

Swaggart opened his car door and looked around. He threw the holdall onto the back seat. The evening sun was setting, and the light was beginning to fade. Raven felt sure they hadn't been made. He was a big fella, a little over six-foot, thinning hair, broad shoulders, pudgy nose and what looked like one-week old stubble. It wasn't like he couldn't have been the guy that Raven had chased after, but something about him wasn't right. He recalled that pale face, the figure lifting from the ground, the shadows becoming darker, the ice-cold air. He shuddered.

'I might have to write down what I'm going to say. Rehearse it, I want to get it right. Practise my voice, make sure I'm not too cockney, be a little bit west end. What do you...?'

Swaggart was pulling away. Raven started up the car.

'Time to roll, Damo. Our man's on the move.'

'Oh shit. Sorry boss. Wasn't paying attention,' he reached round and grabbed his belt, spilling bits of pork pie all over his lap and the floor. 'Oh shit, sorry. I'll clean that up later.'

'Too right you will. Now stop thrashing around, you'll draw attention to yourself.'

They followed Swaggart along Coach Street, keeping a respectable distance between them. They made a few turns down residential neighbourhoods and eventually came out onto the main bypass. They took a right.

'Where do you think he's going, boss?'

'No idea. But if your theory is right then we need to keep close. If he is our guy, we need to catch him doing more than just going out for a late-night cruise.'

The traffic wasn't too bad which meant that Raven could keep to a leisurely pace whilst maintaining a safe distance. There were plenty of vehicles to stay behind while ensuring that he was close enough not to get caught behind one of the many traffic lights and pedestrian crossings on the bypass. He had the air conditioning whacked up and blowing in his face to keep him alert.

'Do you think he's off to meet someone? Maybe his next victim?'

'I think you're jumping to conclusions there, Damo. We have nothing on this guy other than a couple of indirect links with the victims. Let's just keep our minds open to any possibility for now. I hope to God it's him and we can nail him planning to do something hideous but I ain't convinced, not by a long shot. I think there's every chance that we are wasting our time tracking this fella while the actual killer is out there doing God knows what.'

'But you've got to admit, it is odd,' Barber seemed thrilled by the chase, 'he knew two of the victims and was seen with one of them the night before she was killed. That can't just be coincidence, can it?'

'Of course it can. This isn't China. There are tens of thousands of people in this town, sure, but that chippy has most of the locals through its doors at one time or another and well over a thousand work or study at the school. I bet if we looked hard enough, we could find scores of people who knew one or more of these victims, and what do we do then? Put them all on the suspects list?'

They took the third exit at the roundabout, towards the motorway.

'Looks like he's heading out of town.'

Raven didn't like this at all. It was a waste of police time and resources. He could be back at Lisa's, having dinner, talking about their lives, maybe even thinking about the future and generally playing nice. He knew that she was not going to be happy about this, might even break it off with him. *Again.* He had had to work extremely hard last time to mend their fractured relationship and he knew that he was on his last life. He really needed a drink.

They joined the M3 and the little Punto accelerated away. The guy was pushing the 1.2-litre engine about as hard as it would go. Raven gently touched the accelerator, his two-litre Mondeo easily keeping pace, but stayed a good distance away. If this really was their man, he knew that he would be on high alert.

It was almost completely dark now, the last hint of the sun dipping down behind the horizon.

'I've got a good feeling about this, boss. If we play our cards right, we may be able to catch him in the act.'

'Let's just focus on keeping on his tail for now. He could be going anywhere.'

'I just feel it in my bones. We could be all over the press by the morning.' Raven silently cursed the young Detective's thirst for glory. That was the last thing they wanted. Press crawling all over their bust and inventing scandalous and misleading headlines that could potentially derail any chance of a successful prosecution.

Swaggart came off at the next junction and they tailed him along the slip road and turned left at the roundabout. There was a little village about a mile and a half from where they were, lots of Tudor homes, oak beams, thatched rooves and large, landscaped gardens. The type of place that Raven hated.

'This doesn't feel right. This is all wrong. All three of the murders were in town. Why suddenly change? It just doesn't feel in keeping with the previous crimes. They were dark, grimy, horrible places. This is too… upmarket. Too… Downton Abbey. This is the wrong guy, Damo, I'm sure of it.'

They wove their way down the country lanes, darkness enveloping them. Raven cursed that there were no street lights down the 'goddam B roads'. Sharp, high hedged, blind corners meant that Raven had to stay alert. They had to pull over to let a tractor through, the road barely wide enough to allow it to pass.

'You're going to lose him, boss!'

The little Punto was now out of sight, disappearing round the next bend. They could faintly see the red hue of its rear lights, but they were fading fast.

'Don't worry, these aren't fast roads. We'll catch him.'

The tractor had barely squeezed past them when Raven floored the accelerator. They tore round the bend and almost ran headlong into an oncoming Porsche.

'Fucking idiot!' they heard the driver shout through his open window as they swerved around him. They took the next two bends at fifty and eventually saw the Punto poodling along at twenty-five.

'Well, wherever he's going he's not in a rush.'

As they took the next corner the road widened and several large, stately detached homes came into view. There were around six or seven of them, set back from the road and fronting onto large, open fields like brick and timber ogre guardians of the village. The street was lit with black, wrought iron street lamps and Raven watched as Swaggart indicated and turned into a large, stone paved driveway. The expanse at the front of the house was littered with high-end cars; BMWs, Mercedes, Lexus. The garden lights glistened off of the chrome and polished glass. Barber looked across at him as they pulled up alongside the kerbside, directly opposite the front door.

'Maybe he's been grooming a posh bird.'

'Or maybe he is completely innocent and we've been wasting our time.' The radio came into life.

'Come in car number three, come in car number three.'

Raven kept his eye on the Punto as it parked next to the black Lexus and watched as Swaggart hauled himself out of the tiny vehicle. He reached into the rear of the car and pulled out his holdall. Raven grabbed the radio.

'This is car number three. We're a little busy tailing our suspect at the moment. We're in Betchley Village. Looks like our man is attending some sort of... function.'

The door opened to let Swaggart in. Raven strained his eyes to see who it was. He didn't recognise the face but wondered whether the guy was wearing some sort of…costume?

'You'd better get back here, Raven. There's been another… incident.'

'What do you mean by incident?'

He couldn't make out whether it was leather or rubber? The man opening the door was wearing some weird bondage shit. He was almost naked except for a black leather codpiece, black peaked leather cap and something on his nipples. Clamps maybe? Raven thought he'd seen it all but not this. It looked like some kind of homoerotic swinger's thing. Barber was loudly groaning next to him in blatant disapproval.

'An abduction. A break in, there's blood and, well, a real mess.'

The door closed behind Swaggart. While the whole thing was a bit…odd, it was pretty clear to Raven that he wasn't their guy.

'What are you talking about, Ruby? What mess? Where?' There was silence at the other end of the phone.

'Well? Hurry up Rube, we've wasted enough time tonight! Please don't waste any more.' Raven was feeling pretty impatient and very pissed off.

He looked over at Barber who was still sitting dumbfounded, taken aback by what they had just witnessed. Raven had to admit; he hadn't expected to see that sort of thing out there in the sticks. It just proved that you never knew what went on behind closed doors. Rich or poor, everyone had to get their kicks some way. And who were they to judge?

'Number 23, Rogers Street.'

Raven frowned. Number 23 Rogers Street? That can't be right, he thought. That was…

'It's Daisy's place. She's gone.'

Chapter 39: Daisy

Luke Raven stood in the living room of 23 Rogers Street. He couldn't believe his eyes; the place was an absolute mess. The coffee table was over-turned, the TV screen had been shattered, a lamp lay on its side, the shade crumpled under foot, a half-eaten plate of food and a glass of wine were dumped all over the rug.

But these things his mind could deal with. Daisy was a feisty girl at the best of times, and it wasn't beyond her to have a fit of rage and destroy everything around her. He had been on the receiving end a few times and it wasn't nice but what was eating into him like bleach on a T-shirt was the blood and lots of it. Blood all over the laminate flooring and pooling in little puddles, blood up the wall in spatters, blood on the door handle as if somebody had grabbed it in an attempt to flee, blood smears in the hallway, blood on the front door and in the street.

He pinched the bridge of his nose between his thumb and forefinger. He could feel a headache beginning to build there and he closed his eyes.

'What do we have?'

'Neighbour's heard a commotion at around nine P.M. A female voice, shouting, very aggravated. They didn't pay much attention as apparently it was a frequent occurrence,' Barber hesitated and looked up at Raven.

'Sounds like Daisy.'

'Bloke next door says when that happens, he just turns the telly up to drown it out. Apparently, he had tried to mention this to her in the past but that she just got verbally aggressive and it wasn't worth the hassle,' again Barber paused. He felt uncomfortable talking about it with Raven. He knew that they were close and he felt odd talking about her like that to the D.I.

Raven simply smiled, 'Well, I couldn't blame him on that score.'

'Around ten minutes later they heard the door slam and a car pull away. Neither neighbour looked out the window, so we don't currently have an ID on the vehicle. I've got the team scanning through all CCTV footage of the area.'

'Phone?'

'Found it in the street, crushed. We've taken out the sim card and the guys are going to take a look,' Raven winced and thought of all the text messages he had sent her, 'and we're checking the phone records to see if there are any odd numbers.'

Raven looked around him. So much blood. He wondered whether it could be the same guy. The scene was so much more…clumsy. It was the first time that they had come across the scene of the crime. The other murders had been staged scenes, set up in a particular way in order to send a message to whoever had located them. They were yet to find the actual locations of the murders. Was this, he questioned, just some ex-lover taking out their revenge on a girl who could, let's face it, make an enemy of a saint?

'Have we located any weapon?'

'No, not yet. The crime scene guys believe that if a weapon was used it was probably blunt given the way the,' he bit his lip before proceeding, 'the way the blood has splattered up the wall. More of,' again, an uncomfortable pause, 'an impact spray. Not a high-pressure spray.'

Raven winced. The thought of poor Daisy getting cracked across the head with a blunt weapon left him numb and cold inside. He turned to face the young Detective. 'Looks like she fought back which would certainly not be out of character. This… carnage is probably as a result of a struggle and that means we will have evidence. Make sure the crime scene guys are thorough, this could be our best chance of a lead,' he rubbed his palm across his stubbly chin, 'if indeed it is the same guy. The signs currently point to a different set of events but let's keep our minds open to all possibilities. I want blood samples tested, the place scoured for skin, hair, clothing. If we find anything let's see if it matches the skin sample that the Doc found under Trudy Yates' fingernail. And make sure we have all eyes on that CCTV footage. There is no way that our guy could get in and out of here without being seen.'

'Sure thing, boss.'

'I'll take a look down at the Swan. I'm betting she was working earlier today and there's every chance that whoever did...this was there watching her. I'll have a chat with the landlord,' who hated his guts, 'and the locals. Those guys would spot a newcomer a mile off. There's a good possibility that they may have had eyes on our guy.'

Barber eyed the senior Detective Inspector curiously. Raven was wiping his mouth with the back of his hand which was a sure sign that he was in desperate need of something more than a witness statement. He was visibly feeling the strain which usually meant he was feeling the draw of a whiskey bottle.

Raven looked up at him suddenly, startling Barber into turning his head quickly, not wanting to be caught trying to pry on Raven's inner most wants and needs.

'And cordon off the street. I don't want anybody, *anybody*, disturbing our crime scene. This place is like gold dust, Barber. Let's make it work for us.'

'Okay. No problem.'

A white-suited Crime Scene Officer came through the kitchen door into the living area, urgency on her face. She had what looked like a lighter between her gloved fingers and she was holding it out to Raven. He reached out to take it, but she pulled it away.

'Please don't touch it, sir. You're not wearing gloves.'

'What is it?'

'It's a memory stick, sir. It was gaffer taped to the front of the cutlery drawer.'

Raven frowned. Why would Daisy do that? Then his mind raced back to the discovery of the small wooden capsules with the weird, ancient scripts. Was their guy leaping into the twenty first century? He looked around him.

'Does anyone have a laptop?'

'Yes, sir. Letchworth has one in the car. He's gone out to get it now. I thought we could fire this up and see what it contains.'

'Excellent. Well done.'

Another Crime Scene Officer walked into the living room and held up a hand in greeting.

'I've booted up the laptop in the van, sir. Probably best if we don't crowd around it in here.'

Raven agreed and they all exited outside into the thick night air where the dark had descended and the temperature had dropped, the cold chill seeping through Raven's clothes and into his skin and flesh. His mouth was dry, his tongue rough and worn. He hadn't had a drink in a little under twenty-four hours and he could feel his body screaming out for an intoxicant, anything to fuel the fire inside of him. Where was Daisy, he wondered. Was she alive? Was she in pain? Was she terrified, fearing for her very existence? The thought tore at him like a predator ripping through the skin of a cadaver. His eyes burned with rage and fear. He had waved her goodbye the other night, dismissing any perceived advances, pushing her away. Could he have changed this if he had acted differently? Was that the last time he was going to see her alive with her pretty, impish face, her young but brutally experienced eyes, her quick temper, her cutting wit? He gritted his teeth together and climbed into the back of the van.

The blue hue of the laptop screen lit his face with a death mask, turning his rugged appearance into a pale ghost of a human. Pasty, hollow cheeks, eyes staring into the electronic abyss. The screen was frozen on an image, the background was dark, the figure hunched in front of the camera was covered in a black coat of some sort. But Raven could make out dark, ebony eyes with the faintest hint of white skin.

The eyes peered intently into the camera lens.

The C.S.O pressed play.

*

'Hello detective. Very nice to meet you at last, although we almost met the other day I suppose. You really ought to keep yourself in better shape than that. How are you ever supposed to catch anything other than a cold if you can't run more than a hundred yards without running out of steam?

If you are playing the contents of this flash drive then you have stumbled across the fact that I have one of your...friends. Don't worry, if I have managed to do what I have planned then she is still alive, and she is with me. A little worse for wear, maybe lost a little blood and some of her dignity, but she's not dead. And she can stay not dead for as long as you let me do my... work.

You see you are failing to appreciate the art of what I am doing. The importance of it. Because if I don't succeed then *he* will come, and *he* will not be merciful. *He* will unleash all of the unfettered fury of hell and drag us into its chasm of fear and terror for all of eternity. We will not be saved.

I don't want to kill these girls any more than you want to be involved in all of this...mess. I'm sure that you would much rather be sipping on a whiskey and dulling your senses like you have done a thousand times before. But I have a calling, and my calling will help save us all. All of humanity. If you and your friends get in the way of that then we will all be cursed with eternal damnation. I don't want that, and I am sure that neither do you.

I was once like you. Normal, ordinary, dutiful, calm.

No more.

I am cursed with this the same way that you are cursed with your... addictions and as two cursed individuals we need to help each other. I can help you, I can keep Daisy safe, ensure that no more harm comes to her, that she is fed and watered and doesn't have any further... accidents. And you? Well you can leave well alone. Turn a blind eye and stay out of my way. Yes, a few more will die. But you... *we*... will be sacrificing a few to save the many. It is a simple mathematical equation really. Why risk the lives of millions when you can save them by giving so little?

You see, I called *him*, maybe I regret that but then again maybe I don't, but I'm not sure yet whether I can control *him*. I need *him* to do something wonderful for me, but whether *he* will simply stop at that most simple of tasks remains to be seen. So, I need to give *him* what he wants, and you need to let me do that.

I want us to be friends not enemies, but if you persist in your fruitless efforts to stop me then I will be forced to take alternative action. You will never see Daisy again and I will continue to hunt out your loved ones, starting with your other girlfriend. Yes, I know about her and where she lives. I can assure you that I will not stop until you desist. This is not a threat Luke, this is reality. You will leave me be, and I won't hurt another hair on Daisy's head.

Once my work is done, I will leave, and you will never hear from me again. I sincerely hope that we can end this peacefully.

Please don't think of coming after me. If you challenge me, try to hurt me in any way then *he* will come and then everything you know, everything you think you believe, will come crashing down on you with the weight of all of heaven's many fallen angels.

Adios, my friend. See you on the other side.'

Chapter 40: The Package

Billy stood under the underpass in the town centre. There was a busker at the other end, some hairy, flannel-wearing guy bashing on an acoustic, blowing on a harmonica and singing about how 'the times they were-a-changing'. Billy thought that by the look of his guitar case he'd barely made enough money to spring a coffee and he felt no urge to go over and boost his income. The guy probably didn't even pay any taxes.

Billy was buzzing. The old lady had given him a twenty quid tip, he'd won a few quid on the horses earlier in the day and he'd just finished up a pint of his favourite real ale to celebrate. All things being equal, this was a hell of a day.

His guy was late. He'd said to meet him at eight o' clock and it was ten past. His guy was hardly ever late. Billy blew into his hands and bounced up and down on the balls of his feet. Shit, he cursed, it was getting cold.

He checked his phone. No missed calls, no messages. He considered phoning him but decided against it. He didn't want to seem too keen. Being too eager was a good way of pushing the price up and he did not want that.

Billy West was no fool. You didn't get to run a successful business in this town without any street smarts, and he had plenty of those. His dad had been a crook, a clever one at that, and Billy had those genes. The genes that could see trouble coming a mile off and could avoid it at all costs. The genes that told him when a deal was a good deal and when a deal was bad. The genes that meant you could duck and dive your way through life without busting a gut but while making a nice little nest egg for yourself and your family. Sure, his dad had gotten banged up and had ended up dying in the nick, but he had led a tidy life up to that point.

And Billy was smarter than his dad.

'You got the money?'

Billy looked around. His guy had arrived.

'Yeah, yeah. Thought you said not to be late.'

'Yeah, well, shit happens.'

His guy was not in a good mood, 'Sure, sure. I know that feeling.'

They clasped hands as if they were greeting each other. In one swift motion the money went one way and the baggy went another.

'Enjoy.'

'Will do. Hey, you okay? You don't look so good.'

His guy stopped and turned, glaring at him. He paused, considered and then spoke, 'Family. Rubs me up the wrong way is all.'

'Yeah, yeah. You know what they say. You can't live with them, can't live without them.'

'Well I could sure live without that fucking neighbour of yours.'

Billy held has hand up, 'Oh come on. Tony's not that bad. He's always been a good friend to me.'

'Yeah well, not to me.'

'Maybe you're just too similar. You know, I see a lot of him in you.'

Mitchell Richards got up close to Billy's face and spat out his words, the smell of his breath, all tobacco and coffee, wafting over Billy like some foul, toxic stench, 'I... don't... fucking... think so. The cunt's from a different gene pool, and not one that I recognise. Can't give his own mother the time of day and he thinks he can lord it over us like he's better than we are. Well he ain't! He's a fucking circus sideshow, a freak. And he's going to come crashing down to earth with a bang, I promise you that!'

Billy took an involuntary step backwards and held his hands out, 'Okay, okay. I get it,' his genes were telling him that trouble was afoot, 'you've fallen out. I understand. Totally on your side, brother. We'll just finish up our little business here and move on. I don't want to get in between you both. Your business is… your business.'

Mitchell paused, took a breath and grunted, 'That's right. This is my business, and I would appreciate it if you would not mention it to him. We will deal with it in our way. Just puts me in a… bad mood.'

'Understood, Mitchell. Understood. I'll keep this a secret just as I keep our… dealings to myself. Loose lips sink ships and all that,' he touched his fingers to his lips as if to illustrate the point.

'Yeah, and we need to keep it that way. Shit, if he found out how I earned my living he'd have that over me as well. So,' he wagged a finger at Billy, the other hand in his pocket gripping something tightly, 'no talky talky. My… guys like their customers to be discrete. You know that.'

'I do, and I will. No problem with that, no sirree,' Billy took a big gulp of air and smiled unconvincingly at Mitchell. The hairy busker struck up a rendition of Bad Moon Rising by Creedence Clearwater Revival.

'Don't go spouting off to the wrong people, especially not my dip shit of a brother. And definitely not your wife.'

'I won't, I won't'

'Or there will be… consequences.'

'Understood. No question there. You know me, as quiet as a mute.'

'Well, let's keep it that way.'

The hairy busker hollered out the chorus, 'There's a Bad Moon on the riiiiise!' The words and chords echoed down the long underpass with ghostly reverberation. A crushed can of lager followed it, clattering off of the concrete while bashing out some crazy, samba beat. Billy watched it zig zag towards him and took a deep breath. His genes were telling him to move. His hazard lights were on and he was shifting swiftly into reverse.

'Well, I'll be on my way. Nice seeing you again,' he held up a hand, 'say hi to your Mum,' and with that he turned on his heels and shuffled out of the underpass.

Mitchell watched him go, smiling to himself. Fucking idiot, he thought. Didn't know good weed from street skunk. Mitchell had been overcharging him for months, selling him his dregs for premium rate and convincing the buffoon that he was some high-end drug dealer with South American Narcos style connections. What a fool. And what made it even better was that Mitchell knew that whatever he gave to the village idiot made its way to his half-bastard brother. Hilarious really when you thought about it, which he did. A lot.

The contents of the baggy that he had given to the fat lump in combat shorts was definitely not Colombian hash. He wasn't even sure if there was such a thing. Nope, it was standard street skunk crushed and mixed with heroin. He'd been upping the mixture bit by bit over the last few weeks just to see what would happen and the heroin to skunk ratio in the latest mix was a lot higher than in previous batches. A *lot* higher. He chuckled as he considered the consequences. It was going to give them both a high neither of them would forget in a hurry.

Chapter 41: Robert Charon

Tony sat at his kitchen table. He had been working at his novel, trying to take his mind off of his spiralling, out of control life. He couldn't quite believe the way that every day seemed to bring a new revelation to him, knocking him off kilter, spinning him into a new cyclone, but he couldn't concentrate. He couldn't take his mind off of what his brother had told him, had given him. A name. A person. A bloodline. He didn't know whether it was a gift or a curse.

He had sat there for what seemed like an eternity, considering whether to type that name into the search engine. Did he really want to know? Did he really want to search for someone, a father who had committed such a heinous act? He concluded, after some soul searching, that he did. He just couldn't help himself. The temptation was much too strong.

He typed in the name, Robert Charon, added his town in order to narrow down the responses, took a deep breath and pressed 'enter'. He could hear and feel the metaphorical doorway opening.

A list of entries came up, some obscure, some erroneous and many that weren't even in the United Kingdom. But the one at the top of the page, the one that ticked both boxes, the name and the town, stood out from the page like an entry in ultra, high definition 3D. Like all good searches these days it had an image, a picture of the man who purported to be his father and the resemblance was uncanny.

Tony took a sharp breath.

The face staring back at him was older than he, of course, probably twenty five to thirty years older, but it had the same nose, slightly elongated, a small bulge at the bridge, pursed, thin lips, dark eyes, dark but greying hair which was smarter than his own, clipped into a tight style, a small quiff at the front, thin glasses, dark, trimmed beard, white skin. The photo was clearly posed and the look of the man facing him was confident, successful, knowing and slightly regal even. Tony could almost smell the whiff of his aftershave, something expensive and musky.

He hovered his mouse over the entry and clicked.

A webpage sprung into view bearing the image of Robert Charon, the same one he had seen on the search engine page. The webpage was entitled 'Robert Charon – Life Coach' and had a strikingly black backdrop with red italic writing. The web page claimed that its subject was the purveyor of lifestyle tips and lessons with a twist, describing ancient philosophies and idioms that could be used to improve the way that people led their twenty-first century existences in order to maximise 'personal potential, skills and talents.'

There was a link to tributes and letters of recommendation. Tony clicked the link and what seemed like hundreds of responses came into view. He opened a few; 'Mr Charon changed my life, he made me view myself in a whole new light and now I am free to tackle the world head on', 'Mr Charon helped me achieve things that I could only imagine in my wildest dreams, thank you Robert, you are an angel', 'I have been awoken from my sleep, I am now the person that I never thought I could be. I am so grateful that you, Robert, came into my life'. The tributes went on and on and on and they were global. Jennifer from the United States, Bogdan from the Czech Republic, Hilary from Australia. And there were pictures too, photographs of Robert Charon with his arm around his patients, big smiles, happy campers, some in tears. It appeared as if he conducted large seminars as well as one to one sessions; one of the photos showed him on stage with a head microphone, mesmerising hundreds of onlookers who were entranced with his words of spurious wisdom.

He was tall, just like Tony. Lanky even. Smart suit, smart hair and large hands held out in front of him like a puppeteer controlling the hearts and minds of his hypnotised audience. His tie was held in place by a silver pin and he had large silver rings on each of his index fingers. His teeth were so white that they seemed to illuminate the room with their nuclear radiance. He oozed success.

There was a link to a short video. Tony didn't want to press play, but he couldn't help but gorge himself on this. It was if he had flicked to the last page of a novel to find out who did it. This was the answer he didn't know he wanted, but that he oh so seriously needed. He clicked his mouse.

A booming voice leapt from the laptop speakers and the frozen picture sprang into motion. Robert Charon walked from one side of the stage to the other, large purposeful steps, left hand held out to the audience, head high, big smile;

'And you know people, our ancestors had this licked. They knew how to get the best out of their lives. They had what I like to call Super Empowerment. Did they have oppressors who sought to drive them into the dirt? Sure they did. Did they have famine, disease, pestilence? Yep, that too. But what they had more than anything else was a desire, a willingness, an *absolute right* to control their own destiny and with that they controlled their own fate. They were Super Empowered to do whatever it was that they wanted to do. And they did. They built the pyramids, they constructed great statues, rivers, canals, dams, cities, monuments, walked from continent to continent to locate treasures that they only believed were there, carried water on their shoulders from village to city, hunted wild animals to feed their young, survived when only the strong could survive! And how did they achieve all of this? They were empowered, no, Super Empowered by a will so strong. The will that deep down in the pit of their stomach told them to go forth and do what they wanted to do, what they must do, what *you* must do to become the person that you want, no *need*, to be. Did they have super smart computers? No! Did they have credit cards? No! Did they have automobiles, super-sonic planes, high speed trains, pilot-less drones, frequent fucking flyer miles? No, they did not! They had this,' he pointed to his heart, 'and they had this,' he pointed to his head, 'and they had these,' he held out his huge hands, large silver rings shining in the spotlights, 'hands, hands that could do evil, but also hands that could do good. And they put them to good use. And with these three things you,' he held his hands out to the crowd, 'are empowered. You, my friends, colleagues, are Super Empowered and you must seize the day and *Super Empower your lives!'*

The audience erupted in violent applause, many of the congregation standing up and screaming their delight. Robert Charon held his arms out wide and bathed in the adulation, his fluorescent smile brightening the room, mouthing 'thank you, you're so kind, thank you'. And then the video ended.

Tony sat back in his chair and smiled. Smarmy son of a bitch, he thought, but talented too. He knew that anyone that could sell that kind of bullshit must have something about them.

Just then the door opened, and he heard a bag being dropped on the hallway floor, shoes being shaken off, keys being hung on the key hook.

'Is that you, Jane?'

'Yeah, yeah, it's me.'

'You want a tea?'

'Could murder one, thanks.'

Jane walked into the kitchen, her face flushed, her tracksuit still wet with sweat. She had a towel draped over her shoulders, water bottle in her hand. Tony was at the sink, filling the kettle. She looked down at the laptop.

'Who's that?'

'You wouldn't believe it if I told you.'

'Maybe not. You eaten?'

'Yeah, had beans on toast. You want something?'

'I'll grab something later.'

'How was your class?'

She looked up at him, he thought he saw something in her eyes, 'Yeah, yeah. Good. Hard. That bitch of an instructor really put us to the sword today.'

'Don't know why you do it. Paying good money to be tortured.'

'We've had this conversation. I do it to keep fit and to meet with friends. Wouldn't hurt you to do something you know, tone yourself up a bit,' she waved a hand at his swollen belly.

'No, I, er,' he subconsciously rubbed his stomach, 'I guess not.'

Jane sat down at the table, 'Anyway, you didn't answer me,' she pointed a finger at the laptop screen, 'Who is he?'

Tony pushed the switch on the kettle, 'Well, allegedly that smug looking fella is my dad.'

Jane frowned, 'Your what?'

Tony turned and folded his arms, 'My dad. My father.'

'The rapist?'

'I guess so.'

'Shit.'

'Yeah, shit.'

Jane scrolled across the page and looked at the face staring out at her, 'Life coach, eh? Looks rather swish,' she stared at the photo of Robert Charon, 'but I can definitely see the resemblance,' she paused, frowned and looked up at Tony, 'Tony, I think this really is your dad.'

'I think you're probably right.'

'How did you find him?'

'Mitch.'

'Mitch?'

'Yep.'

'How did Mitch know?'

'Turns out that he and Mum knew all along.'

Jane's mouth fell open, 'And they didn't tell you!'

'That's about the size of it.'

Jane continued to stare at the screen, 'Bloody hell. What are you going to do?'

'Don't know. I need to think on it some more.'

'Yeah, yeah,' she paused and looked up at him, standing with his arms crossed, the steam of the kettle rising from behind him like a fiery dragon about to rear up from the kitchen sink, 'you okay?'

Tony turned and grabbed the kettle, 'Yeah,' he said with his back to her, 'I'm fine. A bit stunned I guess, but otherwise I'm okay.' He poured the hot water into the two mugs and started to stir.

She stood up and put a hand on his shoulder. He flinched slightly.

'I'm going to go up and get into the shower. I'll be down in a sec. You… you sure you're okay?'

'Yeah, I'm fine.'

'Okay. Well, call up if you want me.'

She turned and headed up the stairs. Tony listened as she threw her stuff onto their bed, opened the door of the bathroom and turned the shower taps on. Things were a little awkward between them, but they would get through this, he was sure of it. They were strong, they always had been, and he knew that no matter how emotional the last couple of weeks had been that they would get back to how they were. She had his back and he had hers. That was what being a couple was all about. What being in a relationship was all about. Being there for each other. They were good together and he didn't need a life coach to convince him of that. He smiled.

Just then her mobile phone rang. It was on the table next to his laptop where the page was still open on the picture of his estranged dad. He put the two steaming cups down on coasters bearing the universal sign of 'his' and 'hers' next to it and stared at the phone. One large word peered up at him next to a picture of a tanned, smiling face. 'NICK'.

Tony picked up.

'Hey Nick. It's Tony.'

'Hi Tony. How's it going?'

'Yeah, fine thanks. How's things with you?'

'Oh, you know. Busy, busy. Lots going on. How's the book?'

Novel, he thought, what a prat, 'Oh, going okay. Can't complain. What can I do you for? Jane's getting cleaned up at the moment.'

'Oh, just phoning to make sure she's okay.'

'Okay?'

'Yeah, okay. After her episode at the class.'

'What episode?'

'Oh, didn't she tell you?'

Tony frowned, what was this guy talking about? 'I don't know. Give me a clue.'

'She fainted.'

'Fainted?'

'Yeah,' he laughed, 'I think she was trying to go head to head with my girlfriend, you know, Wendy?'

'Wendy? Yeah, I remember.'

'Well Wendy, *Walenta*, is pretty competitive at this kind of thing and I think Jane got caught up in the whole racing challenge. She may have overdone it a bit.'

Tony bit his cheek. What was Jane doing trying to outrun the Polish gazelle, he thought? And why didn't she mention the fact that she had fainted to him? He knew that she had looked at him oddly when she had walked in.

'You know what, now that you mention it, she did say something. Probably played it down a bit, but, yeah, yeah, she said that she'd had a funny turn. I thought she was just mucking about.'

'No, no, she went down like a sack of potatoes. We were all very concerned about her. Just wanted to make sure she got home okay.'

Yeah, sure you did, Tony thought to himself. More likely that you phoned to gloat. 'She's fine, Nick. Very nice of you to call. I'll let her know that you did.'

'No problem, no problem at all. Give her my love and tell her I'll see her at work tomorrow.'

'Okay then, that's great. Take care of yourself.'

'And you. See you later.'

Nick hung up. Tony stared at the phone. She hadn't mentioned a thing and, now that he thought about it, she had been really odd the other day at the pub. As soon as Nick and Wendy had walked in, she had wanted to beat a hasty retreat. And they had rowed, she had gotten really bitey with him. He had thought it had been about his unwillingness to go to see his sick mother but maybe he had been wrong. Was there…was there something going on here? Something he hadn't spotted before. Was she…was she jealous of this girl? Was it her looks? Her figure? Her lifestyle? Did she have a thing for…for Nick? No, no, it couldn't be that. Not Nick. Not Nick. Nick?

'Thanks for the tea, babe.'

'No problem, sweetheart,' he stared at the phone.

'You okay?'

He paused, stared at the phone, looked up at Jane, back to the phone, 'Yeah, yeah. I'm fine. You feel… better?'

'Yeah, yeah, much cleaner. Thanks. So, what you going to do then?'

Tony looked up at her, 'About what?'

Jane frowned, 'About this bloke?'

Tony looked back down at the laptop, 'Oh. Don't know. Probably ignore it,' he looked out of the kitchen window. He could see the lights on in the den. 'You know what, I think I'm going to pop next door for a bit.'

'What, now?'

'Yeah.'

'But you've just made a cup of tea.'

'Yeah…yeah. I'll microwave it later. Don't tip it. It's just that Bill's got a new motorbike magazine that he wanted to show me.'

She looked up at him through the steam of her cup, 'A motorbike magazine?'

'Yeah. He's thinking of getting one. A Harley I think. Gonna help him pick one out. Won't be long.'

'Famous last words. Don't you think that this is more important?'

'What?'

'This thing with your dad!'

'Oh, that. No. No. Probably just a load of crap anyway. Let's talk about it later, I won't be late.'

He grabbed his jacket from the back of a chair and headed out the back door, leaving Jane sitting at the table behind him, hands wrapped around her cup, confused, unsure of what had just gone on between them.

He stopped on the back step and clenched and unclenched his hands.

Nick.

Chapter 42: Chillax

'Jane? And some bloke from school? Are you sure?'

Billy was sitting on the sofa in the den, a bottle of Stella resting on the arm of the couch. He was carefully rolling a joint on his lap, taking care not to spill the expensive baggy contents all over the sofa and the floor.

'No, not sure. I just don't know why she wouldn't have told me about what happened at her class. Or why she has been acting so weird lately,' Tony was staring out the den window back at his house. He could see that the lights in the kitchen were still on but didn't have a good enough view to see if Jane was still in there.

'I don't know, Tone. It all seems a bit far-fetched to me. She just doesn't seem the-' he paused to lick the edge of the Rizla paper, 'the type.' He pointed at Tony, 'You sure it's not you? I mean, you've had a lot going on lately, what with all that stuff with your mum and everything.'

Tony was rubbing a hand across his chin, contemplating, 'She's just never acted like this before. We've always known what the other one has been thinking, you know? I'm sure you're like that with Sal.'

Billy spat out his mouthful of beer. He rested it on the side while he wiped a hand down his neck and T-shirt, 'Er... I don't think so, my friend. Do you really think anyone could get inside of that head? Not a chance. I'm lucky if I understand what she's saying, let alone what she's thinking,' he paused, reflecting, 'no, what me and Sal have is a mutual respect for the others' privacy. Kind of an unwritten rule. It works well for the both of us. Plus, she scares the shite out of me.' They both laughed.

When they quietened down Tony said, 'Well, me and Jane have that sense, you know? Or... we had it. It just seems like lately we don't know how to deal with each other. I don't know, maybe I've had my head buried in the laptop too much. Maybe I should be paying more attention to what she's doing, how she's feeling, what she needs. Maybe I've been too distant. But every time she sees this guy, especially when he's with this... Walenta girl, she acts... odd.'

Billy was sitting with his beer bottle resting on his knee, looking up at Tony, 'Well, have you asked her? Confronted her at all? That's usually the best way to get things out in the open.'

'I wouldn't know where to start.'

'Well, something like, Jane have you been fucking Nick behind my back? That would work.'

Tony choked on his beer, 'I'm not sure that that would be the best approach, Bill. That angle is likely to end our relationship, not rescue it,' he sat down on the office chair, 'if, that is, it even needs rescuing.'

Billy looked at him over the top of his glasses, his moustache hanging over his pooched top lip. He handed him the joint, 'Here. When all else fails just chillax. You can stress about this as much as you want, but until you know there's anything to be getting all uptight about, what's the point? Just take a hit on that and all your worries will be in your rear-view mirror, and after a few miles and a lot of smiles they will be long gone.'

Tony stared at the joint in his hand, 'I don't know, Billy. I'm not sure that this is good timing. I've got things that I've got to work through, and I need to be of a sound mind to do that. I mean, I've got a mother who's dying, a wealthy father I didn't know I had, who, by the way, allegedly raped my mother, impregnating her in the process, and a girlfriend who barely speaks to me. Oh, and who is also keeping things from me and, I suspect, shagging a bloke from work.'

Billy stared at him, a doleful look on his face, 'And you're out here with your best mate, and all he wants to do is to cheer you up. It's on me. The beer, the dope. You can stay out here all night if you want. Me Casa es tu Casa, or something like that. Just have a beer, have a smoke and the world will seem a much happier, healthier place.'

He leaned over and pressed play on his phone. The Doors kicked in, something about it being the end, my only friend, the end. The keyboards, guitar and drums reverberated around the den, making the room seem smaller, more comforting, relaxing.

Tony rolled his eyes, leaned forward and took a light. That was the last thing he remembered.

Chapter 43: Darkness

Daisy was alone. He had gone, the fucking creep with the white face. He'd left her bound on the bed, her wrists tied to the metal frame above her head, her ankles tied at the other end. Her shoulders ached like a bastard, her fingers had pins and needles and the plastic ties were too tight and were cutting into her skin.

He had caught her off guard and she hated that. Ever since she was a kid, when she had lived at home with her mum and when her mum's many boyfriends, drug dealers mainly, had tried to knock her around, she had learnt to protect herself, to see trouble coming and either avoid it or confront it head on. She knew her way around a street fight and she had won plenty.

But this guy had managed to catch her at a moment of weakness.

She had been settling down after a long shift at the pub and had just sat back on her sofa to watch the TV with her dinner, Tikka Masala for one, when the doorbell had rang. She had thought it was the copper, Raven. They'd almost had a thing the other night which thankfully they had both resisted. She hadn't had a lover for quite a while and God knew she needed some company, but they were bad for each other and they both knew it. It would have been a big mistake. But, nevertheless, when the doorbell rang, she had been sure it was him and, despite her reservations, she would probably have let him in and taken him into her bed.

But it hadn't been him. It had been a tall, skinny, emo' guy, dressed from head to foot in black; black boots, black trousers, long black parka coat and a black woollen Peruvian hat with a snowflake pattern. And a white face, a ghostly white face.

Before she could say 'who the fuck are you' he had punched her in the nose, hard enough to crunch bone and spill blood, plenty of it. She had staggered back into her front room, her head spinning, water streaming from her eyes, her legs turning to jelly.

He had come rushing in behind her, slamming the door as he pushed through. She had had just enough sense left to pick up her dinner tray and smash it into the side of his head. That had knocked him off balance and given her a couple of seconds to ready herself and bring the heel of her foot down hard on the back of his neck. His woollen hat had flown off into the dining area, revealing thin, shaggy blond hair.

He had spun on her then, his black, pin prick eyes showing a cold rage that had burrowed deep into her heart. He had come up from his crouching position in a hard arc and had struck his elbow into her cheek. She had shrieked in pain and anger, loud enough to startle him.

As he took a step back, a befuddled look on his face, as if he had just realised that he was in a confrontation with another human being and not some slab of meat, she had shoulder charged him, knocking him backwards, tripping over his own feet as he fell and crashed through her coffee table.

She had laughed at him. Whoever he was, whatever he wanted, he hadn't counted on coming up against someone like her, someone who didn't take shit lying down, someone who could take a shot and then give two back in return. She had thought that the lanky streak of piss was no match for her. She bellowed down at him, 'Come on then, you son of a bitch! You want some of this? Then got off your fucking arse and…'

That was when he had leapt up, her ceramic Buddha in his right hand, a gift from her friend at the pub (he had brought it back from a trip to Thailand or something) and had crashed the large figurine so hard across her head that the room had turned black and her senses had numbed. She had vaguely heard a thud as she swam into the darkness.

And she had awoken in that dark and dank room, her head

throbbing like a bitch, her muscles sore and her pride dented. And her life, well, her life in the balance.

He had been there at first, the room was so dark that she could barely make him out. She was gagged of course, some kind of damp and dirty linen rag tied tightly around the back of her head, but she had tried to make contact with him, making muffled noises through the gag. Her mouth was so dry that it hurt her throat to try to say anything at all, but she was angry, so angry. 'Who did this guy think he was', she had tried to bellow at him, 'that he could invade her space, her home, attack her, assault her and then keep her captive like this? Why? Why her?'

He had just ignored her. He had been checking something on a computer, the light from the screen had illuminated his already ghostly face. He was ill, she was sure of it, his skin was cracked, sore, his lips were dry and the flesh around his eyes was so swollen that his eyeballs appeared to be tiny, black dots. He was wearing his hat, the black Peruvian hat with a snowflake pattern, but she could see his hair hanging over his forehead, thin, fraying. Old.

She had drifted in and out of consciousness, the knock on her head had left her concussed. At one point, when she had awoken, she had watched him while he stared silently out of the window, just watching, barely moving. Another time he had been sitting across the room, just staring at her, the shadows covering most of his features, but she could still see his small, black, sad eyes. But this time, when she had stirred and slowly opened her eyes, he was gone. She was alone.

She looked up at her wrists and down at her ankles. Black cable ties were holding her securely in position. The only way out was to pull so hard so as to either break the ties or break the metal rails that they were attached to. She shook herself. The bed rattled. It wasn't the strongest frame and she felt sure that if she shook hard enough then she could dislodge something, maybe slip one of her hands free and with her free hand she could work at the other ties. She took a deep breath, bit down on the gag between her jaws and thrashed around furiously. The bed clattered and clanged, squeaked and wailed, but everything was still intact. She lay still, catching her breath. Again. She shook and shook, simultaneously wrenching her arms and kicking her legs and the ends of the bed seemed to bend inwards ever so slightly, the mattress bounced and clattered into the springs beneath, but it did not yield. She cried out in sheer rage, 'Arrggghhhh!' She swore under her breath, all of the bad words, the worst words.

She looked up above her head. The headboard railings were rough, not smooth. If she moved her hands up and down repeatedly she thought that she might be able to wear away at the cable ties, maybe cut through them. Her shoulders and upper arms were burning but she fought through the pain, moving her wrists as fast as she could, rubbing at the rough metal, feeling the heat from the friction on her skin. She rubbed away for what seemed like an age, long enough for the pain to scream through her body like an icy dagger. But when she pulled her hands towards her the cable ties remained steadfast. She was trapped. There was no way out.

She groaned in despair. Was this it, she bemoaned? Was this all her life was worth? Everything she had fought through, all the times she had had to use her strong will and her inner strength to keep going. Was it all a waste? Was it all just killing time, leading up to this desperate, pointless end? She would die there alone, in the dark, with no idea who her captor was. With no idea what it was all for. She would lie there, dead, rotting away like some left-over meal, the cockroaches and the maggots making a banquet of her decaying corpse. No one would even miss her. Not Raven. Definitely not her mother who barely even knew she was there when she visited. Her life would be deemed as just a fleeting visit. Nothing to be concerned about. Nothing that had left any kind of mark. No husband, no kids, no nothing.

She felt tears welling up in her eyes which made her even angrier. She never cried. Not even when her dog, Mutley, had been run down in the street when she was a kid. Never.

She turned her head as if ashamed. And then she saw them. The scissors. Rusty, paint flaking, dull brown and battered, but they looked like they were in working order. There on the wooden chair under the window. Right there. She thought he must have left them behind when he went out. Careless.

But they were just agonisingly out of reach.

Chapter 44: From Beyond the Grave

They were all around him. All three of them. Tracey Webb, Billy Roper and Trudy Yates. Young women with so much to give but with no life force left to give it. Two of them with their throats slashed, dried blood caked around their gaping, jagged and fatal wounds, the other with her face bruised and battered, her skull cleaved in, her nose twisted and broken, her eye sockets shattered, eyeballs rolled upwards like they were attached to puppeteer strings. They were naked but their bodies were bloated and rotting, the flesh decaying, disintegrating, tissue and sinew turning into a gloopy stew of black and odorous gore. They were pointing at him, their heads tilted to one side, their arms crooked and twisted, their fingers jutting at him in sharp poses of vigorous accusation.

'We warned you! We warned you! You didn't listen! We sent you messages in your dreams, but you were too drunk, too self-absorbed to listen! This is on you, Luke. This…is…on…you!'

'NO!' he shouted at them, screamed at them, 'No, how could I know? How could I know what you were trying to tell me? They were… they were just dreams! They could have meant anything!'

The moving cadavers circled him. All around them there was blackness, just a single light emanating from somewhere beneath him, illuminating their pale, sickly faces. They were enraged but also saddened. Their arms were flailing around them, angrily pointing and prodding at him, gesticulating with furious daggers of indignation.

'She will be with us soon! Daisy will be here…with us! And it won't stop there. Lisa, perhaps Lisa will be next. Perhaps others will follow. He will not stop until his work is done! And you let him go! We warned you!'

Raven was holding his head, his mouth drawn down in a sneer of disgust and denial.

'It wasn't me. I couldn't stop this! If you wanted to stop him why didn't you tell me who, *where*, he was! You've seen him, you know who he is. If you knew then why didn't you *tell me?!*'

They turned at each other and laughed, screeching, hideous howls of the dead. They threw their heads back in terrible glee, their slit throats gaping open like the mouths of grotesque beasts. Dead Trudy's split mouth and shattered teeth leered up in a loathsome grin, her black and shrivelled tongue poking out from between her shattered jaws.

'You think that this is a man! A normal man with normal thoughts and normal wants and desires?!' they laughed again, their faces thrust at him, their death breath stinging his throat, 'this is much more than a mere mortal man! This is a thing of such hideous evil that it acts from beyond the grave. This is ancient, omnipotent. It will not stop. It will not desist. It finds a willing host to conduct its bidding and uses it as a puppet, a slave! And when the time comes it will reveal itself, rising up in all of its horrific glory with one sole aim. To destroy. But you, you have the key, you have the answer. You just need to look inside yourself, beyond all of the angst and the anxiety, the toil and the turmoil, the addictions and the inaction, and you will find it.'

Luke Raven looked from Tracey to Billy to Trudy. They were glaring at him, their dead eyes bleeding into his heart like tape worms into his lower intestine. This couldn't be real. These things couldn't be real. This was another dream…wasn't it? And even if it was a dream, well there were dreams before and look what happened. Why were they speaking to him? What could he do that others couldn't? Why was all of this responsibility being levelled at him? Was he really a worthy recipient? He had failed so far, and he had had many failures before. He could barely even look after himself let alone save the world from some… some *what*? Evil spirit? A maniac with a grudge? What? He didn't, couldn't, understand. This was too much.

Too much for his frazzled mind to cope with. 'Remember, Luke,' the terrible trio spun around him like birds of prey circling around a helpless, wounded animal, their arms were ensnaring him, their long hair forming a halo of flowing and matted silk all around him, 'Remember. Remember. Remember. Remember…'

Chapter 45: The Altercation

'Remember who the fucking Mayor is around here, Dave! You want to keep your job; you'd better start by getting some results!'

Raven jumped up from his desk. He looked at his watch. He had sat down around fifteen minutes ago and had rested his eyes, a warm cup of coffee still sat on his desk between his loosely clasped fingers. He had been awake for thirty-six hours and his body was exhausted. Shit, he thought to himself, that was one hell of a creepy dream.

He heard a door open from behind him.

'Three murders and a kidnapping in a month and you have diddly squat on this guy. A few torn pieces out of a scrapbook and a flash drive with some crappy quality video do not a case make, Dave!'

'Well…well now, Chester. Don't forget we have the skin sample,' the Chief retorted unconvincingly.

'Oh yes. That's right. The skin sample. And what did that tell us?'

'Er, well. Nothing as yet. There hasn't been a match, but…'

'But what, Dave? But what? A DNA sample with no matching DNA is about as useful as an ashtray on a fucking motorbike!'

Raven turned his chair and watched Mayor Wood, his slippery lackey in tow, storming out of the Chief's office. Chief Simmonds was following wordlessly with a dour look of resignation on his face.

'If you don't start giving me answers soon then I will have to take matters into my own hands! I pay you to keep these streets safe. The voters put us in these positions of power to keep them safe. And at the moment no-body feels safe!'

Chief Simmonds held his hands up as if to say 'okay, okay.' He turned dolefully towards Raven who shrugged his shoulders. The Mayor span on him.

'And you. You with the addictions and the lack of respect for authority or for the rules. Are you sleeping? Fucking sleeping on the job? Is that what you are doing? Citizens out there afraid to leave their homes, their lives turned upside down and you are sitting in this nice cosy office having a... a what? A siesta? A nap? Is this some kind of fucking joke, Dave? Is this the guy that you entrust the safety of our townsfolk with?'

Chief Simmonds held up his hands reproachfully, 'He's had a rough couple of days, Chester. This nut job is now taking this fight to him personally. That's his friend that's been abducted you know? Our friend. And he and his team have been working flat out to bring her home safely. No time off. No sleep. The guy deserves a rest for Christ's sake!'

'A rest? A REST? What is he, in a fucking care home? Jesus. I just came from the home of the parents of Trudy Yates. You know? The girl that had her face smashed in by this lunatic. And do you think they looked like they had been having a nice REST? Perhaps chilling out in the garden with a nice barbeque and couple of glasses of wine? Michael fucking Buble on the stereo. Oh nooooo! No, they weren't doing that at all. They were... what were they doing again? Oh, that's it, they were crying, sobbing, mourning the loss of their beautiful little girl! Do you think they would say to your team, your Detective Inspector,' he pointed at Raven, spitting the words out as he yelled them, 'that he should have a nice REST on the job? Do you? DO YOU?'

Raven leapt up from his chair. He'd had enough of this. He stormed up to the Mayor, knocking his man-servant across the room as he did so. He grabbed him by the lapels of his tweed jacket, his face so close to his that he could smell the Mayor's expensive aftershave and hair wax. He turned up his nose in disgust and spoke in a low, growling rasp of a voice.

'We will bring this guy in, Mayor. We will bring him in, and we will ensure that he feels the full force of the law. The parents of those girls expect as much, my team expects as much, and I fucking expect as much! But I also expect you and your little…bitch to stay out of my way. You can criticise us, *me*, as much as you want. I'm a big boy and I can take it. But get in my way, put one foot in my fucking path, and we will have… we will have a thing to settle! You and I. Just you,' he pointed a finger firmly in the Mayor's chest, 'and I. You fucking understand that you plumped up, ponced up, pampered piece of sh…?'

'Okay, okay, okay,' the Chief had his arms round Raven's shoulders and was pulling him away, 'we've all said some things but it's because we all care. No other reason. No other reason. Let's not let this get blown into something that it's not.' He was looking at the Mayor over Raven's shoulder, trying to gauge his reaction.

'Get your fucking goon away from me, Dave.' The Mayor had an uncertain, apprehensive look in his eyes, but he was smart enough to know that you didn't back down from a silver back on the rampage, you stood your ground. He took a deep breath and looked at Raven through the eyes of his superiority, 'Your father always said that you were trouble, Luke. Nothing but trouble in a donkey jacket. A disappointment, not up to the family name, talent wasted. You want to make him proud? You solve this case and you solve it fast. Because my patience is running thin. And Dave,' he spoke without turning his head to the Chief, 'don't think I'm going to forget this… incident. This is another nail, Dave. Another fucking nail!'

Raven shook the Chief off, rage over-spilling, furious anger on his red and puffy face, but before he could lean over, grab the Mayor by the throat and pummel his face into the office floor he was blocked off by Webber and Bailey, the Sergeant with his hands on Raven's shoulders forcing him back and Bailey, her large frame blocking his view, her arms folded, an understanding, knowing smile spreading wide across her large ruby lips.

'He's not worth it, boss. Not worth it. You're not going to catch this guy by losing your job now, are you?'

Raven knew that she was right, but the red mist had descended. The fucker had had the cheek, the nerve, to bring his father into this. His father, the man who had spent all of his life working for himself under the guise of doing it for his family. The man who had never had a word of praise for his son, the man who had never come to his son's school to see his school play or watch him play football, the man who had had countless affairs behind his mother's back, the man who liked a drink but would hide his dependency from his family and scold them, often violently, if they ever called him on it. And Luke was a disappointment to him? Is that what he had said? Had he said that to this low life weasel? Really?

'Calm down now, Raven,' Webber had his arms around Luke, bear-hug like, forcing him back against his desk, 'this is over. Crusher's right. You lay another finger on him and you're off this case and waiting in a queue at the job centre. You don't want that and neither do we.'

The Chief was looking across at him, flushed crimson spreading across his large cheeks and neck. His eyes were pleading, imploring him to stand down. Dave was his friend, he had looked out for Raven when no-one else had given two shits, when he had hit rock bottom and had had nowhere else to go. This could lose him his job and he didn't deserve that. He owed him more than that.

Mayor Wood was standing, watching, waiting and seeing where the next move took them. He had the power in this situation, and he knew it. His face was full of smug knowing.

'Is that all, Raven? Are we... done?'

Raven grunted. The anger was still burning but reason was starting to win the argument.

'We're done.'

The Mayor smiled, 'Good. That's good,' his face turned to stone, 'then get on and do your fucking jobs. All of you. I expect results by the weekend or... there... will... be... consequences.'

With that he whirled round and walked out the door, his beleaguered puppy dog in tow.

Raven cursed under his breath as the tension in the room gradually evaporated. He slapped his face hard with both hands. *God he was tired.*

Chapter 46: Time Out

Tony awoke on the couch. He was naked except for his boxers. Sunlight was spilling through the front room window. He reached over and grabbed his phone to check the time. It was one-thirty in the afternoon. Shit, he swore under his breath, he had slept in.

He sat up but quickly laid back down. His head was pounding, and his mouth was so dry. How the hell had he gotten home, he wondered out loud. He didn't remember a thing.

He gradually raised himself to a sitting position, rubbed his eyes and stood up. His legs were like jelly and he saw stars, lots of small, bright dots across his vision. He grabbed hold of the door frame to steady himself, took a minute and let the wooziness pass. Whatever that junk was that Billy had given him, he thought, he was never doing that again.

He walked out into the corridor, looked up the stairs, listened for sounds, and then headed into the kitchen.

He wondered what the hell had happened in there. The place was a disaster zone. There were plates smashed against the wall, cups all over the floor, his laptop flung against the patio door, which was slightly open, letting the morning cold air in.

He snapped himself out of his slumber. Jane.

'Jane!'

He turned and headed up the stairs two at a time. His mind was racing. Had someone broken in and attacked her while he stupidly lay sleeping in the lounge, he ruminated, wasted on some cheap dope that he should never had touched? He would never forgive himself if she was up there in their bedroom, dead, her lifeless body staring at him through dead eyes, accusing him, 'you let them do this to me, you let them kill me.' What was he doing? What the hell was his life becoming?

He crashed through the master bedroom door expecting to see carnage, but the bed was made. The cushions, the ones that they threw onto the floor every night so that they could actually get into the bed, were arranged neatly on top of the duvet, all pink and blue. Teddy bears stood guard at the foot of the small double divan. Don't worry, they were saying to him, we looked after her, not that you care. There were no clothes on the floor, no mess, no disorganisation. The room was perfect, just the way that Jane would have left it.

He crossed the hallway to the bathroom. Nothing. Towels hanging neatly from the towel rail, toilet roll folded over just the way that Jane liked it, seat down, shower door closed. The spare bedroom was equally tidy, the single bed was made, the dresser was organised and clean. Perfect.

'What the hell?' he said to himself, 'where the fuck is Jane?'

He checked back through his memory banks. The video of the guy that was allegedly his father. The discussion. The call from Nick.

She was at work. With him. He felt anger building within him but didn't know why.

He gathered himself. Okay, she was at work. She had left the house that morning to go to work but had left that mess in the kitchen and she hadn't woken him. He couldn't reconcile what was going on, what was happening?

He turned and headed down the stairs, back into the front room. He grabbed his phone, flicked through his contacts, found Jane and hit dial.

She picked up on the third ring.

'Tony, I'm at work,' she hissed down the phone at him.

'I, I've just woken up. What the hell happened here?'

She huffed down the phone, 'Wait a second. Tilly, will you take over for me, just for a minute?' There was a pause of a few seconds. He heard footsteps, kids in the background, and then a door opening and closing. 'What do you mean what happened here?'

'The house. It's a wreck. What happened?'

'You know fully well what happened, Tony. You know fully well!'

'I don't. I really don't!' He wracked his brains. Did he? Could he remember anything at all?

'Well, first of all you went round to see our idiot neighbour. For a chat. And then you didn't come back for hours. You remember that?'

'Well, yeah, I guess. I remember going round there. But I don't remember coming back.'

'Oh, really? Well perhaps that was because you were wasted on God only knows what. As per bloody usual. You go over and you come back off your bloody head. And then you expect to have a normal conversation. Except this time, you were mad.'

'Mad?'

'Yes, mad. Mad enough to tear the kitchen apart. Shouting accusations at me like I had done something wrong.' Was she crying? He could hear a tremble in her voice, a heightening of her usually stable pitch.

'I... I don't remember. What did I say?'

'Oh, I don't know. Something about me and another man. That I was betraying you. That you were going through some kind of living hell and I was turning my back on you like every other woman in your life! That you knew. That I didn't know that you knew but that you did.'

'I... I...'

'And then you started throwing things, picking plates up and smashing them, kicking the chairs, swiping things off of the work surface onto the floor. I... I was scared. You scared me!' She was sobbing now; her voice was shaking. He wanted to reach out and hold her. He didn't remember any of this, not one thing, but his body could still feel the anger, the rage. He could still remember his conversation with Nick.

206

'I'm so sorry, Jane. I'm so, so sorry.'

'You terrified me. I shut myself in the bedroom and left you downstairs. I could hear you shouting and screaming and continuing to throw things around. I… I almost called the Police, Tony. Can you believe that?'

'I do believe it because you are saying it. But I wouldn't believe it otherwise, Jane. I… I don't know what to say.'

'You're not the person I met at university, Tony. You've changed. You promised me that you would look after me, but you aren't, are you? I… don't know what to do any more.'

'Jane, Jane. Let's wait until you get home. We can talk about it then. I'll…I'll make it up to you. I promise.'

There was a silence at the end of the phone, 'I'm not coming home, Tony.' The news was like an icy and poisonous dagger in his heart.

'You're what?'

'I'm not coming home. I've packed a bag and I'm going back to my mother's.'

'To your mother's? What do you mean? What does this mean?'

'It means that I need time. I need to get some perspective. I can't be in the house any more. I need some space.'

Some space, some fucking space. He couldn't get to grips with what she was saying.

'Over this one incident? I make one mistake and you pack your bags?'

'It's not one incident, Tony. You've been distant for weeks. And you never spend any time at home when I'm there. You avoid me. You go out, you don't come home and when you do, you're in a different place. Not with me. Somewhere else. You're neglecting our relationship, you're neglecting me.'

'Our relationship. Our fucking relationship! Do you know what's going on in my life, Jane? Do you even care? Do you know that my whole life has been turned upside down, that I don't even know where I come from anymore? Do you even comprehend that?'

'I do, I do. And I'm sorry. But this has been coming for a long time. I can't let what's going on in your life now cloud that fact. I'm not saying it's over. I'm just saying that I need some thinking time.'

'Some thinking time? Well I need some thinking time too. I need to think about my life, my existence. My family. My mother. My father. Where I'm from. Why I'm here. Why my girlfriend, the person who should be supporting me through this, comes home from a class, doesn't tell me that she has been competing with the girlfriend of some bloke from work, the one that she couldn't wait to get away from the other day, that she raced so hard that she passed out, didn't tell me, her *fucking boyfriend*, her boyfriend who then had to take a call from this guy, this colleague, and get his full on patronising bullshit! And why I get the sense that something more is going on here. Something a little more than just play time at class. Something that has maybe been going on for a while. Behind my fucking back. Maybe I need to think *about that!*'

He threw the phone across the room and it smashed into the TV and shattered the screen. He stood there, breathing heavily, his vision swimming in and out of focus, his temple pulsating to the tempo of his racing heart. He sat down, put his head in his hands and sobbed.

Chapter 47: Revelations and Visitations

'Where the hell are you, Raven? I've been trying to reach you for the last two days. You know? Since you didn't show the other evening. The cat had your dinner in the end. Winston said the steak and kidney pie was very nice. Look, if this is it for us, I would appreciate you telling me. A courtesy fucking call for Christ's sake. Just call me back.'

I hung up and threw my phone on the sofa. I had to admit, I was feeling pretty abandoned and pretty alone. Pretty rejected actually. It was eight-thirty in the evening, the sky was darkening outside, and I hadn't seen my supposed boyfriend or cat for two straight days. Not one contact from either of them. And there I was, hiding out in my flat because the one person I couldn't get hold of had warned me to not go out on my own. Well, who the hell was I supposed to go out with then?

I really needed a cigarette but knew that I shouldn't. A glass of wine would have been nice. It had been five weeks since I'd had either and the pangs weren't getting any easier. Or the queasiness.

I crashed back onto the sofa and flicked on the TV. It was bloody re-runs of Friends. Again. It was like the TV had turned into a machine that simply re-hashed the same old same old shit over and over again until your mind gave up and simply accepted it. And my mind was becoming one big mush.

I stood up, walked into the kitchen and filled the kettle. Well, I remember thinking, if I couldn't have a glass of merlot then a cup of tea would have to do. I flicked the radio on. 'Use Somebody' by the Kings of Leon crackled into life and I laughed to myself. That was bloody ironic.

I was so angry at Raven. Time and time again he had made promises to me, about the two of us, about our life together. Lives together. That was a joke. And then he just vanished, as if the very act of making the promise drained any last commitment or resolve out of him. He could never follow through with what he promised faithfully to do, and I was always just left sitting and waiting. And why? Why the hell did I hang around?

He hadn't been faithful, I had caught him with that tart from the pub on more than one occasion, but then, I guess, I hadn't exactly been faithful either. I'd had the odd boyfriend or two during our on-again-off-again courtship. He wasn't particularly available emotionally, but was I any better? I knew that I could be a hard bitch at times, he had told me as much. And he liked a drink a little too often. A lot too often. And maybe I did like a whiskey or two every now and then.

But... jeez.

My mother, God rest her soul, had always said that I went for the wrong 'uns. That there was something in me that just preferred the excitement, the thrill of not knowing what was going to happen next. I had so hoped that she had been wrong. Raven wasn't the first bad boy that I had hooked up with but somewhere inside of me I had hoped that he would be the last.

I stirred two sugars into my tea and leaned back against the oven. I rubbed my stomach which was giving me hell and thought long and ruefully about the bloody mess I had gotten myself into.

I heard footsteps up the stairs outside and hoped that there would be a knock on my door. That I would open it and Luke would be standing there, a bunch of flowers in his arms and an apologetic smile on his face, but no such luck. I laughed inwardly at my stupidity. I thought that it was probably Mister Jackson from upstairs, the old guy who occasionally popped down for a cuppa.

I turned to walk back into the front room and killed the radio. The station had changed tracks and 'Hello' from Adele had come whining out of the speaker. I fucking hated that song. The TV was still showing a Friends re-run but it was on yet another commercial break, some advert trying to get me to buy a sofa or a bed or some other item of furniture that I couldn't afford.

I heard two feet at my door and spun around. I looked at the door handle but there was no movement.

Silence.

It was odd. I knew that unless there was someone coming to visit me that there was no reason for anyone to set foot outside of my front door. The stairs to the flat upstairs passed by at the other end of the hallway.

I heard a scraping on the hallway floor, something had blocked the hallway light that usually shone constantly through the small gap between the door and the threshold. I knew that somebody was there.

I took two steps towards the door. I could hear breathing, panting really. I could feel something, someone looking at me through the door, as if they could see through the solid object, someone's eyes crawling all over me like fingers caressing my skin through my clothes, through my underwear. I felt…dirty. I shuddered.

There was a tapping against the door. Fingernails? I heard something open and close and then an object being placed on the floor.

I ran a hand across my forehead. I could feel perspiration there and I wiped my sweaty strands of hair from my eyes. What was this?

I took another step forward. There was a loud BANG and I nearly hit the bloody roof. I felt a soft cry leak out from between my lips and I held onto the wall for balance.

I moved forwards towards the door. I so wanted to look through the peephole and see who was out there.

Then my phone rang.

'Lisa, it's me. I'm so, so sorry. I've been meaning to call but…'

'Luke,' I whispered, 'Luke, listen. There's someone here, someone outside in the hallway.'

'What? Who?'

'I don't know, but they're just standing there. Outside my door. I'm… I'm scared.' I wasn't, I was terrified.

'Okay, okay. Stay on the phone. I'm in the car and I'm about two minutes away. Don't… open… the… door.'

'I wasn't bloody planning to.'

'Can you see through the peep hole?'

'I… I'll try.'

'Just be quiet, don't let whoever it is know you're there.'

I crept towards the door, my Minny Mouse slippers dampening any sound from the hard laminate flooring underfoot. I could still hear the breathing. It was slow now, calm, purposeful and yet menacing. Whoever was out there was waiting for me. I was trembling, my mouth was quivering frantically, my heart pounding like a sledgehammer in my chest.

I heard a hand slide down the outside surface of the door.

I was inches away now and I could sense the person standing a foot or so away from me, thin plywood, honeycomb cardboard and timber battening standing between us. I closed one eye and leaned forward. I could almost feel the unwanted visitor's breath on my face.

I put one eye to the peephole.

I saw one black eye staring back at me.

'Fuck, fuck, fuck!'

I leapt backwards, my heart in my mouth, terror screaming from every pore.

The door shook inwards repeatedly. BANG, BANG, BANG. Whoever it was they were slamming their fists into the door.

'Lisa, Lisa, Lisa, Lisa! Are you home, Lisa?'

I backed into the living room and almost fell backwards over the sofa.

'I have something for you. I found it in the street! It wants to come in!'

'Luke, do you hear this, Luke? Do you hear this?'

'I hear it, I hear it. Don't move, I'm maybe thirty seconds away. If it's who I think it is, this guy is very dangerous. Grab a knife from the kitchen and shut yourself in your bedroom.'

'But...'

'Just do it, Lisa! I'll be there. Trust me.'

Another commitment?

'Liiiiissssssaaaaa! I won't wait much longer!'

I raced into the kitchen, grabbed the sharpest carving knife I could find and turned towards the bedroom.

I took three or four steps and then stopped. What was I doing? Was I going to let this creep turn up at my home and scare me into hiding myself away, locking myself in my bedroom like a frightened child? Was this the kind of person I had become? I had been shut away for days on the advice of a guy who hadn't even had the decency to stay in touch, just going to work and back with a friend during the day but staying holed up every evening. And now I was going to listen to him again? This was my home. *My home.* I had myself to protect, two of us to protect. It was time that I started doing just that, wasn't it?

I gripped the knife in my right hand. It felt good. Heavy, solid, deadly. It gave me strength, belief. I turned back to the front door. I gritted my teeth together, my jaw set tight and paced purposefully towards it. If I opened that door and some maniac was standing out there, teeth bared, black eyes raging, I knew with a morbid certainty that I would drive the knife so hard into his heart that his head would most likely explode. No fucking psycho was going to show up at my home, where I lived and scare the shit out of me like that. No-one.

Two paces, three paces, four paces.

I reached over, grabbed the door handle, took a deep breath and pulled....

There was no-one there.

I poked my head out and looked left and then right. No-one.

I cocked my ear and listened. No footsteps. No breathing. Nothing.

My arms were shaking, my breathing hard and heavy.

I looked down at my feet. There was a shoe box. The cheap, white cardboard variety. I crouched down, gripping the knife in my right hand, afraid that something was going to reach out from within that box, grab my ankles and drag me in, kicking and screaming like a wild banshee.

I used my left hand to prise the lid upwards, half a centimetre, a centimetre, two centimetres. I could feel my pulse pounding in my head. My abdomen was aching, my body trembling. Somewhere in my head I could hear Luke calling me, pleading with me to tell him what was going on.

I lifted the lid. There, inside, on a bed of tissue paper stained with gloopy blood and sinew was the head of Winston, my beloved black and white tabby, his mouth open, teeth bared, tongue hanging out like a blackened slug, his eyes dark and soulless, dried blood in his white whiskers, tendrils hanging out from his severed neck.

I screamed and screamed and screamed…

I must have passed out because when I came to Luke was standing over me and I was looking up at his unshaven face, the hallway stairs lying dark and soulless behind him. The cold floor felt soothing against my skin which seemed to be burning up.

I remember shouting at him to call an ambulance.

'Why? Are you hurt? Did he hurt you?' His face was a mixture of concern, worry, fear and anger. I remember thinking how tired and old he looked.

The pain in my abdomen was excruciating. I could feel dampness in my knickers, a loosening in my womb.

'No, you idiot! The baby!'

Chapter 48: Dad

'So… are you going in or what?' Billy was sitting in the driver's seat of his van, two hands on the wheel, sunglasses perched on the tip of his nose, looking at Tony through smiling, inquisitive eyes, 'I mean, we've driven all this way. It's been nice, you know, having company when I'm supposed to be working, but it's a long way to come for a chat when I could have had this conversation with you over the garden fence.'

Tony had his hands on the dashboard, eyes forward, staring at the imposing and yet enticing structure ahead of them.

'It's a big place.'

Billy laughed, 'Yep, yep. It's pretty big. Looks like your old man has done okay for himself. I guess talking twaddle to a bunch of people who believe the shit you're selling pays good. Beats working for a living. When you go in ask him if the place needs re-wiring.'

'I don't know if I can go through with this.'

'Sure you can, sure you can. Just walk up to the door, knock, wait for an answer say 'hi, I'm Tony Richards. I'm the happy product of the rape you committed twenty-five years ago.' I'm sure that will go down a treat.'

'You're not being much help, Bill.'

'Sorry, sorry. You're right. Don't say that. Don't say that at all. Might be a little controversial. But you get my gist, right?'

Tony put his head in his hands, 'I don't know why I'm here. What am I hoping to get out of this?'

Billy looked at him and put a hand on his shoulder. He could see that he hadn't slept properly in days. Jane hadn't been returning Tony's calls, her mum was giving him the cold shoulder. He hadn't even made it into work – Big Al had told him that he had three days to sort his life out or he would be given the big heave-ho. Billy felt a little responsible but how was he to know that that bastard Mitchell had spiked their dope? And, anyway, this incident with Jane wasn't just the product of one raucous evening – he knew it and Tony knew it too. Sal had been predicting something like this for months.

He put his hand on Tony's shoulder, 'What you're looking to get out of this, my friend, is some closure. That's all. No more and no less. You go in there, you meet the guy, you have some small talk, maybe a cup of tea, and then you leave. If nothing else at least you will know,' he smiled pitifully, 'and that's all you'll need.'

Tony looked at him through red, tired eyes, smiled back and nodded.

*

The walk up to the house was quite steep, the block-paved path winding through rolling green lawns and neatly trimmed hedgerows. Tony had been surprised to learn that the front gate had been unlocked, but he guessed that in this neighbourhood the crime rate was probably pretty low.

The house looked Victorian, maybe older, three storeys, a large turning circle at the front which was lined with three vehicles; a Merc', a BMW 6 Series Convertible and a vintage Jaguar E Type. The place was slate grey, dark, imposing. It felt to Tony like the leaded windows at the front of the house, two downstairs, four on the first floor and two bay windows on the second floor, were malevolent eyes looking down on him, watching, studying him like a child looking at an ant through a magnifying glass. The front door was large, maybe eight feet tall, and was made from a dark walnut, heavily varnished. It looked sticky, glossy. There was a large door knocker in the middle, about eye height to Tony, and it was in the shape of an angel, her wings fanned out, her eyes wide and vivacious, her gown enveloping her thin, bronze body.

Tony reached out and held her in his hand. He recoiled as if something had shocked him. It had felt as if the angel had been moving within his fingers. He shook himself, muttering under his breath, 'Don't be so stupid, Anthony. You're giving yourself the willies.'

He reached out again, gripped the angel tightly and knocked loudly.

He stood with his hands folded in front of him for around a minute. There was no answer. He grabbed the angel again and knocked, three, four times. Again, he stood there for a minute or two, like a boy-scout waiting to ask a neighbour for sponsorship money. He couldn't believe it. They'd driven all the way out there and the guy didn't even have the decency to make sure he was in. He felt anger welling within him. What an arsehole. It had taken a lot of willpower for Tony to pick up the phone, call this…this person, introduce himself and suggest that they meet. He had to be fitted into a slot in the guy's diary like any old client, like every other numpty who felt that meeting the great Robert Charon was going to turn their meaningless, pitiful life around. And for what? So he could stand there like a lost little boy waiting to be scolded. No. Not this kiddie, he promised himself, this was his one shot and if this was how it was meant to be then so be it.

From behind him he heard the rumble of an engine, a loud roaring boom. He heard tires on gravel and turned to see a large man in light blue jeans, black cowboy boots, black leather jacket and black motorcycle helmet pull up behind the Merc' on a Harley Davidson Fat Boy, all black paint and glistening chrome with orange flames flickering on either side of the fuel tank.

The rider dismounted, pulled off his gloves, walked over to Tony with large lumbering steps and removed his helmet. Tony took a step back. It was like looking into a mirror that reflected your image twenty or so years into the future.

Despite the differing hair colour and neatly trimmed facial hair the resemblance was uncanny.

Robert Charon smiled and held out his hand.

'Hello son.'

*

They were seated in the lounge, or what would have been the smoking room when the house was originally built. It often amazed Tony how tastes and fads changed in such a comparatively small amount of time. A smoking room now was somewhere where people vaped from cheap plastic, pen-like dispensers, no more single malt whiskey and expensive cigars.

The place was enormous. The ceilings were extremely high, giving the room a regal or vintage feel, the walls were wood panelled, and the place smelt of teak and preserving oil with a faint hint of tobacco. The floors were carpeted wall to wall in a thick, plush pile. The chairs were individual, straight backed, floral patterned, high-armed reading chairs. Not meant for lounging whilst watching the TV. There wasn't even a TV in the lounge. Tony was sitting upright, one leg crossed over the other with his tea-cup perched on his knee. He felt...odd and a little out of sorts.

'How's your tea?' Robert's voice was sultry, deep and ever so slightly hypnotic.

'Good, good. Warm.' By comparison Tony's voice felt weak, thin.

'It took a lot of guts for you to come here, Anthony. I'm proud of you.' Robert smiled at Tony, a knowing, fatherly smile.

'Well, you know. I just wanted to see what you...what you were like I suppose.'

Robert Charon laughed, a laugh like the booming roar of his motorcycle. It reverberated around the room, seemingly gaining volume and intensity as it travelled. He gathered himself, sipped his tea and looked at Tony. 'And?'

Tony rested his teacup down on his thin, porcelain saucer. He shrugged his shoulders and looked around the room, looking for something, someone. A friend maybe. He opened his mouth to speak and then closed it again.

'It's okay,' Robert was leaning forward, peering wantonly into Tony's sullen eyes, 'whatever it is, you can say it.'

'Did you really rape my mother?'

Robert laughed again, this time louder, deeper and heartier. The room seemed to shake with its resonance. Tony shifted uncomfortably in his chair. The room fell silent.

'How is she?'

'She's dying.'

'I heard.'

'Then you know how she is.'

'But how is her... spirit? Is it well, is it intact?'

'That's an odd question.'

'It depends on your perspective. It depends on your belief system.'

'Your belief system?' Tony was astounded at the guy's lack of empathy.

Robert stood up and walked to the large, crammed book shelf. He looked up and along the many volumes of dusty hardback books, many of which looked like they had seen better days.

'Your mother has a good soul, Anthony. A good spirit. Death is just a journey that your spirit has to take. The body is simply a vessel. She will be allowed across the bridge to the other side, I believe that deeply.'

Tony stood up, 'Look, Robert.'

'I had hoped that you would call me Dad.'

'Look, Robert, I know you pedal this stuff and it has served you pretty well,' he waved his hand around him as if presenting the house to a potential buyer, 'but that's not why I'm here. I haven't come here for a seminar or a one to one tutorial. I'm here because a little under three weeks ago I found out that my adopted mother is my real mother, that she is dying and that she conceived me when someone, *you*,' he pointed at Robert, 'raped her. Until that time I didn't even know that you existed, that I even had a father, and at this point I don't know whether I want to shake your hand or smack you in the mouth!'

Robert smiled ruefully, walked over to Tony and placed a hand on his shoulder. Tony shook it off.

'Look, Anthony...'

'It's Tony.'

'I prefer Anthony.'

'Suit yourself.'

'Your mother may well have perceived our embrace, our passion, as an assault, as a rape, your words not mine. I'm sure that over time that is how she has rationalised it, but I can assure you that I have never raped a woman in my life and never would. Never could. There is so much that you don't know about me and so much that I would like to show you, to teach you.'

'Teach me?'

'We have a rich heritage, Anthony. Our ancestors trace back to the very dawn of time, to the very land where our world, this world, began. You are one in a long line of Charon's and the family, our family, has carried our faith through the ages, sharing our journey and our wisdom with as many subjects as possible. As many people, from the very richest to the most humbly poor, as we could connect with. That is what I do, that is what my father did and that is what my grandfather did. We are prophets, preachers, wise-men if you will. I'm not a door to door salesman, not a cold caller. I don't ask for individuals, followers, to come to me. They just come. And they come because they want to learn, they want to feel, they want to truly see,' he smiled at Tony, his large white teeth gleaming like pearls in the bright morning sun. 'Your mother was one such person, one such follower. She came to me, she wanted what I had, what I could give her. I did not force myself onto her. She was a willing listener, an advocate, a disciple.'

Tony walked over to the large leaded window and looked out over the expansive and landscaped driveway. In the distance he could see Billy's white van, he could barely make out Billy leaning against it, sipping from a can.

'Are you saying that she's lying?'

'No, not at all. I am saying that she is mistaken.'

'I'm sure that a lot of men in your position have said that before.'

'I'm sure they have. But what I am telling you, son, is the truth.'

The room fell silent, neither man wishing to fill the void.

'How's Jane?'

'How do you know about Jane?'

'I know a lot about you, Anthony. You would be surprised. I have been watching you for some time.'

'Then you would know that she left me.'

'Yes. Yes. That is unfortunate.'

Tony was still gazing out of the window, not wanting to turn around and face the situation or the inquisition head on.

'But is she okay? Spiritually I mean?'

'I wouldn't know. She won't return my calls.'

'Give her time. She will see sense.'

'I'm not so sure about that. I think there's…there's someone else.'

'Who?'

'A work colleague. I think. I've got no proof. Just a… a sense.'

'And this man has sought to steal her from you?'

'I don't think she was ever really mine to steal.'

'But he has the audacity to covet her and to seek her out, knowing that your souls are entwined? That you have committed yourselves to each other for eternity.'

'I don't think that we ever put it like that.'

'Do you love her?'

'More than anything.'

He did love her. Loved her so much. From the bottom of his heart and from the pit of his soul. But at that moment he hated her too. He couldn't erase the thought of her with *him*, embracing, naked, sweating, his tongue on her body, moaning in ecstasy. He wanted to…

'And you want her back?'

Tony bit his lip. He'd never felt so lost before, so alone. It seemed that everyone in his life was abandoning him. His mother who shunned him, his brother who despised him, his girlfriend who had betrayed him. No life, no career, no family. He felt tears well up in his eyes and he pushed them back. Not there. Not now.

'I do.'

'Then you must fight for her.'

Tony gripped his hands together, clenching and unclenching, fighting the fear and raw emotions that were welling up in him. Hatred. Venom. Bile.

'I don't know how.'

'I can help you.'

Tony turned to face him. Robert Charon was maybe two or three inches from him, Tony could smell his aftershave, could taste his sweet breath. Robert held out his arms, pulled Tony to him and buried his son's face in his broad chest.

'I can help you, son.'

Chapter 49: Jailbreak

She was almost there. One of her hands had worked its way loose, nearly to the point where her palm was free of the binds. The sweat enveloping her body was helping, it was so hot in there, in her prison cell. The arsehole hadn't even bothered to prop open a window for air, probably afraid that she might call for help. She could have bloody suffocated like a spider in a Tupperware container. Her greasy hands slipped easily against the plastic of the cable ties. She had lost some skin from either side of her right hand but that was a small price to pay for her freedom.

She bit down on her filthy, dirty gag as she grunted with exertion. She was starting to truly believe that she would be free pretty soon and then she would get away from the psychopath. She would call Raven and get him over there as soon as possible, catch the lunatic and lock the bastard up for life. Kill him for all she cared. She couldn't be sure, but she was pretty certain that he was the nutter that had committed all those heinous murders, the ones that the police were discussing at the pub. Well, she swore to herself, he was going to rue the day that he had messed with her. Wrong place, wrong victim.

She yanked her arm once, twice, three times. On the fourth tug and with a loud 'EURGH!' her hand came free.

She fought back which would certainly not be out of character the tears of elation and took a moment to gather herself. She had cramp in her hand and she patiently waited while the pain subsided. She opened and closed her fingers over and over until the feeling came back to her fingertips and palm.

The scissors.

She reached over, pulling her body as close to the edge of the bed as the ties would allow. The frame squeaked and rattled as she gradually slid her hand and feet along the railings, just as far as they would go.

The fingertips of her right hand brushed the edge of the loops in the handles. She was smiling to herself from beneath her damp and choking gag. She could do this. She would do this. 'Don't rush,' she repeated over and over under her breath, 'take your time.'

Then she heard the door close downstairs. And footsteps.

Her mind started to race. Shit, she cursed, he was back.

She stretched her arm out as far as it would stretch, every muscle, every sinew in her arm crying out in pain. It was almost unbearable. Her shoulder started to cramp, and her elbow was on fire. She silently yelled for joy as her thumb and forefinger clamped round the loop closest to her.

She hastily pulled the scissors to her, praying that they would be sharp enough to break the thick cable ties. She closed them around the white plastic and then scraped the blades back and forth, back and forth until the tie snapped. She pulled her left hand free, again opening and closing her hand until the feeling came back to her nerve endings.

She could hear footsteps on the stairs. He was coming. He was close. She needed to hurry.

Her breath became ragged, short. Pin pricks of heat started to blossom on her face and chest. She was flushed with terror, panic and the sheer physical exertion of it all. She had been gagged and bound for what seemed like an eternity and her energy levels were low. She needed sugar but there was none to hand. She yearned for a sweet and strong black coffee.

She grabbed her legs. There was one large tie binding both feet together. Her ankles were raw and bleeding, but she pushed through the pain.

Again, she closed the scissors and used them like a hack-saw on the plastic tie, back and forth until it started to give.

The footsteps were getting closer. She could hear his breathing, could smell him, could see his black and ghostly form in her mind's eye. She knew that he was coming to finish her. Whatever he had demanded from the authorities they hadn't provided it and now he was going to follow through on his threat.

Well, she thought, this time he was going to find out that payback really was a bitch. And she was the bitch.

With one hefty pull on her legs her ankles snapped free of her binds. The pain in her feet and legs was excruciating but she didn't care. She was free. She was fucking free! She had to stifle a yelp of joy.

She looked at her hands, at the rusty blades of the scissors. Fuck the police. Fuck Raven. She was going to take matters into her own hands. Show the jumped-up prick who he had been fucking with. No-one messes with her, she swore to herself. No-one. He got lucky at her apartment, but he wasn't going to get lucky again. Once bitten, twice shy with a pair of scissors in the eye.

She heard the footsteps cease outside of the door. She stared at it for what seemed like an eternity. Slowly the handle started to twist round.

She quietly got up from the bed, scissors held above her head like a dagger and hid behind the door jamb. It was show-time.

Chapter 50: Another Chapter

Tony closed his laptop. He thought that was enough for the evening. He'd had an eventful day and his mind was still racing.

He'd learned a lot, an awful lot. A lot about where he was from. A lot about the lies that people told. A lot about manipulation, betrayal and who you could and couldn't trust.

He knew that he couldn't fucking trust that prick, Nick. He knew that as much as he knew how to breathe in and out every minute of every day.

He knew that he couldn't trust his brother, Mitch. Billy had revealed the identity of his top-secret drug dealer. His own fucking brother. The little shit had tried to poison them, had probably been doing it for months. And that had indirectly led to Jane walking out on him.

And he now knew that he couldn't trust his mother. She had sold some bullshit lie to him which he had bought hook, line and sinker. And hadn't she been lying to him all these years, about where he was from, who his parents were, who she was? Had kept him from knowing about and seeing his father. His own father for God's sake.

Liars. All of them.

But he still hoped, really hoped that he could trust Jane. That she had just been misled, manipulated, seduced. By that fucker. He wanted, needed to believe that.

His father had said that he would help him get his life back in order and he hoped that he could trust him too. He had known him for literally five minutes but already there was a bond. Not just a physical bond, sure they looked alike. But a mental connection. His father had said it was a spiritual connection, one that could not be broken, that went back for thousands of years. He had said that now they had found each other that they could never lose each other again. That no matter what happened that they would always know where the other was, how they were feeling, what they were thinking.

He ran his hand through his hair. So many thoughts. So many possibilities. So much to consider.

He looked at his laptop. What would Luke Raven do? The hero of his story. How would he approach this? How would he solve the riddles and conundrums that were swirling round and around in his mind?

When Tony wrote about him and all of the other characters in his little, made up world it was if they were real, like the words were simply pouring from his fingertips like tap-water. The laptop was the bath and it was filling rapidly, almost overflowing with his ideas and fluid imagination.

Would Raven do things differently? Be bolder perhaps? Face things head on rather than sit behind a computer screen pondering life's great tragedies? His father had told him that they needed to take the fight to those that sought to do them harm. It seemed a little dramatic, but now that he thought about it...

What to do, what to do?

One thing was for certain. He was not going to be taken for a fool any more. Weak Tony was dead. Strong, wilful Tony had taken over his feeble body and he was going to get his life back. Fuck them all. If they didn't treat him with respect, then he would treat them with the same level of disdain.

He checked the answer machine. No messages. He checked his mobile phone. No voicemails or texts. He went to the door. No post. It was as if no-one cared if he lived or died. Whether he was there or not.

Well, he pondered, all that was about to change.

For the better.

ACT 3: THE REAPING

Chapter 51: The Hospital

'So, the baby's okay?'

The nurse looked Raven in the eyes. His appearance clearly alarmed her. Unshaven, deep crevices in his ashen face, dishevelled clothes and bloodshot irises. If only she knew about the events of the last few weeks, he thought, maybe she would be a little less astounded by the way he looked. Maybe she would wonder why it wasn't him lying in that hospital bed. After all, if it wasn't one drama it was another and the latest series of events had knocked him for six.

Scratch that, for ten.

'Well, we need the Doctor to confirm it. He's on his rounds at the moment. But I would say, based on the scan results, that the baby is doing just fine. Your partner simply needs to take it easy for a while. You know, carrying a baby around for nine months can be a very stressful thing for the body to contend with. And, add to that the trauma she has gone through this evening, she is lucky that the prognosis isn't a lot worse. She needs to be looked after, taken care of,' she looked Raven up and down, 'you know, you may need to familiarise yourself with the vacuum cleaner and the dishwasher.'

Had Lisa been talking to this woman, he thought, was there some kind of maternal alliance going on here? 'I get it nurse... nurse,' he looked down at her name badge, '...Harmon? Is it? I get it. I'll take good care of her, don't worry. I can be a modern man, not a problem.' He smiled at her through gritted teeth. 'And as for the events of this evening, you needn't worry. It's all been taken care of.'

She smiled at him. 'That's good. She's resting at the moment so don't be in there too long. It wouldn't hurt for her to get a good night's sleep.'

Raven nodded as the nurse walked away. His head was spinning. First Daisy, now Lisa. The guy clearly had some kind of personal vendetta against him. Raven had already arranged for two uniforms to be placed on the door of Lisa's ward. He nodded at them as he passed. Until the nut-job was behind bars he was going to insist that the Chief ensure she have personal protection twenty-four seven. The maniac was nothing if not persistent.

He walked past two pairs of beds, the curtains closed. He could hear the voices of expectant mothers, their partners and parents chatting about nappy rash, breastfeeding, presents their friends and families had bought the babies, sleep rotas, the quality of schools in the area, university funds. Their words echoed around the ward and rattled about in his skull like loaded dice. He could feel pressure building behind his eyes. He smiled at Lisa who was lying on the bed nearest the window. She smiled back but he could see the fear behind the facade. The gravity of the night's events was now descending on her like a dark and ominous cloud.

'How you holding up?'

'I'm okay. I'm fine. I'm just glad the baby's okay. It's just...' she put her head in her hands and sobbed. He took the chair next to the bed and put a hand on her shoulder.

'We've got a couple of police officers on the door. Just a precaution. I think he's done all that he intended to do. He just wanted to give you... me... a message. He wants me to back off, but he won't come here.'

She looked up at him, tears running down her soft cheeks, her eyes red and puffy, 'You were supposed to be with me. You know? Like you said. Like you always say. Where have you been?'

He looked down at his shoes, took a breath and then looked back at her, 'He's taken to attacking people that I know. That I care for. It's becoming personal. Two days ago, he kidnapped Daisy Reynolds,' Lisa's face hardened, 'you know? The girl from the Pub?'

'I know her. You know I do.' She caught herself, 'Why... why would he do that?'

'My guess is that he saw us talking the other night in the Swan. He must have been watching us and in some way reasoned that it was a good way to get at me.'

She looked him squarely in the eyes, her own glare intensifying, burning through his skull and rummaging around in his head, 'And was it?'

'What do you mean?'

'Was it a good way to get at you?'

He let go of her shoulder, 'We're friends Lis'. You know that. Nothing has gone on since...'

'Since the last time you screwed her.'

'Since forever. All that's in the past now. I'm with you.' He reached out to hold her, but she shrugged him away. 'She's the same as any other victim in all of this. Whether I know her or not, in any capacity, I have a duty to protect her. And if there's a chance that she's still alive...'

She looked down at the bed, nodding to herself.

He touched her hand, 'Look, Lisa. We need to talk.'

She picked up a magazine from the bedside table, 'About what?'

'What do you mean about what? About the baby.'

'How do you know it has anything to do with you?'

'Well, does it?'

She put the magazine down on the bed and turned to him. Her voice was deadpan, 'Yes. It does. It's yours.'

He felt his mouth go dry. He tried to swallow but couldn't. He took a sip from her cup of water.

'It's okay, Luke. It was an accident. You don't need to be involved.'

'I thought you were on the pill?'

'I was. I stopped.'

'And you didn't fucking tell me?!'

'I never fucking see you!'

A nurse poked her head in the ward and looked over at them, clearly agitated. Raven held up his hand in apology.

Lisa spoke to him, her voice hushed but the malice in her tone was unmistakable, 'You come over when you feel like it and assume I'm going to put out. You hardly ever call and when you do it's like I'm the 'sex on demand' service. You want to make sure you're not going to become a dada? Wear a fucking condom.'

'But this is for life, Lisa. It's not a game. Do you really think we are going to make good... good parents? Do you really believe that?'

'Like I said, you don't have to be involved.'

He looked out of the window. The night was black, he could see cars streaming up and down the dual carriageway outside the hospital, people getting on with their existences, oblivious to the dangers that existed beyond the glossy veneer of their every-day lives. He wished that he could be like them. Innocently ignorant.

'My life is... complicated.'

'Then *uncomplicate* it.'

'I don't know that I can.'

'You mean you don't know whether you want to.'

He turned to face her, 'I want to be a part of this but I'm going to need time to... get used to it. It's just that it's so... I don't know... unexpected. I don't come from a good family; I don't know whether I could be a good father.'

Lisa reached out and held his hand tightly in hers, 'It's okay, Luke. I know. I know that you need to come to terms with this. But I'm having this baby with or without you,' she looked longingly into his haggard eyes and he was suddenly afraid of what she might find in there. 'You let me know when and if you're ready.'

The silence between them was terrifying.

His mobile phone rattled in his pocket. Lisa grunted and picked up her magazine. He answered it.

'This is Raven.'

'Raven, it's Davis. We've got a lead. A good one.'

'What kind of a lead?'

'We think we know where Ms Reynolds is being held. And we think that he's there with her.'

'Is it a good source?'

'One of the lads on the Chamberlain Estate. Says he's seen our man go in and out of the place a number of times over the last two or three days.'

'Give me the address,' he reached in his pocket and grabbed his notebook.

'Number thirty-six, Silver Birch Crescent.' It wasn't far, a mile or so away from the hospital.

'I'll be right there.'

He switched off the phone and grabbed his coat.

'You'll be safe here, Lisa. Just do what the nurse says. Rest. I'll be back as soon as I can.'

'Where are you going?' She felt a complex mixture of anger, confusion and fear.

He could see her eyes were imploring him to stay but he was resolute. With everything that was going on he knew there was only one rational thing for him to do.

'I'm going to catch this son of a bitch.'

.

Chapter 52: Silver Birch Crescent

Raven's car screeched to a halt outside of the Italian restaurant. It was pouring with rain and Barber was exiting the doorway whilst simultaneously pulling on his coat. He had someone with him. The Doc?

'Hey Boss.' Barber was leaning in the driver's side window.

'Hi Damo. You have…company?'

'Yeah, yeah…it's Jasmine.' Damian was looking at Raven through love-struck puppy eyes, 'I can't leave her here. I drove. She's got no way of getting home.'

Raven picked his jaw up from the floor, 'Okay, okay. But she'll have to stay in the car.'

'I've got no intention of leaving the vehicle, Detective Inspector. Ground work isn't really my forte.' Doctor Chandur had opened the rear passenger seat and was easing herself into the vehicle. She smelled delightful. Jammy sod, Raven thought. He hadn't realised that Barber had it in him. He would have bet good money that his desperate infatuation would have simply put him on a fast track to both crashing and burning.

Barber jumped in the front and they pulled away. The rain was coming down in torrents and the wind was howling violently, making visibility on the road extremely limited. Raven was going as fast as he could without endangering themselves or others.

'So,' Raven briefly looked over at Barber, 'nice meal?' He was grinning from ear to ear.

'It was. It was very nice. Nice, wasn't it, Jasmine?' He was smiling like a child who had been given the best Christmas present ever.

'It was… pleasant. Look, I could get an Uber. I don't want to be an inconvenience.'

Raven looked at her in the rear-view mirror. She was certainly dressed to impress. 'It's not a problem, Doc. Just stay put in the vehicle with the doors locked. We've got two squad cars on their way so you will be very safe.'

'Does our contact think he's still there?' Barber was animated, anticipating the take down.

'He hasn't seen him leave but in these conditions who knows.' He swung the car around the corner and up a steep hill. The Chamberlain Estate was about three hundred yards down the other side of the hill and on the left.

The estate was a post-war series of terraced properties, mainly three-bedroom council houses built to accommodate the many families who worked on or around the dockyard. There was a small park area in the centre of a large crescent-shaped street, lined by forty or fifty of the two-storey buildings, many of which had fallen into various states of disrepair.

Despite the awful weather they could see kids hanging out by the children's play area, teenagers with pushbikes and hoodies. They were looking over at them. No matter how hard you tried to not look like a cop, he thought, you looked like a cop. There was simply no way round it. Raven thought it was probable that Davis' snitch was in amongst that lot, watching them watching him. Or her.

Number 36 had been vacant for around four months. Whoever had been using the building had been either squatting or using it as a base camp. Which meant that Raven and Barber didn't need a warrant.

'Like I said, Doc… Jasmine. Just stay here,' she nodded back at him. 'Barber, let's take this slow and steady. This guy is dangerous and the last thing the Chief needs is one of us coming back in a body bag.'

'No problem, Boss. I don't want that either.'

'And don't get trigger happy. I want this sicko alive and able to talk to us. Our two main priorities are to get Daisy out safely and this maniac back to the Station in cuffs.'

'Agreed.'

'The squad cars will be here in five minutes or so but I'm not waiting. Every second we leave him alone in there with Daisy is another second that he has the opportunity to do her harm or get away,' he looked Barber in the eyes, 'you ready?'

'I'm ready.'

'Then let's go.'

*

The front door was unlocked which was good because Raven wasn't planning on knocking. He pushed it slowly inward with his foot. Both he and Barber drew their weapons, standard issue Glock 17s, as they entered the dark downstairs hallway. The floor was littered with rubbish, cigarette boxes, chocolate bar wrappers, crushed beer cans and used condoms. There was a presence in the house. A sense of unease, of something or someone seeking to do them immeasurable harm.

Raven switched on his torch. The hallway was illuminated with a thin beam of blue/white LED light. Barber did the same.

Straight ahead was a set of stairs, to their right the front room. Beyond the stairs was a door into what he could only assume was the kitchen. He motioned to Barber to take the kitchen while he scanned the living room.

Raven paused briefly by the open door and then swung his right arm into the living space, his left hand holding his firing arm steady. He swung the torch around the room. There were the remains of a mattress, more rubbish, stains on the floor and walls. The front window was boarded up, but Raven could see where intruders had prised the boards away, just enough room to squeeze in and then push the boarding closed against the elements. There was no-one in the damp and dank room.

He walked back out into the hallway. Barber was walking back towards him shaking his head. The kitchen was also clear.

Raven motioned to the stairs. If there was anyone around they would have to be up there which was going to make their approach much more difficult. One creaky step and their location would be given away. Raven looked back towards the front door. He cursed. Where the hell were the squad cars? Thoughts of Daisy, Lisa and his soon-to-be son or daughter raced through his mind. How long had it been since he had anything to lose? Too long. Maybe as long as he could remember.

He took the first step. The stairs were bare, the carpet long since stripped away. He had to place his feet softly against the floor boards to avoid making any unwanted noise. The feeling of unease returned.

Again, litter lined every step. It always amazed Raven how quickly the vultures set in when properties vacated. How many families had lived there over the previous many decades? The walls must have borne witness to laughter, tears, anger, passion. All of the above. Mothers, fathers, siblings and grandparents all stepping their way through life's maze of complex relationships, intricate circumstances and difficult decisions. And now the house just sat dormant, a used up, empty shell full of haunted, faded memories and echoes of long-ago laughter and tears.

His mind returned to the image of Lisa lying in her hospital bed.

A noise emanated from the room above. A grunt, a scuffle maybe? He looked back at Barber who was looking up at him questioningly. Raven took another step, inadvertently kicking a disused can of Red Bull.

'Luke, up here!'

It was Daisy. Her call was followed by a scream and the sound of another scuffle.

Raven motioned to Barber and they made their move, taking the steps two at a time. They reached the upstairs landing area.

There were four doors up there, three bedrooms and a bathroom. Raven couldn't place where Daisy's call had come from so he motioned for Barber to take the two doors on the right. He would take the two on the left. It was dark, the gloom only pierced by the narrow beams of their flashlights. Raven didn't know whether to be relieved that Daisy was alive or afraid for her safety. The situation was precarious to say the least.

As he and Barber stood at the head of the stairs, he felt a chill run through him and a glimpse of a shape, a black shape. A shadow maybe, flitting before his eyes. He looked at Barber who was staring back at him, his eyes alert and focussed but struggling to hide the fear that was twisting a knot inside of him. Raven wondered whether he had seen it too, but he decided to shake it off and nodded to his partner.

He watched him as he slowly opened one of the doors. The bathroom, he thought, judging by the tiled floor. Barber walked inside. Raven turned and peered into the first door on his left. It was a bedroom, a small box-room with space for a single bed. The room had no furniture, the wallpaper was peeling away from the walls and the floor was bare. Again, the window was boarded up. There was a loft hatch above where the bed would have been, and it was half opened. Raven prayed that Daisy wasn't up there. Pulling themselves into a crammed loft space would add a whole new level of complexity to any potential takedown.

He backed out of the room just as Barber came out from the bathroom. Again, he shook his head. The bathroom was clear. Two rooms remained; one to the left and one to the right. Barber nodded and they both took their places. Raven held up his left hand and counted down with his fingers. Three... two... one.

They kicked open their respective doors and stepped in.

Raven walked into a black space. There was a bed with an old rickety frame and a rear window. There was a beaten-up wooden chair. But there were no people. He looked behind the door and what remained of the curtains. Nothing.

Which meant that....

He came out of the room quickly, meaning to cross the upstairs landing and leap into the room opposite, firearm drawn.

What he saw made him stop dead in his tracks.

At the top of the stairs was a tall black shape, its arm pulled tightly across the upper body of Daisy Reynolds. Her mouth was wide open in an expression of sheer terror mixed with stubborn defiance. The tall figure was wearing a black woollen hat with some kind of white, snowflake pattern, a long black parka coat.

Its pale face peered across at him with black, intensely focussed marble-like eyes.

'It's okay, Daisy, it's okay.'

She looked at him imploringly. She tried to wriggle free, but the tall figure had her in a strong hold. With a growing sense of realisation, Raven noticed the long knife held horizontally across Daisy's throat.

'I warned you, Raven. I warned you. Stay away. I sent you two clear messages and yet here you are. Exactly where I told you not to be.'

'Where's Barber?'

'If you mean your puppy dog, he's in there. You ought to teach your friends that if they keep poking a stick at a snake it's liable to bite.'

'Barber! Damian!'

The pale face laughed, amused, 'He won't answer you.'

There was a dark mass behind the white-faced figure, like a black cape enveloping the space above the stairs. Raven wondered whether it was a trick of the light, but it was unsettling. It looked like it was moving back and forth, perusing its surroundings and waiting for its turn, holding court while events unfolded. Raven blinked once, twice.

'You need to put the knife down and let her go.' Raven held his Glock firmly, fighting against the tremors that were rippling through his body. He had his gun aimed directly at what he could see of the white, ghostly mask but he knew he couldn't take the shot. If he missed, he was liable to hit Daisy.

'I don't think so, Raven. I think it's you who needs to lower their weapon. And quickly. Otherwise my hand might,' he made a slicing gesture, 'slip.'

'She's done nothing wrong here. Just let her go and we can work this out. She doesn't need to be harmed.'

'You know, she fucking cut me. She's really feisty. She's given me much more hassle than any of the others. You really know how to pick them, Raven. She stuck a pair of scissors in my fucking shoulder. She's lucky she's not dead already.'

Good girl, Raven thought. 'Listen, listen. I know, she's full of fight. I of all people should know that. You *know* I know that. But she is innocent in all of this. You don't need to hurt her. Just let her go.'

'Oh, I beg to differ. You see, you broke the terms of our deal. An eye for an eye. Any harm that comes to this young lady is all on you.'

Raven watched the black shadow as it curled its wispy, tendril-like fingers around the two figures in front of him. He shook his head, trying to re-focus.

'Not if you let her go. If you let her go now, I can talk to the authorities and they will be kind to you. They will take a more sympathetic look at your sentence.'

Pale face laughed. 'You think I'm going to let you bring me in? Is that how you really think this is going to play out? I don't think so. I really don't think so. I suggest that you lower that fucking gun before I cut this bitch's head off!'

Daisy thrashed around furiously and the knife nicked her neck. She let out a soft scream.

'Shoot this bastard, Raven. Shoot him in the fucking head!' She was crying, he had never seen her cry before. She looked younger, smaller, more vulnerable. But he couldn't take the shot. He couldn't be sure that he wouldn't hit her. He lowered his weapon.

'On the floor.'

He placed the Glock down on the bare boards, always keeping his eyes on the white face in front of him. The black eyes blinked three times. He stood up. 'Okay, now let her go.'

Pale face seemed to consider this but then snapped his head up sharply, 'I tell you what. Let's play a game.'

'A game?'

'Yes, a game. A game of fate.' He was smiling at Raven. The black shadow shook as if frustrated.

'What kind of game?'

'A quiz. One single question. You get the answer right, I let her go. You get it wrong; she dies.'

'I don't...'

'Just play the fucking game!'

Raven held his hands out in front of him as if surrendering, 'Okay, okay. I'll play.'

'I ask the question; you give me the answer. Only the first answer counts, Detective Inspector, so be careful.'

'Alright,' he looked at Daisy, re-assuring her with his eyes. She was deeply afraid but steadfastly defiant.

'You'll have ten seconds from the end of my question to answer it. Otherwise, well... you know.' He smiled a black, haunted smile. 'You got it?'

'Yes. I've got it.' The dark shadow was moving backwards and forwards behind the pale-faced figure. Raven thought it seemed impatient, agitated. What did it want? What was it? A figment of his fragile imagination? Was Raven losing what was left of his sanity?

'Mmm. Let me think. Questions, questions. Got to make sure I pick a good... okay, got it.' He smiled, a black toothed, sneering smile, 'It's a good one,' the white-faced figure peered across at Raven, its black eyes and hateful stare filling Raven with a sense of foreboding and tragedy. But there was something else. A sadness. A reluctance maybe. Or a fear. A fear of the thing that was watching him like a master watching its young student. This is crazy, Raven thought. He was providing the shadow with an identity, a personality.

Pale face spoke in a low, deliberate voice. Raven took a deep breath. 'It can be said that some things improve when they are dead. Maybe the same could be said of you and your Inspector,' the figure stared at Raven with confused malevolence, 'tell me this. What stinks of filth while it is living but in death smells delicious?' Pale face smiled, pleased with himself. This was... amusing him.

Raven gasped. What the hell was this? Was he gambling Daisy's life on some kind of kid's riddle? It was ludicrous. 'I don't get it...'

'Ten.'

'Wait, wait. Let's play another game, this is...'

'Nine.'

'This is crazy!'

'Eight.'

Raven looked at Daisy. Her mouth was set in a hard grimace. She was steeling herself for what was about to come.

The shadow was rippling, fizzing with intensity. It was excited.

'Seven.'

Raven thought hard about the riddle. He had never been good at that kind of thing. He wracked his brains and frantically considered what the lunatic could be referring to? Something related, something to do with their situation. Murder, blood, women, girls, knives…

'Six.'

The house smelt bad but that couldn't be it. A house couldn't die. Could it? The air, the town, the streets… 'Five.'

It was hopeless. He didn't have a clue. Food? Maybe food.

The shadow observed, expectant, elated.

'Four.'

What smelt wonderful when it was cooked? Spices, mum's home cooking. What smelt of filth when it was alive?

'Three.'

Daisy was crying, sobbing. Trying to turn her head away, away from the sharp edge of the knife. He had to think of something. The room was getting darker and darker. Oppressive and menacing.

'Two.'

He thought of roast dinners. Sunday roast. Roast chicken. Roast beef.

Roast… pork. Bacon. Why was it so fucking dark in there?

'One.'

'I've got it!' Sweat was pouring from his forehead, his heart was racing. The figure looked at him curiously. The gloom lifted suddenly.

'And your answer?'

'Pigs! It's pigs! They're filthy when alive but smell great when cooked, when they're fucking dead!' He was elated and angry all at the same time, 'It's a cheap fucking wisecrack at us, isn't it? A cheap joke at the police, at the very people who are trying to stop you! Stop the killing! A tacky riddle to gamble away a young woman's life!'

The expression on the pale face changed from anger to surprise. But he was smiling. Pleased perhaps that Raven had got it right. Maybe, Luke pondered, just maybe he didn't want to kill her after all. Perhaps this was all just a play. The black shadow lifted itself to the ceiling, ready for its escape, the battle seemingly lost. Pale faces' grip on Daisy started to slip. His right arm loosened, and his left hand moved the knife a centimetre or two away from Daisy's trembling throat.

And then Daisy Reynolds made the last and greatest mistake of her young adult life. She had obviously sensed the relaxation in her captor's grip and sought to seize her moment. She let out a loud cry and brought her left foot up hard behind her and into her assailant's groin.

A little to her right and she might have gotten lucky. A hard enough crack there and he was sure to go down in a crumpled heap. But she was too far to the left and she caught more thigh than testicle and whilst Raven was sure that it would have hurt, she was no wilting lily after all, it didn't hurt enough to prevent what happened next. Pale face cried out in furious rage, gripped Daisy hard around the chest, raised his left hand that had a hold of the knife and plunged it deep into her upper torso.

The darkness of the room returned, seeping out of the walls, and covering them all in black syrupy fog. Raven felt the bottom drop out of him, his heart raced, his vision swam.

'NOOOO!'

Pale face turned and then fled, taking the stairs three at a time with his long, lumbering strides. Daisy tumbled behind him, spinning backwards down the steep staircase, bouncing off each step like a terrible rag doll and coming to rest at the bottom, her head propped up against the alcove wall. Raven saw all of it in slow motion, like an action replay on the television. It was as if he wasn't there, like he was observing events from a world away.

The door slammed and the dark matter disappeared. Raven snapped himself back into consciousness and raced down after her. She was still breathing, but her neck was bent at an acutely crooked angle, the knife still jutting from her chest.

Blood was bubbling at her lips.

'Daisy, I...'

'Luke, it's okay.'

'Just lay there, don't talk. Just rest. We'll get you to the hospital and...'

'It's okay. You've been good to me. We had some fun, didn't we?' Blood was trickling down her chin and onto her chest. Her breathing was short, and ragged. Her speech was thin, whispered.

Raven laughed, a tearful, melancholic laugh. 'We did. We sure did. I'm sorry if I ever hurt you Daisy. I'm so s...'

'We had fun. You and me,' her eyes started to close and then sharply opened, her pupils dilating, 'look after Mum. Please. Look after Mum...'

'I will. I promise. But I won't have to. Because we'll get you to the...'

'And look after Lis....'

Daisy let out a long breath, her body relaxed, her eyes closed, and her head tilted. She was gone. Raven cradled her in his arms, brushed a hand through her choppy blonde hair and kissed her forehead.

A few seconds later the door crashed inwards.

Chapter 53: Back Home

'Is she here?'

'Of course she's here, but...'

'Get out of my fucking way'

Tony pushed his brother aside with a force hard enough to send him clattering against the hallway wall. Mitchell let out a shout of admonishment, but Tony didn't hear it. He was hell-bent on an audience with his mother. He sped through the house, across the dining room in a few long, determined strides and into the sunlit conservatory.

Which was empty.

'Where is she?'

'I'm not telling you. Not when you're in this...'

Tony turned and grabbed his brother by his collar.

'I've not mentioned it and I won't. I don't know why you've been trying to poison me, Mitchell, or what I could have possibly done to make you want to harm me, but I'm letting it go. I've got more important things on my mind. So, you either tell me where she is or I'm going to find her. I really don't care.'

Mitchell stared at Tony, his hatred and brotherly love mixed with a cold, weary despondence. 'So, you found him, did you? You went to him?'

Tony relaxed his grip. 'What did you think I was going to do?'

'Let it lie. Come to terms with it and move on. If you had any sense that's what you would have done. What you *should* have done'

Tony stared him down, 'Well we're not the same are we. I'd rather know…know who in my fucked up family was telling me the truth and who was selling me a truck load of horse shit.'

Mitchell smoothed out his shirt, 'And have you decided?'

Tony smiled at him, 'I have.' They exchanged stares, 'Now where is she?' Mitchell nodded to the upstairs bedrooms. 'You hurt her, and I'll kill you.'

'Give me a break, Mitchell,' he waved his brother away, 'I think we've all been hurt enough already.'

*

She was lying in her queen size, four-poster bed, the drapes pulled back so that she had a good view out of the large bay window overlooking the rear of the house. He could see the top of the weeping willow from where he stood, waving him a weary 'good day'. The window was lifted open slightly to let the outside air in, a soft breeze caressing the gently rippling net curtains.

She was propped on several large pillows, the bed sheets pulled up to just beneath her withering breasts. She had a breathing mask around her mouth and nose, a long tube attached to an assisted breathing apparatus by the side of the bed. He could hear her wheezing, laboured breath above the sound of the birdsong and mid-day traffic from outside. Her eyes were closed. She looked so old, so unlike the strong, dismissive woman of his formative years. He stood there for several minutes, staring at her, her body motionless aside from the up and down movement of her chest as she struggled to breathe in and out, in and out.

'You're back.' Her voice was muffled from beneath the mask. She lifted a hand and pulled it up over her head and placed it down by her side. 'I thought that we had seen the last of you after you walked out during our last encounter.' She coughed, a loud phlegmy hack. She lifted a tissue, spat into it and placed it onto a tray on the bedside table. The tray was full of disused tissues.

'That was my plan.'

'Then why change it?'

'Things have… happened.'

She looked him up and down, her face impassive. 'What kind of things?'

'Admissions. Facts have become clear to me.'

She looked at him curiously. 'Had I not made them clear before?'

'Depends on your perspective.'

She motioned for him to take a seat by the foot of the bed. 'Sit down, Anthony. You are making the room look untidy.'

He sat on a wooden, cushioned stool, the same stool he had sat upon gingerly many times as a child. He folded his hands in front of him, still feeling like a young boy being scolded for some adolescent caper but fighting to hide the rage and angst that burnt like an inflamed ulcer in his belly.

She took a sip from a glass of water. 'So, tell me, my boy, what is this perspective that you are referring to?'

'I went to see him.'

'Who?'

'My father.'

She looked surprised, maybe a little flustered. 'Really?'

'Yes.'

'How can you be sure that this man was your father?'

'I had it on good information.'

She cursed under her breath, 'your brother.'

'Yes, Mitchell told me,' he was shaking with nervous anger, 'and… and is that such a bad thing? If you had told me all of this before then I wouldn't be feeling so… so messed up right now.'

'You have no idea why I hid this from you.'

'No… no I don't. I have no idea. None at all. So… so why don't you educate me?'

She picked up another tissue and coughed into it, this time a cough that seemed to tear something loose from inside of her. By the time she had finished hacking, her eyes were streaming with tears and her face was flushed, her body shaking. He fought the urge to go over to her and help her, to comfort her.

After a moment to compose herself she placed the tissue in the tray and looked up at him. She fought to get her words out from within her dry and ragged vocal cords. 'I did it for you.'

He laughed, his laughter created from a concoction of sarcasm, anger and self-pity. 'You did it for me. For me! What a fucking joke.' He stood up and walked to the window.

'Language, Anthony.'

'I think the foul mouth of your son... I am your son, aren't I? Yes, that's right. I am. I forget. You see I have heard so many different versions of this that I forget which one is correct,' he smirked, 'in any case, my foul mouth is the last thing you ought to be concerned about, mother.'

'And what is it that I ought to be concerned about... *son?*'

Tony looked out of the window, gazed down onto the overgrown garden; the lime green, cast-iron patio furniture, now old and rusty, the kettle barbeque that they would use once in a blue moon when the sun was high in the sky and his mother's mood was equally elevated, the shed where he would camp out of an evening, smoking cigarettes and drinking his mother's expensive scotch, the willow tree where he would hide. He spoke slowly, deliberately, 'the truth.'

His mother reached out and grabbed a packet of cigarettes, opened it, drew one out with her white, calloused fingers and placed it between her dry, cracked lips. She lit it, inhaled and blew out a long plume of yellowish smoke. 'And what version of the truth did your father tell you?'

'Well let's just say that it was not the same as yours.'

She flicked ash into an empty cup and smiled at him, 'Hardly surprising, is it?'

'Maybe so. But quite convincing.'

'Let me guess,' she took another drag and the smoke cascaded from her mouth and nose while she spoke, 'he told you that I went to him, that the sex was consensual. That there was no rape, *of course* there was no rape, it was all a figment of my imagination. That I was under some kind of spell, that I idolised him like some kind of god and that I gave myself to him willingly.'

'Something like that.'

'That he didn't even know you existed. That I kept the pregnancy from him, that I stole his son, his only child and heir, away from him through some twisted, cruel act of spite brought on by the fact that he spurned me after our one night of passion.'

'Yes, but....'

'And that my resentment towards you was borne out of my intense and misguided hatred for him. That I hated him for the fact that he didn't want me, couldn't make himself love me and that he had moved on and *I couldn't.*'

Tony turned to her from the window, his face a mask of uncertainty and defiance.

'And did you?'

'Resent you?'

'Yes.'

'Yes, I did.'

He sat on the wide sill of the bay window. The sunlight was behind him, his face and body becoming a shadowed, hazy and emotionless figurine.

'He told me about what he did, about who he is. About what you believed.'

She flicked ash from her cigarette. 'And what exactly was that?'

'He told me about his power.'

She started to laugh, a laugh that turned into a wheezy, raspy cough. She doubled up on the bed, coughing into her pillow. When it subsided, she grabbed a hold of her breathing mask and breathed in and out several times, dragging much needed oxygen into her collapsing lungs. She then placed the mask back down and turned to him. 'He still believes in all of that... that whimsy I presume.'

'He does.'

'And do you?'

'I don't know. He said that he's going to…teach me.'

Her face darkened. Her eyes narrowed and her brow furrowed. 'Stay away from him, Anthony. What he will tell you is… dangerous.'

Now it was his turn to laugh. 'In what way? In what way is it dangerous, mother? Is it any more dangerous than a broken family full of secrecy and lies?'

Her eyes did not shift, 'Much more dangerous. Far more dangerous than you could ever imagine.'

'I don't know. I'm an author of fiction remember. I've got a pretty good imagination.'

'Don't kid yourself, son. This is a power far greater than even your fertile brain could conjure up. It will get inside of you and twist like a knife in your intestines. It will infect you like a venom, like a disease. It will…'

Tony leapt up, 'Oh, for *fucks sake*! Will you stop with the horseshit! How can I believe anything that comes out of your mouth? It's been lies after lies after LIES!' He swiped his arm across the dresser angrily, jewellery boxes, ornamental figurines and photograph frames flying across the room and smashing on the floor and against the walls.

His mother sat up in her bed. 'How dare you!'

He looked at her coldly. 'Oh… I'm sorry. Did I… did I damage one of your precious photos? Did I sour one of your happy memories? Did I once again bring shame on our family?'

He bent down and picked up several photographs, their frames cracked and hanging awkwardly. 'Let's see now…' he threw one back to the ground, 'nope, not in that one,' he took a step towards the bed and threw another, this time against the wall, 'no…not in that one either.' He moved closer to her, again throwing a photograph towards the door, 'Can't see me in that one. In fact, there must be some kind of mistake,' his tone was caustic, ironic, 'I'm not in any of these, mother. Not one. Not even one tiny picture of little ole' Anthony in his rolled-up shorts and dirty T shirt.' He bent down and stared into her haggard, lonely eyes. 'Now I would say that's a little hurtful.' He took her cigarette from her bony fingers and crushed it out, 'wouldn't you?'

She hissed at him, her voice hoarse and full of bile, 'You have always been a hateful boy and here you are, at my end, at my last days, pouring more hatred and villainy onto this family. Get out. Get out. GET OUT!'

She lunged forward in her bed and clawed at his face, pulling at his hair and his shirt. She was coughing and wheezing, her eyes red with furious rage and despair.

He grabbed her by her cold and bony skull and threw her back against the head board. She screamed a loud guttural scream, her cough becoming more wretched, her body in a spasm. She was waving her arms at him vigorously, gesturing wildly for him to go, to leave her.

'Gladly.'

He left the room, descended the stairs two at a time and reached for the front door. Mitchell grabbed him by his shoulders from behind.

'You couldn't do it, could you?'

Tony answered without turning, his mouth drawn down in bitter contempt. He was fighting to control his swirling, acidic emotions. 'Do what?'

'Let her see it out without any more upset. Any more drama!' Tony grunted, shrugged him off and opened the door.

It was the last time he would see his mother alive.

Chapter 54: The Break Up

'It's me.' She spoke softly, barely audible.

'I know. Your number comes up on my phone.'

'Yeah, yeah. True. Sorry. Well, you know. We need to talk.'

'About what?'

'What do you mean about what? About this... this situation.'

'Oh. You mean you walking out?'

'Yes. No. Well... yes. I guess.'

'Well, what's to say?'

'We need to sort out some things. Some logistical things.'

'Logistics? Logistics? You walk out on our relationship, our lives, our bloody history and you think that the issue is in the logistics?'

There was a pause. He could hear her breathing, steadying herself.

'I don't mean to be heartless.'

'I know. I know,' he bit down on his bottom lip. 'Are you coming home?'

'Tony...'

'Well, are you?'

'Tony, I need to get my things.'

'Why?'

'What do you mean why?'

'Why do you need to get your things? They're right where you need them. In our house. In our home. *Our home.* Not my home. Not your home. *Ours.*'

Again, a pause. An empty, chasm of silence between them. A vacuum.

'Not anymore.'

Tony grabbed the steering wheel hard with his right hand. His nails dug into the soft, plastic overlay leaving deep, curved ravines.

'So that's it?'

'I just can't go on like this.'

'Like what?'

'You're so distant. Like you're not there anymore.'

'I'm here. I've always been here.'

'Physically yes. But not emotionally. We've... we've grown apart. Times change. People move on.'

'Have you?'

'Have I what?'

'Moved on.' He spat these words out, fighting to hold himself together. He felt a tear leak from the corner of one eye but swiftly wiped it away with the back of his hand.

She paused. He could hear the cogs of her mind whirring.

'I need my stuff.'

'Then come and get it.'

'I don't want to do it while you're there.'

'Then text me when you're ready and I'll make myself scarce.'

'Okay. Okay, I'll do that.' He could hear the relief pouring from her.

'Will I see you again?'

'Eventually, yes. Yes, of course. But not right now. It's too... too raw.'

'I could change you know.'

'No, you can't.'

'You're probably right. I still love you, Jane.'

She sniffed loudly down the phone. His lip trembled and he bit down hard.

'I loved you, Tony. I really, really did. I just…I just don't know that I do anymore.'

The past tense. God, he hated the past tense. It was like an ice pick in his heart. He gripped the steering wheel hard. He did not want this to get emotional, irrational and fought the welling of grief from within him.

'Well. You can't change how you feel. If it's gone, it's gone. I'll… I'll get over it.'

'What will you do about the rent?'

'I'll sort it.'

'But you can't afford it.'

'I'll sort it, Jane. I'll figure it out. Work some more shifts at the bar or something. You never know, maybe this novel thing will work out.'

'I hope so, Tony. I really do.'

'I know.'

Another pause, both of them considering how to end the conversation.

'Anyway,' he took a breath to control himself, 'you didn't answer me.'

'What do you mean?'

'I asked you a question and you didn't answer. Dodged it like a skilled politician actually.'

'Did I?'

'Yep. Sure did.'

'What was the question?'

'Have you… moved on? Is there… someone else?'

A long pause. An awkward pause. A suspicious pause.

'No.'

'Are you sure?'

'Of course I am. I'm not that... that kind of person.'

'I can take it you know.'

'I know. But there isn't'

'I might understand if you...'

'There isn't.'

'Okay.'

'I... I've got to go.'

'Okay.'

'I'll text you when I'm coming over.'

'Okay.'

'Tony?'

'Yes?'

'Don't hate me.'

'I don't.'

'I want to be friends when the dust has settled.'

'Me too.'

'That's good. That's really good.'

She breathed deeply, he could hear it down the phone line, bouncing off some lonely satellite orbiting the planet in a cold, dark void. He wondered if this call was being listened to by some random employee of the secret service, eavesdropping with some amusement as the bottom of his world fell away from beneath him. But that was the thing with a phone call wasn't it, he mused. You didn't ever get the full picture with only one of the senses in play. You could hear what was going on, but you couldn't see it, smell it, touch it. Couldn't see what he was seeing.

'Bye Tony.'

'Bye Jane.'

He hung up.

She looked beautiful. As pretty as ever. God, he loved her in her gym clothes. He had to admit; her body had really toned up since she had been going to spin class. He had noticed it; everyone had noticed it and she had changed both physically and emotionally. But the length of the car park was between them and it may as well have been the whole universe. He couldn't touch her.

But *he* could, he thought as he ran a hand through his hair, his nails digging shallow crevices into his skull. Nick could. Fucking Nick.

Tony watched as the smarmy son of a bitch put an arm around her waist and opened the passenger door of his BMW 3 Series. She smiled at him, touching his cheek tenderly as she got in. Nick closed the door behind her, a smile of smug satisfaction reaching from ear to ear. He was clearly pleased that he had destroyed Tony's world. Tony resisted the urge to turn the ignition, floor the accelerator and run right over the prick. But he held back. His time would come.

His time would definitely come.

Chapter 55: The Aftermath

Raven took a long, yearning draw on his hip flask. The cold, acidic liquid burned satisfyingly as it slipped down his gullet, the warmth growing in his belly like a wildfire as it spread throughout his bladder and intestines. It was like air to him. Like the sweetest spring water.

It wasn't that he wanted it. He needed it. Needed it now more than ever.

He leaned back in the car seat and shut his eyes. He blew out a long, tired breath fermented with single malt scotch and cheeseburger and rubbed his face with the stained palm of his hand. Dried blood caked his fingers and forearm. He had helped lift Daisy's corpse up onto the gurney and she had still been warm. If it wasn't for the blood, so much blood, he could have believed she was simply sleeping, just taking a nap. He had envisioned her sitting up and putting her arms around him, kissing him lightly on the cheek. He would have given anything for that moment, just one more tender moment with her. He had burdened her pretty soul with so much angst, so much unrest. It was all so unnecessary. She hadn't deserved this. The guilt hung around his neck like a heavy weight. He knew that he would carry that with him, like a deep scar, for the rest of his life. He took another swig from his flask and wiped a tear from his cheek.

He looked out at the scene before him. There were several squad cars, crime scene units, an ambulance, dozens and dozens of officers and squaddies. He looked beyond the cordoned off area and could see reporters from newspapers and television, all streaming the day's latest tragedy around the country on internet wavebands that delivered the gore, the drama and the tears straight into the living rooms and the hand-held devices of the masses. The glossy faces of the TV networks all beaming sun-kissed smiles into their virtual world of digital imagery and typography, 4K high definition pictures of their beautifully prepared facades providing detailed renditions of the tragedy at Silver Birch Crescent earlier that evening. He imagined families watching events unfold while they ate their supper, people returning from work on the train, watching it on their iPhones and PDAs, drivers in their cars listening to the news updates on their DAB radios. They would make assumptions, form opinions (often unjustified) and interpret in their own personal way what had happened that fateful night and who was to blame. They would judge those involved; the murderer, the girl, the authorities, the police, the officer in charge. And, he contemplated, could he blame them for pointing the finger? What plan did he have? Where was he going with this? He had had the guy in his grasp twice now and both times he had let him slip away.

It was beyond him. He was in way too deep. Way over his head. People in his life were suffering because of his failings, his basic inability to close it down. They were no closer. Nowhere near catching the guy and now he was seeing things. Weird things. Shadows. Creatures. Dead people. His mind was a mash of images and memories, emotions and creations, details and confusion. He was losing it.

He looked at his flask, inhaled from the neck, and then screwed the top back on. Perhaps his days of heavy drinking were catching up on him. God knew he had been chasing the devil hard for a long, long time. He didn't know why, or even when it had started, but once that demon had gotten his hooks into him, he had been a tough little bugger to shake off.

But then again, he mused, perhaps it wasn't that at all. Perhaps, just perhaps, he was simply headed for the scrap heap like so many before him. Over the hill and sliding down the other side like a kid on an oily sledge. His dad had always said to him that you had to watch out for those behind you, the people that wanted what you had. Because they would catch you fast. They were a lot quicker and fitter than you and you had to use your wits to out-manoeuvre them. Your cunning and your guile. You needed to be prepared to do whatever it took. *Whatever* it took. Because if you didn't and one of them got their hand on your shoulder and pulled you back? Well then, that was your time done son.

'I'm sorry about the girl, Raven. I know that you two were close.'

'Yeah. Thanks Chief.'

Chief Simmonds had leaned into his car. Raven shoved the flask between his seat and the centre console and pushed it out of sight with his foot.

'You need to see the counsellor?'

'What? No. No, I'm fine. I'm fine. I'll shake it off. I just wish I could have saved her. Maybe if I'd gotten here sooner, made some different choices. I don't know. Maybe I should have taken the shot.'

'You did all you could,' the Chief put a hand on his shoulder, 'you can't blame yourself. This maniac was hell-bent on killing someone tonight and, unfortunately, he did what he set out to do. Nothing you could have done.'

Raven pulled himself out from the car and shut the door, encapsulating the sour odour of whiskey and desperation in its upholstered cocoon. 'How's Damo?'

'He's okay. A knock to the head but it was too far from his brain to hurt. His pride's a little dented but he'll get over it.'

'And our guy?'

'He got away. Took off down a side street,' the Chief shook his head, 'sure has a good pair of heels on him. It's like he just vanishes into thin air.' He rubbed a hand across his five o' clock shadow and frowned, 'but listen, the guys are questioning everyone in the area. If anyone saw anything, I'm sure we'll find out soon enough. And then we'll go get this son of a bitch.'

Raven looked at the blood on his hands, his arms and his shirt. Daisy's lifeblood, her essence, her vitality. He wondered whether that was all that she had left behind for him. Her blood. Blood that could be washed away like so many faded memories. He couldn't let that be true. He just couldn't.

'Boss, I spoke to Jas. We might have something.' Barber, his head wrapped in a bloodied bandage, had pushed his way past the crime scene team and was standing behind Raven.

'Damo. You look terrible.' Raven put an arm on his shoulder, 'You took a nasty hit there.'

Barber looked at the floor. Raven could see the embarrassment in his eyes, the regretful shame. His cheeks were flushed, and his lips pursed tightly together. 'I'm sorry, boss. So sorry. I shouldn't have got caught cold like that. My hot head got the better of me.'

'It's okay, it's okay. You had no way of knowing, you did the best you could. It was a difficult situation, kid. You were there for her and she knew that.' There was a moment of silent contemplation between them.

Raven looked over at the reporters and didn't hide a sneer as he watched the Mayor holding court. It was, he thought, as if the guy had some kind of media GPS or something. The bloke just couldn't resist an opportunity, no matter how grotesque. Raven's unsettled stomach turned.

'Barber, you should be in an ambulance. You're concussed.' The Chief whistled to one of the male nurses.

'I'm okay, Chief. Seriously. It's just a knock.' He turned to Raven. 'Look, I spoke to Jasmine. She was in the back of your car, remember?'

What? The Chief spun on them. Raven winced like a stray dog about to take a beating. Why, he inwardly cursed, did Barber have to mention that in front of the Chief? 'You brought a civilian to a takedown? Do you know how many code of conduct rules and regulations that violates? Jesus, Luke. Are you kidding me?' The Chief's face was red with rage.

'Dave, Dave. It's okay. She was parked down the street. She was nowhere near the scene.'

'She was in your bloody car, Raven! What if the killer had…what if she had… Jesus bloody Christ. You'd better keep this to yourselves you two or the Mayor will have my balls in a vice.'

'Well that's just it, Chief,' Barber was visibly excited, 'I don't know that we can.'

'What do you mean, Barber?' The Chief looked from Barber to Raven and back again, 'Come on, spit it out. And you'd better make it good.' He was leering across at Barber like an angry bear, claws drawn and ready to pounce.

'She saw him come out of the building. She was in the back of the car and he ran past her. Even looked in the car at her.'

Raven's jaw dropped. 'He saw her? Did he harm her? Is she okay?' The Chief shook his head, his mouth agape and his face flushed.

'No, no. I mean, yes. She's fine,' Barber smiled reassuringly, 'he just turned and ran off.'

'Well thank God for that.' Raven couldn't help but feel that they had just dodged a bullet.

'Yeah, but you haven't heard the best part.' Barber was jumping up and down on the spot like he needed to pee.

'There's a best part? Oh, I hope that there's a best part, because the rest of it is pretty bloody awful.' Chief Simmonds looked like he was on the verge of cardiac arrest.

Barber paused for dramatic effect.

'She thinks she knows him.'

Chapter 56: Contemplation

He wasn't proud of that. That had not gone according to plan. Something had gone wrong. He hadn't intended to kill her. The Detective had forced his hand and he had acted swiftly, mercilessly and a little irrationally.

Now he had lost his bargaining power and that was not good. And what about the girl? The girl in the car. He had thought about grabbing her as collateral, but something had stirred in his memory. She had felt it too. They knew each other but neither could remember how, he knew that much. He had been frantically wracking his brains ever since. If she knew him, she would have to be dealt with and quickly.

He wouldn't let anything get in the way of obtaining his prize. No, not when he was so close.

He had promised him that when this was all done, he would get what it was that he so desired. What he needed. What he had to have. It was an aching inside of him that tore at the very fabric of his being.

His shoulder hurt. He had come home and washed the deep slash with antiseptic. He had cried out as the cleansing solution attacked the naked, raw flesh. He hadn't lost a lot of blood, but the wound was red and sore. But it would heal. All wounds healed eventually.

What to do next? It was a delicate situation. One wrong move and everything would come undone, like the stitches on an old wound.

Everything would unravel.

He could kill the Detective, but one Detective could easily be replaced by another. And he liked this one. He knew all about him. Every little precious detail. And he should. They had known each other for such a long time. He could use that. Use his weaknesses against him. They had a bond.

He could kill the kid. But what would that achieve? One dumb copper. Who would care?

He could go back for the woman, the one who'd had the cat. He hadn't enjoyed killing the animal. Not one of his finer moments. And she would have twenty-four-hour protection now. He had shown his hand and they would act on it. The D.I. wouldn't let lightning strike twice, now would he?

No. There was only one solution to his problem, and it was staring him in the face while he watched events unfold on the TV. It was obvious. He stared transfixed by the evening news, the bright LCD screen illuminating his gravely, ashen features. He knew what to do. And when it was done, he would have everything he wanted. *He* had promised him.

Chapter 57: Date with a Mate

I hadn't meant for it to happen. You probably don't believe that and I'm sure that you think badly of me. I can see it in your eyes. Maybe, maybe I caused all of this. Maybe it's all my fault. But I'm not a bad person, really, I'm not. You can ask my family. My friends. I am a good person with a good heart.

He changed; you have to see that. He was different. And I suppose I had changed to, I needed something more. Emotionally. And Nick was there for me.

Since that day at the gym I couldn't get him out of my mind. I had felt something that day. Jealousy maybe. I'd never been a jealous person before, so the feeling was brand new to me. Tony had had lots of female friends and I had never resented him for that, never held a grudge against any other woman for talking to my boyfriend, so the feelings I had that day had really taken me aback. I was... confused.

After the argument with Tony I had moved back in with my mum. She had never really liked Tony anyway, she thought he was a waste of space, and so I knew that she would welcome me back with open arms. I felt guilty. I had always defended Tony vehemently to her and now there I was, sleeping with the enemy. But I had nowhere else to go and I knew it wouldn't be permanent. I was absolutely convinced that we would sort something out.

When I had turned up for work the next day it was almost as if the news of my break up with Tony (if that's what it was, I didn't really know at the time) was public knowledge, like someone had posted an infomercial on the notice-board at the school – guess what, Jane is now available! The kids were looking at me through warm, sympathetic eyes that only five to ten-year-olds have. 'Aaah, has miss chucked her boyfriend? Never mind, you can always come and play hop scotch with us.'

I remember going to make myself a coffee at break. God, I needed the caffeine. I felt like I had been turned upside down, shaken violently and all the ingredients of my life had fallen out of my pockets and been scattered all over the staffroom floor.

'You look awful.' Jemima was all over me like paparazzi around royalty. She hugged me tightly and kissed my forehead. 'How's things with Tony?'

'Awful. I think this is definitely it, Jem. I think it's over.'

She waved her hand dismissively, 'Give it time, Jane. It's probably just one of those things. A few days from now and it will probably all blow over. You've made your point and if he's too dumb to get it then you're probably better off without him.'

'I'm not sure I'd go back even if he did.'

Jemima rested herself on the arm of a chair. 'Sounds serious.'

I sipped my coffee, hugging the cup like my life depended on it. 'I think it is.'

'You've got a lot of history, you two.'

'I know. But that's just it, isn't it? All we've got now is history. It's in the past. I think all of our good times, our best times, are behind us.'

I wanted to cry but held myself together. Crying at work wasn't the done thing and I didn't want the kids or other staff members to see. The room was filling up with teachers and TAs and the school was a hotbed for gossip and rumour mongering. I didn't want to be on the list of that week's dramas, controversies and scandals.

Issy wandered over.

'Well if it isn't the spin class world champ. Look at those tight buns.' Jemima wiggled her bum like Iggy Azalea in a music video.

'Okay, okay. That's enough. I'm sure next time one of you two will take the trophy home.' Issy's face was flushed red, almost a permanent fixture for our demure friend.

'I don't know if I'm going back,' I poured the remaining contents of my cup into the sink. 'I think my spinning days are over.'

'That might be for the best, Jane,' Jemima was smiling, 'I mean, if you're going to lie down on the job like that every week it could get embarrassing for Issy and I.'

'Oh, ha bloody ha,' I gently slapped her on the shoulder, 'I just don't think I'm the exercising type.'

'Sure you are, Jane-o!' Nick breezed into the room with his usual mixture of pizazz and fireworks, 'We all are,' he held his arms out as if to say *look at me*. 'Everyone needs to grunt and groan a little bit. How else would we get tone-tastic?' He pumped his hands on his flat stomach rhythmically.

Jemima giggled like a little girl and Issy's blush turned from pastel pink to an odd shade of violet.

'You all okay? It feels like I've walked in on a private discussion. You been talking about me?' He laughed but a genuinely concerned look spread like a blush across his usually beaming and ultra-confident face. 'Did I...did I miss something?'

I looked at the girls, squinting my eyes and softly shaking my head. I didn't want my business out in the public domain so my attempt at sign language was simply me saying 'keep it to yourselves.' But, love her as I do, Jem's never been one to keep her mouth shut.

'Jane and Tony are going through a bit of a rough patch.' Issy kicked her in the ankle and Jemima yelled at her, 'Ow. What was that for?'

Issy rolled her eyes, 'I don't think Jane wants that to be broadcast around the school, Jem. Honestly.'

'Well sorry for breathing. Jeez.'

'It's okay you two. It's not a problem. Just keep it amongst the four of us. Definitely don't tell that lot,' I pointed at a couple of the younger TAs.

Nick was standing silently, seemingly dumbfounded. His hands were shoved deep into his pockets and he was looking from Jemima to Isobelle to me, his mouth open. He turned to face me.

'I'm really, really sorry to hear that, Jane. That truly is sad, sad news.' He touched my arm and stupidly my heart skipped a little, 'How are you... holding up?'

I felt my cheeks getting warm, 'I'm... I'm okay, I guess.'

'Is it permanent?'

'I don't know... maybe.'

The four of us fell silent. I could hear the hustle and bustle of the other staff mulling over the morning's events at school; teachers discussing the syllabus, which kids were doing well, what to do about the naughty ones, had they heard about the parents of little Billy Thorpe etc. The world around me seemed to swim. I could see Jemima smiling at me with her wink-wink, nudge-nudge grin, Issy looking at me like a parent looking at a sickly child, Nick bearing down on me, the corners of his mouth twitching, his eyes like those of a sad puppy. I wasn't stupid. I knew this was what he had wanted to hear.

He put a hand on each of my shoulders, gripped them gently, and looked me deeply in the eyes. I could smell mint on his breath and the warm scent of his aftershave. 'You look distraught, Jane. You look...you look like you need cheering up, doesn't she girls?'

Jemima and Isobelle silently nodded.

Nick snapped his head to the side as if he had just come up with the world's best idea. 'Tell you what. I've got a friend who runs a beautiful Italian restaurant in town. He does the best seafood tagliatelle I have ever tasted,' he grinned at the three of us, 'it's just what you need, Jane. A good hearty meal and maybe a glass of expensive red wine.'

'I don't know Nick, I...'

'Nonsense. Of course you do. This is exactly what you need. You agree, Jem, Issy, don't you?'

They both nodded, smiling.

'Pick you up at seven thirty?'

'I... I guess...'

'Your mum's place. Over at West Street, yes?'

'Yes, I…' I had no idea how he knew where my mother lived. Or even that I was living there.

'Good, it's agreed then. Seven thirty at your mum's and I'll take us down to Giovanni's for a bite to eat. My treat. Don't worry, I won't keep you out too late. We have school in the morning after all,' he laughed, 'you won't regret it, Jane. You'll come out of there feeling like a celebrity.'

I felt like I'd just stepped off of a high-speed merry go round.

'Okay, sounds… sounds good. I guess.'

'Good, good. Must get back to class. The little urchins won't teach themselves now, will they? See you later, Janey. Jem, Issy…' They both fluttered their hands as he walked out.

Issy looked at me, 'You sure you're okay with this, Jane? Looked to me like you were railroaded into that a bit.'

Jemima waved her off, 'Don't be silly, Issy. Where's the harm? A free dinner, good company and a ride there and back. What more could you ask for?'

I was so unsure. I wondered whether Issy was right. Maybe he had pushed me a little harder than he should. But then, he was a good friend and it wasn't as if it was a date. It wasn't a date. It was just an innocent rendezvous really. A meal with a mate.

I wasn't doing anything wrong, was I?

'This does mean one thing, however,' Jemima placed her cup on the counter and picked up her folder.

'What's that,' I asked.

'Gypsy tart is definitely off the menu.'

*

That had been the start of it really. We had a great night that night. He treated me like a lady. He was smart, sophisticated, he had money. I felt spoilt. He really laid it on thick but with real class. If it had been pre-planned he had planned it meticulously, there was no doubt about that and I'm afraid that like a dumb fish in a small pond I had been hooked.

We didn't kiss that night, but we did agree to meet again. I was still wracked with guilt over the break up with Tony but half of me had moved on already. I don't know, maybe I had been moving on day by day during the whole of the previous year. Maybe I hadn't wanted to admit it but my subconscious was already there.

Nick had broken up with Wendy. He told me that they too had grown apart. I don't know whether I believed that, but it seemed plausible and my needy heart let me fall for it all the same.

My mum was over the moon. Here I was, seeing a guy who had his life sorted. He had a nice car, his own place, some savings behind him. Okay, he was only a primary school teacher like me, but Nick had the air of someone who was on the move. He had a direction. Tony had never had that.

I think it must have been around our fourth date when we first kissed. We had gone to the pictures to watch some rom-com. It had been soft and gentle. It was during an emotional scene in the movie. I had a box of popcorn propped on my lap. Nick's arm had moved across my shoulders and he had leaned in. I didn't stop it. Secretly I had been waiting for it. It was passionate, needy, wanting. We couldn't keep our hands off of each other.

We had made love that night. Nick was only my fourth lover, but it felt natural and right. He was gentle, loving and sweet. It was everything I had hoped it would be. Does that make me sound bad? I'm not comparing Nick to Tony or Tony to Nick but the relief it gave me was immense. It was like my life had finally gotten back on track after it had been crawling down a cul-de-sac for such a long time. I don't know, maybe I'm just a run-around, but I didn't feel that way. I felt... I felt looked after.

But I need to let you know that I also felt a heavy weight of guilt sitting on my shoulders. Still do.

Especially after... you know.

Chapter 58: Fatherly Love

'You don't need to defend yourself, son.'

'I just got so angry. Enraged. She brings the worst out in me.'

'I understand.'

'I'm not normally an angry person. Calm. Placid really. Jane…Jane used to say that it would take a nuclear explosion up my arse to get me going. But one word…one word from her and I want to combust.'

'I see.'

'I know she's ill. Terminally ill. And I'm trying. I really am.'

'I can see that.'

'I think I just need to stay away.'

'That's probably for the best.'

Robert Charon poured the Earl Grey and handed Tony a cup. Tony took it and sipped the hot, sweet liquid.

'Thanks.'

'Not a problem.'

'Am I disturbing you?'

'Never.'

'My heads in a spin really. I feel like I've fallen into a hole and I can't see the bottom. I'm just dropping like a lead weight, falling and falling and it's dark, really dark, you know?'

'I do.'

Robert sipped his own tea and placed his cup back down on his saucer. He leaned back in his chair.

'And what of Jane?'

'She's gone.'

'Gone where?'

'She's just gone. She's with… with him.'

'He's been desiring what you have.'

'He has what I had now. I've seen her with him. I don't know how far it's gone but she's moved bloody quickly.'

'Maybe it hasn't gone as far as you imagine.'

'I saw the way she looked at him. Her eyes. I've seen that look in her eyes before but not for a long time. Not since we first started going out, back in uni. She used to look at me like that,' he looked into his teacup. 'I miss that. This isn't supposed to have happened. I'm going to be a success and she knows this. This is what we had been planning for. Now it's all… ruined.'

'You can't be sure.'

'I am sure. As sure as I am that my life to this point has been one long, cruel lie.'

'And I am truly sorry for the part I have played in that.'

Tony sighed, still looking into his cup. It shook ever so slightly on the saucer. He felt a burning in his gut, a ringing in his ears.

'I've lost her.'

'And how does that make you feel?'

Tony stood up and went to the window.

'Come on, son. If you hold it in it will only make you feel worse.' Tony bit his lip and clenched his fists. He felt his face flush with a warm heat.

'How do you feel deep down inside?'

Tony rested his hands on the wall and dipped his head. He spoke quietly and deliberately.

'I feel fucking angry.'

Robert stood up and picked up the phone. He pressed the intercom.

'Davis, would you open up the Church... yes... yes, now if you would... no, no there's not a problem...thank you... no, you won't be needed... that would be good. Thank you.' He turned to look at Tony.

'I've got something to show you. Something that might help you.'

Tony's knuckles were white from gripping the window sill hard. His shoulders were clenched so tightly that his muscles ached. His father's hand fell on his shoulder.

'Come on, son. Come with me.'

Tony turned and looked into his father's eyes. They were dark. Mahogany. He could see his own reflection in there and he felt small, child-like, like he did when he was a little snotty nosed boy.

'Where are we going?'

'Not far.'

*

They had walked through to the rear of the house. Large French doors opened up onto a huge patio area. A pond with a huge, ornate fountain stood in the centre of the large veranda, surrounded by neatly trimmed hedges. Garden furniture was scattered here and there, long tables with huge parasols and comfortable looking recliners. Beyond the fountain the hedges opened up and led out onto a long, stone pathway. It stretched across an open lawned area and out onto what looked like a full size eighteen-hole golf course with water hazards, bunkers and copses of coniferous trees and bushes. A powered golf cart stood waiting for them at the entranceway.

'Hop on, son. We're going to take a short ride.' Tony climbed in next to his father.

'This place is amazing.'

'Yes, I'm quite pleased with it.'

They lurched forward and rolled out across the course. The day was bright and sunny with not a hint of a breeze. Tony let the sun warm his face, the sunshine ease his spirits and the blue sky comfort his soul.

'How do you afford all of this?'

'Well, you know that my line of work puts me in touch with a lot of successful people. Wealthy people. People with power and influence,' he steered around a large lake. Tony could see carp, lots of them. Trout too. The lake was full of fish. There was a jetty on the far side, a fishing rod leaning on a tripod rest. An elderly man was sitting on a folding chair holding a mug in one hand, waving with the other. Robert waved back 'These people pay a lot for a little help. An awful lot. And clearly I am glad to oblige.'

Tony couldn't take it all in. The place was like a five-star holiday retreat and it was all owned by his dad.

'I've seen your talks on the internet. They're good. But does that line of work really pay this well?'

'It depends what you mean by line of work. What do you think my...line of work is?'

'You're some sort of life coach, aren't you? Motivational speaker? That sort of thing?'

Robert laughed. 'Something like that. If you boil it down to its basics.' They passed a couple of golfers at the eighth tee. 'Sorry fellas,' Robert yelled at them, 'just passing through. Enjoying the sunshine?'

'Loving it, Robert. Thanks for your hospitality.'

'Not a problem. Not a problem at all. Watch out for the bunker to the right. I normally hit a three wood to the left. Sets you up nicely for an eight iron onto the green.'

'Thanks. We'll give that a go, although Alfonso's wood play isn't what it used to be.'

'Ha, ha. I'm sure he'll do just fine. See you at dinner. Davis is cooking his salmon gratin speciality.'

'Sounds great. We'll see you then.'

Tony recognised one of the golfers. 'Isn't the guy with the flat cap a politician? I recognise him from the TV.'

'Maybe. But if you do recognise him, I suggest you keep it to yourself. We have a strict confidentiality policy here at the Lodge.'

'Why's that?'

'Because my clients want to keep their personal tutorage away from public scrutiny.'

'I don't understand.'

'You will.'

In the distance Tony could see a small stone building with a timber-pitched roof. The building was maybe no bigger than ten feet by ten feet.

'Is that where we're headed?'

'It is.'

'That's what you referred to as the Church?'

'It is.'

'Doesn't look like much of a church to me.'

'Appearances can be deceiving.'

Tony shielded his eyes from the sun. It was directly above the building, illuminating it like a barren oasis in a perfectly landscaped desert. The sun glistened off of its flint walls. It looked like a large, jagged jewel in the middle of a large green baize.

'I'm going to show you some of my personal possessions. They are collections from my...*our* family history, handed down from generation to generation over thousands of years. When I'm gone, they will be passed to you as my only heir. You will need to take great care of them.'

Tony didn't know what to say to this. All he could muster was a lilting 'Okay.'

Robert swung the cart up the slight incline to the doorway of the Church and hopped out.

'You can go in, son. The door is unlocked. But be careful. It is quite dark inside and there is a steep staircase.'

Tony climbed out and walked over to the door. It was a dark

wood. Heavy. There was a large black handle. He gripped it with his left hand, it was cold, even in the heat, and he pushed downwards. He felt the latch give and he pulled the door outwards. It groaned like an old ogre being awoken from a deep sleep. He felt air escaping, a soft whoosh. He looked back at his father. Robert was smiling and nodding. 'Go on, I'll follow you in.'

He walked into a short entranceway which led directly onto a staircase. The stairs led downward into a dark abyss. 'What's down there?'

'One step at a time, Anthony. You will see.'

He placed one foot on the slippery stone step, using both hands to hold the walls either side as he carefully placed his feet. The sound of each step echoed off the walls either side of him. He strained his eyes, trying to make out how far down the stairway led but the hole just grew darker and darker, the air colder and more damp. Ten, fifteen, twenty steps. The walls were slick with oily water, the air was musty. He could just make out a doorway, around ten steps further. The door was closed.

'That door is also unlocked, son. There's no handle. Just give it a hefty push.'

Tony stood at the bottom of the stairway and placed both hands on the door. The wood was warm to the touch. He looked behind him. His father was above him, maybe seven or eight steps, and the dim light from outside was irradiating him. He was a large, dark, faceless and ominous silhouette.

'A big push, son. And then you'll be inside.'

Tony turned back to the door, took a deep breath and heaved.

Chapter 59: Guilt

Nick watched Jane load the dishwasher. To him, reclining on his sofa and watching her firm buttocks bobbing up and down while she stacked the dishes was just about the best thing in the whole, wide world. He felt that he had finally scored a home run and he was planning to hang onto her for all it was worth.

'Do you need any help, love?'

'No, it's fine. I'll just get this loaded and then I'm going to go out for quick run.'

'You don't need to. You look in great shape to me.'

'Well it's your fault, Daddy-o. You got me into this fitness malarkey. Now I feel that if I stop then everything will just…sag.'

She turned to face him, her hands on her hips, hair tied back in a loose bun.

God, he thanked the heavens. She was gorgeous.

'Okay, but don't go making yourself too attractive to the rest of the male population,' he stood up, walked over to her and put his arms around her waist, 'you're mine now. All mine. And I won't let anybody else have you.'

She put her arms round his neck and kissed him on the cheek. 'You silly sod. I'm doing this just as much for your benefit as well as mine. Anyway, I'll only be thirty minutes. Just a run round the block.

I need to clear my head anyway.'

'Why's that?'

'I spoke to Tony earlier,' she looked down at the floor, 'he's so…'

'So what?'

'So… hurt.'

Nick put his hand under her chin and slowly lifted her head. 'You did nothing wrong.'

'I ran out on him.'

'He ran out on you. Maybe not physically, but mentally. You deserve better.'

'But does he deserve this?'

'You can't look out for everyone, Jane. You need to look out for yourself.'

'I'll need to go round there. Get my stuff.'

'I can do it for you.'

'No. That would be a bad idea. I can do it. I'll just call ahead and he can make himself scarce. I'm not ready to see him yet anyway.'

'Okay, but I'll be in the car waiting for you. Just in case.'

'Yeah, yeah. That would be good. Maybe tomorrow?'

'Not a problem.'

She kissed him on the lips, softly. 'Thank you.'

'For what?'

'For rescuing me.'

He smiled down at her. 'I think it was you that rescued me, not the other way around.'

'Well, let's just be rescued together. I'll see you in a bit.'

'Okay, sweetheart. I'll get the vino ready.'

'You'd better. Make it a big glass.'

She waved and set off down the road. He watched out of the bay window as she bobbed along. God, he couldn't believe how fit she was, and he didn't mean healthy.

He checked his mobile phone. No calls. He flicked open his emails. Nothing for him to be concerned about.

He was worried. It was all going so well with Jane. His plan had worked a treat and not only were they dating, which by the way included having amazing sex, they were now bloody living together. He had really aced the hole. The thing was, he mused, it had all moved a lot faster than he had planned and he still had stuff to…clean up. He had tracks to cover, trails to clear and he'd be damned if he was going to let his past interfere with his future. All it would take was one misplaced text, one email, one knock on the front door while Jane was home alone. No, he swore to himself, he couldn't have that. That would not do at all. He needed to act and act fast.

He scanned down his contacts list. First things first. He needed to make a call.

Chapter 60: Jasmine

'Are you sure?'

'Pretty sure.'

'You've got to be more than pretty sure, Doc. If we're going to bring this guy down, we need you to be one hundred and ten percent sure. I won't get an arrest warrant on pretty sure.'

Doctor Chandur frowned, 'Putting me under pressure is not going to help my powers of recollection, Detective Inspector.'

Raven gritted his teeth. 'Look, I know it was dark, I know it all happened in a blur. I understand. I get it. But people are getting killed, *my friend* has just been killed, and we need this guy to be stopped,' he leaned forward on his desk, 'so I want you to be absolutely clear with this. Crystal bloody clear.' He folded his arms and leaned back in his chair. 'Are you sure?'

Jasmine sipped her coffee, 'It was a long time ago. We only went out a couple of times. He looks different now. He was never that white, that ghostly. He looks…ill.' She glanced over at Barber who was perched on the edge of a meeting room chair, encouraging her passively. 'It was a long time ago, Damian.'

'You can do it, Jas. Just tell them what you told me.'

She looked at her feet. 'I met him around four years ago. I was just out of university; he was still studying. We met in a bar, can't remember the name. He was tall, good looking. Good fun actually.

We had a great time that night, dancing to a band. I remember getting pretty drunk.' She paused, took another sip from her coffee. 'We agreed to meet again, the following weekend in fact. I was out of town, in the city actually, attending a police training course on developments in DNA technology, so I wasn't due back down south until the next Saturday. I remember him being pretty disgruntled with that, but it didn't really strike me as odd at the time.' She picked at a thread on her jacket. 'Anyway, we met up, went out again to the same bar. Had another good evening, but this time he was different. A little more... clingy. He started to get quite possessive actually, quite jealous if anyone spoke to me. Another guy asked to buy me a drink while he was in the toilet, and when he found out his mood changed dramatically. He started to get aggressive. Not physically, but verbally. Again, it wasn't a big thing. Didn't strike me as odd at the time. Just a little... uncomfortable. I'd had a few drinks, so I just laughed it off. Told him not to be stupid, that the guy didn't know that I was there with him. We had another dance and he seemed to calm down.'

The Chief walked out of his office and sat on the edge of Raven's desk, listening to the story with interest.

The Doctor continued, 'Anyway, during the week, it was Tuesday or Wednesday, he showed up outside where I worked. He said he wanted to see me. I thought it was strange, I hadn't even told him where I worked so I was pretty unsettled that he had found out somehow. He looked agitated. He said that he had seen me that morning with another man and wanted to know what was going on. I didn't know what he was talking about, but he insisted. He said that he had seen someone drop me off that morning at work. Again, I was astounded that he had been watching me and alarm bells started ringing immediately. I said to him, how dare he snoop on me like that? It wasn't as if we are an item. We had two dates, and two dates did not make us exclusive. I asked him how the hell he knew where I worked and what the hell was he doing there, waiting for me to turn up in the morning. I was furious. I am quite a private person and the thought of some... some stranger really, spying on me, stalking me, enraged me. I told him, for what it was worth, that the man dropping me to work was my brother, but that it was none of his business and that we were done.'

'And was that the end of it?' the Chief was leaning forward now, desperate to hear what happened next.

Jasmine rubbed her shoulder. 'He grabbed my arm, really quite hard. Said that I didn't get to end it like that. I told him to...' she looked up at Barber.

'Go ahead, Jas.'

'I told him to go fuck himself. That if he gave me any trouble that my brothers would find him and mess him up.' She looked over at Raven. 'I've got a big family, Detective Inspector. A big, over-protective family. They wouldn't think twice about hunting a guy down and giving him a severe beating. I have to be very careful about what I tell them,' she looked up at Barber as he shifted a little uncomfortably on the edge of the chair. She smiled at him reassuringly. 'Anyway, he shirked that off. Told me he didn't care anyway. That he already had a girlfriend and he was just using me for a bit of extracurricular fun. I told him that I pitied her if this was the way he treated women. I told him that he was a sad, pathetic excuse for a man and that he should go and find himself a life. I was furious. He gave me the finger and smiled. Can you believe that? Anyway, I turned and stormed back into the office and never saw him again.'

Raven crossed his legs and took a sip from his water. 'And you know that this is his name?'

'It's the name he gave me.'

'Benjamin Bailey. Sounds a bit odd. There's no guarantee that this is genuine.'

'I know, but that's not the point. You see, I did a bit of stalking myself. Well, one of my brother's did actually. Just to make sure that if anything... untoward happened that I knew where to find him.'

Both Raven and the Chief leaned forward. 'And?' they both spoke in unison.

Jasmine and Barber smiled. She folded her arms.

'I know where he lives.'

Chapter 61: The Performance

Mayor Chester Wood sat in his sun lounger, the summer sun just taking a nap beneath the horizon, and took a drag on his cigar. He had a cognac in his other hand and a smug smile the width of the Amazon slicing a path through his goatee. He had just watched the evening news and by God had he put on a show. A real firework display you could say. His mother had said that he had a knack for the dramatic and she was right. The soap opera that was on just before his interview at the top of the news couldn't touch his extravagance, his panache, his perfectly clipped delivery. Leo had even given him a rapturous round of applause when it had finished and rightly so.

He wasn't surprised. He had practised the speech in front of the mirror several times during the last two weeks. Sure, he hadn't expected it to be required so soon but the death of the girl had meant that it was needed much earlier than planned. This wasn't just the local rag, he rapturously told himself. This was the national fucking evening news. His face would be beamed across the country to millions of families sitting down to have their supper. He was no longer just Chester Wood, Mayor of a small town at the arse end of the country. He was Mayor Chester Wood, the guy in control of a man hunt, the man responsible for taking charge of the situation, the man who would make tough decisions when needed.

He could feel Whitehall beckoning.

He sipped his cognac. The slow burn in his throat felt pleasant, invigorating.

He played back his speech over and over in his mind.

'Mayor Wood, what is your take on what has happened here this evening?'

He had gazed at the young female interviewer, a look of calm solemnity spreading across his carefully preened face.

'A terrible turn of events. We feel, and I am sure that the whole country feels, the effects of this savagery so deeply. Our thoughts and condolences go out to this poor girl's family. It is so, so sad.'

'We understand that the woman in question is one Daisy Reynolds, a barmaid who works in the town. Can you give us any more details?'

'Of course, I cannot comment on the specifics of the case, Sarah. You know that. But what I can say is that we will work tirelessly, use every man and woman at our disposal, every ounce of energy that we have, every waking minute of our long, long days to bring this murderous villain to justice.'

'We also understand, Mayor, that this woman was a close friend of the D.I. in charge. A Detective Inspector Luke Raven?'

'Again, Sarah, I cannot comment on the specifics of the case. But whether she was a friend of one of our officers or not, the determination of the town's police force will not falter. We have been, and will continue to be, absolutely committed to finding the person or persons responsible for these heinous crimes.'

'The murder count is now at four, Mayor. The women of this town are living in fear for their lives, afraid to go out onto the streets alone. Meanwhile the investigation drags on and on with no discernible progress. What can you say to the women of Westhampton to help them to, well, sleep at night?'

'Well Sarah, I say this…'

At this point he had turned to face the cameras, a carefully rehearsed look of both stern authority and fatherly compassion.

'Citizens of Westhampton. I feel the pain that you are feeling. I understand deeply the concern that each and every one of you has for your safety and for the safety of your friends and loved ones. Be sure that I feel this from the moment I wake to the moment I rest, and I will continue to feel this way until we have brought this situation to a satisfactory close. I assure you that you can trust in me, as your Mayor, to make the right decisions, to put in the extra effort, to be righteous and speedy in my judgements. I know that you feel that the authorities in this town have let you down so far, that they are failing in their attempts to locate and incarcerate the perpetrator of these crimes. They, *we*, have made bad decisions. They, *we*, have not been as clinical as we ought. Well, it is now time to act. I will personally be reviewing the methods and practises of the team in charge of this case and if I find that mistakes have been made, if procedures have not been followed and if the skills of the officers involved are in question, then I will act. I will act decisively. This will go on no longer.' He then turned to the reporter.

'And…Sarah, I will keep you and the rest of your colleagues briefed at all times. I want the media to know that there will be no secrets here. I will provide full and frank disclosure. That is why you voted for me, why the people of this wonderful town voted for me and why I am in this very, *very* privileged position. We are, after all, on the same team.'

And jeez, he had thought to himself, would he like to give her a private brief. A behind closed doors brief. An official brief.

He rubbed a hand across his goatee and considered the position he had placed himself in. He had planted the seed and now he had to do something about it. He knew that he needed to take full control of the case, remove the idiot Simmonds and painfully carve out Raven. He would make a show of it too. A public execution if you will. Full and frank disclosure. Their downfall would be his glorious uprising and he would leave no stone unturned, no matter how insignificant it might appear. Once completed he, and only he, would take the glory and enjoy the voracity of the public frenzy. When he brought the maniac to justice and paraded him around town like a stupendous trophy then he, Chester Wood, would be the unrivalled hero of the hour, just as he had always known that he would be, one day. It was his destiny.

He chuckled under his breath and finished his brandy. Times were good and he planned to enjoy them.

*

He watched. Watched his smug face through a brandy glass and cigar smoke. This would be a momentous climax to what had been *his* willing. A fitting finale to their long journey.

The Mayor's head on a platter for all to see. *He* would be happy. Very happy.

And then he would get his prize. The one thing he longed for more than anything on earth. He yearned for it. Needed it. Had to have it. He felt sure, no he knew, that *he* would give it to him when this was completed. But first, he needed to put things in place. Set things right.

He needed to see her one more time.

Chapter 62: Vengeance

'You spoke to him.'

'Of course I did. He came to me.'

'You told him about... what I do.'

'I warned him off.'

'That was a mistake.'

'He is our son for God's sake.'

'He is my son. You were just the carrier, the bearer. You kept him from me for all these years and I will not let you turn him away now.'

'You will destroy him.'

'Quite the contrary, my dear. I will empower him.'

'Empower him with what? With evil? That is not empowerment, Robert. That is conditioning. Brainwashing his poor mind with your hedonistic heresy.'

'You forget who you are talking to, my darling.'

'No, no. I remember. You almost took me along for the ride until I saw, I saw what you did. What you stood for. The heinous acts that you were willing to commit for your... your heritage.'

'We are a blessed people.'

'You are murderers.'

'We continue a bloodline. We cement a legacy.'

'Of fear and of killing.'

'You have always been ignorant of what I, what *we*, stand for.'

'I prefer to call myself enlightened.'

'On that I am afraid we will have to disagree… I hear you are dying. How does that feel?'

'It will be a relief.'

'A relief from what?'

'From all these years, trying to keep him from you. To keep you out of our lives.'

'Well on that count I am afraid you have failed. I have shown him.'

'Shown him what?'

'Everything.'

'What? When?'

'Today.'

'Why? Why would you do that, Robert? He is young. He doesn't need this. He doesn't want it.'

'It is his right, Helen. You know that.'

'I know no such thing.'

'Then you are a fool.'

'A fool that knows to leave this kind of stuff alone. It has infected you, Robert, made you into a monster. Do you really want that of your son?'

'I want him to respect his family.'

'Pah! A family of thugs and hoodlums. Murderers and rapists. Evil incarnate.'

'As I say… ignorant.'

'And how did he react?'

'I don't know. Shocked, surprised. But not repulsed. Certainly not repulsed. Interested.'

'Interested?'

'He wants what I can give him.'

'And what is that?'

'The one thing he yearns for, more than anything.'

'Which is…'

'To be desired.'

'My father was right about you. You are rotten to the core.'

'Your father was an imbecile also. I made a mistake in choosing you.'

'I rather see it the other way around.'

'Again… let's agree to disagree.'

'Why are you here, Robert?'

'To see you one last time.'

'Before what?'

'Before my son and I join in an infinite union. You are unlikely to ever see him again.'

'*Do not do this to him. Do not.*'

'I'm afraid, my dear Helen, that you cannot stop me. You see, as you know only too well, you are dying.'

'I will warn him off. His brother will intervene. He will prevent this…this foolishness. Anthony will listen to Mitchell. You'll see. You cannot corrupt him.'

'Aah Mitchell, yes. Young Mitchell. The drug dealer. Well, I'm afraid that sweet, innocent Mitchell is otherwise indisposed.'

'Indisposed? What do you…?'

'Heroine is such a savage drug. Overdoses can occur quite regularly. Especially when the burden of looking after your dying mother is thrust upon you. It's so hard to be a full-time carer when the caree is so weak, so sick, unable to do even the simplest things for herself. Such a weight on a young and fragile mind. So easy to just… overdo it.'

'*YOU KILLED HIM?*'

'Not me, my dear. His addiction.'

'NOOOOOOO! No… no… no…'

'I'm afraid so my darling. Now, don't get so upset.'

'My son…'

'You stole a son from me. Consider this retribution.'

'You won't get away with this… I will make sure that you pay… you… *you devil…*'

'You will do no such thing, Helen. You see, as I said, you are not long for this world.'

'There is plenty of life in me yet you bastard! I will see to it that you…'

'That I… what?'

'I won't let you… Robert… NO!'

Robert Charon raised the pillow to Helen Richard's frail and terrified face and pushed down.

'Sleep tight, Helen, my dear.'

Chapter 63: Catch Up

'He did what?'

Billy West was gazing at him from the other side of the bar, his mouth agape, his expression dumbstruck. He held a pint of dark ale in one hand and a packet of pork scratchings in the other.

'I told you, he took me to his... workshop, I guess.'

'I... I don't get it. What kind of work does he do again?'

'He's a motivational speaker. But he's much, much more than that.'

'Sounds weird.'

Tony wiped the bar and collected the empty glasses. He looked over at the singer who was picking away at a battered old acoustic guitar and wailing about lost love, broken hearts and other such pitiful tragedies. There was a group of onlookers gathered around the stage. One of them, a pretty blond, kept glancing his way.

'It's not as weird as it sounds. He makes a lot of sense.'

Billy crunched on a pig skin and then took a large swig from his dark, flat beer.

'Sounds odd to me.'

'Well think what you like. He's helping me... a lot.'

Billy wiped beer froth from his moustache. 'I just don't see how some religious mumbo jumbo is going to help you get over Jane. The best thing you can do is to move on.' Tony whirled on him.

'I've fucking told you, Billy! That is not an option!'

Billy held his hands up in defeat, 'Okay, okay. I know. She's your life partner, your soul mate, a yin to your yang. I get it. But she doesn't want you back, Tone. You said she told you as much,' he glanced sympathetically at his despondent friend, 'and jeez, she hasn't wasted any time in moving on now, has she?'

Tony poured a glass of scotch for a punter.

'That's not her fault. He's got to her.'

'Well, that might be true. But she could have fought him off a little harder. That's all I'm saying.'

Tony took the money for the whiskey and handed the thirsty customer his change.

'Sometimes it's not as easy as that,' he brushed his hand through his too long hair, 'and I haven't exactly helped myself now, have I?' He shot Billy an accusatory glance.

'Now, come on, Tony. You came over to me voluntarily don't forget. Don't start trying to lump any of that blame on me, my friend. I'm not the one in this mess.'

Tony looked at the floor in defeat and Billy thought better of himself. 'Sorry mate, I didn't mean that. I know this is tough for you,' he reached over and gave Tony a manly pat on the shoulder. 'Hey, talking of which, I haven't been able to get hold of your brother for days. In fact, I haven't spoken to him since the end of August. Have you heard from him?'

'No. Why would I?'

'Well,' Billy looked over at him with a mock 'duh' expression on his face, 'he's your brother?'

'He's no brother of mine.'

'I think the gene pool begs to differ.'

'We may have the same blood, but we are not brothers.'

'Okay. Well, he ain't answering the phone. Very unusual for Mitch. He's normally super quick to pick up,' Billy rubbed a hand through his moustache, 'might be something to do with the vast sums of money I hand over to him on a regular basis.'

'He's probably avoiding you after he gave you that dodgy dope.'

'Maybe.'

Tony looked over at the singer again. His whining was getting him down. Just one up tempo song, he inwardly pleaded. That's all he asked for. And that girl was still looking at him.

'How's your book going?'

'Novel.'

'Yeah, that's what I said. How's it going?'

'Well, despite of all of this...crap, it's actually still progressing pretty well. I'm starting to think I might even finish it.'

That was true too, he thought. Surprisingly the pain and angst of the last few weeks had actually positively affected his creativity. He had been hammering away at the keyboard for hours at a time. It was as if putting words down onto virtual paper was cathartic to him, like some form of subconscious pressure valve was being released.

'Well, that's great. When can I have a look?'

'When it's done.'

'Awww, come on. Not even a sneak peek? A private preview?'

'Nope.'

'One chapter?'

'No way.'

'A sentence?'

'Piss off.'

Billy watched as a young couple walked down the stairs into the bar.

'You want a drink?'

'I shouldn't,' Tony wanted one, he really did.

'Just keep it under the bar.'

'Oh... okay then. I'll have a pint.'

Tony pulled them both a pint of dark ale and rested his on the shelf beneath the worktop. He looked around to make sure Big Al wasn't watching them.

'Cheers.'

'Cheers.'

They both gulped greedily at the slightly warm, malty liquid and placed their glasses back down simultaneously. Billy burped loudly.

'Pig.'

'Well you know what they say. It takes one to know one.'

'Yeah, I know what they say.'

Billy polished off the rest of his pork scratchings.

'You sure you don't want one, Tone? They're good.'

'They're a heart attack waiting to happen, that's what they are.'

'Bring it on.'

The singer wailed some lament about the love of his life cheating on him and putting an arrow through his heart. People actually like this, Tony thought to himself. It was exactly what his father had warned him against. Wallowing in self-pity. Letting your emotions rule your life. Letting someone else's rules rule your life.

If you want something, he had asked him, why not just take it?

'So, who would have thought it? Tony Richards has royal blood.'

'Leave it out, Billy.'

'Well, that's what you said. Admittedly, way, way back in some country that I haven't even heard of. But royal, nonetheless. Anthony Richards for king.'

'It's not Richards. It's Charon.'

'What? You changing your name?'

'Maybe. Most people take their father's name. Mine was robbed from me so why not take it back?'

'I s'pose.'

'And anyway, I would prefer it if you keep this to yourself. I don't want anyone knowing my private business. Especially this.'

'Your secret's safe with me.'

'Even from Sal?'

'Especially from Sal.'

'You swear, Billy?'

'I swear.'

'No. I mean it.'

Billy raised his left hand and placed his right on the bar menu.

'I solemnly swear, on this Stooges bar menu, within which describes such south coastal delicacies best left for the cast iron of stomach and the unhinged of mind, that I will keep the crazy bullshit that Anthony Richards, *nee Charon*, is buying from his long lost father a secret for all of eternity,' he laughed, spraying pork shavings across the top of the bar, 'and even if I didn't, no-one would believe it anyway.'

'Fuck off, Billy.'

'What? What?'

Billy continued to laugh loudly while Tony turned away, mock anger on his face but daggers of doubt in his heart. Maybe Billy was right, he thought, maybe this was all bullshit.

He looked up and was thankful to see that the singer had finished his encore and the crowd was dispersing. He collected a couple of glasses from the bar and there in front of him was a folded piece of paper. He picked it up curiously and opened it. Written inside were two words and a telephone number.

Call Me.

Chapter 64: In Position

This was it, Raven thought to himself. This was it alright. Despite what that idiot Mayor might think of them they had the bastard's home address. Yes, he thanked his stars, luck had a big hand to play in it. Who would have guessed that the classy doctor had gone out with the lunatic back when they were studying? But, as he always heard the football pundits say, you make your own luck in this game and someone had finally been looking out for them. At long last.

The Chief had helped rush through the warrant overnight, woke some local official up and got the approval he needed, and now there they were, all of the gang. He and Barber, the Chief, Spidey, Wodge, Lola and the heavyweight Crusher, plus two armed units. The road had been blocked off quietly in the early hours of the morning and his officers were all in position. All he had to do was give the word and the whole world would come crashing down around their guy.

The place looked wrong, really. Too nice. Too suburban. The kind of place you would settle down in, raise a family. Barbeques out the back on a Sunday, washing the car out front, painting and decorating to make your house your home, kids playing in the garden. The kind of place he wanted with Lisa. That realisation hit him like a hammer, but in a good way.

All of the... horror had really affected him and shook up his perception of his own life. He knew that he needed to get himself straight and do right by Lisa. Lisa... and the baby. He had hardly had time to sit down and think about that. He was going to be a father and rather than terrify him, it excited him. Warmed him. Made him feel… whole. He couldn't believe how his whole world could turn on just two words. *I'm pregnant.*

'What's the plan, boss?' Barber was perched next to him behind the tight copse of trees just four houses up. He was animated, excited. He needed to teach the kid how to control his emotions. Raven made a mental note to invite him round for a game of Texas Hold 'Em when it was all over.

'We wait until the second unit is positioned at the rear of the building and then I give the nod. Unit number one kicks in the front door and unit number two simultaneously bursts in through the back. No way out. It's what the army call a pincer movement,' he smirked with grim contempt, 'we're not taking any bloody chances this time. No more mistakes.'

Raven gritted his teeth together. No more deaths. The loss of Daisy hung heavily on his heart and he couldn't forget how the fucker had almost got to Lisa too. Lisa and the baby.

No more.

'I'm excited, boss.'

'I can tell. You look like you're going to wet yourself.'

'Who would have though it eh? Jasmine and this guy?'

'Yeah, we got lucky.'

'We sure did. Do you think we could get an award for this?'

'For what?'

'Bringing this loonie in?'

'We'll be lucky to keep our jobs at this rate, Damo. Let's just worry about the job in hand, shall we?'

'Okay, yeah. Alright, boss.'

Raven's radio squawked into life.

'Unit number two in position, over.'

'Unit number one also in position, over.'

Raven picked up his radio, pressed the intercom and spoke with authority.

'Does anybody have a visual on the suspect?'

'Unit number two. No visual. The blinds at the back are closed.'

'Unit number one, no visual from this end either. The curtains are drawn. No sign of movement.'

Shit, Raven thought, were they really going to be lucky enough to catch him in bed? Was it really going to be that easy?

His mind took him back to the dark stairway, the thing that he saw behind the killer. The black, ominous shadow. Prior to that, the chase where the killer seemed to rise up from the ground, darkness enveloping him, his long arms, his clawed hands. The dead, mutilated girls, their blood drained, their lifeless bodies positioned meticulously. His face. His pale, white face. The dreams. Scratch that, the nightmares. The ghosts of the girls haunting him, blaming him. No, he knew that it wasn't going to be that easy. No way. These things never were. And he had the feeling that there was something else at play here.

'Okay guys. Keep your wits about you. This guy should not be underestimated and he's almost certainly armed and prepared. Take no chances.' There was silence over the radio.

'Requesting confirmation. Is that a shoot to kill order, sir? Over.'

Raven sighed. Taking a life was not something he considered lightly. But the lives of his men were in danger also and if it came down to it then it was an easy decision.

'If the situation necessitates it then yes, that is a shoot to kill order.'

'Roger that. Over.'

'Unit number 2, roger that also. Over.'

'On my signal, guys.'

Raven looked up at the house. This is where it would all end, he thought to himself, for all of them.

'*GO, GO, GO!*'

Chapter 65: Morning Glory

Tony sat in his front room, his head in his hands. Another night with very little sleep. Tossing and turning. Faces in his head. Jane, his mum, Mitch, Billy. All laughing at him, pointing. Taunting him. What a loser, what a bum, no job, no girlfriend, no life. Couldn't even afford the rent on his house. And *she*. She had well and truly ruined his life. He felt angry. Bile and acid burned in his stomach and up into his oesophagus. He felt sick.

The sun was up, cutting laser traces through the gap between the curtains in his living room. A slither of light slashed his face in two, an illuminated path walked down his forehead, the bridge of his nose, his lips and down his chin. He blinked. He felt lost, alone. He needed guidance.

He stood up and walked to the window, pulling the curtains back just an inch in order to peer out onto the street outside. All was quiet. It was a glorious day.

The kind of day that should lift your spirits, make you feel joyful, happy to be alive. Elated even. Tony felt none of those things. He had a mild hangover; he was tired, and he missed Jane. The pain of that great loss tore handfuls of tissue from his bleeding heart. She hated him and he hated himself.

He turned to the phone.

*

Nick had crept downstairs. Jane was sleeping. They had had friends round the night before and they had both shared too many bottles of red. She had gone to bed three sheets to the wind, but he hadn't drunk as much as her. He had been tipping the odd glass away when she wasn't looking actually. He needed to keep his head.

He'd had a letter. He had seen it on the sideboard when he had got back from work the day before. Jane had asked him what it was, but he had made up some kind of humorous response, something about MI5 coming to get him, and had swiftly changed the subject. But there it sat. On the cabinet by the front door. Just sitting there. Glaring at him. Taunting him.

He picked it up gingerly, as if it were hot to the touch. He knew that the bloody thing could ruin his life. Their lives.

He ran a hand across his face and walked into the lounge. It was already bathed in beautiful sunshine, the early autumn sun pouring through the front curtains like golden sand. He chanced a peek outside. All was quiet. He was afraid. Afraid that they were out there. Watching him. Waiting. Waiting for the right moment to ruin him.

He couldn't let that happen.

He walked into the kitchen, flicked the kettle on and then returned to the lounge, still clutching the letter like his life was dependent upon it. Maybe it was.

He fell onto the sofa and gripped it in his hands. He tucked one finger under the corner of the folded lip and peeled it back.

*

'It's me.'

'Hello son.'

'I need guidance.'

'All you have to do is ask.'

'I'm lost, Dad. I feel so alone.'

'Then you need to consider what we discussed.'

'I… I don't know.'

'I understand. It appears… strange. Wrong maybe.'

'So wrong.'

'To the ignorant man it is wrong. But to the enlightened man it is the only way. Natural. The order of things.'

'How do I know…?'

'How do you know what?'

'That it will work.'

'Because I told you that it would. Do you not believe me?'

'Of course, of course. But… I don't know.'

'We have succeeded where others have failed for millennia, my son. That is not an accident. That is a birth right. And where others sought to bring us down, we were always victorious. That isn't luck. That is a blessing handed to us by our maker. What man has not given he cannot take away. We are taught that in the scriptures.'

'I don't think I have it in me.'

'It will come.'

'I'm not so sure.'

'Then you need to consider what they have done to you. How they have viciously driven a stake through your heart. How they have sought to do you harm, deliberately and maliciously. If you truly want to put your things back in order, then you need to make the hard decisions.'

'I know. I know. I'll…'

'You'll what?'

'I'll think about it.'

'Don't take too long.'

The phone line went dead. Tony replaced the handset in the receiver and cried.

*

No! No! This couldn't be. How had they found him? How had they found out where he lived? Who the FUCK had given him away!

Nick threw the letter across the coffee table and punched the cushions on the sofa. It was his worst fear. His worst FUCKING nightmare. How the hell had this happened? He had been so careful. So meticulous. Since the beginning. Since before. Way, *way* before.

He knew he had to keep this from Jane. Somehow. He wasn't sure how just yet, but he needed to make a plan. A carefully laid out plan. Jane should never know about this. Because he knew that would be that. Over. Finished. *Caput.*

He reached out and read the letter again.

'NO!'

He put a hand over his mouth and swore under his breath. Shit. He sat and listened. He heard bed springs compress, floorboards creak. He was a fucking idiot. Not a good place to start, he cursed to himself, waking up the one person who it all needed to be kept from. He swiftly folded the letter and tucked it into the pocket of his pyjama bottoms. He would ensure he dealt with it later.

He stood up and gathered himself. He needed to be calm. Calm. Calm in the face of adversity. He counted to twenty and took in deep, soothing breaths,

He walked over to the front window and grabbed a hand on each curtain. He knew that with each new day came a new challenge and he was never one to avoid facing down his enemies. Life, he smirked, was just going to have to come up with something else to throw at him because this was not going to cut it. Life could just *fuck off*.

He threw the curtains wide open and let the light pour in.

Chapter 66: The Break In

Both doors burst in simultaneously with a thunderous crash. There was a chaotic and frenetic energy to what happened next; heavy boots hitting the floor, seemingly random shouting and hollering from the armed response unit, rooms being aggressively entered one by one, stairs being vaulted two and three at a time, doors opening and closing hard enough to rattle in their frames, household items such as chairs, plates, lamps and the like being knocked asunder, radios being shouted into in an evolved musical crescendo of whiskey, tango and bravos. The house throbbed with frantic activity.

The orgasm of adrenalized disorder lasted for only a few tumultuous moments and then subsided like storm waves from a vessel in distress. No-one was home.

Raven entered through the front door, Barber in tow.

'*Shit.*'

'Roger that.' Barber looked as deflated as a party balloon after the wedding party had long since departed.

The hallway led past a living room on the left through to the kitchen out the back. The place was a mess. Dirty clothes, used cutlery, unread mail and empty takeaway cartons strewn across the floor, sofa and kitchen worktops. The house was illuminated by dim light through the curtains in the front room and the half-opened blinds in the kitchen but Raven could see enough to confirm that the place had been empty all night. Their suspect hadn't been home since the day before at best.

'What now, boss?'

'Well Damo, we have a quick look around and then we clear the place for the CSI to do their thing,' he sighed, 'and we hope for all of our sake's that they find something. Otherwise....' He knew that 'otherwise' didn't bear thinking about.

He waited for two armed officers to pass him and then entered the kitchen. It was small, poky and more than a little pungent. The rear window looked out onto a fairly long, narrow and not very well-tended garden. Aside from the careless abandon in which the occupier had treated the place, Raven thought the house actually looked kind of homely. No gothic furnishings, no images of the devil on the wall, no bloody daggers hanging from meat hooks in the ceiling and no satanic pentagram on the floor. But then he knew from his years of experience dealing with the disturbed and socially rejected, it was almost always the quiet ones. The guy next door, the polite one, the nice one, the gentleman that would give handily to charity and help the old lady across the road with her shopping bags. It was very rarely the guy with the scar down his face and the tattoo on his neck.

He walked back down the hallway to the stairs. Barber followed him up and they both stood perusing their surroundings on the first-floor landing.

Bathroom to the left, spare room to the right, master bedroom straight ahead. Raven covered his hand in a handkerchief from his pocket and pushed the door inwards. He immediately touched the handkerchief to his nose. Maybe, he thought to himself thankfully and with more than a little grim relief, CSI wouldn't have to look too hard.

The room was as messy as the others with dirty sheets strewn across the floor, the mattress laying crookedly on the bed, wardrobe doors hanging open and askew and ruffled clothes falling awkwardly from tatty hangers. But there were two telling factors in the room.

The first 'out of the ordinary' things he saw were the pictures. Photographs of a woman. Large prints, multi shot prints, colour or sepia, standard printer, tattered sketches, head shots, full body shots.

All pinned to the walls of the room, covering them like a creepy montage of female adoration, a mosaic of body parts and idle glances. Raven was struck with how pretty she was, casually so but captivating nonetheless.

It was clear to him that the owner of the house had some kind of unrequited obsession with her. Raven nodded to Barber who started taking photographs. He was sure that they needed to swiftly ID the woman and that if she wasn't already dead then she was in serious and mortal danger.

The second, more disturbing thing he noticed was the blood. Old, dark and crusty blood. Not rivers of it, but plenty of splatters. On the wall, on the floor, on the sheets and even a little on the ceiling. Enough. Enough to know that somebody had been hurt in there. Hurt very, very badly. And enough to know that whomever had committed the act hadn't been as careful as perhaps he ought. From the way the splatters appeared, Raven was sure that whoever had done the deed had been in a fit of intense rage, almost as if it were an act of desire or vengeance. Yes, he mused, the scene confirmed it. The perpetrator had been unleashing some sort of pent up anger and violent consequence on the victim, a release of intense pressure spitting out spite, poison and fury. In fact, he pondered as he cracked his knuckles in turn, if he was a betting man, which he quite regularly was, he would put down some pretty hefty stakes that the blood in the room belonged to more than one victim. Very possibly three victims. In fact, three young female victims. Namely Tracey Webb, Billy Roper and Trudy Yates. Yes, he nodded ruefully, he would bet his pitiful yearly salary that those poor girls breathed their last, fearful breaths in that tiny, God-forsaken place.

Raven spoke into his radio. 'Spidey, Bailey?'

They both responded in unison, 'Boss.'

'We need feet on the streets and quick. Our suspect has long since departed. My guess is sometime during yesterday but maybe earlier. Get his face and name out there. Anyone that encounters him needs to be urged to call it in. Make it known that under no circumstances is he to be confronted. He is extremely dangerous.'

'Sir.'

'He's shown himself to be a local lad, picking on local females so I would guess he is still somewhere in the vicinity. Pull in units from all over the county. We need to flood the town with as many foot soldiers as we can.'

'Yes sir.'

Raven could feel the net closing in on their suspect and he guessed that their prey could feel it too.

'And Lola?'

'Yes boss?'

'Get your feelers out. I want as many of our contacts, kosher or otherwise, to keep their eyes peeled. Make it worth their while. If he's planning something, maybe something big, then my guess is he's going to need supplies. The kind of supplies you can only get from the type of people that you and your pals deal with.'

'Will do.'

'I don't want any 'honour amongst thieves' bullshit here. This guy is no organised criminal. Looks to me like this is a whole new ball game to him so they won't know him well, if at all. Anyone looking the other way will be treated like an accessory. Make it known.'

'No problem, boss. I'll get onto it right away.'

'We're bringing this fucker in, and soon.'

Raven's flow was interrupted by a tap on his shoulder. Barber was standing behind him looking exhausted and a little defeated, latex gloves on either hand. He was holding something.

'This look familiar, boss?'

Barber held the book out to him with enough care not to contaminate the evidence.

'What is it?' Raven took a look at it. It looked like an old bible or a seldom used and ancient encyclopaedia to him. Brown cover, frayed, tattered pages and a thin layer of dust. The front of the book was embossed in gold leaf. It was thick, maybe a thousand pages, and it smelt musty like old people. 'I can't read it, what does it say?'

Barber turned his hand and held it so the dim light emanating through the bedroom window fell on its cover. He was grinning unsurely.

The title read: The Book of Ahriman.

'What? What is this, Barber?'

Barber's slightly demonic grin expanded, almost slicing his head in two.

'It's our hook, line and sinker, boss. This book belongs to our Angra Mainyu.'

Raven frowned, the cogs in his brain whirring like an old, beaten up engine in need of oil and attention, and then something clicked, and he smiled. He recalled the capsules, the scraps of paper, the words that were foreign and other worldly to them. In the woods, in the warehouse and on the street during his first encounter with the bizarre stranger with a pale face. Those messages that had confused and befuddled them until Barber had researched them and made the link to the ancient scriptures and myths.

'This,' Barber exclaimed, pointing to the book, 'confirms that the door to Āz is open after all and it's time to take a peek inside.'

Chapter 67: Breaking News

It was a bad day. A really, really bad day. I was driving home from work, I had stayed a little later to mark some papers, when I noticed Tony walking up the street to our house. He looked awful. Really thin, thinner than I had ever seen him before. He had never been a great eater, always picking. He preferred a drink to food. I had tried to instil a healthy eating regime into him but had failed dismally on several occasions.

I drove past him, not stopping, hoping beyond hope that he would just walk on by Nick's house. He looked so ill, like he hadn't been outside in weeks and he looked mad, really mad.

I pulled up onto the driveway next to Nick's car and looked down the street. I could see Tony's tall, thin silhouette striding towards our house. I turned to the front door and pulled out my key, frantically trying to slot it home and get inside. I remember fumbling it at least three times and dropping it more than once. I don't know why but I was terrified. Tony had never hurt me, not physically, but he had always been challenging. He could fly into a fit of rage at a moment's notice. I hadn't really paid it any mind when I was with him, just believing it to be how things were. It wasn't until I met Nick that I recognised the kind of mental torture that Tony had been putting me through for so long.

The door swung inwards as I surged through. Nick was already home, sitting at the table. I remember he put the phone down really quickly. I didn't think much of that at the time either. I guess you think that I'm not very observant and you're probably right. I've always just gone along with things. Trusting people that were close to me. I can tell you that much has changed since… well, you know.

'Nick, Tony's on his way round. I don't know why. I have no idea. But he doesn't look like he's coming around for a cup of tea.'

'What?' he gasped, flustered, 'round here?'

'Yes, round here! Where do you think I mean?'

'Okay, okay. Not a problem. I'll… I'll talk to him.' I could see that Nick was visibly shaken and more than a little on edge. Again, it didn't occur to me at the time that perhaps the call he had taken had something to do with his anxious demeanour.

'No. No. That would be bad. I'll talk to him. I can calm him down from whatever mood he's gotten himself into.'

'Can you do that?' Nick had his arms on my shoulders.

'Sure,' I tried to steady my trembling voice, 'sure I can. I've done it before; I can do it again.' But I hadn't seen him like that before.

The door banged loudly, like someone was trying to bash it in with two hands. Both Nick and I jumped, and Nick even let out a little cry.

'It's okay, Nick. I can handle this.'

I turned and went to the door. There was a loud bang again. This time I jumped so high that my heart caught in my throat. I took a deep breath and opened it.

Tony was standing there. He looked like death. Literally.

'Where is he?'

'Where's who?'

'That bastard you're fucking.'

'I…I'm what? How dare you!'

'Don't mess with me, Jane. I know what's been going on. I'm not an idiot. Now where the fuck is he?'

I was taken aback, and I mean a long way back. He was being so direct, so unlike the Tony that I knew. I was angry and intrigued all at the same time.

'How dare you speak to me like…'

With that he shoved me aside and walked past me into the front room. Nick was standing, halfway between the lounge and the dining room, looking like a lost little boy scout. Tony wasted no time and walked over to him, swinging a vicious punch which connected with Nick's nose causing a crunching, popping sound. Nick cried out in agony and fell to the floor, blood streaming through his fingers.

'Wot ze fug!' Tears were rolling down his cheeks and blood was spilling onto his pale blue shirt and tie.

'Have you told her yet?'

'Tole her wot?' Nick was sitting upright, his legs out in front of him, one hand over his face and the other holding a leg of a chair to steady himself. Tony was looming over him like a giant beanstalk, pointing one long, bony finger at Nick and the other at me.

'You know what, you arsehole!'

'I dorn no.'

I tried to grab Tony's shoulder, but he shrugged me away without looking at me. He was focussed on Nick.

'I know, you bastard. I know. I know everything. Who do you think put them on to you?'

I could see Nick's eyes open in bewilderment.

'It woz yow?'

'Yes, it was me, you dipshit. Do you think I was going to let her go that easily?'

I was confused, angry and dumbfounded. I didn't know what to think. All I knew was that my ex-boyfriend had shown up, walked into my new home and hit the man that I was slowly falling in love with. And yet there was something new and different going on. I just felt all over the place.

'Tony, I have no idea what you are going on about, but I suggest you leave. If you leave now, I won't call the police.' It was all I could think of to get him to go quietly.

'Not until he tells you.' He was still staring down at Nick, refusing to make eye contact with me.

'Tells me what?'

'Nick?'

Nick looked at me and shrugged his shoulders, but I could tell that something was up. His eyes gave it away.

I looked at the dining room table, the phone still lying where Nick had left it. There was a letter next to it. The letter I had given Nick the day before. The one that he had gotten all weird about. I walked over and picked it up.

'No, Dane. No. Dorn reed id.'

Those words, muffled and nasal as they were, dug needles into my spine. What didn't he want me to know? What had he been hiding from me? I pulled the letter from the envelope and slowly opened it. The letter heading made me shudder.

DIVORCE PETITION

I dropped the letter onto the table and took a step back as if I had just taken a solid blow to the ribcage. I looked at him, sitting there on the floor, blood down his shirt and trousers and tears and snot running down his cheeks and chin. I remember mouthing *what?*

'He's married, Jane. He's fucking married! He's even got two kids, two young girls. Alice and Olivia. They didn't know anything about you or any of the other women that he has been with. They just knew that he had walked out on them two years ago and had never come home. Didn't even have the decency to tell them that he was leaving or where he had gone. The first that they knew he was still in the country, or even still alive, was when I called them.'

'I'm dory, Dane.'

My vision went blurry, my blood turned cold. I can still recall that feeling of desperately needing to sit down before I fell down, to curl into a defensive ball. My life had been turned upside down in the previous month but at least I knew, or believed, that I had somewhere to go. Someone to be with. Now this? I looked at Nick.

'You fucker...' I whispered the words.

'Dane...'

'Don't speak to me you… you FUCKER!'

I stood up and kicked him hard. Once, twice, three times. I was crying by this time. Crying with rage and remorse. I was so, so angry.

Tony reached out to me. 'I'm sorry I had to do this, Jane. I….'

'FUCK YOU, TONY!! FUCK YOU!'

I was so angry at them both but, probably and insanely, more angry with Tony for destroying my new idyllic life. I knew it could never be the same again and he had brought this terrible revelation and realisation through *my* front door. Delivered it to me by hand with a smile and a 'have a nice day'.

'But I…'

'But what? You think this changes anything? You think I'm going to come back to you because of this? Really? REALLY?'

'But…'

I laughed at him then. Walked right up to him, put my face up to his, standing on tippy toe, and laughed. A mocking, bitchy, horrible laugh. Laughed so hard it hurt my throat and strained my stomach muscles.

'I wouldn't come back to you if you were the last man on earth, you pathetic loser. What would I be coming back to? Working my backside off to support your good for nothing arse!' I frightened myself. I sounded just like my mother. 'So that you could spend all of your time with your bezzy next door and spend as little time with me as possible! And wait on you hand and foot, all so that you can write a book which you will never finish, and even if you did it probably wouldn't be any bloody good.' I pushed him back towards the door, '*NOW GET OUT OF MY HOME AND LEAVE US ALONE!*'

He stood in the doorway, dejected and desperate, a tear running down one ashen cheek, his shoulders slumped forward in pathetic defeat and looked down at me. He looked displaced, lost. I think I still loved him a little, probably still do. But I couldn't go back. I could *never* go back.

He looked at Nick and then back at me. His eyes were burning with some kind of intensity, but I knew that I had hurt him. Probably more than I had meant to. But there we were, three people whose lives had been inexorably and irreparably destroyed. And for what?

'I'm sorry, Jane.'

And then he was gone.

Chapter 68: The Girl

'It's Tony. Tony from the bar.'

'Tony?'

'Yeah, the bar man. I was serving drinks two nights ago at Stooges. You were watching that singer. Izzy something or other.'

'Mojo.'

'What?'

'That's his name. Izzy Mojo. I went to school with him.'

'That's him.'

'His name's actually Tim. Timothy Brent. Bit of a geek but he has a nice voice.'

'He drones on a bit.'

She laughed, 'True, true. But still. He's a mate.'

'You left me your number.'

'Did you think I was being forward?'

'A little.'

She laughed again, 'That's what my friends tells me. They say I come on a bit strong. Sorry.'

'Don't apologise.'

'Okay, I won't.'

There was a pause. Tony broke the awkward silence. 'So, do you want to meet?'

'Sure.'

'Where?'

'S'up to you.'

'You hang out anywhere?'

'Sure. Yeah. Gold-Diggers. It's a club in town. We go there most Friday and Saturday nights.'

'Can't say I've heard of it. Did it used to be something else?'

'Mmm, I'm not sure. Something like Prance and Dance?'

'Trance n' Dance. That's the one. My friends and I used to frequent that place quite a lot a few years ago. Will you be there this Friday night?'

'Yep, sure will. Me and my girls. We're practically part of the furniture.'

'Then maybe I'll meet you for a drink. I'll buy you one…maybe even two.'

She laughed again. He thought she had a nice laugh. The kind of laugh that he found infectious and invigorating. 'Sounds great. I'll keep my eye out for you.'

'No need… I've got your number.'

Chapter 69: Salutations and Confrontations

Raven and the Chief stood at the Mayor's front door, waiting for someone to let them in.

'Do we have him yet?' The Chief looked visibly uncomfortable. He knew that both he and Raven were on borrowed time if they couldn't swiftly bring the whole bloody nightmare to a close.

'Not yet. But we will.'

'How soon?'

'Very soon,' Raven was sure that they would have the killer behind bars within hours, 'now that we have a face and a name it's really only a matter of time.'

'You know he won't see it like that?'

'He never does.' Raven decided to change the subject. 'How's Stu?'

The Chief's mood lifted instantly, and he smiled, 'Yes. Really good. Thanks for asking, Luke. He's doing good.'

'You two going away on holiday this year? After... all of this.'

'Hoping to. Yes, hoping to get away. Maybe on another walking holiday. Just the two of us. And the dogs.'

'That's good, Chief. You need a break.'

'Don't we all, Luke, you especially. You look like you're on edge all of the time. This thing has taken it out of all of us,' he paused, and then changed the topic of conversation. 'Why don't you just go ahead and make an honest woman of Lisa? You could do a lot worse you know.'

'I know, Chief. I just might do that.'

'That's good. Really good. The office could do with an event to look forward to. An upbeat event, a real shindig... like a good wedding.'

'Ha. Well, don't go sending out invites just yet,' he scratched his head awkwardly, 'we might just have one other big event... a really big event, prior to that.'

'That being?'

'Well,' Raven took a deep breath, 'I wasn't going to say anything but turns out that,' he smiled proudly, 'we're going to be parents.'

The Chief's jaw hit the floor. 'Parents?'

'Yep.'

'You and Lisa?'

'The very same.'

'Well I'll shit the bed!' The Chief put an arm around Raven and hugged tightly. 'Congratulations, my old friend. Congratulations! Oh,' his face was flushed red, 'I'm so pleased for you, Luke. *So pleased*. You will make a great dad.'

'I sure hope so.'

'Well, I believe you would. I really do. What great news.'

With that the door opened and the Mayor's man servant greeted them.

'Hello gentlemen.'

'Hello Leo. Is he in?' The Chief gave the well-dressed lackey a look of mild contempt.

'He sure is, gentlemen. As a matter of fact, the Mayor is reclining in the lounge and he has asked if you wouldn't mind joining him. If it's OK I'll take you through now.'

The Chief and Raven glanced at each other, nodded and followed him as he glided across the entrance hallway and through to the large sitting room with its assortment of lamps, Kashmir rugs and mock Tudor beams. The Mayor was reclining on a long, pale leather sofa, an expensive looking brandy in his pudgy, right hand. He beckoned them in.

'Hello Chief Simmonds. D.I. Raven. Come in, come in. Have a drink.'

'Not for me, Mayor,' Raven looked around at the gauche opulence the Mayor surrounded himself with. He thought it was good to know that the taxes he paid out of his meagre salary were going to good causes. He huffed under his breath. It didn't go unnoticed and neither did he intend it to.

'Chief?'

'I'll have a small scotch please. On the rocks.'

'Excellent, excellent. Leo, please do the honours. Come gentlemen. Come in and take a seat. You're making the place look untidy.'

The Chief reclined onto the couch next to the Mayor and Raven sat in what looked like a throne manufactured from dark mahogany and heavily polished brass. He placed his hands on his knees and attempted to look as uncomfortable as possible. He didn't plan to stay too long. He had promised Lisa that he would meet her after the meeting and take her out for dinner. They had a lot of catching up to do. And planning. Lots of planning.

'So, gentlemen,' the Mayor took a sip of his brandy and paused for effect, 'status update if you will.'

The Chief took his scotch from a silver tray. He nodded to Leo, 'Thank you. Well, where shall we begin? I should start by saying that things are looking up.'

'Are they now?'

'Yes, they are,' the Chief glanced at Raven, 'at eight thirty this morning we raided the house of an individual who is now our chief and only suspect.'

'Chief and only suspect eh?'

'That's right. We were given a name and address by a key witness and, whilst the suspect was not at home when we conducted our raid...'

'Not at home?'

'No, not at home. Whilst he was not at home during the raid, we were able to locate several artefacts that link the suspect to at least three of the four murders.'

'Three of the four.' The Mayor was nodding in a matter of fact way.

'Yes,' the Chief glanced at Raven again who was notably becoming more and more agitated, 'three of the four. And the team located several blood stains which are at the lab being analysed as we speak.'

'Blood stains.'

'Yes sir. Blood stains.'

'Any weapon?'

'Weapon?'

'Yes. Was there a weapon? Knife. Axe. Something sharp? Please tell me we have a weapon.'

'Er…' the Chief sipped his scotch, 'no sir.'

'Any idea of your suspect's whereabouts?'

'Not as such but…'

'Yes or no?'

'Then I would have to say no.'

'And your chief witness is?'

'Er,' the Chief looked at Raven again, this time more in hope than for any moral support.

Raven chipped in, 'Doctor Jasmine Chandur, Mister Mayor.'

'Doctor Jasmine Cha…wait,' the Mayor sat forward on the couch and rested his brandy glass on a side table, 'Leo, more Brandy please! I know that name, don't I?'

'You might do, sir.'

'Yes, I might. Let me think.'

'Maybe you don't know her after all.'

'No, I'm sure I do. It's on the tip of my tongue. Something… official.'

'Well, there are a lot of official types in the town sir. Maybe if you could narrow it down a bit…'

'Don't fuck with me, Raven! You know damn well who she is! She's on our fucking payroll you imbecile!'

Raven sat back in his chair, disgruntled.

The Mayor looked from Raven to the Chief and back to Raven again. 'How do you two think this is going to look in the press? Police force get so desperately frustrated by their own lack of progress that they rely on public official to fabricate a lead?'

'Fabricate a lead?' It was Raven's turn to lean forward in his chair.

'Yes. Fabricate a lead. We've been at this for weeks. No, months, and have come up with diddly squat. So much so that I, the Mayor of this town, felt compelled, no obligated, to put myself in the spotlight on national television in front of millions of people, bare my soul and defend my good name, *our* good name.' The Mayor puffed out his chest, 'And yet just hours after a fourth murder takes place, the murder of some barmaid that, by the way, you had been fucking on and off for years, Detective Inspector, we suddenly come up with a name, an address and some sketchy evidence that links our suspect to the crimes. Leo, more brandy *PLEASE!*

'Sketchy evidence? Are you fucking kidding me?'

'Luke, calm down,' the Chief had necked his scotch, set down his crystal tumbler and had both hands held out submissively in an attempt to placate his D.I.

'Some blood and an old scrap book about some eons old middle eastern mythology that allegedly links the crumpled-up notes at the crime scene to our suspect? Is that it? IS THAT REALLY IT?' The Mayor's face had turned an odd shade of purple and his neck was red and blotchy.

'And what were you expecting, Mayor? The guy to be standing there, a knife in one hand and a severed head in the other? Is that how you think this works? Nice and clean, just like the movies?' It was Raven's turn to turn crimson, 'Oh, that's right, you wouldn't know having never spent any time doing an honest man's work… EVER!'

The Mayor stood up and Raven joined him.

'What I do know, Detective Inspector,' the Mayor growled the last two words, 'is that this will not stand up in court. Any good lawyer, shit any half good lawyer, will poke holes in this so wide that even you could fit your fat, pickled head through them,' he pointed a chubby, heavily ringed finger in the direction of Raven. 'No leads, I mean NOTHING AT ALL, and then all of a sudden your fuck buddy gets murdered and our chief pathologist miraculously remembers that she once had a couple of dates with the guy. While she was lounging in the back of *your* car while the murder was taking place which, by the way, *is against all police protocol.*' The Mayor paced from side to side, 'No, no, no. This is all wrong. All so horribly wrong. It's got conspiracy written all over it whether you like it or not,' he threw his glass at the wall where it shattered and sprayed Glencairn crystal all over the polished, hardwood floor, 'LEO, WHERE IS MY FUCKING BRANDY?'

'And you think I would do that?'

'It's irrelevant what I think. Irrelevant. This is a court room fuck up waiting to happen and a libel case against the police force and the council to boot,' the Mayor ran a hand through his beard, 'and, as you asked, I do think you would do it. Yes, I do. You've been dodging the IPCC for years but that doesn't mean that I don't know what goes on. You're corrupt to the core and this is well within your capabilities.'

The Chief raised his hand as if in need of the bathroom, 'But Chester...'

'DON'T FUCKING CALL ME CHESTER, DAVE! THIS IS WAY, WAY BEYOND FIRST NAME NICETIES!'

Raven took two steps swiftly forward and grabbed the Mayor by the collar, 'Leave... him... alone.'

The Mayor looked at Raven, a mixture of fear, surprise and defiance spread across his carefully polished features. He leant into the D.I., his goatee scratching the surface of Raven's chin and spoke quietly and deliberately. 'I suggest you let go of me or you will be an ex D.I. quicker than you can say *dead barmaid.*'

Detective Inspector Luke Raven hollered a shout of pure frustration and rage and hurled Mayor Chester Wood backwards through the antique trestle coffee table which splintered in half.

'WHAT THE FU...'

There was a soothing voice from the kitchen doorway. 'Now, now people. Let's just take the steam out of this, shall we?'

Raven, the Chief and the Mayor spun round. They had all seen Leo, the manservant, head to the kitchen just minutes earlier, picking fluff from the collar of his expensive designer suit jacket as he went, but the voice wasn't Leo's.

There, in the shady nook between the semi-circular low-topped bar and the open doorway, resplendent in a long black parka coat and a black, Peruvian hat with a white snow-flake pattern was a tall, thin man with a ghostly white face, shrouded in an ominous shadow so deeply black that his dark angular frame seemed to melt into it.

Pale Face leaned forward, his cracked white countenance folding into a hollow grin, and held his long arms out wide, his right, milky fist gripping a bloodied knife. He spoke in a thin voice, like wind whistling through dry reeds.

'Surprise...'

Chapter 70: Confession

'I need to tell you something son and I don't want you to be upset.'

Tony and Robert Charon were walking across the fairway on the ninth hole and were deep in conversation. The sky was full of clouds the shape and texture of cotton wool, the October air was brisk and there was a light, soothing breeze.

'What is it, Dad?'

'You may find it shocking.'

'I won't.' Tony was tired. He had never felt so tired in all his life. He had made a big play with Jane and it hadn't gone to plan. It had made him feel good, but she hadn't gone for it, not in the slightest and he hadn't known whether to laugh or cry. His sleep had suffered further as a result. He was starting to think that the damned insomnia would never end. The insomnia and the bad dreams.

'You might son, you just might.' Robert was wearing black jeans, black cowboy boots and a black, figure hugging sweatshirt. He had a silver chain with a small, bronze pendant around his neck and his hair was slicked back with perfumed, hair wax.

'I've had everything thrown at me these last few months, Dad. One more uncomfortable surprise isn't going to make much of a difference.'

'It's hard to put into words.'

'Just try me.'

Robert stopped and turned to face him.

'It's about your mother and your brother.'

Tony looked at him impassively, 'Is she dead?'

Robert's features solidified into a mixture of shock and pride, 'She is.' Tony looked at the floor.

'I'm sorry, son.'

'Did you kill her?'

Robert Charon's face was impassive.

'And Mitchell?'

Again, no emotion or reaction. Tony paused and took a deep breath. He felt the oxygen burning his throat and his lungs, a deep-seated burn that filled his torso with a strange, sweetly acidic sensation.

'Why did you do it?'

'They were trying to come between us. I couldn't allow that. Not again.'

'I wouldn't have let them.'

'Some things are unstoppable.'

'But you told me that your power was unstoppable.'

'I couldn't take any chances.'

Tony felt a tear roll down his right cheek. He swiftly wiped it away. 'She was dying.'

'Then perhaps I helped her pass without suffering.'

'And Mitch? Did he suffer?'

Robert placed a large, sun-kissed hand onto Tony's shoulder. 'He died of what had been killing him all along. Some people cannot be saved. It is in their destiny. They are not blessed with the grace of our legacy. It is…unfortunate, but unavoidable.'

Tony looked up at his father's face. 'She hurt me, Dad.'

'I know, son.'

'For so long. She hurt me for so, so long.'

'I know.'

'But I loved her.'

'I know that too.'

'Deep in my heart, in spite of everything, I loved her.' Robert Charon nodded again.

Tony looked across the golf course, its rolling greens, its perfectly trimmed putting lawns, the golden sandy bunkers, the fir trees swaying idly in the breeze. He looked back at the house, its large, sweeping wings, windows like eyes, dark, ominous stone, wide entranceway and jutting angular architraves. He looked ahead at the church, like a shining diamond on the hill. He loved it there. It was mesmerising.

'I won't miss her.'

'And neither should you.'

Robert grabbed his son in his long arms and pulled him to him. Tony buried his face in the crook of his father's neck and wept.

'Come now, son. It will all be okay.'

'I don't know if I have the strength.'

Robert ran his hands through his son's blond, tousled hair.

'Then I will give it to you. I will be your strength. Let us finish what we have started.'

Chapter 71: Neighbourly Love

Tony got home at around six o'clock. He was due back at work that evening, but he didn't think he had the energy in him. He decided he was going to crack on with his novel. It was the only thing that was keeping the horrible images in his mind at bay. Horrible thoughts. Dark, ominous, oppressive thoughts. Scary thoughts.

He dug deep in his pocket for his front door key and opened the gate onto the pathway.

'Tony, can I have a word?'

He turned around to see Sally West standing on the road behind him. She was wearing beige slacks, a loose-fitting black top and long, silver earrings.

'Er... yeah. Sure Sal. What's up?'

'I had a call from Jane.'

Tony frowned and took a breath, 'Really?'

'Yes, really.'

Tony couldn't help but think that her tone was a little disrespectful. 'And what did she say?'

'You know damn well what she said!' Sally's eyes were burning with an uncontrolled rage.

'Well, well... you see, now, I don't, do I, *Sal*?' Tony was also fighting to keep his cool, 'Because if I did, if I knew what she said, I wouldn't be asking.' He clenched and unclenched his hands. 'That would just be stupid now, wouldn't it?'

'You bastard.'

Tony stepped out from his garden onto the road. 'What did you call me?'

'You forced your way into her house, accused her of some horrible things and then attacked her new boyfriend? It's not right, Tony. It's not right,' Sally's face was burning red, her voice cracking with emotion, 'she was in hysterics. She was barely able to control herself.'

Tony took a step towards her. 'I did it for her own good.'

'Her own good? Her own bloody good? Do you really think that was helping her in any way whatsoever?'

'He was cheating on her.'

'He was going to tell her.'

'Easy to say that now.'

'That's not for you to decide. That's not for you to judge.'

'Somebody had to intervene. Somebody who cares for her!'

'It's over, Tony. She has left you. Can't you see that? It's finished. Let it go!'

Tony grabbed her by her shoulders. 'Don't you dare say that to me!'

Sally's eyes widened. 'Let go of me, you idiot!'

'Take back what you said!' Tony's desperately sleep-deprived features were haggard and drawn. His eyes were bloodshot, his unwashed hair was greasy and slick, and his skin was red and flaky.

'I'm telling you the truth. For your own good. You need to move on.' Sally glared at him imploringly.

'She is mine.'

'She is not your possession, Tony. She is not for you to own.'

'She loves me!'

'She doesn't! Not anymore.'

'Don't say that!'

'You need to hear it, Tony. You need to accept it. You can't keep going on like this. It's not good for her. It's not good for you!'

Tony gripped her tighter, digging his sharp fingers into her shoulders. 'I will NEVER accept it!'

Sally shrieked. 'Tony, let the fuck go! You're hurting me!'

From behind Sally a freshly showered and bathrobe-wearing Billy West came crashing out of his front door. 'What the fuck is going on here? Tony, what the fuck are you doing?'

'Stay away, Billy.'

'The hell I will. That's my wife!' Billy West took two steps forward and shoved Tony back hard. Tony released his grip on Sally.

'Stay out of this, Billy!'

'You lay one more finger on my Sal and I'm knocking you out, pal.'

'She was lying to me!'

Billy looked at Sally. 'She was what?'

Tony pointed a finger at her, his lips curled up in a hateful snarl. 'She's a fucking liar!'

'I told him the truth!' Sally looked at Billy, eyes wide and full of hurt, 'I told him the truth about him and Jane!'

Tony lunged at her, 'You filthy fucking liar! You're all filthy fucking liars!'

Billy grabbed him by the collar and threw him to the ground. 'What the hell has gotten into you, Tony? Is this about Jane, because if it is you've got to get past it! I told you. *I told you*! It's fucking over!'

Tony lay on the floor, staring at them through a haze of tears, loathing and confusion. 'It's not over. She still loves me. She's just confused. That bastard Nick. He wanted what we had. He got into her head. She just needs time.'

Billy took a deep breath, kissed his wife on the cheek and then knelt next to his neighbour. 'Then you have to give her time, Tony. You just have to give her time and space, my friend.'

Tony pulled himself up off of the floor and gingerly got to his feet, his eyes never leaving Billy's. 'You're no friend of mine, Billy

West. If you were you would see through this. See what they,' he pointed at Sally, 'are up to. All of them.' He grinned at Billy, a sneering, deceitful grin, 'Just stay out of this and stay away from me. Away from my business and my life. I am taking care of it.' And with that he crashed through the front gate and threw open his front door, slamming it behind him.

As he passed the bottom of the stairs, he grabbed the phone and hit speed dial. He was panting heavily, sweat droplets forming on his face and arms. He felt sick. Sick of everything.

'Hi… yeah. It's me. I'm in. I'm all in. Let's do this.'

Chapter 72: The Text

As usual he let me down.

I thought, stupidly as it turns out, that now he knew that the baby was coming, that it was his, that he would change his ways. Become more... reliable. But that just wasn't Luke Raven at all. Not in the slightest. Reliability was most definitely not his middle name.

I was back at my place, a police guard at the door twenty-four, seven. A young kid named Ashley. Tall and handsome but with no common sense. He was okay for the odd chat, good looking, smelt nice, but for all intents and purposes I was alone. Luke had said that he would pick me up at eight and we would go out for pizza. We would talk. You know, about the baby and stuff? I had got the feeling that he was kind of emotional about the whole thing. Excited even.

The baby had been kicking all day. Pushing and shoving just like it's dad, never able to sit still. I couldn't get comfortable and it was making me pretty irritated. I remember really yearning for a cigarette and a glass of wine. I couldn't believe I had been stood up again.

I had been out of the hospital for a couple of days and I hadn't seen Luke in all that time. Not one visit, not even for a moment. I had been given a lift back to the flat by a uniformed officer, but I had been expecting Luke to be there. But... no. Yeah, he had called to check on me and stuff and he had sent me some flowers but, you know, I wanted to see him. Needed to talk to him. Face to face.

I had texted him, three or four times. You know? Where are you? Thought you said eight o'clock? I'm hungry, should I make myself some dinner? But no answer. Nothing. Nada. You might think that perhaps I should have been worried, but you don't know Luke like I do. Disappointing people was second nature to him and disappearing for days was not unusual.

Eight o'clock turned into eight fifteen, eight fifteen turned into eight thirty, and before I knew it, it was almost nine. I went out to the kitchen and looked in the freezer. There was nothing in there but a Weight Watchers chilli for one, so I took it out, looked it over and then put it back. Given that I knew I was now eating for two, a fat-free meal for one really wasn't going to cut it.

And that's when I got the text. My phone beeped twice. I reached over to the worktop by the kettle, unplugged the phone from the charger (the battery never seems to last for more than ten minutes these days) and picked it up.

I read it and I really didn't understand it at first. It didn't seem to make a lot of sense.

Just a few words.

At Mayor's. He's here. Get Damo x

Chapter 73: Hostages

'Who the hell are you?' The Mayor defiantly confronted the intruder with a wary unease.

'You don't know me, Chester?' Pale Face was standing in a crucifix pose, his arms outstretched, his pasty features twisted and contorted in a grotesque grin, 'Surely you know who I am, because I know you. I know all about you. Things that you don't even know about yourself. What a story I could write. The hookers, the drugs, the violent and, verging on non-consensual, sex with your eager butler,' he laughed to himself, 'and you have been looking for me for so long. Hell, the whole town has been looking for me. It's *meeeeee.*' He drew out the last word, long and piercing like the cry of a baby fox.

'I know who you are.' Raven took a step forward.

'Well of course you do, Detective Inspector. We're firm friends now, aren't we? Especially after that little chat we had before. You know, at number 36?' Raven winced. Pale Face wiped the blade of the knife on his coat and held it up so that he could look at it, 'Such good, good friends. I feel like I've known you all my life. I even dream of you. See you in my dreams, dancing with dead, pretty girls in nightclubs. Bizarre really,' he laughed, 'freaks me out a little.'

Raven was taken aback with the distinct similarity with his own, disturbed dreams but shook it off. 'Thankfully that's not the case.' Raven inched further forward, 'We are not friends. I couldn't think of anything worse than having a friend such as you. A murderous, hateful, villainous individual. Able to flick a switch on a human life without a moment's hesitation. Carrying out these hate crimes on such young, young women. Young, innocent women with their whole lives ahead of them.'

'Like Daisy?'

Raven recoiled. The simple mention of her name caused a pain like pins being pushed brutally into his heart. 'Yes, you bastard. Like Daisy.'

'And you think the way that you treated her when she was alive, using her when it suited you, discarding her when it didn't, you think that was first class I assume?'

Raven eyed him venomously, 'What the fuck does that have to do with you?'

'You're throwing stones, Detective Inspector. Make sure that you step out of your glass house when you do so.'

Raven's face flushed red. He felt anger and self-loathing all in an instant.

'This is all very nice, very nice indeed, Mister....?' The Mayor took two steps forward, his palm facing forward in a conciliatory manner.

'I don't think that I shall be offering my name, Chester. That would be pretty dumb now, wouldn't it?'

'Yes, yes. I suppose so, but as I was saying, this is all very nice. A nice chat and all. But what the fuck are you doing in my house? And what the hell do you want?'

Pale Face turned and peered at him through sad, rueful eyes, his gaze penetrating through the eyes of the Mayor and seemingly foraging through his blackened soul. 'What do I want?'

'Yes. What do you want? I mean, you've broken into my home by some means, and I have to say that I don't know how given that the place is alarmed to the eyeballs,' the Mayor nodded to the kitchen door, 'I believe it is very possible that you have killed my butler judging by the bloodied weapon in your hands, and now you stand before us, the Mayor of the town and two senior police officials, one of which is armed by the way,' he glanced at Raven affirmatively, 'and it seems that you are expecting us to be afraid,' he chuckled non-convincingly, 'you have brought a knife to a gunfight my friend.' The Mayor was gritting his teeth. Raven smirked at the balls of the guy. He was irritating, self-centred, egotistical and all manner of horrendous things that Raven despised, but he was amazed at how brazen he was.

Pale Face squinted his eyes and smiled. 'Well, that's very interesting. Very interesting.' He looked from the Mayor, down at the Chief who was still sitting on the sofa, his shaky hand gripping his glass of scotch, and back to Raven. 'Firstly, the butler's not dead. He might bleed out before we're done, but he's certainly not dead yet.' He wiped a bloodied hand across his mouth. 'Secondly, I don't really want anything from you at all. No demands from me.' He held his hands out and chuckled. 'But I do need a finale.' The shadow behind him moved and shifted. '*He* demands it you see, and *He* must be obeyed.' Raven caught sight of Pale Face looking from side to side, his eyes flitting and furtive. Was he afraid?

The Chief stood up. 'What... what kind of finale?'

'A fitting one, David. One that brings this all together. Gives *Him* what he wants and shows *Him* that I am worthy.'

The Chief walked to Raven's side. 'Worthy of what?'

Pale Face laughed. It was a brittle, nervous cackle. 'My prize, David. My prize. The thing that I have been chasing all along.'

'And,' the Chief's tone was subtle, inquisitive but comforting, 'what is this prize? Maybe it's something that we can get for you. Without having to go through all of... this.'

Pale face was looking at the Chief impassively. His maniacal smile had disappeared. He was listening.

He pondered something for a moment and then almost jolted as if being woken abruptly.

'Ha ha. You want me to tell you? Ha ha. Do I look like an idiot? I tell you and then you take it away from me. Take it *aaaall* away. Make all of this... this effort, this drama, this fucking tragedy into a stupendous waste of time. No way. No fucking way!' Pale face pointed to each of them in turn, 'You see, what you don't realise is that we are all connected. Connected by a common thread, by all of these events, by death, by fate, by transcript,' he looked at the fingers of both of his hands, 'by life.' He paused, contemplating. 'Whatever you might think, whatever you believe that you can do individually or collectively to turn things around, this evening will turn out exactly the way I expect it to,' he inspected each finger curiously and then smiled. A grim, painful smile, 'And there's not one fucking thing that you can do about it!' Raven slipped a hand into his pocket.

'Don't do that, Luke! DO NOT DO THAT!' He pointed at Raven's right hand and slipped his own right hand into the pocket of his parka. 'You do that and then we all die.' With that Pale Face pulled out a small, rubber handled device with what looked like an X-Box style trigger switch.

'Ka... fucking... boom!'

Chapter 74: The Date

Tony stood on Waynes Street, just opposite the club. There were tens of kids out front, boys and girls in their late teens and early twenties, smoking cigarettes, laughing and joking, calling each other names and flirting vivaciously. There were already a few clearly a little worse for wear. He spotted two bouncers on the door, six feet plus tall and three feet wide, dressed in black combats and looking at Tony like they were ready for a tussle.

He didn't want to go in. He'd been to these places before and the music really wasn't his cup of tea. Tuneless songs, trancy synthesisers, bass and drums way up in the mix and no real discernible vocal melody. And besides, he thought, he wasn't feeling great. His head hurt, his eyes hurt, he felt pretty useless as a matter of fact and he didn't really know why he was there. But he was going in, nonetheless.

His dad had convinced him to go.

'It's your time, Anthony. This is your time.'

'I don't know, Dad. I just want to curl up in a ball and silently wait until it all goes away.'

'That's the child in you. Push it away. You're a grown man now. You can make your own choices, stand up and be more than just a number. Nothing comes for free, Anthony. Nothing comes in a gift bag with a little bow on it, a sign saying take me, I'm yours, no charge.'

'Maybe now's not the right time.'

'Now is the only time.'

'But I...'

'No buts, Anthony. Only action. If you want to get everything you believe is rightfully yours then you have to believe in yourself.'

'I don't know that I do.'

'Then believe in me. I got to where I am today through positive action. Erase all negativity, be decisive, be creative and be a better version of yourself. That is the way our family has always been, that is the way we always will be.'

'I guess you're right.'

'I know I am.'

And here he was, standing out in the October cold, his coat zipped up to his neck, three pints of Doombar and a double bourbon inside of him, his body frail and weak from lack of sleep and food, his mind still on other things. Hiding in the shadows.

He walked up to the two doormen.

'Evening, boys.'

'Evening, sir. We're going to need to pat you down.'

'Not a problem, gents. I've got nothing on me but my wallet and my phone.' The big guy ran his hands down Tony's sides and legs and winked at him.

'All good, sir, you can go in.'

Tony made his way up the stairs, handed his money over to the young girl behind the counter with piercings in her lips and cheek and pushed open the large double doors.

He squinted. The space beyond was black with flashing red, blue and green lights, lasers tracing shapes up the walls, loud, thumping music, so loud it beat a drum pattern in his chest, sweaty bodies rubbing up against each other, queues of people around the bar, scantily clad dancers cutting shapes on high podiums, young waiters and waitresses with utility belts holding test tube shaped containers full of colourful alcoholic drinks. He hated these places.

He stood in the doorway, not wanting to enter while people

pushed past him to get to and from the toilets. He looked around. He was sure he would find the girl easily. He remembered her long blond hair, her dainty features, her dark brown eyes.

He felt eyes on him as if he was being stared at through some kind of giant looking glass. He felt as if he were an actor in a movie, like the scene before him was from a long-forgotten dream, the distant memories coming back to him in tiny, distorted snippets. His body felt clammy and claustrophobic and his skin tingled as if roaming, icy hands were running up and down his stomach and spine. He shook it off and looked around.

He spotted her, further back in the room amongst a throng of writhing people, dancing around some bloke in a black T shirt and blue jeans. She glanced over at him and he raised a hand. She smiled back at him and called him over.

He grinned.

*

Tony got them out of there as quickly as he could. It was a suffocating environment for him; dark, oppressive and intensely claustrophobic. He grabbed her hand as they descended the stairs and exited into the street. She was in a little black dress, black heels, long blond hair, tiny clutch bag. She looked like…like Jane. Maybe a few years younger but… he could see the resemblance. She was shivering.

'You look cold.'

'I am. It's fucking freezing out here.'

'Then let's get out of here. I've booked us a table.'

'Where?'

'Rizzi's. It's a little Italian place I know. Nice and quiet. We can talk.'

She laughed. 'Italian? Most blokes only want to go for a curry or a kebab.'

He smiled, 'Maybe I'm a little bit classier than most blokes.'

She giggled, 'Let's hope so.'

He laughed and waved down a cab.

The restaurant was less than a mile away, but Tony didn't feel like he had the energy to walk. It was up hill most of the way and he hadn't had any exercise in weeks. His head was pounding and his stomach was churning and besides, he thought sheepishly, she was cold and he was buggered if he was giving up his coat.

They chatted all of the way there. She told him about her friends and how she had left them behind when she had spotted him. He asked her why she hadn't introduced him and she had told him that she already had a boyfriend that she was trying to get shot of. She didn't want her friends gossiping behind her back and for him to find out before she had had a chance to tell him.

'I thought it was best if I slipped away unnoticed.'

'Maybe you're ashamed of being seen out with an older bloke.'

'I'm not ashamed of anything. I do what I want, when I want.' She winked at him and ran a hand softly down the inside of his leg. He shuddered. Jane's face appeared in his mind like an unwanted intruder. Jane, her legs wrapped around that imbecile Nick. Jane, on top of him, writhing in ecstasy, her hips grinding into his, her small but firm breasts bobbing up and down like rubber ducks in the bath. Jane and Nick, covered in sweat and smelling of sex. Jane and Nick.

Fucking.

The cab pulled up outside of the restaurant and Tony handed the cab driver a twenty.

'Keep the change mate. Pick us up in a couple of hours, yeah?'

'No worries, buddy. I'll be parked out front.'

'Cheers.' Tony got out and walked round to the other door. He opened it and took her hand as she peeled herself from the car.

'Ready?'

She smiled at him as she smoothed down her tight-fitting dress. 'Ready.'

Chapter 75: Negotiation

'Whoah there, buddy! Just ease down. Just ease down!' The Mayor had both hands out in front as if trying to protect himself from the impending blast.

'I think it's you who needs to…ease down, Chester. If you freak me out, I am liable to slip and press this little switch here.' Pale Face smiled at the Mayor, his creamy, cracked and ragged complexion creasing into tiny folds, flaky skin peeling from his nose and neck. Raven could see blisters at his nape and across his forehead.

'Listen, friend. Let's just all calm down and find out what you want.' Raven had taken his hand away from his jacket and was holding both palms up in a gesture of surrender.

'I told you, Luke. I don't want anything. *He* wants it. It has always been *Him*. Not me.' Pale Face looked around at the darkness slowly enveloping him.

'Okay, okay.' Raven was watching for movement, the memory of number 36 Silver Birch Street etched in his mind like a bloodied stain. 'And who is *He*?'

'I told you.'

'You told me?'

'In my notes.'

'Your notes?'

'I left you fucking notes, Luke. Didn't you read them?'

The Chief intervened, 'The scraps of paper, Raven. At the murder scenes.'

Raven slapped his head. 'Sorry, sorry. The notes. In the strange language. Something... foreign.'

Pale Face laughed. 'Your ignorance is a thing to behold, Luke. You're not an educated man, are you?'

Raven blushed. 'I fail to see how my schooling has anything to do with this.'

'If you had listened in class you might have learned something. The notes I left you were from ancient scrolls. Clues if you will.' Pale Face grinned, 'If you had completed your research you may have gotten to me sooner. Might have even saved your friend.'

The Mayor gave Raven a reproachful stare. 'What is he talking about, Detective Inspector?'

'The notes. Barber looked them up. It was religious bullshit. Something about an ancient people. A time before Christianity.'

'Way, way before that nonsense.' Pale face turned his attention to the Mayor, 'It's dawn of time stuff, Chester. Creatures that existed before humanity saw fit to drag itself out of the primordial soup. Beings that created us, that still exist here,' he waved his arms around him, his right hand still gripping the trigger switch, 'amongst us, around us, within us.'

'You're not making any sense.' The Mayor had his gaze firmly fixed on the detonator.

'Have you heard of the prophet Zoroaster?'

The Chief looked at the Mayor and shrugged his shoulders.

'Ignorance all around me.' Pale Face pointed his knife at the Mayor, 'If you were less ignorant you would know that he spoke of ancient beings, creatures that created us. You would know of Ahura Mazda, the monster that cast my family aside and drove us from our homes. And you would know of *Him*. *He* is around me,' he looked from side to side, 'if you look closely you will see *Him*. *He* is not completely here yet, but *He* is coming. The door is open. You will see.'

Raven looked at him curiously, 'The door. The door. Damo mentioned it to me. And some other creature. Anger... Angra...'

'Do not speak his name!'

'Jesus kid. I couldn't if I tried. This just sounds like bullshit to me. Something you use to justify your acts of horror!'

Pale Face turned to him, 'You think this is bullshit? You think this is bullshit, Luke?! Do you think that I am doing this for fun?'

Raven took a step closer, 'No. No, I don't,' he paused and smiled with regret, 'I think you're doing this because you're two sandwiches short of a picnic.'

Pale Face laughed, his head thrown back, maniacal shrieks emitting from his fractured lips, 'Angra Manyu will be here soon, Luke. And then you will see. We will all see! You will feel his wrath; it will be thrust down onto us like a shower of a thousand knives. We will not survive,' he pointed his knife at Raven, 'unless I am able to appease him.'

'Is that what all of this has been about? You've been sacrificing young women to stave off some fictional being that only exists in the warped recesses of your mind? Is that why you have been doing all of this?' Raven was astounded.

'You know nothing!'

'I know everything, you crazy son of a bitch. You think that by taking the blood of those girls that you could deliver it as a...an offering to the... the Gods? For what? To stop some kind of end of days scenario? Armageddon?'

'No!'

'Then what?'

'You've got it all wrong!'

'Then educate me!'

'You wouldn't understand!' Pale Face was pacing up and down, the darkening shadow behind him swirling like a whirlpool of tar-like soup.

'There will be no end of days! Not now, not for many, many eons. *He* doesn't want that. *He* feeds off of mankind's greeds, its lusts, its desires. *He* feasts on the depravity, the despair, on man killing man, woman killing woman, tearing at each other like wild dogs. *He* laughs at hunger, famine, disease, pestilence. Wars give him strength. Pain gives him energy. Why would *He* want to destroy the very thing that keeps him alive?'

'Then why is *He* doing this?' Raven watched as the Mayor slowly slipped behind Pale Face as he paced the room, the black cloud attached to him like a grisly, demonic cloak.

'*He* is not doing anything at all.' Pale Face seemed annoyed, confused.

'Then why is *He* coming?' Raven stood in front of Pale Face, distracting him so that the Mayor could stay out of view as he grabbed a wrought-iron candle stick.

'BECAUSE I ASKED HIM TO!'

Raven and the Chief glanced at each other. 'You what?'

Pale Face laughed. 'I... called... *Him*. Because he can give me something that... I... want.'

The Chief cast a sideways glance at the Mayor and realised in a moment of clarity what was about to unfold. He interjected, 'If you told us what you wanted then perhaps we, rather than this... thing, erm... well, perhaps we could get it for you.'

'It's not a thing, David. It's a person.'

The Chief looked dumbfounded, 'I don't understand.'

'It's my love.'

'Your love?'

Pale Face looked at the floor. 'Yes.' He sighed, 'My one true love.'

And then, seeing his opportunity, the Mayor raised his arm high above his head and gave out a mighty scream.

The dark shadow surrounding Pale Face wrapped its tendrils around its host's body and yanked him to one side just as the Mayor's hand bearing the candlestick sought to connect with Pale Face's skull. The momentum of the Mayor threw him forward, a look of dumbfounded surprise on his face, allowing Pale Face to whirl round and thrust the knife into his throat. The blade tour through the

Mayor's skin, bone, sinew and cartilage and up through the back of his skull, creating jets of thick, dark-red blood spraying three feet into the air and onto the extravagantly adorned walls and carpet.

The Chief cried out in shock and disgust and Raven turned his head away. Pale Face looked down at the chief in surprise and anger.

Then the front-door crashed in.

Chapter 76: Dinner Date

'Shit. I don't even know your name.'

The girl laughed as she swallowed her food. 'It's Tracey. My friends call me Trace.'

'I can't believe I hadn't asked that already.'

'You new to this?'

'No. Just out of practise.'

'You have a girlfriend?' Tony looked down at his plate, 'It's okay if you do. I won't judge.'

'Split up actually. Kind of on a break.'

'Aren't we all?' She laughed again. Tony was starting to find her laugh a little irritating. Nothing, he thought, was that funny. 'I know your name.'

'Oh. How so?'

She smiled as she sipped her wine. 'I asked around. I've seen you a few times in Stooges. You worked there long?'

'About three years on and off. It suits me.' He took a mouthful of tagliatelle and meatballs.

'Is that your job?' She laughed again. He bit down on his fork.

'It's not my career if that's what you're asking.' *Bitch*, he thought to himself, who was she to mock him?

'Then what is?' She stopped and pointed at him. 'Wait. You're not one of those vloggers are you?' She wiped her face with her napkin and smiled inanely.

'I'm an author.'

'Really?' She seemed impressed. 'What have you written?'

'I'm in the middle of something.'

'Is it any good?'

'I don't know yet.'

'What's it about?'

He sipped his beer and took a deep breath. 'I'd rather not say.'

'Embarrassed?'

He was starting to sweat. He could feel his clothes clinging to him. 'No. I would just rather wait until it's finished.'

'My friend wrote a book last year. Man, it was pants. The guy could hardly string two sentences together let alone a whole book. We all took the piss out of him for weeks,' she laughed again and had another bite from her pizza. Hot, stringy cheese hung from her bottom lip. 'I don't think he's going to write a book again. We told him to stick to Facebook.'

Tony could hear his dad's words in his head. This is your time, Anthony. Take the next step. Don't be distracted. You can have anything you want. Just be bold. Be empowered.

Be a better version of you.

He swigged greedily from his glass, his head flushing with heat, his vision blurring, his body oozing with sweat and fever.

'Well, I hope mine will be...somewhat better than pants.' He smiled but he didn't mean it. His whole body was burning up and his stomach acid was raging a war throughout his intestines.

'Let's hope so.' She grabbed his hand, 'Maybe I can get a signed copy later.' She laughed loudly and took another swig from her wine.

'I need to... er... go to the loo. I'll be back in a second.'

'Sure,' she waved her hand at him, 'take your time.'

He got up from his chair, almost tripping a waiter over behind him, and rushed to the back of the room where the 'Customer Toilets' sign was hanging. He burst through the hallway door and into the gents. He raced to the cubicle, which was thankfully empty, and threw up. He retched for what seemed like an eternity, black bile tainted with thin strings of blood filling the bowl, and then wiped his face with tissue paper.

He stood up and his vision distorted. He felt a rush of heat rise to the top of his skull. He grabbed hold of the edge of the basin for balance and counted to ten, his eyes closed. When he opened them he could see again but what he saw before him in the bathroom mirror terrified him.

He was white. White as a sheet. His hair was slick with sweat, His lips were dry, his eyes black. He felt awful.

'Do I have to go through with this?'

He could hear his dad's voice. *You must do this for your own sake son. It's for your own good.*

'I feel... awful.'

This is how it always feels. The first time.

'Will it get better?'

It always gets better.

'I feel like I'm dying inside.'

Not dying. Just changing.

'I miss mum. I miss Jane.'

Stay strong, son.

Tony splashed his face with cold water, undid his shirt and wiped his armpits. Jesus, he thought, it was amazing this girl found him attractive at all. He looked a mess. He wiped his face on the towel hanging from the wall, took a deep breath and strode back into the restaurant.

The girl was finishing off her pizza as he sat down, and he poured her another glass of red wine. He folded his arms and smiled at her.

'So, clearly you know my full name. It's Tony. Tony Richards. You know that already. But I feel at a disadvantage,' she looked at him, confused, 'I only know your first name.'

'Well,' she laughed, 'maybe I like the mystery.'

It was Tony's turn to laugh. 'Oh, come on now. That's hardly fair.'

'Life's not fair, Tony.'

'Give me a break. How can I take you out to dinner and not even know your surname? That... that's just not right.'

She held out her hand and he took it. She smiled at him, her red lips carving a beautiful, crimson river across her face. 'Well, if we're going to get all formal about it, I'm Ms. Webb,' she chuckled, 'Ms. Tracey Webb.'

Chapter 77: Sacrifice

The alarm was wailing like a banshee. The houselights had dimmed and warning lights were spinning frantically in the doorway, giving the house an otherworldly glow.

The Mayor was lying face down on the floor in a spreading pool of blood and ooze. Raven noticed that there was a puddle around the Mayor's groin where his bladder had given way at the point of penetration.

'I told you, Luke. I fucking told you. You do not FUCK with Angra Manyu. Now the door is well and truly fucking open!' Pale Face had the detonator in his hand and was thrusting it towards Raven. 'If I have to push this I will. I WILL!'

Barber came through the living room door, his gun drawn.

'What the fuck?' Pale Face thrust the detonator at Barber. 'Why are you here?'

Barber looked at Raven, fear etched across his face like a ghostly tattoo, but he never lowered his gun. 'You okay, boss? Chief?'

The Chief put a hand on his shoulder. 'We're fine, Damian. But I suggest you lower the pistol. The place is rigged with explosives.'

'But...'

'Do as the Chief asks, Damo! This guy's got us cornered.' Raven had to yell to be heard above the chaos.

'Fucking right I have!' Pale Face looked from the Chief, to Raven to Barber.

The alarm continued to wale and the spinning, warning lights continued to whir. '*He* is coming now. There is no stopping it. He,' he pointed to the Mayor's prone body, 'shouldn't have done that and he,' he pointed to Barber, 'should not fucking be here. I should have killed you when I had the chance. This was supposed to be simple. I should be done by now and gone. But no, you had to fuck it up! Now give me that fucking gun!'

Barber lowered his gun hand.

'Throw it on the floor and kick it to me.'

Barber looked at Raven and Raven nodded. 'Do as he says, Damo.'

Barber bent down, glanced up at Raven who was still nodding, and put the gun on the floor in front of him. 'You sure about this, boss?'

'It's the only way.'

Barber slid the gun across the floor to Pale Face who knelt down and gripped it in his calloused fingers. 'Thank you very much, Damian.'

The thick black cloud behind Pale Face began to glow a dull red with a bright orange star-like shape at its centre. Pale Face looked at it. '*He* is coming.'

Barber looked at the Chief and at Raven. 'What is he talking about?'

Raven shrugged his shoulders, but his gaze was transfixed on the growing star and deepening crimson of the cloud.

'Oh shit, oh shit, oh SHIT!' Pale Face tried to back away from the swirling darkness but wherever he went it followed him.

The Chief started to feel an impending dread in the pit of his stomach. He wanted to be back at home. Why, he cursed, didn't he take that goddamn retirement when he had the chance? He thought of his family, his partner, the dogs, the tranquillity.

Raven thought of Lisa. He felt a desperate need to get back to her. He couldn't die here, he thought. He was starting to feel the air in the room begin to thicken, the temperature plummet. His own despair and deepest anxieties began to rise in his chest like a tide of dark and acidic regret.

Barber couldn't look away from the spinning redness. He could see something dark at its centre, a misshapen thing rising up from the burning light. He could hardly comprehend what he was seeing. Could he really see claws, horns, an eye?

'Oh Angra Manyu, I am here to do your bidding. Tell me what it is that you want, and I will offer it to you. You know my wants and desires. Tell me what you want in return for the gift that I so long for. I have provided the blood of the women as you asked. I have slain them in your name. Your name was the last words they heard before I passed them to you through the gift of death. I offer myself to you. Tell me, tell me oh great one...'

Pale Face was standing with his back to them, facing the black thing that was rising higher and higher in the orange centre of the red and black spinning cloud. His arms were held out wide, welcoming the oncoming thing that swam towards them. A torrid wind had whipped up all around them, making it hard to stand upright. Raven was gripping the back of the sofa, the Chief was leaning against the fireplace and Barber was standing, legs apart, staring directly into what now appeared to be a glowing abyss.

Barber looked at Raven. He mouthed 'what the fuck.' He looked terrified and mesmerised all at once.

Raven had had enough of the insanity and reached inside his jacket for his gun. Pale Face hadn't thought to ask for it and he hadn't offered it. Now, with his back to them, he was a sitting duck.

He gripped the handle and yelled in agony. He dropped it to the floor and stared at his hand, which was now red and blistered, sores torn open along the lengths of his fingers and across his palm. Watery pus poured from the wounds.

Pale Face did not turn. The room was now a throbbing red, the swirling mass now filled the whole space and the black, rising shape was enormous. It was horned, thorny, it had arms and legs like a human but like no human they had ever seen. Its eyes were a burning hateful red. Its body was black and green, but scaly like a lizard. It had a long twisting tail, taloned wings, fiery breath, teeth like long knives, a tongue like the tail of a shark. It roared at them. It was looking at Raven and Raven was staring at it. Raven knew that it was drawn by his dark soul. His own dark core was pulling the thing towards him. It wanted him.

The realization dawned on Pale Face.

'It's you!' He pointed at Raven. 'I must sacrifice you, Luke!' Raven backed away.

'If I give you to him then he will give me her. That's it. That's the answer!'

Pale Face drew the gun from the pocket of his parka and screamed as the cacophony continued around him.

'Oh, thank you great one! Thank you for giving me the guidance of your wisdom and greatness! Through reverence I will make the ultimate sacrifice such that you will graciously afford me the wondrous prize that you have so generously spared me!'

Barber looked at Raven and back at Pale Face.

Raven had nowhere to run. He thought of Lisa. He thought of his unborn child. He thought of all the shit that he had allowed to be borne by others on his behalf. He deserved this. If anyone deserved it, he did. Not Daisy, not those other girls. No. Just him. Now was his time. He closed his eyes.

'Sorry Luke.' Pale Face looked torn. 'Nothing personal.'

The gun fired just as Damian Barber lunged forward.

Chapter 78: Realization

Tony was thinking. The cogs in his brain were whirring. That name. That fucking name. It was like someone had smashed a very large hammer against a very large bell in his head.

'Say that again.'

Tracey looked at him, confused. 'Say what again?'

'That name.'

'My name?'

'Yes, your fucking name.' Tony rubbed his hands across his eyes like he was trying to rub away the burning that he felt there.

'No need to be rude.' She looked agitated.

'Sorry, sorry. I didn't mean to be rude.' He grabbed her hands. 'I just…I just didn't hear you properly. That's all.'

'Okay. It's just your tone was so…'

'I know. I know. Sorry.'

'It's Tracey. Tracey Webb.'

Tony took a deep breath and then a big sip from his beer glass. It cooled him down but only for a second.

He looked over Tracey's shoulder at the mirror behind her. It was on the far wall, but he could still see his reflection. He was pasty. White. Pale even. He could feel sweat rising to his face.

His hair had gotten thin. When had that happened, he wondered? It was slick with a mixture of hair gel and perspiration. And he looked so skinny. So sickly.

He looked behind him at the coat rack. His black parka was hanging there like the skin of long dead animal. It goaded him.

He looked next to him where he had placed Tracey's clutch bag and his hat. His woollen Peruvian black hat. With a snowflake pattern.

He thought of his dad. Of the teachings that he had bestowed on him. Of his Persian ancestry. The church. The artefacts that he had shown him. Books, scriptures. Images. Horned devils. Gods. Not like the God that he had known when he was growing up, but ancient mythological Gods. Good and bad. The stories of the Charons. His family. How they had been cast aside by the Amesha Spentas. Cast into the wilderness.

And Tracey Webb. That fucking name. He knew it couldn't *not* be a coincidence, but he reminded himself that it was just fiction. It was in his fucking head!

'Are you okay, Tony? You look like you've seen a ghost.'

How had he not seen this, he asked himself ashamedly? How had he not known? It had been there for all to see. How could he have been so naïve? So foolish?

'Tony. Are you okay?'

It was a circle. A vicious circle. How it began would be how it would end. Only he had no ending. Not yet. It was unfinished.

'Maybe I should go.' Tracey was staring at him. She looked disturbed.

If he was to go through with this, he realised, he would have to write the ending. It could not go on and on. It had to be done. It had to end. No more, he swore to himself. No more.

'I'm gonna go.'

He had just wanted to be a writer. A writer of stories. But, he pondered agitatedly, this was... this was...

'See you later, Tony.'

'No!'

'What?'

'I mean… no. Don't go. Sorry. I was just… distracted.'

'You're bloody right you were. It was like you had left the building.' She was glaring at him, clearly angered but also more than a little confused.

'I get like that sometimes. I apologise.'

'You'd better.'

'I do.' He gathered himself. 'It's just your beauty. It's so outrageous it just stuns me into silence.'

She squinted her eyes and pursed her lips. 'That's bloody cheesy, that's what that is.' She leaned over and slapped him, laughing as she did so, 'But I like it.'

'Sorry, sorry. But I mean it, really, I do,' he laughed back, but the icy chills were still running up and down his spine.

'Shall we… get out of here?'

He took a deep, shuddery breath. He could see Jane. He could only see Jane. He longed and wanted Jane. His dad had told him that this was the only way. He didn't want to do it at first, but he had convinced him. Hell, he thought, that was his dad's job wasn't it? And he was bloody good at it. He could get into your psyche. And Tony wanted it. He needed it. He couldn't be without her. She was his. She was fucking his after all. How dare she walk out on him. How fucking dare she. Who did she think she was? But he loved her. And he would do anything. *Anything.* Anything at all.

'Let's.'

Chapter 79: The Ending

'Damo!'

Barber lay on the floor, his lifeless eyes gazing vacantly up at the ceiling, a bullet-hole the size of a ten-pence piece through the centre of his chest.

'NO!' Pale Face was distraught. The red cloud had disappeared, the giant, black figure had gone, the violent, gale force wind had dissipated. '*He* didn't want him. *He* wanted you, Raven.' Pale Face was sobbing. '*He* won't give me what I want in exchange for Barber. *He* didn't fucking want Barber!'

Raven had Barber's head in his hands. 'Hang in there Damo. It'll be fine. We'll get you fixed up.' He looked around the room frantically. There was no-one there that could help and those that could may as well have been a thousand miles away. Barber was gone. His distant stare and the lack of any discernible pulse told him as much. The fucking kid was dead. And all because of the lunatic's crazy obsession with his ex-girlfriend. He felt the anger raging in his belly.

'It's ruined. The whole thing is ruined. What a waste. What a fucking waste!'

Raven looked up at him, Anthony Richards, lazy, no life, son of a bitch who had spent his formative years abandoned by his father and ritualistically abused by his mother, his later years taking out his deep seated hatred for women on every female who had had the misfortune to encounter him. He was both psychotically possessive and sadistically creative with his warped version of reality. A fucked-up kid who had grown up to become a monster. Someone who had killed people close to Raven. Who had almost killed Raven's unborn child.

Both Richard's and Raven's lives had come crashing together in such a tragic and violent, twisted mess and now, Raven regretted deeply, Barber had paid with his life. And for what, he asked himself? To save Detective Inspector Luke Raven, a fuck up who had alienated pretty much everyone he had ever gotten close to. Everyone, that is, save the Chief who stood over them, Raven's gun in his hand. His arm was shaking but his face was resolute. 'Anthony Richards, I am placing you under arrest on suspicion of the murders of Tracey Webb, Billy Roper, Trudy Yates, Daisy Reynolds, Chester Wood and...'

The Chief looked down at the lifeless form of his Inspector and sighed, '....and Damian Barber.'

Tony Richards refused to look up, continuing to sob silently as the Chief read him his rights.

Raven's radio crackled into life.

'Boss, are you there? Over.'

He could barely muster the energy to raise the radio to his mouth, 'This is Raven, over.'

'We have an armed response unit in position, over.'

'The coast is clear, Spidey. We have the suspect under arrest. We have two men down in here and a man in need of urgent medical attention, over.'

'Entering through the south entrance now, over and out.'

Raven looked down at Barber. All the kid wanted to do was to become a D.I. and, he knew in his heart, he would have made it too. He looked over at Richards. Another kid whose life was in tatters. And for what?

'Tony?'

Raven looked up and saw the doorway filled with armed officers.

Standing amongst them was a civilian woman, dressed in a grey sweatshirt and blue jeans.

'What the fuck, Webber?'

'It's his girlfriend, boss. She... insisted.'

'Jane, Jane?' Tony stood up, straining with the exertion but his face illuminated by her presence, 'you came?'

Jane Butler pushed past the two officers in front of her.

'Tony. What the hell have you been doing?' She was sobbing. She looked around at the carnage in front of her and raised her hands to her face.

'I did it for you, Jane. This is all for you.' He stood up and reached out for her.

'Easy there, Richards. I suggest you back off,' Raven put his arm across him to prevent him from going any further.

'For me? For me? You killed all of these poor people for me?'

'Yes, my darling. To get you back. So that you would come back to me.'

Tony was smiling. He was happy. It had worked, he thought, everything his dad had told him. Everything he had done. It had worked. The magic had worked. He had come through for him.

'Why the hell would I come back to you after this, Tony? What have you become?'

'I found out what my true destiny is, Jane. I found out what I am, what I truly am,' his face was a beaming ray of distorted sunshine, 'I am part of an elite. You and I, we are meant to be together. It's all written down for us.' He held his arms out, his long, thin fingers reaching out for her, his beloved.

'Written? You... you sound crazy, Tony. Whatever it is that has gotten a hold on you, you need to push it away. Far away. You...' she held her hand to her lips, 'you need help.'

'Not any more, Jane. Don't you see? I needed help but I found it. After all this time and it was there for me all along. Help found me and now I've found you.' His eyes were open, his grin wide and boyish, his mood elevated.

'But Tony...' she sobbed into her hands.

'Don't cry, my love. I am a changed man. I'm not the loser, the waster that you once knew. I've been taught how to succeed. How to get what I want. You'll never want for anything again.'

'Tony...Tony,' she looked at him, 'Tony, they hurt you so bad.'

'No, no. I'm not hurt. I'm saved. I've been saved.'

'Your family. They destroyed you. I never saw it but now it's clear. This has been eating you up since you were a little boy.' Jane was crying tears of sadness and of frustration.

'Yes, yes. But not anymore. Now I've got past that. I've been shown the way.'

'The way to what, Tony? The way to hurt people? The way to kill people?'

'The way to be all that I can be. Don't you see?' Tony was crying now, the desperation etched on his face like a surrealist painting.

'I see all too much, Tony. And I am grateful that I got away when I did. I only wish that I could have prevented this.'

Tony cried out in pain. 'Jane, no. Please.'

'I can't...'

'Don't go back to that... that Nick, Jane. Please.'

'I won't. You did that much for me. We tried to work things out after your... intervention,' her mouth turned up at the corner in a leer, 'your *assault*. But I couldn't get past it. Couldn't get what you said out of my head,' she looked down at the ground, 'Nick and I are over.'

Tony's smile widened, 'Then you are free. *You are free.* You can come home.' He held his hands out to hold her.

Jane took two steps towards him. Sergeant Webber placed a hand on her shoulder. She spoke to Tony Richards through a sneer and gritted teeth, 'If you think I am getting anywhere near you ever again, Tony, you are sadly, sadly mistaken. This... is... *finished.*'

Tony stared at her, the cruel realisation spreading across his face like an ugly, black cloud. His lip trembled and his body shook. Jane turned and walked back towards the doorway. He looked at the floor, glanced sideways at Raven and took off his hat, revealing his thinning hair and cracked and scaly scalp. His eyes focussed on something far away and a tear rolled down one, ragged cheek.

'Jane?'

She turned to face him. 'Yes, Tony.'

'I finished my book.'

'Your book?'

'Yes, my novel.' His voice was wavering.

'Is... is this relevant, Tony?'

'You'll like the ending.'

He reached into his parka and retrieved Barber's pistol. Raven launched himself between him and Jane. 'Richards, NO!'

Tony Richards lifted the pistol and held the muzzle under his chin.

'See you on the other side, Mum and Dad.'

He pulled the trigger.

EPILOGUE

Jane Butler finished her interview with Inspector Dawes, sipped the dregs from her coffee cup and stood up to leave. She pulled on her jacket as the Inspector switched off the tape recorder.

'Do you think I'm a bad person, Inspector?'

'For leaving him or for not coming forward sooner?'

'Either.'

'I think you did all you could. It seems to me that Anthony Richards didn't really stand a chance from birth. The fault doesn't lie at your door.'

'But if I had stayed...'

'Then you might have been his first victim.'

'I still don't understand how he knew all of that... stuff. In his book I mean. It was like he was... predicting the future.'

Inspector Dawes smiled sympathetically at her, 'He was writing down his fantasies, Ms Butler. Writing them down and then acting them out. It's odd but it's not uncommon. He was sick.'

'He never hurt me.'

'Not physically. But often it's the mental abuse that's the most difficult to spot.'

Jane Butler nodded. She understood the point, but the guilt still wracked her body and soul, keeping her awake at night and gnawing at her like a hungry tiger. She still believed that she could have saved him, but she hadn't had the emotional energy or patience to do it.

The Inspector stood up from the table and threw his empty water cup in the waste bin. 'Where do you go from here?'

'Oh, I've got a car outside.'

'No, I mean where do you go from here? Personally.'

'Oh, well,' she laughed at the misunderstanding, 'back to work. Back to my mums. You know. I'll be staying away from men for a while.'

The Inspector laughed. 'Probably not a bad idea,' he smiled an empathetic smile at her, 'thanks for coming in, Jane.'

'Not a problem. Glad I could help. It's the least I could do. You know... for the families.'

The Inspector reached over and grabbed the door handle. 'I'll see you around.'

'I sincerely hope not, Inspector.' They both laughed as she walked out into the cold corridor.

A door opened further down the hall and a heavily pregnant lady stepped out of another interview room. She had a shock of red hair, colourful leggings and a vest top, a piercing in her lip and a tattoo on her right shoulder. Lisa Clancy turned to face Inspector Davis.

'Was that any help, Inspector?'

'It sure was Lis. Thanks for that.'

'That's okay. If you need any more just call.'

'I will. Take care of that baby now.'

'I sure will. That is if Luke will let me do anything. I'm sure he thinks I've got an illness. I keep telling him that millions of women have babies every day.'

'It's good to see he's looking out for you, Lisa,' the Inspector shook her hand firmly, 'take care of yourself.'

'And you, Ray.'

She turned down the corridor and saw Jane. The two women exchanged glances and smiled. Lisa held her hand up to wave and

Jane waved back.

Luke Raven appeared from behind Lisa and placed his hand on her shoulder.

'You all done?'

'Yeah. All done.'

'Come on then. I promised the Doc that we would go round to see her. She misses Damo pretty bad. God, we all do. I said we'd take her out for lunch.'

'Sounds good. Poor girl. I wish we could do more.'

'I wish I could have done more. He saved my life, Lisa. I wouldn't be here for you, for the baby, if it wasn't for Damian Barber.' Raven had been to see Barber's family two days earlier and it had been the hardest home visit of his career. Damian had been like a brother to him and the pain he had witnessed in Mr and Mrs Barber's eyes was emulated in his own.

He still couldn't shake what he had seen during those final moments at the Mayor's house. The dark shadow, the thing rising from the raging inferno, its black manifestation emerging from a swirling, angry, dark mass. He and the Chief had spoken with the police psychologist at HQ and had been educated in the ways of communal hallucination, how one man's visions could be superimposed on your own semi-conscious state, how you could be convinced, through subtleties of tone, specific vocabulary and cleverly manipulated body language, to see what the other person believes he or she could see. It was some freaky shit and he wasn't convinced but, for his sake and the sake of his unborn child, he had inwardly agreed to reconcile himself to it. As had the Chief. There were just some things that he didn't want or need to understand.

'You did all that you could, Luke. All we can do now is remember.'

'Well, I spoke to Crusher about the winter inter-departmental games and we're going to dedicate the charitable donations in Damo's honour. It's the very least we can do. He was a good police officer. He would have become a hell of a D.I.'

'I know. And that's nice. That really is. His family would appreciate that,' she sighed. 'Now let's get out of here while my bladder holds up.'

Raven laughed, 'I love you Lisa.'

'I love you too, Detective Inspector.'

Jane Butler smiled to herself as she watched the young couple hug deeply. She threw the long handle of her handbag over her shoulder and walked out through the front office, pushing through the double doors and stepping out into the sunshine.

The cool autumnal air gently caressed her neck and face. It was soothing and much needed. Her car was parked just out front, between a Honda Civic and an Audi A6. She fumbled for her keys, unlocked the driver's side and pulled herself in, closing the door behind her.

She slumped her head onto the steering wheel and sobbed. So much pain, so much fear, so much loss. She wondered, with a searing and desperately painful regret, how it had all come to this.

Wiping her tears from her face, she slotted the car key into the ignition and pushed down on the clutch. The car roared into life. She slipped into reverse and backed out, wiping warm tears from her cheeks as she did so.

Behind her, just out of view and sitting on a bright, chrome Harley Davidson Fat Boy with black paint and orange flames down either side was a tall man with dark hair, a dark, trimmed beard, black pleated trousers and black sweatshirt. He had waited as the treacherous, adulterous woman had gotten into her car and keyed the ignition. He watched as her red Vauxhall Corsa turned left out into the street and waited patiently and silently to observe where it was headed. He smiled as he pulled on his gloves and helmet and then kicked the bike into life, the gentle throbbing of the engine helping to dull the deep-seated desire for vengeance and destruction burning within him. He pulled left out of the station and praised *His* name.

ABOUT THE AUTHOR

Stacey Dighton is a married father of two from Kent, England. He and his wife, Jo, enjoy hiking with their Bassett Hound, Lily, and spending time with their adult children, Jayden and Harley. The family are keen music lovers and love spending time at gigs and music festivals whenever they can.

Printed in Great Britain
by Amazon